Stephen Deas

THE HOUSE OF CATS AND GULLS

BLACK MOON, BOOK II

ANGRY ROBOT

ANGRY ROBOT
An imprint of Watkins Media Ltd

Unit 11, Shepperton House
89-93 Shepperton Road
London N1 3DF
UK

angryrobotbooks.com
twitter.com/angryrobotbooks
Batten Down the Hatches

An Angry Robot paperback original, 2022

Edited by Eleanor Teasdale and Paul Simpson
Cover by Kieryn Tyler
Set in Meridien

ISBN 978 0 85766 878 3
Ebook ISBN 978 0 85766 879 0

Printed and bound in the United Kingdom by TJ Books Ltd.

9 8 7 6 5 4 3 2 1

For Nigel, Matt, Sam, Ali, Pete, Tony & Michaela

MAP OF
ARIA

FEB . 2022

PART ONE
MYLA

Our actions and their consequences define us. Words are nothing.
— Tasahre

THE MONTH OF STORMS

"It's simple enough," said Myla. "About halfway through the Month of Contemplation, the Imperial Guard stop patrolling the roads from Varr to the City of Spires. After the festival of the Equinox, they start again. In between, anyone who can pick up a big stick and shout a lot indulges in their seasonal pastime of mugging travellers stupid enough to be out on the winter roads. It fits nicely between the end of harvest and the start of planting, when the locals really don't have enough else to keep themselves busy."

Orien stifled a yawn. "But we're past Midwinter and the patrols are still out. I've *seen* them."

"Yes. This year is different. I don't know why. Something's going on."

For the last two days, Myla had sat on a boat and drifted down the river Arr, current, sails and oars all pushing them onwards. On the first day, she'd been alone, thinking it had been the right choice, that she'd done the only thing she could, given where she was going and what would be waiting when she got there. But then, on the second morning, as the boat was about to leave, Orien had appeared. He must have ridden through the night and close to murdered both himself and his horse to do it, but there he was. And in truth she was glad, even if Orien had spent most of the rest of that day wearing an expression of confusion, curiosity and an irritating smugness.

"Do you have any idea how long it takes to ride from Varr to Deephaven?" she asked. Orien didn't know much about anything except starting fires and who was stabbing whom in the back in the Imperial Court in Varr. "I didn't want to get stuck in Neja or the City of Spires for three months."

"Pah!" Orien waved a hand. "Ice and snow and banditry are but petty trifles to a fire-mage."

"I seem to remember that when we *had* some ice and snow and bandits, I had to rescue you and haul you to the nearest waystation because you could barely sit straight in the saddle." Myla hid a smile as she thought about pushing him into the water. In coves and inlets around the riverbanks, the ice was almost thick enough to take a man's weight. But no. Orien was a paying passenger as much as she was. There'd be difficulties with the boat's crew if she pushed him overboard.

And, for better or for worse, she liked him.

"Anyway," said Orien. "That's not what I meant. What I meant wasn't *why are you here* as in why this boat at this particular place and time; what I meant was why did you leave Varr in such a hurry, and why did you go without telling anyone?"

Typically for Orien, he'd waited most of the day before asking, dedicating the rest of their time to how clever he'd been. The last time they'd been together had been on Midwinter's night, the two of them standing on an old forgotten bridge over a canal in the dead of night, handing over a dead Emperor's crown to an unsettlingly young slip of a sorceress who happened to be the same dead Emperor's daughter, all on an unlikely off-chance that it might stop a war. Everything afterwards had apparently gone exactly the way Orien had said it would: Midwinter had passed; the old year had died and the new had bloomed into life; Ashahn II, six years old, sat on the Sapphire Throne and had been crowned Emperor of Aria; later, in a quieter but perhaps more significant ceremony, his elder sister had been named Princess-Regent. The Levanya, her uncle – great-uncle, actually, and whom half the court had expected to take the throne for himself – had prostrated himself and pressed his head to the feet of his new Emperor and Regent, just like all the other courtiers, and that had been that. It *would* have meant war if the Butcher of Deephaven had taken the crown. The consensus according to Orien was that the Levanya now planned to marry his grand-niece and take power that way instead; having met their new Regent, albeit briefly, Myla wasn't at all sure she fancied his chances.

The next morning, while the merchants of the Spice Market nursed sore heads and sipped tea and wondered loudly among themselves whether this new regency would see out the year, Myla had quietly left the city. Elsewhere, the Princess-Regent had given her Imperial Seal to a new guild: The Guild of Fire-mages. Since this was exactly what Orien had wanted all along, Myla imagined he was now going to be insufferable about it all the way to Deephaven.

Closer to home, she knew Fings had managed to keep three bags of the Emperor's silver, enough to set him up for life if he was careful, which he wouldn't be. Arjay and Dox had taken over the *Unruly Pig*. Even Seth had been different, although Myla wasn't sure why. No one had been thrown into the Kaveneth. Everyone was happy who wasn't dead, and she didn't think Blackhand would be missed for long. There might have been a few tears for Wil. All in all, everyone had got what they wanted except her, because what *she* wanted wasn't possible. The closest she could get was waiting for her in Deephaven and was very unlikely to have a happy ending.

"Well let's see... On the one hand, I *did* help return the Emperor's crown. On the other, I *was* one of the people who stole it in the first place."

"But you didn't *know* what you were stealing!" interrupted Orien.

"You think that will save me when the Guild Mages come

calling? Yes, we didn't know until we had it in our hands, but I can't pretend I didn't have a shrewd idea we were stealing something that might have been more than a little important."

"Lady Novashi is clearing up that little matter for you."

"And then there's Sulfane." Sulfane, who'd put Blackhand up to the theft, telling him there was a fortune to be made while all along setting him up to take the fall. "I did ruin his plan and stab him a couple of times, so he's probably quite annoyed about that. And *then* there are the Torpreahns who came after us in the snow. *They're* probably annoyed too." She rounded on Orien then, the one thing she was truly angry at him about. "I left Sulfane alive for a *reason*, you know! You were supposed to make sure the Guild got him. They were supposed to have someone to blame that wasn't me and Fings; and Sulfane was supposed to give them the Torpreahns and get *them* off our backs too. When I left him, he was bleeding and could barely stand. How did he get away?"

Orien had the decency to look sheepish. "He can't have gone far. The Guild will find him." He didn't sound much like he believed it.

"Whatever Sulfane was doing ran deep. Something to do with a priest and something called the Twelfth House, not that I know what that is, or care. And *then*," moving quickly on, because Orien looked all set to interrupt her again, "most of all, there's the small matter of Jeffa Hawat's headless corpse. Sulfane saw me kill him, so thanks *again* for letting him slip through your fingers. Between the Torpreahns, Sulfane, the Imperial Mages and House Hawat, frankly it's the Hawats that trouble me the most."

"Yet here you are, heading straight for them."

Yet here she was, doing exactly that. And yes, it *had* been tempting to stay in Varr. To sit quietly on her hands and say nothing; to stay where she was and see what happened, or maybe wait for spring and then slip away, further east to Vyan and Tzeroth, or south to Torpreah, somewhere where House Hawat might not reach her.

"Are you going to kill him?" Orien asked.

She looked at him long and hard, puzzled until she realized he was serious. "Kelm's Teeth, Orien! I'm not an assassin." At least, so she kept telling herself. "Besides, even if I did, what then? Kill his whole extended family and all his friends too? Because they *would* come after me."

"Then... what?"

Myla looked across the river, at the water rushing steadily by. Truth was, she didn't know. "Did Fings never tell you why I ran from Deephaven? Why a washed-up sword-monk ended up in a place like the *Unruly Pig*?"

Orien shook his head.

"Well. Long story short: Sarwatta Hawat did something I didn't like and so I stabbed him in the balls. He got quite angry about that. Unfortunately, he's rich and powerful, so I made it look like I'd burned to death in a fire and ran away. When Sarwatta discovers I'm still alive *and* that I've killed his brother, he'll have my entire family arrested, tortured, and eventually executed, and he'll do all of that to try and lure me in. He'll go after everyone I care about until he gets what he wants. So, Orien, the reason I left without telling anyone is that I'm going to save us both that trouble and put an end to this, one way or another. I didn't tell you I was leaving because, frankly, I'm most likely walking straight towards a lingering and unpleasant death at the hands of someone I despise. It's as hard to live with as it sounds, and I didn't want to have to deal with you trying to stop me."

She watched the expressions flicker across Orien's face as he caught up with what she was saying. Sardonic amusement, then more serious, then looking for the trick, then seeing there wasn't one. Shock as it hit him that she mostly expected to die. Refusal and outrage. And then finally, the dawning realization that there wasn't a single thing he could do about it.

"Show me another way and I'll take it," Myla said.

"I'll talk to my mistress... She has the ear of–"

"A pardon from our new Princess-Regent?" Myla laughed. "Even if you had that power, Orien, which I don't think you do, Sarwatta would never accept it. He'd simply find another way, and if he can't touch *me*, he'll take it out on my family. No. I have to find something he wants even more than revenge, then find a way to give it to him." Which, frankly, would be impossible.

"That's really why you left Varr without telling me?"

"You would have tried to talk me out of it. I was afraid you might succeed." She touched his cheek. His skin was warm. "I'm glad you came, though. Truly. Even if you should probably have stayed at home. Oh, and… please *don't* try to talk me out of it."

2

THE CITY OF SPIRES

To begin with, Myla decided it was better not to let Orien get too close. Not that she didn't want a friend – those would soon be in short supply – but, for all his cleverness, there really *wasn't* another way out. She'd go back to Deephaven and visit her brother Lucius and they'd have one last riotous evening together. She'd visit her sister Soraya, plead for forgiveness, and probably wouldn't get it. She'd go to her old sword-mistress, Tasahre, and hand back the two Sunsteel swords that marked her as a sword-monk, blades she no longer deserved to carry. After all that, she'd try to make a deal with Sarwatta; and most likely she'd fail, and he'd take his vengeance in blood, and that would be the end of the matter. If she let Orien have what he wanted, he'd only get hurt; so she hid in her closet-sized cabin, wrapped in layers of fur, walled away from the icy air and the relentless snow that muffled sound and sight and even life itself. She dozed and stared at the walls and thought the same thoughts over and over, round in circles until she was ready to drown.

It was a small boat, though. When she gave up avoiding him, he wasn't exactly hard to find.

"I see what you mean," he said, looking out across the water at the wall of white that was the shore. "Only an idiot would travel in this."

7

She thought about nodding, or at least making some sort of vague noise to let him know that she was listening, but nothing happened.

"I'm not going to let you kill yourself," he said.

"I don't plan to." No, *that* would be the easy way. "But I have to keep my brother and my sister safe. I only stayed in Varr after Jeffa found me because we'd done something stupid that I could actually put right."

Orien took her hand. To her surprise, she didn't pull away. "We'll be at the City of Spires in a week," he said. "You could get back to Varr from there a lot faster than if you travel all the way to Deephaven."

"Not true: it's actually easier to work a passage back to Varr from the coast than from the City of Spires. But neither of those things is going to happen. I hope we both know that."

Orien squeezed her hand. "Find a way to delay. I will convince my mistress to intervene on your behalf. Not a pardon. Something else."

Myla pulled her hand away. Sometimes Orien could be so naïve and it made her cross. "House Hawat may not be one of the Eleven Houses, but the Hawats wield a lot of influence in Deephaven. You won't be able–"

"My mistress is Lady Novashi of Neja. Fourth in line to the Nejan throne, mistress of the Order of Fire and conceivably the most powerful voice in the Empire after the Princess-Regent herself! She does not–"

"Stop!" Myla rounded on him and glared; and then, when he actually *did* stop, took his hands in hers and spoke more gently. "Orien. Stop. Your precious Princess-Regent sits on a precarious throne. Deephaven is a city she will depend on in the months to come. There will be no intervention. Not for me. Nor, if it might tip the scales to war, would I want there to be." The thought led her back to Sulfane. *The Crown. If she has it, they will come for her. It will be a war like nothing you can imagine. A war of mages.* The last words he'd said to her, right after she stabbed him. She had no idea what he'd been on about.

Orien smiled, a weak little thing, and nodded. "Let me know if there are a few things you'd like set aflame out of sheer spite."

They both laughed at that. "No, but thank you for the thought. Although, on the whole, I'm in agreement with Fings on the subject of mages."

"That we're to be avoided?"

"That you're a strange and unpredictable species. Not to mention smug, arrogant and self-obsessed."

"More so than mysterious merchant-girls with uncanny aptitudes for sword-fighting?"

"I *had* decided not to hurl you into the river. Should I reconsider?"

"When you get to Deephaven, I can see to it, perhaps, that at least you have fair hearing."

Hard not to laugh; and maybe, with an unpleasant death likely waiting for her, laughter was good. "It won't make a difference. But again, thank you."

For the next few days, a biting wind blew sleet and ice across the decks. Myla and Orien hid below, idly sipping tea – leaves from the *Unruly Pig* and Orien's sorcery to heat the water. A simple, easy ritual, he said, but the sailors worshipped him for it. Then the wind died and the skies cleared and, with the confident timing of a master actor, the City of Spires glided from behind a bend in the river and revealed her glory. The sailors, who'd been up and down this river for most of their lives and knew each twist and turn better than their own hands, barely noticed, but Orien and Myla stood transfixed at the prow like children, hands gripping the rails, heads tilted back, eyes wide. Myla felt a wave of something warm wash through her. She'd done the same on the trip to Varr, coming the other way, seeing the five spires of the city for the first time. They were so fantastically, unimaginably tall, three or four times the height of Talsin's spire in Varr, gleaming white against the piercing blue of the sky. Tiny bridges, invisible from such distance, joined them at different levels. They made her think of Seth and his strange question on the night the Spicers had taken the *Unruly Pig*, asking whether she'd ever been here.

"They say that when the first explorers came this far up the river, the spires were already there," she said. "Abandoned. Shunned by the people who lived nearby."

"Haunted by ghosts of the fallen half-gods," said Orien. "I know."

"I've heard some say they still are."

Orien snorted and shook his head, and, for him at least, the magic seemed to fail. "Hardly. The Princess-Regent was born in one of those towers. Her mother's family live there now, those that haven't moved to Varr."

"The Path of the Moon have their home here too."

"And their hall of records." Orien turned away. "I have a delivery to make and an errand to run. We'll be stopping in the city for a few hours."

"We will, will we?"

"Yes." He grinned at her. "And I've already bribed all the sailors far too well for you to do anything about it."

He left. Myla stayed, letting the spires hypnotise her as their pointed tips scratched their way across the heavens.

An hour later, the riverboat pulled into the Spiredocks. The deck became a frenzy of activity for a few minutes and then all the sailors were suddenly gone, off about their own business; and since the alternative seemed to be sitting on the deck twiddling her thumbs, Myla agreed to walk with Orien to wherever he was going. There was always a chance that Lucius *wasn't* in Deephaven, that she'd find his house shuttered up for the winter and that she'd need Orien's help, if only for a place to stay.

No. You'll go to the temple and Sword-mistress Tasahre. But she went with Orien anyway.

He stopped on the docks and asked for directions, followed them for a few minutes, somehow confused them, ended up going the wrong way, tried again, got it wrong again, and got them lost for a second time. Since the spires were visible from almost every corner of every street, and since it was one of the spires they were heading for, this struck Myla as quite an achievement. After they got lost for a third time, she let slip a quiet comment about some people not being able to find their way off a plank of wood. They had a bit of an argument after that, which ended when she asked for directions of her own and marched him briskly off. Ten minutes later, she had him at the entrance to the Moonspire. Orien gritted his teeth and muttered something about luck and Myla suggested he might thank her for being so helpful. To his credit, he managed it, although from the palaver he made, you might have thought she'd asked him to cut off his own head.

Up close, the spires were disorientating. She looked up and up, felt herself tipping backwards, caught herself and had to look away. When she glanced at Orien, she saw he was watching her, swaying and smiling; then he shook himself down, arranged his self-important mage-face, and went inside. Myla stayed where she was. A Moon priestess had once told her that anyone who wanted – who had the strength for it – could climb the Moonspire all the way to the top. From there, on a clear day, you could see to Deephaven and the sea, to Varr, to the mountains in the north, to the Werey Forest in the far east, to the line of The Fracture, clearly visible to the south and almost all the way to Torpreah. If you were lucky, one of the white stone arches built into the walls would shimmer; instead of stone there would come an image of the far side of the world, or a vision of the past, or of the future. It was a place to cleanse your soul, the priestess had said. A place to see your fate.

To cleanse her soul? Myla paced the white stone steps, chewing her hair and tossing her head, arguing back and forth whether she should go inside. In the end she didn't. Right now, she didn't much fancy seeing her future.

When Orien came out, his errand complete, she walked with him, back turned to the spire. A wave of sadness struck her. She wanted to curl up and cry at the unfairness of it, at Sarwatta and Soraya and everything that had happened between the three of them. She wanted someone to sit beside her and comfort her. It wasn't a very sword-monk sort of feeling.

"So how did you end up a mage?" she asked with brittle brightness. "You weren't born in a city."

"How do you know that?"

"Your under-developed navigation skills."

Orien made a sour face. "I was born in Khrozir. It's all different now, but when I was a child, the town was still being built and the whole place felt like one great market. Every summer it grew tenfold, filled with tents and makeshift huts, all higgledy-piggledy on top of one another, people coming for the Emperor's coin. The walls of Varr were almost finished, but they were still building the fortresses of Ratan and Lytha. It was a mad place. And then, every winter, they went away again. It was as though the town died and was reborn each year. My father was a stonemason. One summer, a rope snapped and stone the size of a horse landed on him. Squashed him flat and that was the end of him, although I'm told there's a stone in the walls of one of the fortresses with a stain that looks just like him." He shrugged. "A school for children of the Imperial Guard had started in Khrozir but the fortresses weren't finished. The Guard weren't there yet, so they took children off the street instead. Orphans and such like."

"I've heard of places like that." When Orien talked this way, when he forgot about being a mage and how important he was, it was possible, Myla conceded, to like him really quite a lot.

STEPHEN DEAS 13

The mage shook his head emphatically. "It made us feel as though the Emperor had chosen us for something. It made us feel special. Those of us they thought were the cleverest got sent to the Guild of Mages to serve them. We were all about twelve, thirteen, starting to think we were men. We were so excited! But it was a disappointment. We thought we were going to learn sorcery and rule the world, but the closest they ever let us to anything arcane was into the alchemy rooms to clean up after something went wrong. I watched and listened, hid in lots of places I wasn't supposed to be, and taught myself how to do some of what *they* could do. I can tell you from my heart, I would have returned the Emperor's crown, sun bless him, and asked for nothing in return. The Imperial Guild of Mages is entirely another matter."

Myla raised an eyebrow. "Feisty words for a loyal servant of the throne. They say the Guild has ears everywhere."

"I *am* a loyal servant, and proud to be. I'm just not content to wipe the shoes of someone who is my intellectual inferior simply because he happened to be born in a castle instead of a back-alley." He stopped. They were back at the barge already. "Are the Moonspire and the Spiredocks really so close?"

Myla laughed. "Navigation skills!"

"Sometimes I don't know why I like you."

"Oh, I ask myself that question *all* the time."

Later, as the barge pushed away and floated down the river, Myla watched the Moonspire and her four sisters gleam in the setting sun. She imagined one of those spires, shorn through at the base, the rubble removed until all that was left was a gleaming, seamless white ring of stone.

Like the one in Varr, she thought. And as she did, she reached a decision.

"Listen," she said. "You know that my going back to Deephaven probably only ends one way. But if you're so determined to fight for me, then fight."

Orien beamed at her like a small boy given a treat.

"And Orien... Sarwatta will have his judgement in blood, most likely; and if he does, and if that's what it takes to save my brother and my sister, I won't stop him. But I'd have some joy in my last days, too."

She took his hand and led him below.

3

MYLA'S GHOST

Deephaven sat on the northern bank of the river Arr as it reached the sea. On the South shore, the estuary reluctantly gave way to tidal mudflats and a scattered township of wooden houses built on stilts. This was Siltside, home of the mudlarks, men and women who scraped a living through what they could dig out of the mud. Or, more often, what they could steal from the ships anchored on the north side of the river, where a granite monolith enthusiastically known as the Peak butted into the sea. The city-dwellers – Deepies, as the mudlarks called them – occasionally put together a militia, sailed across the river and set fire to a few huts; but since the river marked the border between two of the Eleven Houses, while the city itself was under direct Imperial administration, the mudlarks largely endured under a confusion of authority and bureaucracy, along with an uneasy suspicion that the last real attempt to eradicate them and the civil war that had followed shortly after were, somehow, related.

North again of the Peak was the sheltered, deep-water bay from which the city took its name, where ships from across the oceans harboured. On the Peak itself, sitting between them and safe from the floods that came with monotonous regularity from both river and sea, some of the richest men and women of the Empire made their wealth, buying and selling across the scrap of land that separated salt water from the fresh. The rest of the city sprawled inland. A string of fishing villages spread up the coast, while thickets of inns sprouted along the north bank of the river, along with more docks and warehouses for those who aspired to riches but had yet to find them. Over time, these eruptions of activity had grown so close that it was hard to say where one ended and the next began; and so, one day, there was a city.

Myla watched as the riverboat drifted past them all; warehouses she knew, inns she'd visited, docks where she'd once helped load and unload barges with Lucius and Soraya while her father looked on. Orien stood beside her, comfortably close and agreeably silent. The air smelled of the sea, of fish and rot and smoke. The weather had changed too, warmer here on the coast than a Varr winter. It was raining, of course. In Deephaven, it was always raining.

The boat pulled into the shore. Myla climbed up to the pier. The feeling was strange, as though she'd never left, and yet different and alien. Home, but not home. Not anymore. Not ever again.

"Do you have a place to go?" she asked Orien.

"I'll find somewhere."

"You'll *find* somewhere?"

"Yes. Do *you* have a place to go?"

"I'm supposed to be searching for a guild house, remember?" He'd been talking about this on and off on the journey, how his mistress, Lady Novashi, intended Deephaven to be home for her new cabal of fire-mages. It all sounded horribly vague, and Myla had gradually come to understand that Orien had left Varr in far too much of a hurry, simply so he could be with her.

"You never told me why Deephaven. It's a long way from the Sapphire Throne. Isn't your mistress concerned about losing her… influence?"

Orien's expression was pained. "There's already another fire-mage in Varr. There's also already another Guild. We prefer a... a fresh start. As for losing her influence..." He smirked. "No fear of *that*, I'm quite sure."

There was something Orien wasn't saying, something he wanted her to pry out of him, but she couldn't muster the interest to try. Whatever the consequences of what she and Orien had done at Midwinter, whatever machinations and manoeuvres he hoped to share, she didn't think herself likely to live to see them. It rather spoiled the excitement.

"So," he said when she didn't reply. "*Do* you have a place to go?"

There was Lucius if she could find him. There was the temple. They'd take her in if she asked, although she doubted they'd let her go again.

"We'll see," she said, and set off to walk into the heart of the city, and then stopped. Something wasn't right, and it wasn't simply that she'd been away for so long. The docks were subdued, not as busy as they should have been. When she looked around, she saw grey tatters of cloth hanging limply from masts and nailed to doors. She saw a tavern, *The Waterman*, whose gates should have been wide open, a raucous noise of merriment and singing spilling out across the docks at all hours of day and night. Except it was silent and its gates were closed, a grey strip of cloth nailed across them. The grey banner of death.

"Oh, bloody Khrozus," she said.

"What is it?" asked Orien.

Myla shushed him. She looked up and down the river. It was the same everywhere; and the feeling of the waterfront was wrong, and yet oddly familiar, as though it had been this way once before, a long time ago... And then she sighed. It was back, was it? Again. She turned to Orien and pushed him back towards the boat.

"Go back to Varr," she said. "The boatmen will take you."

Orien looked bewildered. "What? Why? I'm not–"

"The sickness is back."

"*What*?"

She pointed to the grey banners. "The River Plague burns through Deephaven every few years, usually down here by the river docks. People turn feverish, erupt in boils and then start dropping like flies. Lasts a few months and then just... goes away again. Some sickness from over the sea, brought in by one of the ships decades ago, most likely. Comes and goes and then comes back again. Can't ever get rid of it, like we're cursed. Looks like it's bad this time."

"Then we should *both* go."

"I need to see my brother and my sister are safe." Myla gave him a weak smile. "Besides, I should at least stay and find out whether it got Sarwatta, don't you think?" Which was far too much to hope, of course.

Orien wasn't having it. Mages, he told her, didn't get sick, which was an outright lie and they both knew it; but she didn't have the energy for a fight, and so half an hour later they were sitting together in Deephaven Square, in the cold sun, sipping some bitter infusion that had yet to find its way into Varr's Spice Markets. Across the wide-open space stood the Solar Temple, magnificent with its low gold domes and its grand Spire of the Sun. Beside it stood the Overlord's Palace, equally magnificent and with a tower of its own. The towers were the tallest in the city and, by careful design, the exact same height.

"That's where I was trained," Myla said.

On the opposite side of the square stood the Guild Hall, walking the line between magnificent and gaudy. Along the other two sides, the houses of the Empire's merchant-princes competed for attention; bright colours and murals and statues; bronze and marble and even gold fought with each other, blending into a confusion of glittering opulence.

"You shouldn't stay," said Myla, but her heart wasn't really in it, and Orien didn't reply. Her eyes kept settling on the House of Hawat. Was he in there, right now, the man who'd ruined her sister? The man she'd stabbed and who wanted her dead? Did he have some inkling that she was back? Unlikely, but she enjoyed imagining that he did, that some nagging unease stalked him like a shadow.

A couple of houses flew grey banners. Unusual for the River Plague to spread as far as the Peak. But no grey banner flew from House Hawat. The gods were never *that* kind.

"We used to come here all the time," she said, after they'd stared at the square for long enough, at the thin crowd of the rich and their retainers gliding through one another across the marble paving. "My brother and my sister and I." A lot of the people in the Square, she saw, wore cloth over their faces, covering everything but their eyes. The new fashion, was it? "It changes so quickly. New colours, a bit added here, a bit knocked off there, everyone following the latest craze. Every summer." Six months away and everything had changed, everything except the temple and the palace and the Guild Hall.

Orien gave her a sheepish look. "You used to live *here*?" he asked with a hint of disbelief.

Myla laughed. "Us? No! Lucius and I used to dream of making our fortunes, enough to elbow our way up here. Then we'd set up in competition, make out we were deadly rivals. No one would ever know we were brother and sister, working together in secret. And then Soraya..." she stopped, a sudden lump in her throat.

She felt Orien's hand on her arm. A light touch. She took a deep breath and pointed across the square to House Hawat. "That house, there. Sarwatta is their eldest son and heir. They were far above and beyond us, the sort of people who expected to marry into one of the Eleven Houses, for the most part. If you look hard enough, they probably have some distant connection to the Emperor. It was quite a coup when Soraya turned his head. Too good to be real, you might say. My mother and father had left and moved to Torpreah to be close to the Autarch. Very religious people. Soraya was the head of our house. Mother's letters were ecstatic when she heard. All the prestige and status it would earn. How Lucius would be able to expand our business." She had to stop, collect her thoughts. The words were tumbling over each other inside her to escape, to tell Orien everything and then beg and weep for forgiveness, not for what she'd done, but for how these would be their last days together.

Orien touched her arm again. A question without words.

"What wouldn't I give to take it all back." A part of her wanted to flee, run across the square and out, away from Deephaven and back to Varr. And at the same time, another urge welled up to cross the square to where it had started, to simply wait outside House Hawat until someone realized who she was. To give herself up and get it over with and bring an end to it all.

"You're shaking," said Orien.

"There was a fight." Myla forced herself to breathe, looked Orien in the eye, then dropped her gaze to the ground. "Sarwatta was toying with her. Another pretty girl to take to bed and toss aside. He'd done it before. Had a reputation for it. Soraya knew, of course. She wasn't stupid. But for some reason, she thought she was different. I went to him. I... I think I was testing him. So I tell myself, although... Things were said afterwards that weren't true but... they weren't entirely lies, either. When she heard... Soraya went to him as well, and Sarwatta did what he'd done so many times before: took what he wanted and then threw her away, like some toy that no longer amused him. He was cruel about it, too – unusually so, even for him. I think... I think that was because of me. That spite. Soraya blamed me for how he treated her. Screamed how it was all my fault. But she was my sister, and he'd hurt her, and so I called him out in front of his friends and demanded an apology; and I would have walked away and let it be if one had come, but... An apology from a man like that? I taunted and goaded him until he tried to hit me, and then I hit him back. He didn't know, back then, what I was. He pulled a knife and tried to cut me, and so I took it off him and stabbed him with it. I don't remember *choosing* to stab him where I did; it just seemed to... happen."

She shrugged and shook her head. "I can pretend it wasn't supposed to end that way; but the truth is that I knew what I was doing, right from the start. I wanted an excuse to hurt him." She looked Orien in the eye again now, tears running down her cheeks. "My sister hates me. He was such a bastard. He didn't deserve her. I told myself I did it for her. There's truth to that, but it's not the whole truth. I'd take it back if I could. Grit my teeth and suffer his lies. I'd make it go away so it never happened; but it did, and I can't, and so that's why I'm here, Orien, and why you can't help me. I'm going to find Soraya. I'm going to put things right between us if I can. And then I'm going to go to Sarwatta, so he can have whatever he needs to leave the rest of my family alone. I'm scared, Orien. I'm scared of what that will be."

Orien lifted a hand to reach to her, then drew back, uncertain. He looked about, as if seeking inspiration, and then stopped, eyes locked on something across the square. A frown spread across his face. He tapped Myla on the shoulder.

"There's someone watching us," he said.

4

LUCİUS

"Lady Shirish?" The man wasn't so much watching as staring in wide-eyed disbelief. He wore a cloth mask across his face, hiding everything but his eyes, and yet…

"Korfa? *Korfa*?" Myla jumped up and hugged him.

Behind Myla, Orien twitched. Myla let go and Korfa bowed, a little uncertain. "Lady Shirish! We all… We all thought you were dead! In the fire…" He flicked a glance to House Hawat, and then his eyes went wide. His mouth opened without any words coming out. There it was: the moment he realized the fire had been staged.

"You know this man?" asked Orien.

"Korfa used to work for my father."

Korfa nodded. "And now for your brother, my lady. Does he… does he know?" Another glance across the square. "You can't *be* here! It's not safe. If they discover you're alive…"

"I'm not a lady, Korfa," Myla said. "I never was. And as for the Hawats, they already know, or will, very soon." He was right, though, about sitting out here in the open. If Korfa could recognize her then so could others. "Yes, Lucius knows. He always did. He doesn't know I'm back in Deephaven, though. I need to see him. Where is he?"

Korfa led them back to the river-docks. As they walked,

Myla asked about the River Plague. Korfa was suitably graphic in his description. "It's bad this time," he said, when he was done talking about corpses coming through the streets in wagonloads to be burned on the temple pyres. "Worse than the Year of Smoke." The River Plague had first come back when Myla was still a child. The year had become known as the Year of Smoke on account of all the pyres around the city that year. The plague has returned every few years since. A few days of fever and then nothing more, for the lucky; boils and pustules for those in whom it took root. Some survived even that, horribly scarred; but most didn't, and there was no telling who would be struck down.

"There's talk of burning houses when people fall sick," said Korfa. "Or even entire streets. It's reached the point where some crews refuse to come ashore."

"Bad, then." Refusing to come ashore after months at sea was quite a thing.

Korfa chuckled. "It keeps the mudlarks at bay, at least. The Violet Pox of twenty years ago – now *there* was a plague. But you were a babe, so you won't remember."

He led them to a part of the river-docks close to the Peak; and there he was: Lucius, the big brother who'd always tried to look out for her, even if towards the end it had more been the other way around. He was standing on a pier, arms folded, watching the unloading of a barge. He was exactly the way she remembered him.

"You shouldn't..." Korfa started, but Myla ignored him; it didn't matter if people saw because she wasn't planning to hide. She walked to her brother and tapped him on the back. When he turned, the change in his face was delicious. That frown at being disturbed, flashing to confusion, then recognition and disbelief, and then love, and then fear.

"Rish?"

She hugged him. After a moment, he hugged her back.

"Rish! What are you doing here? I thought you were in Varr.

Are you mad? You can't *be* here!" He looked around, gestured at the death-banners scattered up and down the barges and piers, but they both knew that wasn't what he meant. "Why? Why would you come back? Why *now*, of all times?"

Myla broke the embrace and stepped away. "I had no idea the plague was back, Luce. That news hasn't come to Varr."

"But..."

"I had to, Luce. I can't spend my life running."

"You won't *have* a life if you stay here!"

"Nevertheless."

"Rish! He will kill you! And badly!"

Myla nodded. "Jeffa Hawat found me. I killed him, but not before he sent word. By now, Sarwatta knows. If I don't reach some bargain with him, he'll come after you and Soraya. I'll not have that."

A chain of men and women worked around them, loading a barge with bolts of what looked like Taiytakei silk, bright colours on their way to the robemakers in the City of Spires. Lucius stared at her, speechless – he was grasping the trap she was in, slowly coming to terms with the same truth she'd realized these last few weeks: that very likely, there wasn't a way out.

"So... you're here to *fight* him? How?"

Myla shook her head. "Not to fight. I'm here to let Sarwatta have whatever he needs to put an end to this."

"*Rish...!*" She saw the sadness in his eyes. "Don't *do* this."

"Show me another way and I'll take it."

"There's no *bargain* here!" Lucius rounded on her. "You have *no* idea what he's capable of. He'll break you into pieces. When he's finally bored of you, he'll pass you around to his friends. When *they're* bored, he'll kill you, and that *still* won't be enough for him."

"Do you think I don't know that?" Myla hissed. "Do you think I need all that rubbed in my face? That I haven't been thinking about what he wants to do to me all the way from Varr?"

"I'm sorry, but... Rish! No!"

"I did what I did, Luce. You and Soraya shouldn't have to pay for that. There has to be a way."

Lucius searched for more to say. When he didn't find anything, he hugged her again, this time like he meant it. Myla held him tight; and when he finally released her, she let out a long pent-up breath. Much more of this and she was going to cry again. She didn't want to cry. Not here. Not yet.

"It's fine." It wasn't. "I'll talk to him. One way or another, we'll find an accommodation." They wouldn't, and Lucius had to know that. "I'm giving myself a few days before I go to him. You, first. Then the temple and Mistress Tasahre. Then Soraya. I want to put things right before I go."

There were tears in Lucius's eyes now. "You don't need to put things right with me, Rish. You never did. As for Soraya..." He shook his head. "I'd say don't bother. But..." He looked around the pier, at the men and women working and the barge being loaded with silks. "Rish... She still thinks you're dead. I never told her the truth. It was better that way."

Myla looked away, trying to hide how much that stung, even if it was probably true. "Best she learns from someone other than Sarwatta." Another deep breath. "Will you tell her? Before I go to her? It might be a bit much, otherwise."

"Of course. If that's what you want."

They stood together, side by side, looking out over the water. Myla was dimly aware of Orien, lurking like an unwanted spare leg, unsure of what to do with himself. Having him for company on the trip from Varr had been a pleasant distraction, but now... Now she wished he'd go away. Leaving him behind was only going to make everything more difficult.

"We were further down the river when I left," she said, waving an arm at the docks. "You've gone up in the world, despite me."

"How long do I have you?"

"Just today, I think."

Lucius squeezed his eyes shut and shivered, and then opened them again and snapped his fingers at Korfa to supervise the loading of the barge. He led Myla across the docks and through the alleys behind them to the old Broken Spar teahouse, the place they used to meet in secret back when Myla had been training at the temple and Lucius had been his father's apprentice.

"Nostalgia?" she asked; but no, it turned out that Lucius had a room rented, that he was living there. "What happened to the house?"

"Soraya has it."

Orien had followed, so Myla introduced him to Lucius; and then, when Lucius seemed about to invite Orien to join them, gently put a hand on the mage's arm.

"I want some time alone with my brother," she said. "Just for a while."

Orien didn't look happy but didn't protest. He promised to return and then walked away, huffing about having plenty of other places be. Myla watched him go; and then for a long time, she and Lucius talked and drank tea, just the two of them, and for a while it was as though the last six months, Sarwatta and Soraya, had never happened. She let him tell her about the family business, how it was prospering. Nothing spectacular, but they *were* about to take their first consignment of Taiytakei silks to the robemakers in the City of Spires. He told her about Soraya, how she was running the sea-docks side of things. He showed her the last letter from their parents, from Torpreah, where her mother had taken Holy Orders and was now a Servant of the Sun. How she talked about Myla, her child who was a sword-monk, with pride and... was that even a little envy? Such a change from the mother Myla remembered, quietly resentful of her unwanted second daughter.

"They don't know?"

"They think you're still here at the temple. I didn't have the heart."

"You know you have to tell them."

Lucius made a sour face. "Torpreah is a long way away, Rish. Maybe let them keep the daughter they remember, eh? The young heroic monk who earned her swords to such acclaim?"

Myla didn't argue. She couldn't see how it would work, but one thing at a time. She asked about House Hawat, then. Sarwatta, it seemed, had left them alone. When Myla pressed, Lucius only shook his head. He didn't know why, only that Soraya had told him in no uncertain terms to keep away both from her and from anything to do with Hawat business. He turned the conversation then, asking about Orien, who he was and should he be jumping to defend his sister's honour? He clearly meant it as a joke, but it almost made Myla burst into tears, because wasn't that exactly what had ripped their family apart in the first place? He fell quiet, after that.

"I should have just let him get away with it," Myla said. "I should have let him use her and then throw her away and left it be. Every single one of us would have been happier. Even Soraya."

That was the bitter truth. She'd seen it coming, had tried to head it off, but it had happened anyway, only she'd put herself between them and given Soraya someone else to blame. And then she'd stabbed Sarwatta, because frankly he'd deserved a good stabbing, but it had made everything a hundred times worse.

And hadn't she been a little jealous, too? But she didn't want to think about that, so she shouted up for a couple of bottles of wine and told Lucius about Orien, how he was a mage, albeit not much of one, and her on-off lover. She told him how she'd washed up in the *Unruly Pig* more or less by accident after her flight from Deephaven, and how that was where Orien had found her. She told him about Fings and Seth and Dox and Arjay and Blackhand and Sulfane, how Sulfane had tricked them into stealing the late Emperor's crown, how she and Orien had managed to give it back and met the Princess-

Regent in person, Sun bless her. They laughed and joked and called for more wine until they were both drunk and the walls were spinning, because that was what they did, her and her brother. Drank and laughed and told stories to each other.

"You can tell mother and father *that*," she said. "They'll like that. Let them think I'm gallivanting around the Empire, doing Important Things."

"Has to count for something, doesn't it?" Lucius slurred, after she told him for the third time about the meeting at Samir's Folly on Midwinter's Night. "Maybe the court in Varr can intervene with the Hawats?"

As if she hadn't been wondering the same thing all the way from Varr. As if Orien hadn't been pushing it at her all that time. But it was dream-thinking. "Don't fool yourself," she murmured. "I'm already forgotten."

She must have passed out after that because the next thing she knew she was tucked up in bed, and Orien was in the room talking to Lucius, and she was far too numb and tingly and warm and comfortable and drunk to move. Lucius, on the other hand, sounded a lot more sober than he had earlier.

"...with that. If you tell me where you're staying, I'll have Korfa draw up a list of possibilities. Then we can inspect them."

"Somewhere a little... isolated," said Orien. "And with access to water."

"That shouldn't be a problem."

Mostly, Myla wanted to go back to sleep; but she didn't because she couldn't work out what in Kelm's name they were talking about. It sounded like business talk.

And then suddenly it wasn't.

"She thinks she can bargain with Sarwatta," said Lucius, "but she can't. Can you help her?"

"I don't know," said Orien. "Can you?"

"House Hawat could take everything we have with a snap of their fingers. I'd be happy with that, if that meant she could walk away, but... Orien, did she tell you what she did? She...

she *castrated* him. In public. I don't know if she meant to, but…" A pause, then: "She told me what you did in Varr. The two of you. Doesn't that count for something?"

"Of course… but I can't make promises."

"Then you have to get her away from here."

"You think I don't know that?" There was a long pause and then she heard Orien again: "Are you sure she's asleep?"

"She drank enough."

"Then tie her up and throw her onto the back of a horse. Start riding and don't stop and don't look back. Do it now."

"What?"

"Because that's the only way you're going to get her to do what you want. And *I'm* not going to do it because she'll bloody well murder me."

"You're her… I don't know, what are you? Her lover? Her partner?"

"I don't know *what* I am to her. Yes, I suppose. Something like that."

"*Talk* to her, then! Tell her she can't do this!"

"Kelm's teeth, do you think I haven't tried? All the way from Varr! Have you *met* your own sister? *You* try telling her what to do."

She heard Lucius laugh, then, although it was an odd sound, as though some part of him was sobbing. "I can't do anything," he said, almost a whisper. "I can't stop her, and I can't stop Sarwatta. All I can do is watch."

"Don't give up."

"She's my sister and I love her."

Another long pause. Then a heavy sigh from Orien. "I have a bad feeling I might have the same problem."

Silently, Myla smiled. And then she fell back asleep and started to snore.

5

SETH

Back in Varr, Seth was in the sort of reflective mood that came when you were possibly about to be murdered and couldn't do anything about it. Working for Blackhand in the *Unruly Pig* as the best forger south of the river had, in hindsight, been a better job than he'd credited at the time. Yes, Blackhand had been abusive, miserly and generally unpleasant to work with, but you could count on the fingers of a severed stump the number of times he'd taken Seth out onto the river, tied a block of stone to his ankles, and threatened to push him overboard.

The woman who'd spent the last few minutes doing exactly that – Seth didn't know who she was and reckoned it best to keep things that way – was currently pacing the deck of her boat. It was a small boat but nicely made, well cared-for and clearly not used for lugging cargo up and down the river or ferrying passengers from one side to the other, day in and day out. It was the sort of boat that belonged to the sort of woman who could afford to have a boat and then not use it very much.

The same sort of woman, it turned out, could also afford to have half a dozen strapping young thugs grab a fellow off the street, tie a rock around his ankles and then drag him out onto the river, next to a freshly dead corpse who'd apparently had a spasm while shaving and accidentally cut his own throat. An appallingly *bad* spasm, by the looks of how he'd cut all the way to the bone.

The woman stopped pacing. They were out in the middle of the water now. The middle of the river, the middle of the night. A part of Seth wanted to point out that the stone wasn't necessary: he couldn't swim, and this deep into the Sulk of winter, the water was so cold that it would kill him in minutes even if he could. Adding the rock was, Seth thought, a little too theatrical to be tasteful.

"You're the one who can make dead men talk?" asked the woman.

This, right here, was the problem with being able to talk to Dead Men. You *tried* to spread the word to the sort of people who wouldn't mind passing over the occasional half-moon for some last words with a recently-passed loved one. What you *got* were psychotic criminals who saw you as a quick and easy alternative to the tedious process of torturing people for information.

Although… There *was* some promise to the idea, assuming he lived through the next five minutes.

She prodded him. "The necromancer?"

Seth wondered what would happen if he said no, but the answer would inevitably be bad, and probably involve the river and the rock tied around his ankles. "Warlock," he said. "Necromancer is such a loaded word." Not that it made a difference. He could call himself a fish-juggler if he liked; one whisper of someone who could talk to Dead Men and the Path of the Sun would turn the city inside out until they hunted him down, burned him for heresy and then stomped on the ashes. He sighed. "For future reference, it helps if they still have a working windpipe. What did you cut his throat with? A pike?"

The woman didn't answer. She was hooded and kept her face hidden, but her accent was from the south, somewhere near Torpreah where they were all devout followers of the

Sun. Which made it all the more dangerous that she was about to make a pact with a warlock.

Except she's not. She's going to get what she wants, then salve her conscience by chucking you in the river. Let's face it, it's what you'd *do.*

"Here's the thing," Seth said. "We're out here in the middle of the night, and I'm all tied up, and you've got your bunch of guards, and I don't know how much you know about me, but if you knew anything at all, you'd know I'm not really the bravest sort. I mean, ordinarily under these sorts of circumstances, I'd be shitting myself. And yet here I am, not really scared at all. In your shoes, I'd ask myself why that was. We're clearly not in any great hurry, so take your time. But *do* have a think, because there's a couple of ways this can go. The best is where we treat each other as fellow professionals: you pay me for my unique services, we go our separate ways, I quietly forget about this little piece of murder next to me, you quietly forget about a little dark sorcery, and maybe we do some more business in the future. Or we do it with threats and rocks and black magic and trying to drown people and see what happens."

It was a good speech, he thought. He'd certainly practiced it enough.

To her credit, the woman put on a good show of changing her mind. She had her henchmen untie the ropes around Seth's ankles, agreed a price, gave him the time and space he needed to do what he did, asked her questions, then took him back to the shore and paid him what he asked. He'd *almost* got to thinking he was wrong about her, until he spotted the men following him.

6

A DEAD MAN CALLED STUPID

There were four of them. Actually five, but the fifth wasn't following *him*, and nor was it really a man. Seth followed the river upstream past the grain silos, although not too close on account of the Imperial Guard stationed there since Midwinter, apparently to stop them from being burned by enemies of the new Regency. By the time he reached the entrance to the undercity in the bowels of a derelict warehouse, he thought he'd lost them.

He waited a bit to be sure. When it turned out he was wrong, he sighed. *Here we go.*

It surprised him they didn't try taking him before he went underground. Seemed like it would have been easier for them. Certainly safer, although he supposed they had no way to know that. On the other hand, being underground effectively meant he was trapped, since the way back home from the derelict warehouse meant going through the sorcerous portal that only Cleaver knew how to open, which meant he couldn't actually *get* home until Cleaver bothered showing up.

He left the door from the cellars of the warehouse open, vaguely hoping that the men following might take that as a hint. Then he walked a little way down the tunnel on the other side until he was almost at the white stone shaft and the spiralling steps that led into the vaults below. He stopped there, took his charcoal stick from inside his coat along with a couple of pieces of paper, and drew some sigils. He drew a handful more on the walls of the tunnel and then waited. There wasn't anywhere else for the men to go, there wasn't anywhere for them to hide once they came through that door, and, unless they knew a great deal more about the undercity than Seth did, there wasn't any way for them to get around behind him.

Eventually they came sneaking in, all quiet and stealthy and slow, which might have worked if Seth hadn't been sitting staring straight back at them as they entered.

"Well come on then!" he called.

They came on. When they were a dozen paces short, Seth raised his hands. He didn't bother getting to his feet.

"I'd stop there, if I were you," he said.

They stopped.

"Your mistress sent you to kill me then, did she?"

"Not at all," said the biggest of the four, apparently imagining he sounded genuine. "We're just here to talk."

"Yes. Well, if *that* was true, we could have talked in the open back when we were all pretending to be friends. So bollocks to that. Look, you were there so you know what I am. Turn around, go home and tell your mistress that I look forward to doing further business together."

The big man made a clucking noise. "Yeah... That's not how this works."

"Isn't it? Why not?"

This seemed to confuse them.

"Honestly, if I were in your shoes, I'd be asking your mistress some difficult questions. It hardly seems fair, ordering you to go out and murder a warlock. Did anyone even tell you how? I mean, you can't just stick a knife into me and expect that to work. You *did* know that, right?" As far as Seth knew, sticking knives in him would work just fine, but two could play at a bit of theatre.

"You don't even have lanterns. If you don't have lanterns,

how are you supposed to see the hideous, deadly necromantic sigils drawn all over this tunnel?"

"Bullshit," said the big man, although he hesitated a moment before he said it, and didn't sound quite as sure of himself as perhaps he'd hoped. Seth shrugged.

"Take a step closer and find out. Do you mind if I call you Stupid?"

"*What*?"

"Because you'll need to have a name, once you're my undead servant. *All* my undead servants have names. So, I'm going to call you Stupid." Seth snapped his fingers. "I'd like you to meet a friend of mine. Stupid, this is Cleaver. Cleaver, this is Stupid."

He wasn't sure how Cleaver was there, exactly. One moment, he had four uncertain thugs in front of him; and then somehow Cleaver was standing behind them with... well, not to put too fine a point on it, with a cleaver stuck through his skull. Seth hadn't actually *seen* Cleaver come through the doorway, yet there he stood. That was how it was with Cleaver. He'd been a Spicer once, but Seth was pretty sure that whatever was in him now, it wasn't human. The big give-away on that score was how Cleaver could open the portals of the undercity, while Seth still didn't have the first clue about how they worked.

A wraith.

Yeah. No. Definitely didn't want to be thinking about how Cleaver just might have the lingering spirit of a dead half-god lurking inside him; fortunately, he had other things to occupy his thoughts: Stupid turned, saw Cleaver, skewered the Dead Man with a short stabbing sword, and then discovered that stabbing Dead Men didn't really achieve anything.

"See what I–"

Cleaver pulled the cleaver out of his skull and buried it in Stupid's face, which very much *did* achieve something.

"Cleaver! What have we said about–"

Cleaver grinned at him and threw Stupid down the tunnel.

As he did, two of the other thugs ran at Seth. The third, apparently a bit quicker on the uptake, held back.

"No! Don't–"

The two running at him crossed the sigils he'd drawn on the tunnel floor and dropped dead.

"Oh, for pity's sake!"

The last one was busy hacking at Cleaver, mostly, Seth reckoned, to try and get past so he could run away. Cleaver caught him, threw him to the ground and jumped on him, ready to rip out the man's throat with his teeth.

"Cleaver! *Cleaver*! No! Kelm's Teeth, can't I have at least *one* of them alive? Let him go!"

There was a lot of reluctance, but Cleaver eventually let him go.

"Bad zombie!"

Cleaver gave him a baleful look.

While the last survivor was picking himself up and staring at Cleaver – still with Stupid's sword stuck through him – Seth slapped a sigil onto each of the other corpses and brought them back as Dead Men. When he was done, he brushed himself down.

"I do think I tried quite hard for it not to end like this," he said. "I hope you can see that. Anyway, you can go now. Tell your mistress that she should know better, but that our little misunderstanding in no way diminishes my interest in her ongoing patronage. Any *further* misunderstandings, however, will be taken very personally."

He stood beside Cleaver. Together, they watched the man go.

"You're going to keep that, aren't you?" Seth prodded the two inches of sword sticking out of Cleaver's back.

The Dead Man grinned and put his cleaver back into the side of his skull.

And this, Seth thought, is how you let the people with the real money know that you're open for business, and also not to fuck with you.

He headed off into the undercity, letting Cleaver lead the way. When they got where they were going, he was going to have a whole pile of questions for his new Dead Men friends. They'd start with who the hooded woman was, he reckoned, and take it from there.

He'd paid attention to the questions the hooded woman had asked – that was the thing – and to the answers the dead man had given. The hooded woman was looking for someone, and Seth reckoned he had a shrewd idea that the person she was looking for was Sulfane. The dead man had known her, too, and had mentioned a priest from Torpreah. If Seth was right, there was a good chance this priest had been the one pulling Sulfane's strings last year when Sulfane had roped them all into stealing the late Emperor's crown, which meant this same priest had had something to do with the late Emperor being *late* in the first place. If *that* was true, he reckoned Myla and Fings probably wanted a word, and probably a lot of other people too, starting with the Guild of Mages and the Imperial Guard and ending with the Sapphire Throne itself.

He grinned to himself. The sort of people who were dangerous, true enough, but would also have a lot of money for information like that, if he played it right.

7

THE SWORD MISTRESS

Dawn prayer had been a part of Myla's daily life back when she'd been training to be a sword-monk. These days she couldn't understand how she'd managed. It was almost midday before she stirred, and well into the afternoon before she nursed herself back to some semblance of civility. Now and then, Lucius came to look in on her. She had no idea where Orien had gone.

"Searching for my new guild house," the mage told her that evening, when she finally saw him.

"Did you find anywhere?"

"I'll show you, tomorrow. Let's eat! I'm starving!"

The light outside the Broken Spar was that peculiar dull Deephaven grey of early evening in the rain. Myla caught his arm. "No." She let go again. "Or rather... Do as you please, but I've got somewhere I need to be. I'd... You can come too, if you want, but it might be better if you didn't."

He came, complaining on and off about how hungry he was, and how the rain was making him cold and wet as they walked side by side up to the Peak and Deephaven Square. Despite herself, Myla was glad of the company. She wore a mask now, since that seemed to be the fashion, a folded square of cotton from Lucius, dipped in aromatic oils to keep the miasma of the

River Plague at bay. He'd given her a charm to wear around her neck, too. As a daughter of the Sun, Myla didn't believe in miasmas or lucky charms, but she *did* believe in the power of a mask to hide her face so that people didn't recognize her until she was good and ready.

The oils smelled of Varr and the Spice Market. They made her think of Seth and Fings. For a while, at least, until the rain soaked through and the mask took to smelling of rot and the sea, same as everything else.

"House Hawat?" Orien asked, as they crossed the square. He had the right one: the ochre-and-yellow painted façade, the balustrades and balconies, the wide arched windows on the upper levels, the stumpy signalling tower on top that was exactly the height permitted by decree of the late Emperor, Sun bless him. In all these things, House Hawat stood among peers and equals, a follower of the fashion of the day, no less and no more. Among the great merchant houses of the richest city in the Empire, they were nothing special. Enough that they *were* one of those houses.

"You should see it when the rains stop and the sun comes out," she said.

Orien made a face. "Does that ever actually happen?"

"It's not like this *all* the time, you know."

"How much power do they really have?" Orien scratched at his nose.

"A seat on the city council along with nine of their peers, bowing only to the authority of the Overlord and the Sunherald – who can usually be relied upon to disagree and thus neuter one another, unless that's changed. Neither would defy the Ten Families if the Ten Families were ever united."

"But these Ten Families... usually they're *not* united?"

Myla shrugged. "Factions and alliances constantly shift. What gives an advantage to one rarely gives advantage to all."

"The Hawats have enemies, then?"

"Don't we all?"

"Who?"

"Ask Lucius. It changes so quickly." Not that it would do any good. She could see where Orien's thoughts were taking him, but he was new here and didn't understand. "In the matter of what I did to Sarwatta, they will unite. Secret smiles and a gleeful enjoyment of his discomfort in private, yes, but in the open..." she shook her head. "They need to set an example. Otherwise, who knows? I might do it again, to one of them."

"Would they mind if the House of Hawat accidentally caught fire and burned to the ground?"

He was trying to make her smile. That was a nice thing about him. It almost worked, too. "I'm afraid they would, and for much the same reason." She smirked and glanced at the sky, the leaden grey cloud, the steady, falling rain. "Also, fires aren't really much of a problem in Deephaven. Not this time of year. They might work out who did it rather too easily for your liking."

"If he so much as touches you, I might do it anyway."

"Well, *I* won't stop you. Just don't get caught."

Orien bowed his head and nodded, as much to himself as to her. "Lady Novashi will expect a place on that council," he said. "When she gets here. Perhaps that might change things?"

They crossed the square through the rain and listened to the temple bells ring. An hour until sunset, warning that Twilight Prayer would come soon. Outside the open temple gates, Myla pointed to the Spire of the Sun, capped in gold. Then to the other tower, the one with what looked like wings sprouting from its peak. She and Orien were both soaked. It didn't bother her but it was clearly making Orien uncomfortable.

"Are you *sure* it's not always like this?" he asked.

She ignored him. "The Spire of the Sun and the Overlord's tower are the same height. Before I was born, they kept being rebuilt, each always trying to be bigger than the other. Before one was even finished, the other had started on something grander. That was after Khrozus took the Sapphire Throne and

STEPHEN DEAS   41

called himself Emperor, and he and the old Autarch down in Torpreah would have gone to war with each other all over again, if they could. When the Butcher died, Emperor Ashahn made it stop, Sun bless him. The Sunherald and the Overlord now have towers exactly as tall as each other and are forbidden from building more. And of course, no one else is allowed to build one that's taller." She pointed around the square at the houses there, all with towers of their own, all the same height as one another. "That's how this city lives, Orien. Everyone looking to show they're better than everyone else. Always looking for some advantage. What you *do*, what you *are*, none of that matters, only the façade in which you dress yourself. I hope your mistress is ready for that."

"She'll eat them alive," said Orien, so quietly that he might have been talking to himself.

With the bells still ringing, she led Orien away from the temple, taking him around the square to the other great arch beside the Guildhouse. From there, she walked him down the half-mile of the Avenue of the Sun until it sprawled them out into the city's second great square, the square of Four Winds. Masked men and women scurried back and forth, heads bowed against the drizzle. Rain hissed into steam from braziers pressed against the walls, tainting the smells of hot fat and butter and onions and spices with the stink of damp streets and dung and the ever-present tang of rotting fish. The noise was a cacophony of shouting, offers of everything from fried dough-balls to strips of pickled fish to spiced rat-sticks and baked weevils, all hurled and battered against one another by the whirl of the wind. The city might be in the grip of plague, but, other than the masks and the charms and the burning incense, there was no sign of it here.

Through the middle of it all was what she wanted Orien to see, the relentless train of carts and wagons that trundled from one side of the square to the other: up the Godsway and the Avenue of Emperors from the river-docks, down the other half of the Avenue of Emperors to the harbour and the sea, then back the other way. Errand boys slipped and skittered between them across cobbles slick with water, splashing through puddles, heedless of angry shouts that followed them.

"Take a moment," she said. "Right here is the blood of this city, the flow that never stops, up and down, river to sea and back again. It fills the coffers of rich men with gold and then fills them again, over and over until there are no coffers left to hold such wealth, and still the wagons roll. The engine of the Empire." She wanted Orien to understand; but now that he was here, she couldn't think of how to explain it. All she saw, when she looked at him, was the rain dripping off his nose and his beard, his drenched robes clinging to his scrawny skin, how he looked like a sad drowned rat. It made her want to hug him and hold him and take him somewhere warm and dry.

"When Khrozus rose against the Sapphire Throne, the Autarch of the Sun in Torpreah denounced him and called upon his priests to resist. In Varr, they whipped the populace into opposition. When Khrozus took the city, he executed every Sunherald, Dawncaller and Sunbright who didn't manage to flee. Yet six months before, when Khrozus held Deephaven and Emperor Talsin laid siege to it, the priests took no side and Khrozus left them alone. Why?" She pointed down the Avenue of the Sun to the Overlord's Palace and the temple beside it. "Because all that really matters here is what you see in front of you, and that it never falters. All through the siege, the ships kept coming. Bring your mistress. Stand her here and tell her all this. If she understands, perhaps you'll survive this place."

It hit her then, the weight of what she was about to do. She'd been expecting it all the way from Varr, the crushing extinction of hope, yet it hadn't come, maybe because Orien had sought her out and resolutely stayed at her side. She'd been born to this, raised to it, a daughter of two worlds, the one ahead of her, filling Four Winds Square, the constant groan and creak of wheels and rope and wood. And the other behind her, the tolling of the temple bells, of prayer and that inner calm she'd never quite mastered, of the scrape of steel and the unflinching obedience to duty. She'd turned her back on both. Now she felt the weight of that choice. The regret for what she'd done. Or, more honestly, for the consequences.

He deserved it.

Abruptly, she turned back to the temple. "I can't do this."

"Do what?" asked Orien.

Myla ignored him. She ran back up the Avenue of the Sun, dashing through the rain, across Deephaven Square to the temple gates. The Sunguard in their bright yellow sunburst shirts saw her swords and gave short nods of respect. She avoided the dome of the Hall of Light, straight to the first Sunguard she saw standing outside, a young man barely more than a boy. Inside the dome, Twilight Prayer had already started. She stood, sodden and miserable.

"Sword-mistress Tasahre," she said. "Is she here?"

"I... I don't..."

"Mistress Tasahre! The sword-mistress!" She shook him.

"Y–Yes! I don't know where she–"

"Never mind." She let him go and undid the straps and buckles that held the two Sunsteel hook-swords across her back. She slid herself out of the harness and handed it to him. The young Sunguard looked at her as though she'd given him a snake.

"Take these to Mistress Tasahre. Give them to her after evening prayer. Take a message, too. Tell her that Shirish profoundly regrets the dishonour she brought and means to make amends as best she can."

She made him repeat the message until he had it memorized, then turned away. Orien stood waiting at the gate to the square; and she was glad for the rain and how and how it hid her tears.

"Come on," she said. "Let's get drunk."

8

SORAYA

By the time Myla woke, Orien was gone again. She lay for a while, luxuriating in the warmest, plushest, most expensive bed she'd ever found, in a room that had, according to the boast of the *Imperial Watchman's Arms*, once hosted the Emperor's cousin. The thought made her smile. From what she'd heard of the Sulking Prince, sharing a bed with him really wasn't much an achievement; still, she let herself linger on the idea as she fell back asleep.

When she woke again, she remembered that Prince Sharda was dead. One of the last pieces of news she'd heard before she'd left Varr: fate had apparently caught up with him only months after he'd murdered the Emperor's brother on the first day of the Winter Court in Tarantor. Hand in hand with news of his death was a rumour that the Sulking Prince was also the Princess-Regent's true father. It was, she supposed, as handy a way as any of undermining the Regent's authority. Men were always so obsessed with who fucked whom.

There *was* a war coming. She could feel it, even if she most likely wouldn't live to see it.

She lay in the bed a while longer, stroking its sheets of Taiytakei silk until hunger demanded she move. Orien hadn't returned, so she went outside and stalked her way to the sea-docks where men with braziers stood in the rain, grilling every part of every creature the sea could think to offer. She moved from one to the next, hiding behind her mask, grazing, not realizing until now how much she'd missed this. The food in Varr, so far from the sea, was dull and monotonous. Mutton and a root vegetable. Pork and a slightly different root vegetable. That was about the extent of Varr's repertoire.

Hunger sated, she left the docks and started up through the Maze towards the Peak. The Maze wasn't a place where a nice merchant's daughter ever went, but she was a sword-monk too, not that either of those things mattered now. Despite the rain, a gang of children took to following her, dancing and singing, half a dozen scruffy ragamuffins chasing each other with sticks, moving around her as though she was an island and they were the sea. The rain didn't trouble them at all. She knew their song, if not the tune; when they started to sing again, she joined them.

Man with no shadow that nobody knows
Comes to harvest that which he sows
Great white tower made of stone that grows
Home to the makers of all of man's woes

The four old mages fall from the sky
Now the dead in peace may lie
Two born low and two born high
Touched by silver, three will die

Dragon-king and dark lord's bane
Each will wax and then will wane
The Bloody Judge lifts his hand
All is razed to ash and sand

Black moon comes, round and round
Black moon comes, all fall down.

They laughed as their song ended, and ran away.

The Maze spat her out onto the Avenue of Emperors halfway between the Peak and the sea, with its statues like the Circus of Dead Emperors in Varr. The statue of the usurper Khrozus was another new one, she saw, because statues of Khrozus didn't tend to last in Deephaven. This one was already scarred, the eyes chipped out by some angry chisel, paint daubed over the base: Usurper. Butcher. Bastard.

The Princess-Regent was Khrozus' grand-daughter. If war came, she'd need Deephaven, and Deephaven wouldn't go easy to a descendant of the Usurper. Maybe the rumours about the Sulking Prince being her father weren't such a bad thing?

Not that you care, remember?

The rain had her soaked to the skin again. Deephaven rain was cold this time of year, but she didn't feel it. She stayed by the statue, looking it over, and saw that someone had had a go at chiselling off the head, too. She wondered why they'd stopped. Disturbed by Longcoats, probably.

The thought took her to Midwinter's night: her and Orien on the bridge in Varr, handing back the Emperor's crown. She'd been sure, then, that it was the right thing to do. Now…?

Well, if she was honest, it had been a penance to set against what she'd done in Deephaven. That was why she'd stayed in Varr. To make something right. Had she, though? *Had* she made something right?

The Princess-Regent had looked her in the eye. The sorceress Princess. The Moon-Witch. By returning the crown, she and Orien had secured her throne, or so Orien claimed. Her eyes had been green and fierce. You didn't see green eyes in natives of the Empire. But skin like her own. Green eyes, dark olive skin. They didn't go.

What else had she seen in those eyes? Fire and resolve and purpose. A lot of anger.

I'm told it was one of your kind who killed my mother.

Yes, well. Everyone knew *that* story. Didn't make it true.

There's a storm coming. From the sea. Can you feel it?

What had she meant by that?

Here she was, standing out in the rain beside the statue of a dead emperor, soaked through, thinking of something that had happened more than a month ago. Why? Oh, but she knew *exactly* why, because she'd known for some time where her feet were taking her, with their meandering path towards the Peak. They were taking her to Soraya, to the last place she had to go before she gave herself to the hopelessness of making peace with Sarwatta. A thing that absolutely had to be done, and which, nevertheless, she absolutely didn't want to do.

What would you *do*, she asked, thinking of those green eyes on that Midwinter bridge. Lucius would tell her to run. So would Orien. Sword-mistress Tasahre would tell her to find whatever made her afraid and walk straight towards it.

The memory of Midwinter made her think of a line from a poem, written long ago by a man waiting to hang. *The murder in my eye is just the will to stay alive...*

You know exactly *what I'd do.*

Yes. She did. Didn't make it any easier, though.

Sarwatta deserved it...

But the nights that went before? There would be no forgiveness from Soraya. Lucius hadn't exactly said so, but he hadn't told Soraya that Myla wasn't dead, either.

So brave. Coming all this way, carefully not looking at how it would end. But you have to open your eyes now. Not so pretty when you look at it. One of you has to die.

She'd known how it would be, even before she'd left Varr.

She kicked herself into movement, and still almost had to drag herself up the last hundred yards of the Avenue of Emperors. She crossed Four Winds Square and headed towards the river, into a warren of small but elegant squares where the river merchants lived. Her old home, when she found it, hadn't changed. There were no annual renovations here, no competing for the gaudiest façade. The only status that mattered was location: the closer to Deephaven Square you were, the richer you must be.

She thought about climbing around the back, the way she – and she had no doubt that Lucius and Soraya had done it too – used slip out in secret in the years before their parents had left for Torpreah. But what if Lucius hadn't done as he'd promised? What if Soraya didn't know her errant sister wasn't dead after all? What if she heard a noise and went to look and discovered a ghost climbing through a window? Probably not the best start, and it was always going to be difficult, this.

She settled for knocking on the door. The servant who opened it was unfamiliar, someone who didn't know her.

"Can I help you, my lady?"

My lady. She couldn't stop a slight sad smile. *My lady. Myla...*

"If Soraya is here, I'd speak with her."

The servant invited her out of the rain and settled her in the little room behind the entrance, the place where her father used to keep men of lower station waiting before he'd see them. Giving them a few minutes to remember their place, he'd call it.

"Who shall I say is here?" asked the servant.

"Shirish," said Myla. "Her sister." She saw the flash of alarm then, but quickly suppressed. She was, to some extent, expected. Good. Lucius had kept his promise.

If Soraya knew she was here, House Hawat would know it too. She caught the servant's arm as he was about to leave.

"Tell Soraya this," she said. "If she has words for me, this may be the last chance she'll have to say them. If she has none, I will leave."

She tried to imagine what her mother would say, if she'd been here and not in Torpreah. Mostly it would be about how disappointed she was, probably, how Myla had brought shame on their house, when what she *really* meant was that Myla had damaged their chances of moving further up the Peak. And then, from her father, more of the same, only this time

Myla would have to work hard not to slap him to silence, because they both knew that all she'd ever been to him was an inconvenience. Finally, her mother would cry, which would probably make *her* cry too, and Soraya would take one look at the whole sorry scene and leave without a word.

But her mother and father were in Torpreah. Five years, now, since they'd left, and she and Lucius and Soraya... they'd all been too young. That was it. That was all it was. Too young.

The door opened. Myla stood. She had words ready, words she'd been thinking on all the way from Varr and which needed to be said. She had them all lined up in her head, ready to–

Soraya was pregnant. Very pregnant. She stood, looking at Myla, waiting for something, and then Myla understood, and all her words dissolved to ash in her mouth.

"You're carrying his child! You're carrying Sarwatta Hawat's heir."

Soraya met her eye. "Yes."

"How *could* you?"

Soraya flared. "How *could* I? After what you did, what *else* was I to do when I discovered it inside me?" She turned to the servant, hovering at the door. "Carry a message. Inform the master of House Hawat that my sister is here, that I will detain her for as long as required."

The servant bowed and backed away. Soraya spat.

"How *could* I? How *dare* you! So I might not be beggared! So Lucius might not be murdered! So my mother and father might not be hunted down in some far away city and kicked to the street with nothing to their name, without ever knowing why!" Her jaw quivered as she raged. "You think I *want* this? *You* did this. You! You did this to us all. Well. Sarwatta will have no other heir of his own. *You* saw to that. Did his seed not sprout in *your* belly too? Or is the rest of you as barren as your heart?" She turned and spat again. "I should have known it was too good to be true when they said you were dead."

"I never–"

Soraya whirled to hiss in Myla's face. "You! All a pretence so you could run, leaving me and Lucius to suffer for what you did; is that what it was? Did you think he'd leave us alone? Are you *that* stupid? How *could* I? Because this unwanted bastard inside me is the only shield I have! Pray to your pitiless god that he comes into the world strong. You care nothing for me, that was always clear, nor for mother or father, but *Lucius...*" She sneered. "Big brother Lucius, who always took your side. Understand what you've done, little sister. I'm carrying his only chance of a son. His child inside me is the *only* thing that has stopped him from ending us all. If it dies, this family dies with it. On *that*, Sarwatta has been very clear."

"No." Myla found herself shaking. "No! He can't do this to you. He can't!"

"*He* is doing nothing. *I* am seeing to that. And when the child is born, I will keep it close, always at my side, always a shield to see that Sarwatta stays his hand, knowing that if he destroys our family, he destroys his own."

"Soraya! He will never allow—"

"You have ruined me, Shirish. Well and truly, but this way, at least you've not ruined *every*thing." Soraya turned her back, as if to leave, then paused. "You should have stayed dead. He'll hurt you, before he kills you. I think of what he'll do, and I feel nothing. You should go."

Myla caught Soraya as she reached for the door and spun her around. "Soraya! You can't—"

"Will you strike your own sister now?" Myla realized she had a hand raised, reaching for the swords she no longer carried.

"Soraya!" *Deep breaths. Deep breaths. Light of the mind and courage of the heart.* "You're right. He was handsome and charming, and yes, a part of me wanted him for no other reason than you were blind with love for him. But you've seen him for what he is now. I saw it too. Honestly, all I wanted was to save you."

"To *save* me?" Soraya almost howled with laughter. "From *what*?"

"From a broken heart."

The words hung between them.

"Then bravo," said Soraya, after a long, long silence. "What a fine job you did."

Myla pushed past her for the door. Soraya didn't stop her. As she left, Myla turned for a moment. "He was beneath you," she said.

Soraya only shook her head, a smile on her lips while poison burned in her eyes. "I think we both know who was beneath whom, Shirish."

9

JUST ANOTHER DRUNKEN BRAWL ON THE DOCKS

A year ago, when Myla had known him, Sarwatta often spent his evenings in the *Captain's Rest* down by the Sea Docks. It didn't quite have the old-guard prestige of the *Imperial Watchman's Arms*, which had hosted not only the late Emperor's cousin but, in years long before Myla had been born, the Emperor himself. *That* had been before the Sad Empress had been murdered on the road between Varr and Deephaven, after which the late Emperor, Sun bless him, had largely kept to his three capitals of Varr, Tarator and the City of Spires. Still, the *Captain's Rest* had played host to more than its share of titles since and, more importantly, it was where the merchant princes of Deephaven met to do business. As the saying went: for politics, *The Watchman*; for money, *The Captain*.

She was already drunk as she lurched into the yard where the servants and the hangers-on passed their time waiting for their masters. The air was cold and damp, the cobbles slippery with rain. When she started towards the doors of *The Captain*, two brutes with long curved swords moved to block her way. She thought about fighting them, reckoned she could, too, but her swords were back at the temple, and besides, what was the point?

"I'm looking for Sarwatta Hawat," she told them. Maybe she should have waited with Soraya. Had it out then and there, her and Sarwatta fighting to the death right in front of her sister. That was why she was here, wasn't it? To put an end to this. To save Soraya from the burden she carried?

I'm doing this for her. She kept telling it to herself, hoping it might eventually sound like it was true.

The two idiots with their flashy cavalry swords – hopeless for fighting in close quarters – didn't move. They were doing a good job of pretending they hadn't heard her.

"He'll be very pleased if you tell him I'm here," she said. "Tell him Shirish is waiting for him."

That got their attention, although whether they knew her name because of what she'd done to Sarwatta – surely the whole city knew about *that* by now – or because of the other thing, she couldn't tell. Probably for Sarwatta, she thought. People tended to remember things like that.

"Stay here," said one of the guards, then darted inside.

Myla lounged against the wall, eyeing the other one. "What does a girl have to do around here to get a drink?"

The guard rolled his eyes and nodded to the serving boys, scurrying about the yard carrying pitchers and mugs.

"Is he here?" she tried. "Sarwatta?"

The guard glared.

He wasn't, as it turned out, but now two men were sauntering towards her with the swagger of sell-swords. They both carried long knives for close quarters brawling and reminded Myla of the men Jeffa Hawat had brought with him to Varr. They stopped beside the idiot with the silly sword and all three looked at her. She could almost see them thinking: *Is that really her?* The *Shirish?*

She pushed herself from the wall and into the path of a serving boy, making him veer to dodge around her. As he did, she snatched the pitcher out of his hand and took a good long swallow. Mead. The good stuff. Strong and sweet.

"Hey!" The boy gave her an angry glare and then looked to the guard with the silly sword. The guard tried to grab her. He was briefly surprised as she swerved around his lunge; and then she smashed the pitcher over his head and down he went. So much for carrying a cavalry sword in the middle of a crowded yard.

The sell-swords came at her then. She ducked around a table, kicked some poor fool who probably didn't deserve it off his stool, snatched it up and jabbed at the nearest. The leg caught him square on his nose, making him bleed everywhere. He swore and said something colourful about what he was going to do before he killed her. A space cleared around them. There was a bit of jeering as Myla brandished her stool again. The sell-swords hadn't gone for their knives yet, but they would. Off to one side, she could already see money changing hands.

"What are my odds?" she called. Men and women were coming out of the *Captain's Rest* now, a trickle leaving their tables inside to come out and watch the fun. The crowd hooted and whistled at the sell-swords to get on with it, it was just some drunk woman after all… But then a whisper started. She heard her name, and the jeers stopped.

"You want to talk to Sarwatta Hawat?" One sell-sword took a cautious step forward. "We can take you to him." Off to one side, Myla saw a tall woman in a long coat stoop and whisper something to a short round man beside her. The short man nodded and trotted off. They'd both come from inside. Reinforcements?

"How about you bring him here?" suggested Myla. "Let's finish what we started. In front of all these people. Let's be done with it."

"We'd prefer to take you to him in one piece," said the sell-sword. "Doesn't *have* to be that way, mind."

Myla scanned the crowd, looking at faces. There were more Hawat men here, there had to be, and others looking for Sarwatta's favour. But there would be Hawat enemies, too.

"Go fetch him!" countered Myla. "Tell him he can bring as many swords as he needs to feel safe from an unarmed woman." Her eyes swept the crowd again. She caught a few smirks, but not many. Mostly they were hostile. She'd been unarmed on the day she'd stabbed him with his own knife, too, but she was willing to bet that *that* wasn't a part of the story everyone got to hear.

The sell-sword with the bloody nose sprang at her. He slashed with his knife, driving her back, then darted in and lunged. It wasn't a bad effort, and he was quick on his feet, but he was no sword-monk. Myla blocked the lunge with her stool, felt the tip of his blade bite into the wood, twisted hard, twisting him, too, as he tried to keep hold of his knife, then took a quick step closer and jabbed the stool at his head, making him punch himself in his already-ruined nose. As he howled, she snapped a kick between his legs and watched him crumple.

"Right, then," she said. She pulled the knife from the stool and circled towards the second sell-sword. He didn't look happy, and the crowd wasn't giving him an easy way out.

"Enough!"

Amyar the Strong was pushing his way out from the *Captain's Rest*, four men at his back. Everyone knew Amyar. It was almost flattering that he wasn't coming at her alone.

"You two! Piss off." He swatted at the sell-swords without even looking. "You." He glared at Myla. "Put that knife down"

"Make me."

Amyar gave her a long moment, long enough to navigate the fog of mead and wine in her head. She didn't want to kill this man. She didn't want to kill *any*one, when it came down to it. Except maybe Sarwatta Hawat.

"Fine." She threw down the knife. "But you want me, you'll have to come and get me." She stalked away. The crowd, such as it was, parted to let her through. When she looked back, Amyar hadn't followed. A handful of others had, though – the second Hawat sell-sword, for one. As she walked down the

Avenue of Emperors towards the sea-docks, they came after her, casual and keeping their distance. For now.

Which was what she wanted. They could finish it here. Once she was dead, Sarwatta would have no reason to go after Lucius and Soraya, right?

Close to the sea, she stopped and turned. "Don't you lot all have other things to do?"

"Do you know how big the bounty is on you?" asked the sell-sword.

"Not as big as it should be," she said.

There were seven, now she had a chance to count, which was too many, and they were all armed and she wasn't, and, now she'd stopped, they were starting to spread out... but this was the Avenue of Emperors, busy right through the night with carts heading up to the Peak and down to the sea-docks, so she evened the odds a little by swinging under a wagon and then coming back over the top, blindsiding some idiot with a sword, kicking him in the head and taking his blade off him, which got her another moment of surprise which she used to stab someone in the leg, deep enough that he stopped being interested in anything more than screaming and trying not to bleed out.

Seven down to five. Not a bad start.

Five men in the middle of the night, in the middle of the Avenue of Emperors, except the one at the back was probably Amyar's and only here to watch, which made it four, and four was still too many, but not so many as to be ridiculous, and by now the traffic had worked out that there was a fight breaking out, and the road was full of shouting and people running away, which all made for good distractions; and so yes, it was going to be messy, but why the fuck not? It wasn't as if she had anything to lose.

The fight seemed to happen in flashes, too fast for her to follow even though she was a part of it: attacking and attacking, taking the fight to them rather than letting them come at her;

a vague nagging thought that she didn't want to kill anyone; a lot of shouting; having someone's face up close to her own and watching the light go out of his eyes and so much for not killing anyone; the smell of blood; something hitting her; a growing fury that she was fighting men she didn't even know when the one person she *did* want to fight wasn't even here...

And then she stood alone in the Avenue of Emperors, covered in other people's blood, a dripping sword in her hand, and it was over, and the man she'd kicked in the head was lying at her feet, out cold or worse, and there were two corpses beside him, cut to ribbons, and one was running away. She couldn't see the last two and had no idea where they'd gone; but the tall woman from the *Captain's Rest* was back, coming towards her at the head of a dozen city Longcoats, all just watching.

Myla turned her back and carried on towards the sea. For some reason, she wasn't walking right and kept nearly falling over, and one of her legs felt wonky, which made her frown, because she wasn't *that* drunk, was she?

She looked down at herself.

Oh.

So not *all* other people's blood, then.

The cut in her leg was bleeding freely, but it was the stab-wound under her ribs that was probably going to kill her. She stopped, trying to remember how it had happened, and found she couldn't.

That was the point though, wasn't it? Get yourself killed?

Couldn't even do *that* right.

The Longcoats were still following. She turned to face them and lifted her sword, reasoning they were as good anyone to finish the job; and then the distant hiss and rush of the sea seemed to get very loud, and there was some strange blast of music for a moment as the sword slipped out of her hand, and then everything went black.

INTERLUDE: ORIEN

Orien looked at the words he'd written, realised there were far too many and that he still hadn't said the thing that actually mattered, and scribbled another few lines:

I therefore require the assistance, at your earliest possible convenience, of a burglar; and, as what I require to be retrieved is quite bulky, frequently stubborn, and currently in the custody of the sword-monks of the Water Dragon, only the best will do. I trust this letter, dispatched with the greatest haste, finds you in good health, etcetera, etcetera. Speed is of the essence.

He signed the message and popped it into a bamboo tube and marched to where the courier was waiting. He showed his letter of authority, signed and sealed by the Princess-Regent herself and given to Lady Novashi on the day he'd left Varr. *Strictly,* it was Lady Novashi's letter of authority, which he'd casually stolen off her desk in case he needed it. She'd probably set him on fire if she ever found out, but he'd been in a hurry.

The courier read the letter carefully, then handed it back.

"How long from here to Varr?" Orien asked. The answer came with a shrug.

"Four days to the City of Spires. After that? Depends on the snow and the roads. Could be another six. Could be a twelvenight. Destination?"

Orien sealed the message tube. "Varr."

"Yes. You said. Where in Varr?"

"The *Unruly Pig* on Threadneedle Street. Close to the Western Spice Market."

PART TWO
SETH

When all else fails, setting something on fire is frequently
a useful distraction.
– Orien

10

A ПICE SPOT OF BVSIПESS

A few days later, the man Seth had let go was back, waiting at the warehouse entrance. The poor sod looked ready to piss himself. He kept a good distance, tossed a pouch at Seth's feet, and ran. Seth picked up the pouch and opened it. A handful of silver moons and a note: *Point made. Tonight. Here. Sunset. We have a proposition for you.*

Yes! *This* was how it was supposed to go: rich folk from across the river making propositions, paying in silver and gold for his services. The Path thought they could hide the truth by kicking him out, but they were wrong. He knew six sigils now. Seven, if you included the one that all priests were taught, the one that set Dead Men to rest. He could make the dead talk. He could make them rise and serve. He could travel back in time to see how they died. He could take a man's will and make him obedient, and he could kill – a life or a memory – but that was only the start. There was more out there. The Heresies of Sivingathm claimed there were Sigils to end anything you could imagine, right up to the Gods themselves, all contained in some mysterious Book of Endings. Even a Sigil for ending creation itself, although that *did* seem a likely to be an exaggeration and, if you sat and thought about it, also not particularly useful.

Still, if *Heresies* was right, they were out there; and though Seth didn't know where to find them or what they did or what they meant, he intended to find out. When he'd unravelled the mysteries of the universe, when he'd untied the knot of creation and looked the gods in the eye and understood them... *then* he'd march right back into the Cathedral of the Sun and show the priests what they'd done. He even knew where to start, once he had some silver in his pocket. Deephaven, and the stories of a warlock driven from the city by Myla's teacher, the sword-mistress Tasahre, sixteen years ago.

Before any of that, though, he needed money. He'd have them all paying soon enough, all the rich fuckers from across the river. He'd start with the hooded woman and the priest who lurked behind her. Unravel their secrets and then sell them the Sapphire Throne. Once he had the ear of someone in the palace, he'd make himself useful until they couldn't get enough of him. Give himself a title, maybe. Court Necromancer or something like that, something to give the self-righteous priests of the Sun palpitations; but by then, he'd be the one ordering some poor bastard tied to rock and threatening him with being tossed in the river.

Still, it was with caution that he came back at sunset, Cleaver and Stupid and his other two Dead Men never far away in case it was a trap. The man from the boat was there again. After some guarded negotiations, he went away and returned with a wagon and a corpse. This time, the corpse had had the good grace *not* to have had a wind-pipe related accident – apparently, this one had repeatedly bludgeoned himself and then stabbed himself in the eye, which Seth took to mean that someone had actually listened to him back on the boat. Money changed hands, questions were asked and answered, and everyone went away happy. *This* was more like it.

Weeks went by and they went a few more rounds of this, Seth and the man from the boat. After a bit, the hooded woman started showing up again, which Seth took as a good sign. She never apologised for trying to have him murdered but she didn't try to do it again. In return, Seth never apologised for turning three of her men into walking corpses but didn't make it four or five. It was ironic, really. There was never a name, but he was quite sure by now that the hooded woman was looking for Sulfane. Seth wondered if he should say something but decided not. He had a good thing going here.

The month of Bitterness slid reluctantly into the month of Storms. The Sulk gripped Varr tight. More weeks passed and people started talking about how much longer it would be before Sulk broke and the weather started to change. Down in his crypts and vaults, Seth barely noticed, until the man from the boat – his regular go-between now – told him they had a new corpse, but one that couldn't be moved, so Seth had to go to *it*, instead. A larger sum of money changed hands, along with a promise from Seth that if anything turned bad, unfortunate happenings would follow. And they *would* be unfortunate. That night on the boat... well, it had been a good speech, but that was about all it had been. Now? Now he was ready.

The hooded woman took him across the river into the Imperial Quarter. Some new men Seth didn't recognize showed up and wanted to blindfold him. Seth politely pointed out that, as a Master of the Dark Arts, they could go fuck themselves. Some shouting followed until some Dead Men conveniently made their presence felt; after that, the whole business of blindfolds was quietly forgotten.

They took him to the Butterfly Gardens, not far from the Cathedral of Solar Brilliance where he'd spent several years of his life hoping to become a priest. There was a man there, waiting. Seth paid enough attention to notice how, although the hooded woman still asked the questions, she wasn't the one in charge this time. And that the man, who very much *was* in charge, had a way about him that Seth found oddly familiar, and at the same time distinctly unsettling.

He asked his questions. By the end, he knew who the dead man was: *this* dead man had been there on the night Myla and Fings and Sulfane had stolen the crown. He'd been with the mage who'd double-crossed Sulfane. He was the one who'd survived. He'd seen Myla and remembered her, possibly because she was the one who'd sliced his leg and left him a cripple. The corpse remembered seeing a third man, too, although nothing useful by way of a description. Which was just as well, Seth reckoned, because the third man had been Fings.

When no one else was paying attention, Seth quickly asked a couple of questions of his own, to be sure. Yes, the dead man had been working for the mage Sulfane had killed that night, and yes, the mage had been working for the unsettling man watching over them both right now.

This was the priest. *The* priest.

Right, then.

After it was done, Seth took his money and left, and then crept back again for a spot of eavesdropping. He heard the hooded woman ask something along the lines of *why not simply let them do all the work and then pick up the pieces when it's done.* The priest's reply was that there might not *be* any pieces if it came to that.

Whatever *that* was. Whoever *they* were.

Seth pondered all this on his way home, wondering whether it was worth his while trying to find out and reckoned that yes, it probably was. That was probably why it took him so long to realise two things. The first was that he'd met this priest before, years ago, although it was the sort of meeting where he'd happened to be in the same room at the same time for a few minutes, nothing more. A priest from Torpreah, if he remembered it right, and not some lowly Lightbringer, either. A Dawncaller, which was only one step below a Sunherald.

The second was that he was being followed again, this time by the men who'd wanted to blindfold him.

Did they *never* learn? Had he not made his point forcibly enough the first time?

Ah well. He had his Dead Men with him, and Cleaver too, not that he had much say in Cleaver's comings and goings. He had sigils on strips of paper in pockets he could easily reach; more sigils on the floor and the walls of the tunnel under the derelict warehouse, and one on his own skin too, a new sigil he'd managed to decipher from the vaults of the undercity, a sigil of protection so he didn't accidentally kill himself with his own traps, exactly the sort of embarrassing fuck-up that tended to happen when you meddled with ancient sorceries you barely understood. If he was going to die, it could at least be in a way that wasn't stupid.

He reached the entrance to his warehouse thinking he'd wait outside this time. He'd make his point, they'd make theirs, he'd probably have to kill one of them, then maybe the others would negotiate, and–

The two sword-monks gave no warning, a sudden whirl of blades carving up his Dead Men before Seth even had time to squeak *I surrender* and curl up tight in a ball and hope they didn't murder him on the spot. It was all too quick.

II

DEMON AT THE DOOR

Fings clasped his belly and frowned. "Am I getting fat?" he asked.

Arjay looked up, cocked her head, nodded, and slumped across the table again. They were sitting in the commons of the *Unruly Pig* in the small hours of the morning. The teahouse was almost deserted, the debris of an evening of eating and drinking all around them. Beside Arjay, Dox was snoring. Fings reached out and shook him but it didn't work: Dox was gone. Fings stood up and patted his stomach again.

"What am I supposed to do?" That was the trouble with having money. He could hardly remember the last time he hadn't been scrimping and saving and stealing whatever he could to look after his ma and his sisters. *Last* time they'd had money was years ago, before his bother Levvi had left Varr, and look how *that* had turned out.

"Nothing," slurred Arjay. She didn't lift her head. "There's floors need cleaning in the kitchen, if you're desperate."

Fings checked to see whether Dox really *was* asleep, then went to where Arjay wouldn't see, stood on one leg, reached out his arms, and bent his knee. He still felt a twinge where Sulfane had stabbed him, but that had been almost two months ago and mostly he didn't notice these days, not unless he looked for it, which of course he did, a lot.

He grimaced, remembering the days before Midwinter. Bad times, downcast and gloomy, always taking care never to put his back to any opening wide enough to take an arrow, once he knew Sulfane had escaped.

You let him live. You should have finished him.

Yeah, but he wasn't a murderer.

Well, yeah, but actually, he was.

He winced. Best not to think about the Spicer in Locusteater yard; but that only got him back to the two sacks of silver Ma Fings had hidden away, which got him back to the last time they'd had money, which got him back to thinking about how Levvi had been gone for more than five years now when he said he'd be gone only two, and how that probably meant he wasn't ever coming back.

He'd been thinking about Levvi a lot, these last few months.

"Is it still snowing out there?" asked Arjay. "Because if it's stopped, you could get a head start on clearing the alley if you like."

Fings shook his head. "On an Abyssday? You want me to slip and break a leg? I already spent the whole of Bitterness hopping and hobbling around the place. No thanks."

Ma Fings had made it clear: no more thieving, no more stealing; she didn't want anything more to do with his dirty money, thanks. Which was easy to say when the *last* haul of dirty money had been enough to set them up for, well, years and years probably, if they were careful and managed to hang on to it. Live cautiously and they wouldn't ever need more. Still, had to respect the choice, right?

"You could run down to old Baffon. See if he's up and baking yet. See if you can annoy him enough that he sticks you in one of his ovens."

Midwinter night and Myla and that mage fellow going off and giving back the crown and coming face to face with the Princess-Regent herself, Sun bless her, or so they said. Not that Fings was all that keen for the Sun to bless a mage, which, apparently, she was. He wasn't sure how he felt about all that. Didn't seem real. *Mostly*, what he felt was that it was none of his business. Glad not to have any part of it, really.

He'd heard an odd story, after Myla had gone, of some mystery archer – Fings reckoned most likely Sulfane, largely because he liked to blame Sulfane for pretty much everything – taking a shot at the Regent as she'd crossed the city back to the palace, of some mage she was with bursting into flames and setting a sizeable portion of Carpetmakers' alight before regaining control of herself.

And then Seth with his weird goings-on in the undercity, strange people visiting him day and night, that weird phase he'd gone through right after Midwinter of trying not to sleep. Some sort of religion thing, Fings supposed. Like fasting, maybe?

He frowned. "Arjay?"

"Fings! *Please* fuck off somewhere else."

"That night in Tombland before Midwinter. When the Spicers had me and Myla. What... What exactly was it you and Dox were doing there?"

Arjay groaned. "*This* again?"

"Well... You said Seth came up with the idea of poisoning all the Spicers, so they'd be too sick to fight. Yeah?" Which he had to admit *did* account for the smell of the place when he and Myla had broken out.

"Aye."

"And then... what? Seth somehow slipped inside and opened the doors to let you in so you and Dox could fight your way through however many Spicers were left and get us out?"

"Aye, except it was me and Brick and Topher, not Dox, and it was that priest friend of Myla's who let us in, or mage or whatever he is. Not Seth." Arjay made a sour face. "And Myla had pretty much finished escaping on her own by then, and there wasn't any fighting, on account of all the Spicers that weren't dead having the sense to run. I can promise you, no one wanted to get in Myla's way that night. I already told you all this about a hundred times."

"But Seth..." He couldn't leave it alone because it was so out of place, Seth sneaking all on his own into a house full of Spicers and knowing Sulfane was there, too.

"You want to know what he was up to that night, go ask him. Or that orange priest."

The orange priest who was a mage, not a priest, not that Arjay and Dox gave a shit.

Seth and a mage?

He shivered.

Maybe that was all it was, though. Couldn't see Seth sneaking into a place like that on his own; but getting a mage to do it *for* him... Made sense, that did. And Orien *had* had a thing for Myla, that was obvious. Still, Seth hadn't been the same since. He'd taken to hiding away in the undercity, where no one in their right mind ever went on account of all the bad luck that lurked there. Always seeped downward, bad luck. The deeper you went, the worse it got. That, Fings reckoned, was the main reason rich folk lived in towers.

"And Myla murdered almost a dozen Spicers?"

Arjay grunted. "They *were* planning on selling her to that Deephaven fellow who wanted to skin her alive or whatever. Do you blame her?"

Something felt off about that too. Yes, he'd seen what Myla had done when they were fighting their way out, when she hadn't had much of a choice in the matter, when there was no doubt it was kill or be killed. But the rest? It wasn't *her*, not something like that, not running around killing out of sheer spite.

Was it? Maybe it was. How well did he know her, really?

He stretched and yawned and patted his belly. All this wealth and inactivity was no good. If he wasn't careful, he'd be looking down at a paunch before much longer.

He missed Myla. Sort of. Having her around had been a bit

like having a big sister who always knew what to do, which made a nice change from his *actual* sisters. Might have known what to do about Seth, for example. But she was gone, and so he'd have to work it out for himself. And, Seth aside, life wasn't so bad, was it? The Spicers shattered, the Unrulys coming back together, what was left of them, Dox and Arjay running the *Pig*, Ma Fings with enough money to keep her and his sisters with a roof over their heads and food in their bellies and a warm fire in the hearth...

The front door of the *Pig* exploded open. An apparition stood, silhouetted against the night, a figure swathed in swirling black like a demon from the abyss. Fings froze where he stood. Behind him, Arjay jerked awake. Even Dox stirred a little. The apparition stepped inside and turned out not to be a demon but a man wearing a voluminous black cloak. Which *was* an improvement, just not very much of one, given the hint and glint of armour and steels underneath.

Fings backed away.

"Er?" he tried.

"I have a message for a Ser... Fings," boomed the man, whose crisp, aristocratic tone of authority was slightly undermined by a hesitation and an evident suspicion that he'd somehow come to the wrong place. He looked around. It didn't seem to help him.

"That's... nice. Er... what sort of message?" Fings couldn't help but think that the *last* time a message had been as ostentatious as this, it had resulted, through a long and complicated chain of events, in him getting stabbed.

"Ser Fings?" Arjay made a noise like an extended fart as she tried not to laugh. "*Ser* Fings?"

The apparition scowled. "This is the... the *Unruly Pig*?" He licked his lips as though the name left a bad taste in his mouth.

"*Ser* Fings...?" Apparently this was too much for Arjay, although Fings couldn't quite see what was so funny about a heavily-armed man crashing into the *Pig* in the middle of the night. The man took three quick steps towards the stairs and then stopped in front of Fings, mostly because Fings was barring the way further, which in turn was because Fings didn't quite know what else to do with himself.

The armoured man looked him up and down. Fings returned the favour.

"Does... does this message involve anyone getting stabbed?"

"Yes. That's Fings," wheezed Arjay. "There. In front of you. Ser Fings..." Another howl of laughter. "Fings, he's an Imperial courier. Imperial couriers don't stab people."

Which was true enough, as far as Fings knew, but on the other hand, Arjay was clearly wrong about what this man was, because Imperial couriers raced messages across the empire, changing horses and not stopping for anything, riding through any weather you'd cared to imagine, bandits, monsters, all that sort of thing. A properly heroic and dashing line of work which, thank you very much, made them for the exclusive use of the handful of incredibly rich people who could afford them. They absolutely did not *ever* carry messages for people like Fings.

"You're... Ser Fings...?" The courier – or whatever he really was – seemed to be struggling with the idea of a name which didn't have fifty syllables, half a dozen titles, and a coat of arms, all of which probably made identification of the correct recipient a touch easier in most cases.

Fine. "Yeh. I'm Fings. I ain't no *ser*, though." Behind him, Arjay made another strangled noise. "What can I do for you?"

"I carry a message from the House of Fire in Deephaven." The man in black handed Fings a leather tube with a cap on each end and spun on his heel.

Seconds later, he was gone.

Fings stood, dazed, holding the tube. There was a moment of utter silence, and then Arjay couldn't hold it in any longer. "*Ser* Fings!" She howled and hooted and hammered the table with her hand, loud enough that Dox grumbled something and fell off his stool. "Ser *Fings!*"

It was a good while before she stopped. While she was getting a hold of herself, Fings opened the tube, mulling over how he and Arjay were going to have some words about this once she'd calmed down. Inside was a roll of parchment.

"Your face..." said Arjay, once she could manage talking again. "Your face, Fings... *Ser* Fings... Who in Kelm's name is the House of Fire, anyway? Some rich tart you've got squirrelled away?"

Fings shoved the roll of parchment at her. All very well, people sending fancy messages and letters and the like, but whoever they were, they obviously didn't know him.

"You read?" he asked. "Because I don't."

Arjay shook her head, still sniggering.

Dox couldn't read. Nor could Brick or Topher, far as Fings knew.

Seth could read, though.

Which meant a trip to the undercity, which he'd been avoiding, telling everyone it was on account of his dodgy leg, but mostly on account of it being cursed and Seth being all different and messing with things that were going to get him trouble.

Well. It *was* about time, wasn't it? And Seth, whatever he was up to, was still his brother, right?

Fings sighed. If he was going to go down *there*, he was going to need to see about getting some new lucky charms.

12

A PAIR OF ANGRY
SWORD-MONKS

They didn't murder him on the spot, which was something.

"Warlock!" hissed one.

"Heretic," hissed the other. They didn't try to hide their disdain. "Get up."

"I remember you," said Seth as he got up. "From before Midwinter." They were the monks he'd seen with Myla, back when he'd been trying to do the right thing and show them what he'd found, when he'd still had some foolish notion that he could be a priest again if he tried hard enough. "Still smarting from when you failed to kill me the last time?"

Stupid mouth.

"Disrobe." The only power he had lay in the sigils in his pockets. But of course, they knew that, being sword-monks.

"I was trying to help, back then, you know?" he said. "You see that, right? *You're* the ones who messed that up. You made this happen. Not me."

He'd shown them the sigil to make the dead speak and they'd tried to kill him for knowing it existed. Myla had fought them long enough for him to get away. He hadn't really spoken to her since. If he was honest, everything had taken rather a turn for the worse after that. If by *worse*, you meant…

Oh, call it what it is. Practising necromancy.

A monk poked at him with a Sunsteel sword. "Disrobe," she said again.

And now Myla was gone, and he still couldn't get his head round how she'd put herself into a fight she couldn't win to protect him, when less than a twelvenight before he'd betrayed her to a man who wanted her dead.

Because she didn't know it was you.

He bowed his head and disrobed. He deserved this, really.

Yes. Don't you just.

And for a moment, thinking of Myla, he was actually ready to give himself up, to let them take him back to the temple on Spice Market Square, to tell them everything he knew and then let them hang him; but Cleaver, it turned out, had other ideas. The Dead Man came loping out of the tunnels with his sword in one hand and his cleaver in the other and launched himself at the monks. Being a Dead Man, he wasn't exactly quick or agile, and so the monks easily shimmied out of his way and stabbed him a few times. They seemed puzzled when this didn't work. It puzzled Seth too. Yes, stabbing Dead Men with *ordinary* swords didn't work, but the monks had swords of Sunsteel, like Myla's, which usually absolutely *did* work, and yet here they were, very clearly *not* working. It was all a bit unexpected, fascinating enough that a part of him might have stopped to have a bit of a theological chat about this turn of events; fortunately, a more sensible part already had him racing back to the derelict warehouse with its doorway and its tunnel and its sigils and its shaft down to the undercity…

Which was, he realized almost exactly as soon as it was too late to do anything about it, a bit of a mistake. At the end of the tunnel behind the door, past his traps, was a long open stair into a vault like the one under the Circus of Dead Emperors, only *un*like that other vault, the only way out was through one of the sigil-ringed portals that he hadn't worked out how to open. And Cleaver who *could* open them – was a busy being cut to ribbons.

He stopped at the top of the steps. By then, the monks were coming through the doorway. Seth's last few Dead Men tried to get in their way; but these were ordinary Dead Men, the sort who collapsed exactly the way Dead Men were supposed to collapse when someone skewered them with Sunsteel, and so they slowed the monks for exactly as long as it took Seth to whisper *Oh fuck* and vaguely remember that he was still naked.

Ah well. There were still the sigils on the walls. He didn't much like it, but in the end, what choice did he have?

There's always a choice.

Not this time there wasn't.

Yes. There is.

Oh, for fuck's sake... He threw up his hands in surrender. Thing was, the men the hooded woman had sent, those he and Cleaver had killed in the tunnels... well, he'd *tried* to give them a chance, but people like that had it coming and so he didn't feel too bad about what he'd done. But sword-monks? Sword-monks were holy. Arrogant and uptight, yes, but deep down he still saw himself as a priest, and monks were the pinnacle of what was righteous, even this pair who were about to murder him.

"Stop! Please?" He turned to face them. "I'm not really a bad person."

Apart from the... how many people is it you've killed and turned into Dead Men?

Shut up!

"I'm sorry... But if you come any closer, the traps I've set will kill you. Even you."

The monks kept coming, although at least they were coming more slowly now.

"What, do you not *believe* me?"

They kept coming.

"I *am* a necromancer, for fuck's sake! You think I don't have hideous sorceries that could turn you inside out? Doesn't mean I want to *use* them! I don't want to *hurt* anyone!"

Liar.

The monks *still* kept coming, and what was he supposed to do? Scrub out his own sigils so they could take him back, have a quick trial and burn him?

"*Damn* you!"

Well, he didn't have to watch, did he? He turned and ran, skittering for the steps as quickly as he dared, the same open steps held up by sheer bloody-minded defiance of gravity as the ones under the incinerators in the Circus of Dead Emperors...

The monks caught him before he even reached them, apparently not bothered by the sigils he'd written over the tunnel walls that should have killed them. One moment he was running, stark naked, cursing himself and the world in general, the next he was flat on his face, all the breath knocked out of him, an angry sword-monk on his back.

Were sword-monks ever *not* angry, he wondered?

One of them smashed his head into the stone floor, and so he didn't have much chance to think about it.

13

A BAD PLACE

Fings got up early and spent the morning buying himself all the luck-charms and talismans he could think of that might keep him safe in the cursed undercity full of old ghosts and spirits and skeletons and all manner of other crap he didn't like to think about. The only good part of this was how it was a Sunday, a good day for avoiding restless spirits and curses and the like, safest day of the week, in his opinion. He didn't much like leaving the *Pig* even so, mostly because the Murdering Bastard was still out there, and while Sulfane probably had more of a bone to pick with Myla than with Fings, Myla had done the sensible thing and buggered off. But it was what it was. Sometimes stuff needed to be done, and that was just the way of the world.

The undercity was about the last place he fancied visiting even at the best of times. Creepy and gloomy, made of a glowing white stone that changed as the moon waxed and waned in the sky, the whole place was old and reeking of sorcery and dead stuff, everything that made Fings's skin crawl. Still, he'd been to see the crazy witch of the White Circle, who'd sold him a charm made of bones and feathers so that any lurking Dead Men wouldn't bother him; he'd been to the Feather Man, who'd sold him what looked like the best feather Fings had ever seen, huge and painted in all bright colours. Suck on a good feather and other people's eyes just slid right off without noticing you were there. He still had his most prized charm, of course, the lucky chicken-foot that made him invisible to sorcery and mages, the one he'd picked up for a single silver Moon back before Midwinter, that evening with Seth at the Solstice Festival. Stank a bit, these days, but that was to be expected.

Suitably protected, Fings made his way through Haberdashers and Seamstresses and Bonecarvers. He reached the Circus of Dead Emperors without any arrow-related accidents and crossed to the solar chapel that sat opposite the Glass Market and the Bridge of Questions. He stood at the steps to the chapel and looked back at the old Constable's Castle and the entrance to Tombland, wondering if the Murdering Bastard still lurked somewhere about, nursing his wounds. You had to admire someone, he supposed, who could be shot in the arm with a crossbow and get stabbed, and then a few weeks later get stabbed again, and still haunt you like a spectre.

One of us should have finished him.

But they hadn't. Myla because she thought she was leaving him for the Guild of Mages to find, so they could ask their questions about who'd been behind the theft of the emperor's crown. Fings because... Well, because he wasn't a killer.

Mostly.

He walked up the steps into the chapel, stuck his feather between his teeth and sucked on it. From there, he made his way to the incinerators out back, where they burned the bodies of the dead so the Hungry Goddess wouldn't snare their souls. Past the incinerators, he climbed the old wall into the abandoned garden, forced his way through the thorn thickets to a long-forgotten building, pulled the foliage aside to reveal an old doorway, and there it was: in the centre of the floor just as he remembered it, like a big old well, a staircase spiralling into the ground.

He stared at it a bit like the way he'd stared across the Circus of Dead Emperors into Tombland. No one apart from him and Seth had come this way for years, possibly no one else at all since that time when Seth, still a novice, although not for much longer, had dragged him here with promises of riches buried under the ground. Fings had come this far and gone no further. Seth had gone alone and come out after an hour, a wild look on his face like he really *had* found something. Three days later, the Path of the Sun had expelled him and cut him off from the light. Shortly before Midwinter, Fings and Seth had returned to the vaults below using a different route, and this time Fings *had* gone down. He hadn't much liked it.

No one had come *this* way for ages. He could see that. Seth must be using the path Fings had shown him, or else found another. No surprise, not with a threat of execution for heresy hanging over him if he ever stepped foot on Holy ground. There *were* other ways down, dotted about.

He took a deep breath and started on the stairs. He hadn't bothered with a lantern because of the whole thing of the walls glowing like moonlight. After a few steps, he was walking down a spiral of stones that simply hung through the middle of an enormous vault as though gravity had been distracted by something more interesting. Fings wasn't usually bothered by heights, but this? This was mage work. He found himself quivering at the sheer drop into nothing all around him.

At the bottom, he crouched by a circular opening in the floor, not much wider than a man, and peered into the second vault. This was where Seth had found whatever it was that he'd found. It looked much as he remembered: some ruined pieces of furniture, not much more than dust and splinters; a mosaic on the floor that had either been obliterated by age or had made no sense in the first place; the three skeletons…

Oh. Bollocks.

There *had* been three skeletons, last time, but now there were only two, and both missing their skulls, which Fings was quite sure had been attached when he'd come here with Seth. Which meant either the third skeleton had got up and walked off all on its own at some point, taking a couple of skulls as souvenirs for some reason, or else Seth had been up to something. He wasn't sure which possibility bothered him more. *Probably* the idea that a skeleton had got up and walked off all on its own, but he wasn't entirely sure.

Seth! What have you done now?

He stroked the charms around his neck, then put his Feather of Not Being Noticed back between his teeth and sucked on it, not that a lucky feather would do much if there were Dead Men about. Skeletons? Skeletons were simply wrong. Sun-fearing men and women burned their dead. Moon-worshippers sank their corpses into water. If there was anyone out there who offered their prayers to the Mistress of Many Faces, they left their dead out in the open, in a high place if they could. No one left their dead under the ground like this.

He shivered again. Bury a man under the ground and his soul was for the Hungry Goddess. No one, not even the worst criminals, deserved that. Yet here they were. Not skeletons of men, according to Seth. Three skeletons of half-gods, or wraiths, or moonchildren, or whatever you wanted to call the creatures that looked like men but carried a piece of Fickle Lord Moon inside them, the god-touched sorcerers that had vanished at the end of the Shining Age.

No, he reminded himself. Not *three*. Two. *Two* skeletons of god-touched sorcerer wraith-things, because there *had* been three, but now one of them was missing, and did he really want to think about that?

He tried it out and decided no, he really didn't.

Another thing that wasn't here was Seth, so Fings settled to wait. He was good at waiting. Patience was one of those things a proper burglar had in abundance.

He'd lost track of how long he'd been waiting when the voices came echoing from above. Voices was another thing he was quite good at; fortunately, these weren't the voices of people who'd seen some scruffy idiot sneak into an abandoned building and wanted to know what he was up to – *those* voices he knew all too well. They weren't the voices of people who knew exactly what they were doing, either. They were the cautious voices of people going somewhere where they didn't know what to expect. Guarded and uncertain, which made them dangerous. They sounded...

Vigilant. Yeah, that was it. Vigilant was bad. Fings stopped thinking about how many steps were between him and the surface and started thinking about how quickly he could take them; the only trouble being that the voices were coming from above.

Four of them.

Bollocks!

It was about then that Fings realised, rather too late, that a perfectly hemispherical vault made of softly glowing white stone was a bit short of dark shadowy corners suitable for hiding. That left him two choices: down to the lower vault with its mosaic and its collection of bones, or one of the tunnels that led away into the rest of the undercity and the different entrances from the streets above. The tunnels were long and straight and made of the same glowing stone, which made them as rubbish as the vault as places to hide. On the other hand, Fings reckoned he'd rather run up to an angry mage and slap him in the face with a wet fish than have anything to do with those skeletons, especially with one gone missing.

The tunnels, then. He went for the nearest, ran down a little way, lay flat, stuck his feather between his teeth and sucked on it while he watched to see what would happen. It wasn't perfect, but if anyone saw him and he had to run, he'd at least have a good head start. He'd counted right: four figures. Two monks with paired swords crossed over their backs, and two yellow-robed priests of the Sun. Fings wondered, briefly, whether Seth had finally reconciled with the Path, that showing this place to them was a part of him becoming a priest again.

He considered this, and then considered Seth.

Probably not.

He watched, wary, to see what they did. Charms mostly didn't work on priests and monks because priests and monks had God on their side, and charms didn't work on Gods. His feather was a *good* feather, though, and so he sucked on it, hoping no one bothered to look his way; sure enough, all the priests and monks did was peer through the hole in the floor, realise they'd need some rope if they wanted to go further, grumble about how many steps there were, and then head back the way they'd come. No one glanced his way. The power of a good feather, that was. Stay quiet and still enough, sucking on a feather, and people would almost tread on you before they realised you were there.

He waited for them to go and then scampered up the steps, quick as he could. He caught sight of them leaving the Circus of Dead Emperors and followed them all the way back to the temple in Spice Market Square, wondering as he went what priests and sword-monks were doing in the undercity and thinking how Seth needed to be warned. Inside the temple, the priests scurried off while the sword-monks stayed in the Hall of Light, pacing back and forth like they didn't know how to stay still. After a bit, another priest joined them, older and wearing the robe of a Dawncaller, which made her the most senior priest of the temple. Fings couldn't make out what was being said but it looked like the monks wanted to do something the Dawncaller didn't like. The monks were going to do it anyway because, well, that was sword-monks for you.

He did catch a word or two, though. *Heretic,* for example. And something about a prisoner in a cell.

He thought about that. Then he thought about Seth. Then he thought about how Seth hadn't been where Fings had expected to find him. After quite a lot of thinking about all those things, he sighed and rolled his eyes, and then sighed a bit more theatrically. He *was* in a temple, after all, so there were probably Gods watching; if that was the case, best they knew he wasn't happy about what he was about to do.

For all the wrong reasons, the Temple to the Sun in Spice Market Square was a place Fings knew like the back of his hand, mostly from when Seth had lived there. He slipped away from the Hall of Light to the cloisters, checked the position of the sun in the sky, squinted as he tried to remember what chores the novices would be doing this time of day, then made his way to the cells. The novice cells were never locked and so he helped himself to a robe. That done, he took his feather out of his mouth and walked bold as brass through the rest of the novice's quarters, to the three cells at the very end that *did* have locks, the cells where Lightbringers sometimes sentenced a disobedient novice for a day or two of being shunned.

A bored young novice stood watch. No one was supposed to talk to whoever was locked in the cells – not much of a shunning otherwise – and there was always a novice on watch to make a point of it. Seth had complained about guard duty, grumbling how dull it was, how it was almost better to be the one *in* the cell, because at least there no one bothered you.

"You can't talk to the prisoner," said the novice as Fings approached, presumably from habit rather than any actual thought.

Right. So there is *someone here, then.* "I wouldn't want to," said Fings, loud enough that anyone who happened to be inside the cells couldn't help but overhear. "I was in the kitchens making sweetbread. Lightbringer Osri caught me with my fingers in the dough, so here I am." Seth had told him this story years ago, growling his way through it. "We're to swap duties. Unless... you'd rather not?" he tried to sound hopeful.

"Lightbringer who?"

Fings gave an exaggerated shrug. "The one who runs the kitchens. I don't know anyone's names yet, not really. Only got here yesterday. I was at the cathedral, you know? It wasn't *my* fault, all the bother there."

The novice looked him up and down. "What's your name?"

"Novice Fings," said Fings. "What's yours?"

"Novice Lalan."

"Nice to meet you, novice Lalan. I think you're supposed to take my place in the kitchen." Kitchen duty, he knew from Seth, was a prize. "If you want my advice, keep your hands where they belong. That Lightbringer is sharp."

Novice Lalan's eyes lit up. Inside, Fings felt the smug satisfaction of a lie well told.

"No one can talk to the heretic. No one at all," said Novice Lalan. "Not even the Lightbringers."

"There's a heretic? That sounds exciting. What did he do?"

"No idea." A glance to the cell at the far end. "No one except the sword-monks. They're allowed."

Fings made a face. "Wouldn't be trying to stop a sword-monk even if they weren't, but right you are."

Novice Lalan trotted off with the happy enthusiasm of someone leaving a shit on the floor for someone else to clean up. Wouldn't be so happy when he reached the kitchens, but it would take a few minutes for him to get there and a few more to realised he'd been fooled, and a few minutes was all Fings needed. As soon as he was alone, he was at the cell door. It wasn't much of a door, nor much of a cell, nor much of a lock. It took him seconds to pick and then he had it open. From inside, stark naked, Seth looked at him.

Fings rolled his eyes. "Why aren't I surprised?"

14

THE KNİFE

For a long time, Myla wasn't quite sure where she was. She remembered the tall woman with her posse of city Longcoats. She remembered the men she'd killed on the Avenue of Emperors. She remembered seeing herself bleeding and thinking she was dying and a sense of relief, because that was always what had been waiting for her, coming back to Deephaven, wasn't it? And at least it had been quick.

Yet here she was, not dead after all, so no such luck.

She *thought* she remembered Orien's voice, and men shouting at each other, and then a quiet place, a cool room, dry and calm, where a young woman in the robes of a novice of the Sun came to her and tutted and brought her water. It was a place that made her think of the old temple, which made it either a dream or a memory. Or so she thought; but as her wits returned, she saw no, that's where she really was, and wondered why. She asked the novice: yes, she was in the Temple on Deephaven Square, *her* temple. As to why, the novice only shrugged; but a few hours later, when the door to her cell opened again, there was sword-mistress Tasahre, looking stern and sad and angry, much as she always did. And that was all the answer Myla needed.

"Hello, Shirish," she said.

Myla bowed her head as Tasahre closed the door behind her. "I returned my swords." Myla faltered and found she couldn't meet Tasahre's eye. "I'm sorry. I should have come to see you. I was… I was ashamed."

"As you should be." Tasahre let out a long breath and then pulled up a stool and sat beside Myla's cot. "It might have been kinder leaving you to die in the hands of the Overlord," she said. "I'm not sure I've done you a service. Oh, Shirish." She took Myla's hand and squeezed. "Why did you do it?"

"To right a wrong."

Tasahre raised an eyebrow. "And did you?"

"No. It was a mistake. In Varr, I made another, but one I managed to put right. I came back here to do the same."

"You can't, Shirish. Not this."

"I can try."

Tasahre squeezed her hand again. "So brilliant and so flawed. So angry. I thought I might take that anger and turn it into purpose."

"You did."

"Certainly not the purpose I had in mind." Tasahre snorted, rose, then bent over and kissed Myla's brow. "You're not going to find what you're looking for, Shirish. No forgiveness. No redemption. Only pain."

Tasahre didn't visit again for a long time after that. Days went by and then weeks. Myla managed to sit, then to stand, then to take a few steps around her cell. She found it barred from the outside, not that she intended to leave. By the time Tasahre finally did return, Myla was exercising, stepping from the floor onto her cot and stepping back, trying to put the strength back into her legs. Tasahre watched, gave a nod of approval, and held the door open.

"Come."

Outside, the sun was low, the cloisters empty, the novices all at Twilight Prayer. Tasahre took Myla up the steps that spiralled the Hall of Light to the peak of the temple dome, to a little niche set with a stone bench, facing out towards the winged tower of the Overlord's palace, then the rocky tip of Deephaven Point, and then beyond that, the endless glitter of the sea. To her left, the setting sun blazed orange fire. To her right, she could see all the way to the sea-docks, its webs of piers and jetties, the forest of masts out in Deephaven Bay. Below her was the yard where the sword-monks trained. There were ten, dressed in their robes, each with a pair of practice swords, moving through forms and patterns that Myla remembered well.

"Would you like to train with them?" asked Tasahre.

"You'd permit that?"

"Perhaps."

Myla tried a few tentative stretches, then shook her head. "It'll be weeks before I have the strength. But thank you."

"You may not have weeks, Shirish."

"Then why did you bring me here?"

Tasahre didn't answer. She sat, watching the setting sun until it touched the sea and set it alight. "A sorcerer keeps coming to the temple, asking after you," she said, her lip curling with distaste.

"Orien?" Despite herself, Myla felt her heart skip a beat.

"I think that's his name, yes. He seems very keen to know what your fate will be. And when."

"I'd like to see him. If you would permit it."

"This is a temple of the Sun, Shirish. Mages aren't welcome." As far as Tasahre was concerned, every mage was one bad decision away from being a warlock.

"I can ask him not to come, if you like."

"He tells a story about you and a crown, and the Moon-worshipping witch-princess who now sits on the Sapphire Throne. Is it true?"

"He likely exaggerates." His own part most of all, Myla thought, but kept that to herself.

"He thinks he can help you."

"Can he?"

"I doubt it. The only thing saving you right now is the Sunherald, and only because he baulks at the idea of one of his sword-monks being publicly humiliated, which is what the Hawats want. He'd prefer a quiet and private execution."

"Which is the best outcome I can hope for, I suppose."

The sun sank slowly into the sea.

"Why *did* you bring me here?" asked Myla again.

"To make peace with yourself before what comes next."

"I've already made my peace."

Tasahre laughed, a strange noise from someone who rarely even smiled. "I can smell lies from far more accomplished deceivers that you, Shirish. You've done no such thing."

"I came back, didn't I? I came to–"

"Face the consequences of what you did? No."

Myla bit her tongue.

"You think yourself brave, but getting yourself killed is simply another escape, is it not?" Tasahre held her eye, then pulled a knife from her sleeve and offered it, hilt first. "Is that what you want, Shirish? Merely to rid yourself of the burden of guilt? Your sister was the one he wronged, not you. Now she carries his child as penance for what you did."

"I know."

The offer of the knife remained. "Half the city knows, Shirish. Make no mistake, you destroyed them both. Was it worth it?"

Myla looked at the knife. How easy to take what Tasahre offered. To end it.

"He deserved it," she whispered.

"Perhaps, but did she?"

Myla closed her eyes. "No."

The sun set. When Myla still didn't take the knife, Tasahre led her back to her cell.

"Why did you come back, Shirish? The truth, this time."

"To make whatever bargain must be made. Whatever it takes for that man to leave my family alone."

"Bargain?" Tasahre snorted her derision. "Shirish, you crippled the heir to one of the most powerful fortunes in Deephaven. You *un-manned* him! He wishes you to suffer in every way. The longer you endure, the more he will dismantle everything that you are and everything in which you believe. He will not be content until he annihilates every shred of meaning your life ever had; yet even then, it will not be enough. Even your death will not be enough, because what you did to him cannot be undone. Find your strength, Shirish. He will not spare those you love."

As Tasahre left, she placed the knife on the floor by the door.

15

A QUICK EXIT

They fled the temple together, Seth brazening it out wearing Fings's stolen novice robe, Fings slipping between shadows, sucking on his feather and, when he had to, making out like he was one of the temple servants. Once they were out, Fings hurried Seth into the alleys behind the Spice Market, through the maze of Haberdashers and didn't stop until they were in Bonecarvers. Bonecarvers was a good place for fugitives: no priests, no Longcoats, and alleys cleared of snow, unlike most of the rest of the city.

"I need to get out of Varr," said Seth. "Right now. You got any money?"

Fings rolled his eyes. Seemed like he spent half his life bailing Seth out of whatever trouble he'd found for himself and then giving him money. "Why? What did you do this time? What you been up to, anyway? Ain't barely seen you since the whole business with the Spicers and Sulfane."

"Yeah. Well. Avoiding Myla, mostly."

Fings snorted. "She buggered off for Deephaven ages ago. Right after Midwinter. Long gone. And before you ask: no, Dox and Arjay don't know it was you who let the Spicers into the *Pig* that night. No one does. Except me."

Seth flinched at that.

"So. What you done?"

He knew from the way Seth went all shifty that he wasn't going to get the truth, and also, for the same reason, that it was something to do with the tired old drum Seth had been banging for years, how there was something going on in the Path of the Sun that they didn't want anyone to know.

"You know what," he said. "Don't bother."

Seth took a deep breath. "You remember when you sent Myla off chasing after a crown that wasn't there?"

Now it was Fings's turn to look shifty. "Course I remember!" Hard not to. Hard not to remember how murderously angry Myla had been about it, too, and how she'd still put herself in harm's way to get him out of trouble.

"Yeah. Well. After she came back, before she went looking for *you*, we went to the temple. I was going to show the sword-monks those papers you lifted at the same time you lifted the crown. I thought that if I had Myla with me, they'd listen long enough to hear me out. Long story short, they didn't. Myla got in a fight with them, I got away, and they've been hunting me ever since. I *told* you those papers were important, to the right people. Anyway, they found me, and now I need to get away. If they catch me again, they'll burn me as a heretic. Do I need to say that again? I *need* to get away. So, you got any money?"

Fings kept walking. From the sound of things, the more distance they put between the two of them and the Spice Market, the better.

"Yeah. Read this, would you? Tell me what it says. Was how come I was even looking for you."

He handed Seth the letter. Seth read it for him, and they both learned that Myla was in Deephaven, and in trouble, and that Orien wanted Fings's help. The conversation that followed was short.

"Right then," said Seth. "Deephaven, then."

It was all a bit abrupt, Fings thought, but then again, it *would* get him away from Varr and the sneaking fear he had every time he went out that the Murdering Bastard would show up out of nowhere and stick him full of arrows. And he *had* been thinking of going there anyway, on account of Levvi.

He frowned. "What day is it? Sunday, right?"

Seth nodded. Fings nodded too. Tomorrow was Towerday. Towerdays were the best days for hiding out, and also the best days for starting on a journey.

"Deephaven then," he agreed. "But tomorrow."

Seth argued, wanting to go straight for the river. Fings pointed out certain practical issues, starting with how he didn't have that sort of money *on* him, and following up with how Seth was wandering the streets wearing nothing but a novice robe and would catch his death of cold before they even reached the river at this rate. Seth fussed, but there wasn't much point in arguing; he *was* shivering, and river barges were well known for not giving free rides, even to people pretending to be novices; and anyway, Fings wasn't leaving Varr without seeing Ma Fings and his sisters first, and so that was what they did; and by the time they reached Locusteater Yard, it was already dark, and Seth was blue in the face and shaking with cold like a dying chicken, all of which Fings reckoned made his point rather nicely, thanks.

Felt like it took half the night to explain everything and get Ma Fings to hand over a fist full of their stolen silver, tucked away under a loose board. All the time, he had Seth twitching in a corner like he could feel the hue and cry from the temple, like it was some sort of beast, reaching out its arms to devour him. Everyone seemed to want to make life difficult and awkward, mostly by asking a hundred questions that he couldn't answer, until Seth finally snatched the letter back from Fings and read it aloud.

"See," he said. "Urgent business. For someone important." He said the last with a bit of a smirk and a wink.

"'The Esteemed *Ser* Fings.' *Ser* Fings?" Ma Fings looked at him in disbelief, and then it was exactly how it had been with

Arjay all over again, only now from his sisters, all of them at once, which frankly Fings could have done without, especially when Seth started on about it as well; and then, of course, he had to explain who Myla and Orien *were*, and how Myla was the one who'd helped them that night they'd had to flee Varr, and all of that with Seth hopping from one foot to the other in between smirks, banging on about how they *really* needed to leave Varr as soon as this was done, on account of all the angry sword-monks who'd surely discovered he was missing by now.

"How *you* need to go right now," muttered Fings. The two of them were going to have a long talk, he reckoned, about why Seth had been naked in a temple cell and had angry sword-monks looking for him. About them papers too, and what the bloody Khrozus Seth had been up to.

"Was thinking maybe I should go see if I can find Levvi," he said as he made his farewells. The look Ma Fings gave him said she thought he was wasting his time with that, that five years was several years too long, but she nodded anyway and told him yes, she supposed he should give it a go.

"We got plenty to see us through for now. You just make sure you come back."

He thought briefly about trying to convince them to all come with him; but Seth was tearing at his hair again, and his sisters kept sneaking looks at him and whispering *Ser Fings* and then giggling like it was the funniest joke they'd ever heard. Weeks of that, trapped on a barge together, he was probably going to end up wanting to murder something, and so he quietly dropped the idea. Turned out to be just as well, what with the docks swarming with Longcoats and priests and sword-monks by the time he and Seth arrived.

Fortunately, Fings knew how to slip unnoticed through almost anything, and so three hours later, there they were, on the river, on their way to Deephaven. Odd how, for weeks after Midwinter, limping around the *Pig*, he'd been thinking of making this trip. Truth be told, he'd been thinking about it for a lot longer; and now, here he was. Was all a bit sudden, but maybe that was for the best. Felt a bit like… Well, felt a bit like fate, really. Like he was *meant* to go, so maybe he was meant to find Levvi, too.

He watched Varr dwindle down the river. When there didn't seem to be boats full of angry priests and monks giving chase, he took Seth aside and asked exactly how it was that Seth had ended up locked in a cell in the temple on Spice Market Square. A *proper* talk this time. Seth sighed and huffed and made a big song and dance of it all, then went through the same bollocks he'd spouted in Bonecarvers, how it was all some silly misunderstanding because of the papers Fings had taken that night he'd lifted the Moonsteel Crown, how Seth had simply been trying to return them to their rightful owner, how the temple monks had got the wrong end of it and now they wanted to burn him. Fings, who'd known Seth for a long time, listened quietly, letting it all sink in.

"You know," he said, when Seth finally finished talking, "that this is *me* you're talking to."

"What do you mean?"

"What I mean is, I reckon there's a few bits you're conveniently forgetting to mention here. And I suppose you might have your reasons, but I *did* just get you out of a cell and out of Varr, and get you money and some sensible clothes and all that, and I *am* your brother, or as close as it gets, right?"

"Yes. And thank you." Came hard to Seth, saying that, Fings reckoned.

"So?"

"So?"

"So, in all the stuff you *haven't* said, is there anything you really *ought* to be telling me? Given where we're going, and all that. Because there *is* more, and we both know it. You want to keep secrets, that's your choice. Just… Well, seems to me that running away from one bunch of angry sword-monks only to immediately irritate *another* bunch of angry sword-monks by burgling Myla out of their prison... Maybe not the cleverest idea? I mean, that Is, *if* there happens to be a bit more to whatever was going with you and them in Varr than a simple misunderstanding." Which Fings was quite certain there was.

Seth shook his head and said he'd leave the burgling to Fings. He'd stay well clear of all that, thanks.

"When you get Myla, I'll tell you the rest. Her too. I don't think anyone else can help."

Fings wrinkled his nose. "Alright."

"Just don't let Orien know I've come with you," Seth added.

Fings reckoned he could let that be the end of it, at least for now, until the business with Myla was sorted. Brothers were brothers, but that didn't mean they had to share *every*thing – Fings certainly didn't.

"Just... Keep your head down and keep quiet. And don't be bothering any priests and don't be getting up to stuff." He gave Seth what he hoped was a hard look, then frowned and huffed and huffed and frowned and went to sit by himself for a bit. People, he thought, could be such a *bother*.

16

THE MOONSPIRE

Seth stood alone in a place he shouldn't be, somewhere deep within the Earth. A circle of archways lined the walls around him, blank white stone ringed with sigils. Beside each stood a hazy figure, some men, some women, a few perhaps... something else. The one-eyed god with the ruined face stood beside him, looking silently on. He was missing a hand, too, this time. Seth jabbed a finger at him: "What do you–?"

He jerked awake. Lying in an out-of-the-way corner below decks, lulled by the rhythm of the river, he'd dozed off and the visions had ambushed him again.

"Wanker," he muttered.

He supposed he shouldn't be surprised. Not given where he was going and why he'd left Varr. If it hadn't been for Fings, he would have taken whatever barge was the next to leave. Probably would have ended up in Tzeroth or something. But instead, he was on his way to Deephaven where Myla's warlock had once lived. He didn't like that. True, if Fings hadn't shown up when he did, Seth reckoned on being a pile of ash by now, being swept up by some novice to be thrown in the nearest canal. A cautionary tale for young priests. *Remember Seth the heretic? Remember what happened to him?* And yes, he'd been planning on going to Deephaven one day, but like this? *This* felt like the Gods giving him a good hard nudge and yelling at him to get on with it. Whatever *it* was.

After what felt like a month but was probably closer to a twelvenight, the barge put in for a day at the City of Spires. First chance he got, Seth was off, heading for the heart of the city. Chances were good that he could never go back to Varr; once word of his escape got out, maybe he'd never be able to come back *here*, either, and so while he *was* here, he was going to climb the Moonspire. Anyone who could make the ascent – exactly seven thousand and one steps – would be granted a vision of their future by Fickle Lord Moon; or at least, that was the story. He reckoned he could do with a bit of that. A bit more about the sigils would be nice, what they were and why they'd been on that barge. Or about the hooded woman and the priest who'd set the sword-monks on him. Mostly, though, he wanted to know about the one-eyed god. A vision of his future, he reckoned, might go a long way to fixing that. Might even show him how to make the irritating fucker leave him alone.

For a while after Midwinter, he'd tried to stop the visions by not sleeping. He'd managed three days of that, Cleaver poking him every time his head drooped, until he'd ended up curled on the floor, weeping with desperation; and of course, he *had* fallen asleep in the end, and the one-eyed arse-stain had got him like he always did. Then, for a while, they'd stopped. They'd stopped for quite a time. He'd been about ready to think they were gone...

Until the sword-monks took him. As he'd sat in his cell, waiting for the monks to decide he was no longer useful and that it was time to burn him, he'd dozed off; and *that* was when the one-eyed piece of shit had had the audacity to show up again and mock him. He'd told the monks when they returned, partly in the hope that they'd have a way to make it stop, but mostly out of spite. They *did* have a way to make it stop, after all, and when they were done with their questions, they were inevitably going to use it. Presumably, after he'd been burned or hanged, the one-eyed bastard wouldn't have any more use for him.

The stories of his visions had troubled the monks, gratifying in a hollow sort of way. They'd come at him with their questions, and he'd answered honestly, taking his time, dragging it out, not bothering to lie because what was the point? He'd told them about the hooded woman and the questions she'd been asking, about the priest and the sigils from the barge that had carried the late Emperor's crown and treasury. He'd told them about Sulfane and the Unrulys. When it came to all that, they knew as much as he did.

He'd tried to keep Myla and Fings out of it. Thought he'd be clever, biting his lip until it bled, then dipping his finger in the blood and drawing a sigil on himself, ending his memories of the theft. After that, all he knew was that the theft had been Sulfane's idea, that Sulfane had gone and not come back. When the monks asked after Sulfane's accomplices, Seth answered honestly that he didn't know who they were, that he didn't remember how the sigils had ended up in his possession after it was done.

The monks had stripped him and found the sigil on his skin. At dawn, they'd taken him out into the sun and made it go away. The memories hadn't returned but he suspected they'd got most of what he'd been trying to hide simply by asking about the sigil itself, why he'd done it and who he was trying to protect. Like an idiot, he hadn't made himself forget *that*, only what had actually happened. And, of course, he had no idea what he'd forgotten that they *hadn't* managed to winkle out of him.

A lesson for next time, he supposed.

Their vigilance hadn't been perfect. He'd managed another sigil, later, more careful about how and where he drew it. When they asked about the disappearance of Lightbringer Suaresh, Seth had shrugged his shoulders and told them honestly that he knew nothing about it. They hadn't liked it, but he wasn't lying. That sigil they hadn't found.

He'd volunteered what he knew about the Undercity in the vain hope it might save him from being burned alive. Stupid and desperate, because they were *always* going to burn him when they were done, but then again, maybe it *had* saved him. It had delayed them. It was what had led Fings to find him.

And there it was: fate again. The guiding hand of... something. And so now he was at the Moonspire, hoping to find out who and what and why.

He left Fings skulking at the bottom and started the climb. It took most of the day. By the time Seth reached the top, his legs were useless. He could barely breathe. He walked through the door into the Chamber of the Moon and found himself surrounded by polished white stone, which, frankly, was a bit unsettling, because it was *exactly* like the white stone arches of the undercity in Varr, which in turn were like the white stone arches of his visions. To the north, south, east and west, archways opened to the sky, leading to a balcony that ringed the tower, the setting sun streaming through them. Between the open archways were more arches, blank plain things of white stone ringed with sigils.

The same sigils as the arches under Varr? He wasn't sure. Couldn't tell. Couldn't quite remember. There was something very odd about this place, though. Something not quite real.

"Come outside."

A woman's voice, soft and melodious, out on the balcony. He took a deep breath and walked out. He didn't much like it there. The wind was strong, the balcony wasn't wide and didn't have a rail or anything to hold on to. It was a very long way down.

The four other spires stood about him in a circle. The city lay spread below, and the great river, as wide again and aswarm with ships and barges. Faint sounds wafted up, muffled almost to extinction, merchants selling their wares, the singing of street-corner bards, criers shouting news and imperial edicts, the clatter of horses, the distant blare of cavalry horns. And with the sounds came the stink…

Shit! He'd never been good with heights.

Wait… cavalry horns?

He looked again, disorientated, because this all felt like a summer afternoon, and yet it had been the last dying days of winter only a few hours ago, and the climb had taken so long that surely it must be near dark by now, and…

The sun was in the wrong place.

"Where am I?" he asked.

When no one answered, he inched around the balcony until he saw a woman sitting with her feet over the edge. She wore tight breeches in a deep lush red, black riding boots and a short tunic of white and gold. Her skin was brown, her long black hair tied in a plait that reached to the small of her back. Her eyes were an emerald green and the gold circlet she wore across her brow blazed with power. He knew this woman because he'd seen her a couple of months ago, standing in front of the Hanging Tree in the Circus of Dead Emperors. Except… She was older now. A decade, maybe?

"The question you should be asking is when," she said, without looking at him.

He knew her circlet, too. The circlet she wore was the Sunsteel Circlet of the Moon. The twin of the circlet Fings had stolen before Midwinter.

He sighed.

"Ice Witch!" growled another voice. Seth spun around to see who'd spoken. A second woman emerged onto the balcony. A plainly dressed Taiytakei, very angry, with swirling snakes of dark shadow writhing around each of her hands. The Taiytakei didn't seem to have noticed that Seth was there. She hurled her snakes of nothingness, and then seemed surprised when they fizzled harmlessly away.

"I learned that trick a while back," said the woman in red

and black and white and gold. "Have you learned *this* one?"

The whistle of the wind fell silent. The noises of the city too. When Seth looked at the river, the ships had fallen still and the gleaming ripples on the water had frozen. Birds hung motionless in the air between wingbeats. Someone had stopped time.

Is there a point to this, or are we all just taking it in turns to show off?

And there he was, right on cue. The one-eyed god with the ruined face and the missing hand, standing there beside him. Was the missing hand new? Or had it always been that way. Seth wasn't sure.

"I'd *love* to eavesdrop," he said. "But best not. She has a way of noticing when I drop by." He grinned. "She drew you here to see this. But we can hide things, you and I. We can hide what we know. We're very good at that."

"Piss off!" said Seth.

"But you came here to find me, did you not?"

"Fine. Who are you and what do you want?"

"I'm you. And what I want is for you not to make such a fucking pig's ear of everything this time around."

Seth gave this a moment of considered thought. "Fuck you," he said, and pushed the one-eyed god off the balcony.

There was a short, fading scream. Seth peered tentatively over the edge. He hadn't really expected that to work.

"You're not me," he said; and then suddenly he was back in the room where he'd started. Through the arches, he saw a dark moon rise from the southern sky to chase the sun, catch it and hold it tight; he saw the earth burn and dragons fly, saw fire and death and ash, and glass ground to sand, saw darkness fall and endless snow until all became ice and still. He saw a half-god blaze across the sky, heard names he didn't know spoken by unfamiliar voices; and then through those voices, one rang through, stronger than the others. She was standing beside him. He couldn't see her, but he knew she was there.

"You can stop this," Myla said.

"What? Me?" The Regent was standing behind him too. He could feel the blaze of unstoppable power that shone out of her like the light of a star.

No, you can't, whispered the one-eyed god.

"Fuck's sake! Just fuck *off!*"

"Use the sigil," said Myla. "Not on her. On me." And then she was gone, they were all gone, and he was in the room where he'd started, alone, and the arches looked out onto a peaceful winter twilight, and he was shivering with cold, and a priestess was wrapping a blanket across his shoulders.

"You're back," she said. "You should come away before you freeze."

"I had a vision," said Seth.

"Fickle Lord Moon spoke to you." She guided him out. "That's what happens here."

"I think I saw the end of the world."

The priestess smiled as she led him from the room of arches, down some steps to the room below where a brazier burned. Stools were arranged around it. Two were occupied, two women, both priestesses, both wrapped in blankets, warming themselves.

She probably thinks I'm a madman. Deranged. Good chance she's right.

"I used to be a priest," Seth said, not sure why but too cold and disorientated to care. "I saw the Black Moon. I thought it was just a story. But it isn't. There really was a Black Moon. It's going to come back."

He felt the quiver of her hand on his back as she guided him to sit. "Wait here a while. Warm yourself."

Another priestess passed him a bowl of something that turned out to be hot porridge, sweetened with a lot of honey.

"It's a long way down," she said. "You'll need your strength."

"I saw a one-eyed god." Seth sat and stared at the flames. "Half his face was a ruin of scars and he was missing a hand.

But the only gods *I* know are the Constant Sun and the Fickle Moon and the Infinite Mistress and the Hungry Goddess. I pushed him off the balcony and watched him fall."

Neither priestess answered, so he ate and warmed himself and, when he had his strength again, he left. On his way down, whenever he saw a priestess, he asked whether she knew of a one-eyed god with a ruined face. It was what Fings would have done, but he didn't have Fings's luck, and so none of them had an answer.

Eventually, he made his way back to the barge. Fings wasn't there, which was something of a relief. He went to sleep.

In the morning, Fings poked him awake. They were moving again, he could feel it. Back on their way to Deephaven.

"Did you get to the top?" Fings asked.

Seth nodded.

"So, what's up there?"

"I saw the future, Fings."

"What? Really?"

"I should have been a priestess."

Fings seemed to give this some thought. "But you're not a girl."

"Maybe I should have been."

Fings seemed to give *this* some thought, too. "You really saw the future?" he asked, after a bit.

"I think so."

"So... what happens then? In the future?"

Seth sighed. "Frankly, it looked a bit rubbish."

17

DEEPHAVEΠ

While Seth climbed the Moonspire, Fings waited at the bottom, reckoning that seven thousand and one steps was about seven thousand more than he fancied, and also that only an idiot went and looked at their future, because what if it was shit? Eventually, a Moon priestess pointed out that climbing the Moonspire and coming down again took an entire day and most of the following night.

"You should put in something so you can slide down," he said.

The Moon priestess winked at him. "We did. But you have to live here to be allowed to use it."

He wasn't sure what to make of that. Priests and priestesses were supposed to be serious-minded people which, as far as he could tell, was the main reason Seth had been thrown out. Well, and breaking into forbidden vaults and crypts and getting Fings to steal forbidden books and so forth... Actually, probably mostly all that.

Anyway, once he knew he had a wait on his hands, he left Seth to get on with his god-stuff and went back into the city to have a proper explore of the place. He soon found markets and crowds and busy streets and all the things he missed from Varr, and had a fine old time helping himself to whatever took his

106

fancy. He made his way back to the barge in the small hours of the morning, purse fatter than when he'd left, his satchel full of things he didn't need but which had looked interesting at the time and generally feeling a lot better about life. He found Seth fast asleep and left him alone, reckoning the last thing you wanted after climbing seven thousand and one steps was having someone give you a poking while you were trying to recover. In the morning, after they'd left and Seth was *still* asleep, Fings poked him anyway and was rewarded by Seth claiming to have seen the future and that it was rubbish and that he should have been a priestess. Fings spent the rest of the day trying to imagine Seth done up as a Moon priestess and, once he managed it, wishing he hadn't.

Eventually, he badgered Seth into telling him everything he had seen, and then largely wished he hadn't managed *that*, either. Then he went to sleep.

The last stage of their journey to the sea passed more quickly. The weather changed. The deep snow that had covered everything all the way from Varr became patchy, then vanished. The air was still cold but no longer bitter. Between Varr and the City of Spires, the north bank of the river was dredged and shored up, one of the Emperor's Roads kissing against it, a wide stinking towpath for all the barges that moved between the two cities. Beyond the City of Spires, towards the sea, the road disappeared inland. The river became wide and slow, the banks alternating between stretches of forest, thick and tall and dark, and wide flat grassland that flooded into water-meadows every spring, while every boat on the water was powered by oar or sail.

He noticed these things because Myla had told him about them, back when they'd been travelling together. He wasn't at all sure whether her fascination with how the world worked was healthy. Seth had the same, and it hadn't brought him anything but trouble.

It rained, a steady grey drizzle that never seemed to end.

The first Fings knew they were close to Deephaven itself was a small, vicious-looking fort on the bank, built in a hurry out of tree trunks, piers spilling into the river like some dead wooden monster made of tentacles. He saw soldiers idling away their time by the water, fishing and smoking pipes, close enough as the barge passed for Fings to make out their colours: silver and black. Not that he had the first idea what that meant.

"We'll be in Deephaven by the end of the day," the sailors said.

Later came the smell. Every city had its own stink, and Deephaven's was the rank odour of rotting seaweed, hanging like a roof over everything and sending tendrils of warning for miles at the whim of the wind. Fings sat at the prow, swinging his legs, watching the first fringes of the city as they rolled past, makeshift huts strung along the waters' edge, spreading back into the trees, jetties and piers reaching into the river. And boats, dozens and then hundreds, mostly tiny rafts made from a few hollow poles of bamboo lashed together. The rafts swarmed the edges of the river while larger sailing boats lumbered back and forth along the deeper channels further out. Each raft had one man and a string of large black birds they used to fish the river. A simple, easy life. He liked the thought of that.

Some of the buildings along the waterfront, he noticed, had grey banners hanging over the door. Warnings of death. He liked that less.

A mile further on and a mass of stonework jutted into the river. Here were the walls of Deephaven and the River Gate and, somewhere between here and the sea, the infamous Pelean's Gate, where the Levanya had nailed up Emperor Talsin's son back in the war; and then the river-docks, a solid mile of warehouses and piers and barges and shouting and chaos. For some reason, the first hundred yards or so were a heaving mass of people and carts all streaming down some road leading up to the heart of the city, and then the next hundred

were almost deserted; and then after *that*... After that, what
he saw was a constant cacophony of noise and motion, barges
pulling in and pushing away, armadas of crates and barrels and
bales being hoisted on and off and carried back and forth, a
heaving mass of people and enough noise to make the Spice
Market on festival day look like a contemplative dawn prayer
in the Temple of the Sun. The steady drizzle and the fact that
everyone and everything was somewhere between damp and
sodden didn't seem to bother anyone in the least.

He wasn't sure about the rain. Could get tedious that, he
reckoned. But as for the rest...? As the boatmen nosed their
barge into a pier shortly past the bit that apparently no one
used, Fings drank it all in. Deephaven wasn't as impressive to
look at as the City of Spires, with its towers, or Varr with its
cliffs topped by the Kavaneth and with the Sapphire Palace
looming across the river, but the buzz of life! The energy! From
the water, he saw the peak of rock rising towards the sea at
the far end of the river; obviously, from how it was covered in
stumpy little towers, it was where the rich folk lived. He saw
the walls of a fortress, glimpsed through the rain and the masts
of ships moored up at the seaward end of the river-docks. As
he stepped off the boat, he saw tell-tale signs of secret circles
and underworld communities, marks and symbols scratched
on wood and stone; and it didn't matter that he didn't know
what they meant, the sight of them was enough. Stepping
off the barge and feeling his feet on dry land again felt like
climbing into a warm cosy bed after being stuck out in a storm.
He'd never thought of himself as a boat person. Being stuck on
one for the best part of a month with only Seth for company,
well, all *that* had done was convince him he was right.

More banners, too. Limp wet rags of grey hanging over
closed doors. Drooping, here and there, from the masts and
spars of the boats. He shivered. Death was here.

"Right then, *Ser* Fings, where do we start?"

"Are you *ever* going to stop with that?"

"Probably not."

The sensible thing, Fings supposed, would be to find Orien, given that Orien was the reason they were here, the only trouble being that Orien was also a mage and... well, he didn't know where to look. And these banners, what *was* all that all about? Dead Men? Because if it *was* Dead Men, he might turn around and go right back to Varr.

He'd lost track of what day it was, so he went to where a stooped old man with a brazier was selling grilled scraps of... well, Fings wasn't sure *what*, exactly, but they smelled somewhere between fish and vomit.

"What day is it?" he asked, scrunching his nose.

The stooped old man scooped a handful of whatever it was straight from the hot coals, popped one in his mouth and dropped the rest onto a scrap of wood. He offered it to Fings.

"I don't... Oh. Right." Fings dropped a coin into the old man's waiting hand and took the sliver of wood. It still amazed him that he could pay for things and still have money in his pockets. The whole concept was going to take some getting used to.

"You won't find better anywhere this side of the Peak."

"Really?" Seth gave him a hard stare, one street-vendor to another. "I used to say that about the pastries I sold in the Spice Markets of Varr. Truth was, if I'm honest, you probably could have scraped better off the cobbles."

The stooped old man gave Seth a look, the two of them eyeing each other like a pair of tomcats sizing up for a fight. Fings warily stuck one of the hot vomity fish-things into his mouth. "It's..."

He bit down and then stopped, taken by surprise. In part by the texture, which was unexpectedly gritty. But mostly because whatever it was, it was delicious.

"That's amazing!" He grabbed Seth. "You have to try this!"

"Oh, here we go." Seth rolled his eyes. Fings ignored him, paid the old man another three bits for the rest of his vomity fish-things, and then asked whether he'd ever met Levvi. The old man said no, not that he knew, but it didn't sound like a local name, and had this Levvi fellow, whoever he was, come in off the river? Fings explained that Levvi was his brother, come from Deephaven five years ago, looking to make his fortune. The old man huffed and puffed and reckoned Fings should try his luck across the city at the sea-docks, since that was where all the idiot fortune-seekers ended up.

"Working the river, good steady work that, but no one ever got rich who wasn't already rich to begin with. Now the sea, on the other hand? Taking up with the Taiytakei traders on their Black Ships? Death or glory, that is."

Fings asked about the death-banners hanging about the place. Deephaven, as it turned out, was in the grip of what the old man called the River Plague, something that rattled by every few years, ever since the year the dragon monks had come from Torpreah, as it happened, but most likely that was a coincidence and it had been brought by all the foreigner-types clogging up the streets these days. Nothing to worry about for a godly fellow who took the right precautions. Fings asked him what those might be.

"Saying your prayers to the Sun at dawn and dusk, that's a good start," the old man said, "and steering well clear of that cursed place down by the River Gate."

After that, it got long and complicated; coincidentally, by the time the old man had finished suggesting places Fings shouldn't go and things he shouldn't do and charms he should wear, he'd conveniently managed to sizzle up a fresh batch of vomity fish-things, dredged from a chipped urn full of water by his feet. Fings, who'd conveniently munched his way through those he'd already bought, handed over another few coins and walked away happy, almost forgetting why he'd stopped to talk to the old man in the first place.

"It's Moonday, by the way," called the old man at his back.

Fings gave this some thought and decided *not* to try and find

Orien. Moonday was a bad day for closing circles, which was sort of what they'd be doing if they went looking for Orien. On the other hand, Moonday was absolutely the *best* day for finding things which, Fings reckoned, made it the best day to search for Levvi.

He scanned a nervous eye to the doors with their death-banners, and to the quiet spot on the waterfront towards the River Gate, uncomfortably close now that he knew there was some cursed house down there which was presumably what everyone was avoiding. He should be getting some of those charms the old man had been banging on about, he reckoned. Sooner rather than later, too.

Figuring it couldn't be *that* hard to find the sea-docks, and that there was no one more superstitious than a bunch of sailors, he set off, leaving Seth to follow. He had no idea what to expect, since Levvi had never sent a letter back home and none of them would have been able to read it even if he had. But there were always stories, and so he looked around as he crossed Deephaven, eager for the triangular houses, the upside-down temples, the part of the city that floated and was made entirely of old ships, the roofs of white feathers, all the while keeping a nervous eye open for the giant sea-birds he'd heard about that would swoop down and tear off the occasional finger if you weren't careful. Doubtless there were charms against that sort of thing; after a while, when he hadn't seen any, he noted how most of the population seemed to have a full complement of digits and supposed a watchful eye might do for now.

By the time they reached the sea, he'd accumulated a feeling that was part excitement, part trepidation, and part disappointment. Disappointment because he'd been looking forward to upside-down temples but, so far, Deephaven's temples had been disappointingly the same way up as the ones in Varr. Trepidation because he hadn't been ready for how *big* this city was, as big as Varr or even more, which meant

finding Levvi was going to be difficult. Excitement because...
because... because he'd never imagined anything like the
Deephaven sea-docks could even exist! They were *enormous*,
five times the size of the docks in Varr; and the crowds were
huge, and the people...! All colours and sizes, people with
bright orange faces, people with black and white stripy hands,
bald men with hundreds of feathers sticking out of their scalps,
tattooed from head to toe, women with their hair braided to
their knees and tiny blades at the ends. He got a bit spooked
by the ones who were dead but still walked and laughed and
jabbered in some strange language that might be the language
of the underworld, until Seth pointed out that they were
simply foreigners who didn't know that grey was the death-
colour, and thought the funny looks they kept getting were
because of the spiked bands around their necks and wrists.

He looked at it all in awe and wonder. Hundreds of ships.
Thousands of carts and wagons. *Tens* of thousands of people.

And then, because you had to start somewhere, he picked a
random sailor and asked: "You know Levvi?"

18

THE OΠE-EYED GOD

"You all right?" Fings sat down beside Seth with a heavy thump. At least, it *sounded* like Fings. They'd been here what, half a day? Less? Already, Fings had taken to wearing a scented mask and a bizarre, tasselled hat on top of his usual assortment of charms, apparently to keep at bay whatever disease gripped the city.

The River Plague, was that what the idiot old man had called it? Seth reckoned it was just his luck to run away from angry sword-monks only to wash up in a city gripped by plague. He was starting to wish he hadn't come.

On the other hand, none of the locals seemed particularly concerned. And... well. Angry sword-monks.

"You know those are all useless, right?" Seth had met a few Moon priestesses over the years before he'd been kicked out of the temple. They'd even had a priestess coming to the *Pig* before Midwinter, putting Arjay and then Dox back together, and being all weird about Seth and avoiding him and then telling him she knew what he was going to do, whatever *that* had meant. Point was, Moon priestesses dealt with sick people all the time, and you didn't see *them* wearing masks and funny hats and a dozen stupid charms round their necks and smelling of six different types of incense all at once. Prayer and holiness, *that* was what kept sickness at bay. That and a ruthless policy of extermination of all vermin.

You'd better hope they're just as wrong because you're fucked if they're not.

Fings gave him a funny look, then shrugged. Whenever Seth did something or said something that Fings didn't like, he'd put it down to "weird priest shit" and leave Seth to deal with it on his own. Which Seth agreed was largely for the best: of the many ways he might have described Fings's likely reaction to the idea that you could kill people by drawing funny squiggles on bits of paper, and then bring them back to life and make them talk... well, calm and collected weren't likely to be among them.

Another thing that didn't sit well with calm and collected was what he'd seen at the top of the Moonspire. Presumably, he wasn't the *only* one who could stop whatever needed stopping; if he was... well, the world was probably a bit fucked in that case, but also, you might think that if it was *that* important, something as powerful as a God might, well... actually *do* something. It wasn't as if Fickle Lord Moon didn't have thousands and thousands of priests and priestesses and followers and worshippers, all of whom were likely a sight better suited for stopping any end-of-the-world shenanigans than Seth would ever be.

You do *know what you have to do, though.*

Yeah. The one thing the vision had made clear, but only up to a point. *Use the sigil* was all very well, but *which* sigil? *Not on her, On me.* On Myla? Right, because using sigils on sword-monks had worked out *so* well in Varr. What was he supposed to do? Wander up and stick random sigils on her until something happened, all on the say-so of some enigmatic divinity that could have chosen to be perfectly clear if it had felt like it? No. Fuck that. He *liked* Myla.

"Found Levvi yet?" Seth asked, since Fings was still looking at him like he was expecting an answer to some question he hadn't yet put into words. Fings's approach to looking for Levvi – wandering from place to place, asking random passers-by about some bloke that might have passed through five years ago – struck Seth as ridiculous. Trouble was, he couldn't think of anything better. What did people *do* when they came to Deephaven to make their fortune? Well, they went to sea, didn't they? Even in Varr, he knew *that* much. And since the Empire didn't have many ships of its own, and since the Black Ships of the Taiytakei were always looking for crew, the sea-docks seemed as a good a place as any to start.

Knowing Fings's luck, he'd stumble into Levvi on his way to the privy a few days from now. A city full of people, spread out over miles, and they'd bump into each other, just like that.

"Since you're awake, you can give me a hand with this bloody thing."

Seth rubbed his temples. For some reason, Fings had bought a carpet. Even Fings didn't seem to know why.

Fings caught his look. "I had a good feeling about it," he said, sounding vaguely defensive.

He'll probably unroll it and find a note from Levvi inside.

Some God wanted someone to save the world? Should have picked Fings. He'd do it, right enough, probably through a string of unlikely accidents.

Why *him*? Why, of anyone, pick *him*? The Path of the Sun had cast him out. Gods weren't even supposed to notice that he existed.

So maybe it wasn't *a God. Maybe it was something else.*

Yeah. *That* sounded more like it. That one-eyed fucker again. He *had* been there too, after all, even if Seth had pushed him off the balcony. Too much to hope for that the shit-spirit had plunged to his death.

They moved to the next tavern and then the next. The taverns all smelled a bit odd, and all in the same way, until Seth worked out it was because they were all burning the same scented candles and incense sticks. He didn't recognize what it was, which was curious given he'd grown up in Varr's Spice Market, so he took a leaf out of Fings's book and asked random strangers. The looks he got were like he was asking what the sea was made of. Some resin or other the Black Ships were bringing in, it turned out, supposedly the ground-up remains of men who'd been turned to stone by dragons, mixed with spices to make it smell better. *Supposedly* stuff to keep the plague at bay. Seth didn't recognise the name, but he *did* recognise a scam when he saw one.

After a bit, he got bored, borrowed some more money from Fings and left him to get on with it. He rented a room and sat in it and wondered what he was supposed to do. Hadn't given it much thought on the barge. Get away from Varr. Well, he'd done that. So now what?

The hooded woman and the priest in Varr had been looking for Sulfane. The sword-monks clearly hadn't known the first thing about any of that, not until Seth had told them. Seth quite fancied tracking them both down and introducing them to some sigil-related unpleasantness; but they were in Varr, and he was a thousand miles away. Then there was the book he'd found in Sulfane's room back in Tombland, written in a cipher, but *that* was in Varr, too. Most likely, the monks would have found it by now, along with Seth's money and everything else. Then there was the mystery of where Fings had found the sigils themselves, and the strange death of the late Emperor, and the unlikely ascent of his daughter, and... But the fact was, he really couldn't find one good reason to give a shit about any of that. Like it or not, he wouldn't be returning to Varr in a hurry.

Would he?

He had no doubt Fings would find a way to help Myla. That was who Fings was, and what he did. Lucky bastard would probably find Levvi too. And, if past performances were anything to go by, in a few days they'd all be getting out of Deephaven in a huge hurry on account of people being all

angry at them, probably sword-monks again, and then what?
Go somewhere else and do the same again? Over and over?

He thought about this. It felt immensely depressing.

He sighed. He was here now, right? Best make the most of
it. Which meant… Well, there *was* the whole thing about the
warlock who'd once lived here. The one Myla's sword-mistress
had chased off. Probably knew a thing or two about sigils if
nothing else.

He stretched and waved his arms and then jumped up and
down a bit, mostly because he could. Having his own space felt
strange after all the months of sleeping on the kitchen floor in
the *Pig* and then in the cold, dead bowels of the Undercity. A
nice strange, though, to have a bed and warmth and a fire and
not to have to share it with anyone. He even had a working
window, and never mind that his view was mostly of the
constant rain. He *even* had a mirror!

He got up and started to pace circles. Maybe seeing the
future – *if* that's what it had been – was all part of life's rich
tapestry when you were one of the chosen; for all *he* knew,
the Autarch of the Sun spent the whole time in his palace in
Torpreah doing nothing else. Perhaps the Sun was constantly
in his head, yelling at him. If that was true, the Path hadn't
thought to tell Seth before they'd kicked him out. Nor had
they thought to tell him what to do about it.

Except, the more he thought about it, the more likely it
seemed that he *hadn't* had a divine vision, and that, most likely,
this was just the one-eyed god fucking about again. The half-
blind shitweasel had first shown up on the night Fings and
Myla had stolen the Emperor's crown. For a while, Seth had
taken as a blessing every night where he didn't find himself
on any icy ridge, or in some secret underground chamber,
or somewhere that hadn't happened yet. Then, shortly after
Midwinter, the visions had almost stopped. Three in pushing
two months, and that was counting the one he'd had in the
cell in the temple on Spice Market Square, which frankly had

been more of an orchestrated replay of all his various failings than anything you could call a *vision*. Since the Moonspire, though, the one-eyed god had decided to get busy. Cross about being pushed off a balcony, probably.

Well. Weighing it all in the balance, Seth reckoned the one-eyed god could go fuck himself, and Fickle Lord Moon could go fuck himself too. They were here to find Myla, right? Right. First chance he got, then, he was going to tell her everything. Start to finish, all of it, the good *and* the bad, not that there was much good. When he was done, he'd let her choose. Either they could work it out, together, side by side to save the world or whatever, or else she could take his head for being a murderer and a heretic and a warlock.

He sprawled on the bed. A bed! True, he'd had a cot in his cell when he'd been a novice, and yes, Myla had let him use her room when she wasn't at the *Pig*, but he'd never had a space with four whole walls and a roof and bed that was all *his*.

The people in the next room were talking, loud staccato volleys of questions and counter-questions. He had a vague idea they were arguing about getting out of the city. He closed his eyes and ran his hands through his hair.

He *was* a long way from Varr. No one here knew him. Maybe... Maybe he could get away with masquerading as a priest? Get into a temple, find a Dawncaller or a Sunbright and see if they could make the one-eyed privy-accident go away?

Or... he *could* track down the warlock who'd once lived here...

His head felt heavy. He closed his eyes as his chin sank to his chest.

Here we go again...

19

SİPPİNG TEA WİTH A MAGE

Finding Orien turned out to be easy, once Fings got to looking. There were plenty of people not keen on the idea of a mage on their doorstep, so Orien's arrival was Being Talked About. Even on the sea-docks side of the city, people remembered the *last* mage to set up shop in Deephaven, some warlock who'd lived down by the river-docks until a bunch of Torpreahn sword-monks had chased him off. So yes, word had spread quickly of the mage who dressed in orange and strutted around and acted like he was all important and seemed to like to set things on fire, even if it was mostly himself. Admittedly, Fings *had* got confused for a while, on account of there being *another* mage apparently skulking near the sea-docks in what used to be an old chapel to the Moon. But this other mage had been in Deephaven for ages and didn't have a burgeoning reputation for setting things on fire, so that was easily settled.

The *other* mage was apparently some sort of healer. Fings knew for an absolute fact that this was bollocks because he'd met healers. Moon priestesses were healers, albeit expensive ones. Witches, sure, they could do a bit of healing now and then.

Herbalists too. Even alchemists, if you were desperate, although they were just as likely to explode you. But mages? Never.

Best keep well clear of *that* one, then.

He traipsed through the rain. Orien's house – the Guildhouse of the Order of Fire, to give its full title, which Fings had no intention of doing – was in a tiny square sandwiched between the fringes of the sea-docks and some part of town called The Maze, which Fings rather fancied exploring. Turned out to be a big run-down old mess of a place with rooms for servants, three separate entrances, the sort of fancy house obviously built by someone who'd had money, long ago. Someone who'd had money and then lost it, Fings reckoned, from how run-down it was, with a leaky roof and bits falling off the corners.

He wondered if Orien could magic them back on again. Then he moved to wishing Seth was with him, so Seth could be the one to knock on the door in case it exploded. Seth *wasn't* with him, though, having exhibited a perfectly sensible reluctance to have anything whatsoever to do with Orien under any circumstances, so Fings took a deep breath and knocked on the door himself.

Nothing exploded. After a long pause, a servant in orange livery opened the door and led him inside to where Orien and some well-dressed fellow were sipping tea. Fings did all the right things, of course: walked into the room with his hands clasped together and held out in front of him, said "Morning, mage," even though it was late evening and dark outside, and then turned his back like you were supposed to, waiting for Orien to tell him it was safe to look. The real face of a mage could make you go mad, *every*one knew that, so you had to be careful the first time you saw one. Give them time to put their masks back.

"Fings?"

Fings could almost feel Orien staring at him like he had some weird growth sprouting out of the back of his head. He tried not to look. "Is it safe?" he asked.

"What?"

"Is it safe to look?"

"*What*? Yes… what do you mean? Of course it is."

Fings turned. Orien was in an orange robe with enough embroidery to made him look like the priest of some fruit-god, but his face was a perfectly normal face, the same face he'd had in Varr, so that was a relief. The man sitting across from him had skin the colour of deep dark honey, which was turning out to be fairly typical for Deephaven. He had a hawkish nose and eyes that reminded Fings of Myla, and dressed as though he carried crowns and maybe the occasional emperor in his purse, although with the air of someone who sometimes kept a poisonous centipede in there too, just for fun.

Probably puts a curse on his purse each morning.

A rich man's parlour with a mage was about last place Fings ever thought he'd find himself. Thing was, it reminded him of the Bithwar woman's place in Bonecarvers, except here was full of scented candles burning to keep the miasma of disease out of the air. He took a deep breath and then wished he hadn't. The smell was almost overwhelming.

"This is Lucius," said Orien.

The eyes and the face and the name all came together in a moment of happy understanding. "You're Myla's brother," mumbled Fings from behind his mask, trying not to breathe but relieved that Lucius wasn't some other mage Orien had already befriended, because one was quite enough. "Right?"

"Pardon?"

Fings pulled down his mask, said it again, and then pulled it back up.

"I am," said Lucius.

"Good. That's good. Talked about you sometimes, she did. I'm Fings," said Fings, still looking nervously at Orien. One mage was still one mage too many, even if he'd seemed mostly normal back in Varr.

"The burglar." Lucius raised an eyebrow. "I've heard of you."

Fings took a step back in case he found himself with a sudden urgent need to run. Usually that was what happened right after *I've heard of you.* He risked lowering his mask. He *probably* didn't need it, not here, not given there was enough incense in the air to make his eyes water. Probably did a good enough job of keeping the plague demons at bay, right?

"Heard... what, exactly?" he asked.

"You're Myla's friend."

"Yeah. Right. That's me. Um... So, anyway." He forced himself to look at Orien. "You wrote a letter. Said to come. Here I am."

There was lots of talking after that, mostly stuff Fings already knew about what Myla had done. He spent his time watching Orien. He supposed, grudgingly, they might manage to get along, at least as long as it took to do whatever needed to be done. Orien obviously had a thing for Myla, and Fings reckoned he could respect that; although it *was* still a bit of a discovery that mages could have feelings like ordinary people in between all that contemplating of Things Best Left Alone they got up to.

After that thought, he moved on to being distracted by the bad smell lurking behind all the incense. There were a lot of bad smells in Deephaven, and he was just heading off into a bit of idle speculation as to whether he'd start seeing people with no noses – didn't seem all that unlikely after all he'd seen around the sea-docks – when he realised Orien and Lucius had stopped talking and were looking at him.

"What?"

Orien reached across and patted him on the arm, which was a bit disturbing. He was looking at Lucius, though. "Fings's brother spent years as a novice, some of it in a temple in the south of Varr, some in the Cathedral of Light itself. The way Myla tells it, Fings used to come and go as he pleased and none of the priests or the other novices ever knew." He gave Fings a wink. "*Apparently*, someone stole a book from the Sunherald's private library?"

Fings gave Orien a stare. He couldn't imagine how the mage could possibly know about that; except he *could* – he'd obviously heard it from Myla, which meant Myla had picked it up from someone in the *Unruly Pig*, which meant Seth had been flapping his gums, which meant the two of them would be needing to have another talk about Seth keeping his bloody mouth shut.

"Get me a robe and I can get inside," said Fings, thinking of Seth and how he could make himself useful while he was swanning about on Fings's coin. "I'll find a way to get her out."

"Your brother was a priest?" asked Lucius.

"A novice, but long enough for me to know my way around a temple." Fings shrugged. "While I'm helping you, maybe you can be helping me in return." He told them about Levvi, how Levvi had come to Deephaven looking to make his fortune and had never returned. Lucius listened politely while Orien yawned and fidgeted. When Fings was done, Lucius shook his head.

"He probably signed with one of the Black Ships. One trip and you'll come back a rich man, they say. What they *don't* say is that most don't come back at all."

"Or he got mugged and murdered and dumped in the river," said Orien.

"Levvi ain't dead," Fings said, although he knew he was probably wrong. Ma Fings had come to the same way of thinking a couple of years back, which was why she didn't talk about Levvi nowadays.

After a bit of awkward sitting in silence, Orien got up and showed Fings to an upstairs room and told him he could use it for as long as he wanted, all furnished with a proper bed and all manner of rich-man stuff. The mage conjured a flame out of nothing, lit a candle which had the same smell as the rooms downstairs, told Fings it was to keep the miasma of the sickness away, and then left. Fings considered this. Sicknesses, as *every*one knew, were caused by bad spirits who liked to suck the life out of one person for a bit and then jump into another, and that was why you wore a mask, so they couldn't get in, and also why you stayed away from anyone who wasn't well. He hadn't come across the notion of keeping bad spirits away using a smell they didn't like, but he supposed he could see the sense to it since *he* didn't much like the smell either. And Orien *was* a mage and so maybe he knew what he was talking about.

Maybe.

Still, he blew out the candle and then lit it again, properly this time, from a firebox. Unpleasant smells were one thing, but if he was going to have a candle burning in his room, it was going to have a normal flame, lit properly, not by some sorcery nonsense.

He let the candle burn and tried to get his head around the rest of his new room. A place to hang enough clothes to dress a whole village. A hatstand, which was handy, given he had a new hat. Beside it was a mirror, cracked and grimy. Cracked mirrors being bad luck, Fings turned it to face the wall. He dropped onto the bed and then jumped up again in panic, sinking so deep into feathers that he thought he must have broken it. He looked around, bewildered.

This was how rich people lived, was it? He tried to imagine Ma Fings and his sisters in a place like this. He could see his sisters easily enough, running about like over-excited clowns; but Ma Fings... she'd find a reason why they couldn't stay. It would make her feel small, like she hadn't earned it.

As if anyone who lived in a house like this had actually *earned* it.

A knock on the door and then Myla's brother came in without being asked. He sat on the bed, causing the whole thing to sag again. Fings eyed him suspiciously.

"Shirish tells me that the two of you stole the Emperor's crown from right under the noses of the Imperial Guard."

Instinct had Fings check the window, looking to see how quickly he could get out without having to use the door.

Seth blabbing about that book from the cathedral, now Myla blabbing about the crown? He'd have to be having that talk with *both* of them. Emperors, he reckoned, even dead ones, could be touchy about people stealing their crowns, and had long memories and held grudges. Sunheralds too.

"Help my sister and I'll do what I can to look for your brother. Was he a righteous man?"

"Um?" Fings wasn't sure what to say about that. "Didn't go to temple much, if that's what you mean."

"Anything about him people might remember?"

"He worked in Tanners for a while, curing hides. Did no favours for the skin on his hands and arms. Don't know if that might all have healed up by the time he got here." He shrugged. "Hadn't when he left. Broken nose. Missing a couple of front teeth."

Thinking about it, it *was* possible that Levvi had dropped himself into the first dubious get-rich-quick plot he stumbled across rather than look for honest work. He'd always been a thief at heart, same as Fings. Maybe he'd found himself some gang like the Unrulys, and then got himself in trouble. Maybe Orien had it right. Maybe Levvi *did* get stabbed and dumped in the river, and that was the end of it, and no one would ever know.

"What do the Longcoats do with thieves here?"

"Cut off a finger, maybe." Lucius shrugged. "Hang them, sometimes, if they annoyed someone important. Most get sent to the mines. The Nejans pay good coin for a solid worker. But if you're caught trying to help Myla, it'll be temple justice that–"

Fings snorted. "*I* ain't getting caught. Was thinking of Levvi."

"Oh. Well. Then the mines, most likely. But those are a thousand miles away. Up the river Arr and then the Torea and the Lasot, all the way to the Dragon's Teeth. No one ever comes back." Lucius shifted. "There's a fort up the river a little way. You must have seen it if you came by boat, about half a day upriver? They keep ledgers and accounts. If your brother went through, there might be a record of him, but... It's full of Nejans. They keep to themselves. It'll be difficult. And five years is a long time. I don't know if they keep records back that far."

Fings thought of what he'd seen from the boat, coming towards the city. "This fort. The one with all them jetties?"

"Piers. But yes."

Was that how it was? Levvi got himself wrapped up in something, got himself in trouble, got himself caught? But no. Levvi had done honest work in Varr before he left. He wasn't *that* stupid.

"Got to ask this," he said. "But... you sure Myla *wants* to be rescued? Because the way she was talking, last we spoke... I got to wonder." He supposed he could see how stealing people out of prisons looked much the same as burgling, but it wasn't. Gold didn't make a fuss about whose pocket it was in, or go wandering off, or start talking about crap that could very definitely wait until later, or generally do anything except stay exactly where it was put.

Lucius looked away, and right there was Fings's answer. He *wasn't* sure.

"Look... I can get in and I can find her and everything. I can give her the choice. But I ain't forcing her to do something she don't want. Doubt I could even if I tried."

That brought a chuckle. "Me neither. Never could." Lucius got up. "Thank you, Fings."

"What for? I ain't done anything yet."

"For being her friend. For answering Orien's call."

Fings stared at the door after Lucius left, trying to remember the last time anyone had thanked him for something. Hadn't seemed like such a big thing, leaving Varr to come here, but maybe it was, when you thought about it.

Thinking about it got him thinking about Orien's courier, bursting into the Pig like some confused monster. And Arjay, laughing, and his sister too. *Ser Fings!* He headed back to the big fancy room with the writing desk and the fireplace, looking for the mage.

"Can you do another one of them letter things?" Fings asked. "If I get someone to write it."

Orien shrugged. "If it's truly important to the wellbeing of the empire then yes, I can."

"Yeah." Fings nodded. "It's definitely... all that. Can't be helping Myla without it."

In his head, he was already telling Seth what to write. *For the attention of Her Grandness the Lady Ma Fings and all her Royal Daughters...*

They'd like that. They'd have to find someone to read it for them, of course, but he wasn't going to be another Levvi, vanishing without a word.

20

ACCEPTANCE

Tasahre came every day and walked the temple with Myla. Myla relished it, the whip of the wind and rain on her skin. *This* was home. It made her feel alive again. Each evening, when the sword-mistress took Myla back to her cell, she left the knife. Every morning, when she saw it still lying where she'd left it, Tasahre picked it up without a word. Eventually she stopped. Once Myla's wounds had healed enough, they went into the exercise yard after dark each night, after the other monks had gone inside. Tasahre watched Myla stretch and run through her forms, tutting and correcting everything. The days passed this way until the month of Storms gave way to the month of Rebirth and with it, the coming equinox. Spring gnawed at the last dying edges of winter, and all that was left of the wounds Myla had taken on the Avenue of Emperors were two ugly scars.

"The Hawats petition the Overlord daily to have you given into their custody," said Tasahre. "The Overlord wants this done with, so the Sunherald delights in thwarting him while he looks for a way to spare himself the embarrassment of a sword-monk put on public trial. The Autarch in Torpreah sends messages in secret. It's not hard to guess what they say. There will be war between north and the south before long;

and when it comes, the Autarch will call on his swords to fight against the throne. I had thought to use that, but somehow the Sunherald knows the story of what you did in Varr. Had you taken the crown to Torpreah and given it to the Autarch, I have no doubt that every sin you ever committed, no matter how dire, would have been forgiven. But you didn't."

"I did what was right," said Myla.

"Yes. What you *thought* was right, at least. I'm sorry, Shirish, that you will be punished for that."

"Will you?" asked Myla. "Fight against the Sapphire throne, I mean?"

"My swords stand against the enemies of the path." Beyond that, Tasahre wouldn't be drawn.

"Does Orien still come?" asked Myla later.

"Your sorcerer? Yes. Every day, always the same. And every day, he's turned away."

"Will you allow me to see him?"

"I will not."

Myla stamped her foot. "Why?"

"*There's* my Shirish." A smile played across Tasahre's face. She crossed the yard to the armoury, came back with four wooden practice swords, and tossed a pair at Myla's feet. "I will give you an hour with your sorcerer if you can do one of two things. Accept the burden of your choices, or spar with me and win."

"I *have* accepted my guilt! That's why I came back!"

"You have courage, thinking you can strike a bargain with Sarwatta for your family's safety; and yes, yes, your brother has been here begging my ear almost as often as your mage. But I do not speak precisely of *guilt*. The burden both you *and* the Hawat must accept is that what each of you have done to the other cannot be undone. He must take his legal retribution and let it go. The burden *you* have yet to accept is not his retribution, but the truth that such a letting go is immeasurably beyond him. Thus he *will* hurt those you love, no matter what you do, because no punishment can ever be enough."

Myla watched her, waiting, the two practice swords held loose and low. "What do you want from me?" she asked.

"I've already told you."

"I don't understand what you're looking for."

"And there lies the problem."

"And there *you* are," snapped Myla. "The inscrutable sword-mistress with her riddles that no one understands, that don't even make any sense!"

Tasahre's smile grew a little but there was steel in it, even a little venom. She lifted one sword and stroked her knuckles along the scar that crossed her throat.

Myla bared her teeth. "Do you know what he did?"

"Of course, I do."

"*Do* you? Or have you heard only *his* story?"

Tasahre raised her other sword and stood ready. Myla did the same. "You think me an idiot? Perhaps you think, because I live in this temple, I am naïve?"

"Then you should know he deserved it!" Myla launched herself, a whirl of the swords, snapped slashes high and low as she went straight into the Kraken Rises form. Tasahre batted her away without bothering to riposte.

"Should I?"

Myla stood panting. "He *used* my sister. Does *that* feature in your story?"

"It's what men like him do." Tasahre tossed one of her swords aside, an obvious goad. "So?"

"So? So he deserved it!"

"Did he take anything not freely given?"

Myla levelled her swords at her old mistress. "Freely given in exchange for promises that were false. In both his world and mine, that becomes theft."

"Were those promises witnessed?"

"Do you call my sister a liar?" Myla feinted and then jabbed. "*Do* you?"

Tasahre took a step back as she parried. "I do not."

"Then what?"

They exchanged more blows, until Tasahre shook her head and let out a little sigh. "Ah, Shirish. I cannot teach you." They stepped apart.

"Perhaps this time the fault lies with the teacher, and not the student," Myla flared. They were Tasahre's own words, spoken long ago when Myla had been not much more than a girl. The sword-mistress clearly didn't like having them thrown back at her, either, attacking with a sudden series of cuts and lunges.

"Insolent! Arrogant!" She came hard, forcing Myla back. "You rightly put those words on the man you despise, yet you wear them so well yourself!"

Another flurry. Myla dug in her heels and forced herself to focus on Tasahre's centre, blocking and sidestepping until she saw the glimmer of an opening and took it, dropping low under a cut and then snapping upward, clipping the sword-mistress on the wrist as she whipped back from a lunge. "He deserved it," she hissed. "And *you* have over-extended, sword-mistress."

Tasahre stepped back, rubbing her wrist and wearing a half-smile that had Myla's heart thumping. "And still you shy away from the truth, Shirish. A man who believed himself entitled to whatever he wished chose to seduce your sister. Through lies and deceit, he succeeded. You sought to teach him a lesson? Was that it? To this man steeped in his own selfish arrogance? Raised and bred to be so? You have wasted yourself on him, thrown your life away on a futile effort to teach a man something he cannot learn. What will change, Shirish? Will he be better because of you? Will he be kinder? No. This city has a hundred others like him. Will *they* be any different? No, they will not. You have thrown your life away for nothing. This makes me angry with you, Shirish, because *you* were worth something!"

"It's *my* life to do with as I choose, and my sister was worth something too!"

Tasahre scooped up her second sword. "And what is she worth now?"

"As much as she ever was!" But it wasn't true. It *should* have been true, yes, but it wasn't.

Tasahre came at her again now, both swords high. "If there was ever a lesson I thought to teach above all others, if there was ever a lesson that I thought that *you*, of all my students, might learn, it is to commit to your cause!" The swords came in a blur of blows, fast and furious. Myla danced back, blocking what she could, dodging what she couldn't, feet wary and uncertain on stones slick from the afternoon rains, splashing in puddles. "A sword-monk is slow to attack; but when that attack comes, it is *final*!" She flicked a flurry of cuts at Myla's face and then dropped low and whacked her on the knee. Myla jumped back before Tasahre could hit her again. "We do not leave our opponents crippled to lick their wounds and come at us a second time."

"I should have killed him, then?"

Tasahre twirled her swords. "If you were so sure of your righteousness, yes!" She sprang and swept at Myla's legs, then chopped at her knees, then at her hands, forcing Myla back until she ran out of yard. Myla skittered sideways as a wooden blade clattered off stone beside her head. A hard blow caught her on the thigh. Tasahre bared her teeth.

"But that wouldn't have been enough, would it, Shirish?" Again, she attacked; again, Myla gave ground, batting away what she could. It was a fight she couldn't win, not this way.

"No!" She snarled. "It wouldn't." Abruptly, she reversed, pushed herself forward into the rain of blows, taking a hard hit to the ribs and another to the arm as she crashed through Tasahre's guard and slammed into her, staggering them both. Tasahre tried to skip away, but Myla dropped her swords and grabbed her.

"So, what then, Shirish?" Tasahre twisted, trying to throw her. Myla jumped through the twist and turned it back on her mistress. For a moment, they were locked together, faces inches apart, teeth bare, eyes wide. "Kill *all* of them? His family? His friends? His house? Everyone like him? Every man in Deephaven? The empire? The world? Where do you stop, Shirish?"

Tasahre slowly forced Myla down, and then suddenly something took away her legs and she was falling, and Tasahre was on top of her, pinning her, holding one arm twisted behind her back and pressing her face into the wet stone.

"Who are you to judge us all and find us wanting? For that, I contend, is the provenance of Gods. Are you a God, Shirish? Is that how you see yourself? Must we all bow down before you? Do only *you* know the right and truthful way?"

She was angry. Furious, twisting Myla's arm close to breaking it.

"*Are* you a God, Shirish?"

She let go. Myla picked herself up. She saluted and brushed herself down. Tasahre, she noted, didn't return the salute.

"No, sword-mistress, I'm not a God. I am but one lowly sword prepared to speak truth to power and back my words with action. Exactly as *you* taught me. And yes, he still deserved it."

Tasahre tossed her head as if searching for inspiration from the heavens. "And you *still* don't understand. Yes, Shirish, perhaps he did. I cannot judge that; but you *will* be judged, in front of all, and *he* will be the victim. In crippling one man, you have empowered a hundred others and brought ruin to the one person you sought to save. It's not your *actions*, Shirish, that make me angry with you. It's your lack of consideration for their consequences."

She came close then. "What I want from you is that you take sanctuary here. Become one of us, where the Hawats cannot touch you. You will become what you were always destined to be; and in the reckoning that approaches, you will be called to fight, and you will probably die, as will I; but you fight *well*,

Shirish, and you will not die easy, and so at least your life will have mattered. But I cannot take you if you won't let this go, and to let this go, you must accept that you cannot save your family from whatever vengeance the Hawat chooses. And that, I fear, you cannot do."

To Myla's surprise, Tasahre put a hand on her shoulder. Despite her words, she didn't look angry, only sad.

"You fought well, Shirish. I will allow your sorcerer to come to you."

21

THE POPİΠjAY

Seth slipped away after he'd written Fings' stupid letter, leaving Fings giggling like a novice who'd heard a priest say *penis*. The Deephaven docks after dark reminded him of the riverside in Varr, only bigger and louder and smellier. He dressed himself in the robe he'd worn escaping from the temple in Varr, and then took a leaf out of Fings' book and asked random people about the old warlock of Deephaven and who might know anything more about him. Mostly he got blank looks, or signs to ward off evil, but the robe of a novice of the Path gave him an authority and, more to the point, allowed him to deflect the obvious answer that if anyone knew about the old warlock, it would be the priests in the temple on Deephaven Square.

The answers gradually coalesced around two possibilities: the warlock had had some connection to a thief-taker, back in the day, who'd left the city at the same time. The city thief-takers all knew each other and a few of them were still around from back then, a couple working as Justicars for the city Overlord, one running some sort of refuge somewhere in someplace called the Maze. Alternatively, there was the healer who lived in the old Moon-chapel down near Reeper's Gate, a mage who'd been in Deephaven longer than anyone could remember, and who was obviously the other mage they'd heard about when Fings had asked after Orlen.

A mage or an old thief-taker sounded like a choice between a rock and a hard place, and Fings would surely have run a mile at the idea of going to see either; but Seth wasn't Fings, and so he took directions and headed for Reeper's Gate and the old Moon-chapel where this mage who might or might not be a healer supposedly lived. If anyone knew about the old warlock, stood to reason it would be another mage. Yes, there were the sword-monks who'd chased the warlock away, but Seth preferred his chances with a mage who only *might* decide to murder him. The man *was* known as a healer, after all, so how bad could it be?

The visions from the Moonspire dogged him – enigmatic, apocalyptic, sneaking around the edges of trying to tell him something without ever actually coming out and saying it. If he ever *met* this one-eyed god with the ruined face, Seth reckoned the first order of business would be a punch on the nose. But what was the point?

Well… It would *be quite satisfying.*

Was the Fickle Moon having a laugh at his expense, trying to leave him with a riddle that had no answer? The Moon could be like that, so he'd heard. More likely, the Fickle Lord had been ignoring him and what he'd seen was all the work of that one-eyed stain on the chamber-pot of divinity. If so, what he ought to do – certainly what he *wanted* to do – was the exact opposite of what he'd been told. Myla had stopped a pair of sword-monks from casually murdering him. She'd been kind to him, as much as anyone had ever been kind, and he'd repaid that kindness by selling her out to mercenaries from Deephaven. If he was honest with himself, he admired her. Admired, resented and envied. She knew what it was like to be cast out of the light. She was, more than anyone he knew, a good person.

Makes you wonder why she'd have anything to do with someone like you.

I'm not about to start throwing random sigils at her without the first idea why I should be doing it.

He reached a rambling piece of old stonework that had obviously once been a temple to the Moon. The door hung open. He wondered why he was doing this. Why was he even here?

You mean apart from messing around with Dead Men and being caught and the whole business of some sword-monks looking for a good dose of heretic-burning?

Yeah. Apart from that. Probably best not mention all that to this mage fellow.

He knocked on the door. After a bit, when no one came, he went inside. The old chapel was abandoned and dark, but he could see light coming from a passage behind the altar.

"Hello?"

No answer. Seth sighed. One thing Fings had right: mages were troublesome buggers. He took a few more steps, then reckoned that if he'd come this far, he might as well keep going. He crossed the temple, passed the old altar, and followed the light. It led him into a cloister. He stood in the moonlight, wondering which way to go.

"Before you ask," said a voice behind him, "yes, this did indeed used to be a temple."

Seth spun around, trying not to die of fright. As he did, whoever was doing the talking unhooded a lantern, shining it in Seth's face.

"Don't get many visits from your sort."

For a second, Seth toyed with the idea of slapping a sigil on whoever this was and turning him into a Dead Man, mostly because Dead Men – with the one glaring exception of Cleaver – could largely be relied on to do as they were told and not suddenly murder you.

"My sort?" he asked.

The man hung his lantern from a peg on the wall and stepped into the light. He was younger than Seth had imagined, almost the same age as Fings from the looks of him. He was also Taiytakei. No one else had skin so dark. Better dressed than most, though. Like a popinjay.

Yeah, but try not to say that to his face.

"A long time ago, this was a temple to the Sun," said the popinjay. "Your lot would mostly like to have me burned. Why are you here?"

"Again, *my* lot?"

"Lightbringers, Dawncallers, Sunbrights, sword-monks. All that."

Oh. Right. Seth had sort of forgotten that he was wearing his stolen novice robe. He grunted. "I *was* a novice once, but not anymore. They kicked me out." *Oh, why did you go and tell him that?*

"What do you want?"

There was an edge to the man's voice, an urgency. Seth almost came out and told the popinjay his name, then stopped himself. Did mages talk to each other? They probably did, didn't they? What if this mage knew Orien? Because if he *did*, there was the whole business of Seth not wanting Orien to know he was here on account of the last time Seth and Orien had met, back in Varr, when Orien had seen some things that Seth rather wished he hadn't, and Seth had had a go at making him forget. The sigil had worked out well enough on himself a couple of months later, removing his own memory of... well, that was the thing, he had no idea. He remembered *doing* it, that he'd done it to protect Myla and Fings and to forget... something else which he had a sneaking suspicion had to do with the mysterious disappearance of Lightbringer Suaresh... But what if Orien *did* remember? He *was* a mage, after all, and so was this Taiytakei. What if they'd talked?

Fuck. Fuck!

"Are you *really* a healer?" Seth asked. At least the popinjay didn't have a missing eye and a face all fucked up by scars, although that might have been something of a relief because at least then Seth could have thumped him.

"Ah. You're one of *those*." The popinjay gave a weary sigh. "I'll show you," he said, after another moment of hesitation. "Don't follow too closely. But you'll have to see to understand."

Against his better judgement, Seth followed across the cloisters to a door; when the popinjay opened it, a stench bowled out: shit and piss and vomit and rotting flesh and candle-smoke and incense, all rolled up together. Even standing outside, Seth wanted to gag. He forced himself up the last couple of steps and into the doorway as the popinjay went inside. A little moonlight followed and there were candles mounted on the walls, enough that he could make out what looked like a temple dormitory. Which sort of made sense: what he *hadn't* expected were the cots laid out in a neat straight line, all of them occupied. He heard snores and moans.

"Don't come inside unless you want to catch it yourself," said the popinjay.

"Catch *what*?"

"The River Plague." The popinjay walked among the cots, pausing to lay a hand on each sleeping figure as he passed. The smell of death and disease grew stronger with every breath. Seth found himself wishing he had a mask like Fings. Whatever this was, he wanted no part of it. In the end, he retreated down the steps to wait in the yard.

"They inevitably die," said the popinjay when he came out. He shook his head. "Of course, they only send me the worst cases."

"You're a… *Moon* priest?" asked Seth. He frowned. There was no trace of the incense he'd smelled everywhere else. The popinjay didn't wear a scented mask or any charms that Seth could see. So why wasn't he sick like his patients?

The popinjay snorted, then looked at Seth, keen and expectant. "Seen what you came to see?"

The popinjay's look set Seth on edge and made him want to run away. His fingers curled around the strip of parchment in his pocket. *Can I trust him? No, of course I bloody can't. I can't trust anyone. No. But I came here to ask a question.*

"I came to ask you about the warlock who used to live in Deephaven," said Seth, then tensed, ready with a sigil in case he needed it. "I thought you might know something."

The popinjay laughed. "*That* place? They should burn it out, turn the whole stretch to ash and start from scratch."

"What place? What are you talking about?"

"The House of Cats and Gulls. The source of the River Plague."

The expression on the popinjay's face shifted, calculating, balancing two answers one against the other, weighing them up to see which would get him what he wanted. "I've been in this city for a long time," he said at last. "An exile from my people. I'm... *tolerated* here because of what I do. I *am* a healer of sorts. But such talents run to... darker places, now and then?"

Sigil him. Sigil him now!

What if it doesn't work?

Alright, then run, *you lemon! Don't stand around like a fool!*

"You're a curious fellow for a priest. *Former* priest." The popinjay bared his teeth as he corrected himself, an expression that was trying to pass itself off as a smile but mostly looked like he was about to bite someone. "I'll show you the rest of what I do if you like. Follow."

No. Don't. Don't... Oh, what are you doing, you daft twat?

Following, it seemed.

Why, so you can roll your eyes and tell yourself that yes, you certainly should have seen that *coming when he turns you inside out?*

Shut up! I need to know what he knows. Inner voices, if they couldn't stay quiet, could at least be helpful.

The popinjay stopped suddenly and turned, eyeing Seth closely. "How old do you think I am?" His eyes didn't flicker. Never left Seth's face. Didn't even blink.

Sigil him! "I don't know."

"I lived through the civil war. I remember it." Which made

him at least a few decades more than the twenty-odd years he looked. "So yes, I know the man you mean."

Seth's skin prickled. "You do, do you?" *Sigil him while you still can!*

"Knew of him, at least." The popinjay turned away, nodding to himself as he did. Seth forced himself to let go of the sigil in his pocket.

"If you consort with warlocks, why would you help a failed priest?"

The popinjay snorted. "But I *haven't* helped you yet, have I?" He led Seth back through the cloisters to what might once have been the High Priestess's quarters, a cluster of humble rooms squashed together against the side of the old Hall of Light. Inside, he gestured to a seat at an old table in the middle of what might once have been a private chapel. Through narrow open doors, Seth saw a tiny room with a cot and a well-stocked pantry, and what looked like a study full of books. The popinjay wandered into the pantry and came back with a plate of bread and cheese, all pleasantly fresh, then came back a second time with two battered old cups and a bottle of wine. He poured them each a cup, and by Kelm it was good. Strong and rich and nothing like the watered dregs Blackhand had served in the *Unruly Pig*. Or rather, nothing like the watered dregs that Blackhand had served to *him*.

"How… *well* did you know him?" Seth asked.

The popinjay ignored him. "They still teach history to priests, yes?"

"A version of it," said Seth carefully. "Emperor Khrozus murdered most of the priests in Varr when he took the throne. They have some quite particular views because of that."

"Khrozus? Nasty piece of work," said the popinjay. "Far too interested in anyone who had a whiff of mage to them. Yes, I knew right away that I wanted nothing to do with *that* one. Tried to turn his sons into mages, I hear, although not with any great success. Did something right when it came to his grand-children though. The oldest one, at least."

Seth took a sip of wine. "I wouldn't know."

The popinjay held his eye for a long time, then seemed to reach some sort of decision. "So, you want to know about Saffran Kuy, do you?"

"Who?"

"The warlock of the House of Cats and Gulls."

Seth nodded. "Everything you can tell me."

"Why?"

Which was, Seth supposed, a reasonable question, and one for which he didn't have much of an answer. "Because I heard he could speak with the dead."

"Yes. He could certainly do *that*. A lot more, too." The popinjay took a deep breath and then let out a long sigh. "Until a few years before the war, there were Dead Men in Deephaven, same as everywhere else," he said. "And the priests dealt with them, same as everywhere else. A couple of years before the sicge, the Dead Men stopped coming. No one knew why. Just... no one ever saw any. But then, if you were really once a priest, you'd know all that."

"I served the Path in Varr, not in Deephaven. Enlighten me."

The popinjay made a non-committal face. "The war came. Khrozus occupied Deephaven. The siege lasted for half a year. No one who lived through it will ever forget, but this is where Emperor Talsin lost the war. He never managed to cut us off from the sea, that was the thing. Khrozus made a deal with my people. Their ships kept coming, and so we never *quite* starved. In the end it was the Emperor's army that fell apart... but I'm sure you know all this. They must have taught you *that* much, at least?"

Seth nodded. "The gist."

The popinjay shot Seth a sharp glance. "If my guess is right, it wasn't only *my* people with whom Khrozus made bargains." He took a large slug of wine and poured himself another cup, gestured at the bottle for Seth to help himself.

"What do you mean by that?"

Another shrug. "No Dead Men when half the city was starving was something of a blessing. After the war, people just… forgot, I suppose. That was when I started to hear about the mage who'd set himself up on the waterfront of the river-docks. These days, your lot tend to a general policy of take-no-chances, stab-it-if-it-looks-like-sorcery towards our kind, but it was different back then. There were no sword-monks in Deephaven, only priests. Your warlock – and he *was* a warlock, no doubt of that – had already been here for years by the time I heard his name. Everyone around the river-docks knew of him, but he didn't seem to be doing any harm and so he was left alone. Then the Autarch and the Torpreahns turned their minds to taking back the Sapphire Throne. The Autarch sent sword-monks to Deephaven to prepare the city for revolt. It all came to nothing, but one took it on herself to do something about our warlock. Chased him out of the city but didn't manage to kill him is what I hear. Got her throat cut by a thief-taker for her trouble." He paused, giving Seth a moment to raise an eyebrow at this.

"And that, my priestly friend, is as much as I can tell you about Saffran Kuy, the warlock of the House of Cats and Gulls." He nodded, cocking his head in the vague direction of the Hall of Light. "In that same year he was driven out, the River Plague struck for the first time and Dead Men returned to Deephaven. I think he was keeping both in check."

Seth considered this. Myla had told him, back in Varr, how Deephaven had once had a warlock who could speak with the dead. And that, until now, had been the sum of what he knew.

He contemplated his cup of wine. It was a good wine, and the popinjay made it all sound so reasonable. Almost as if this warlock hadn't been such a bad person.

And yet…

It was all too easy. Life didn't work that way. Somewhere, in all of this, was a trap.

"Would you show it to me?" Seth asked. "This House of Cats and Gulls?"

The popinjay blinked. Apparently, he hadn't expected this. "I suppose I could do that," he said, after a bit of thought. "If you'll do something for me in return."

22

TASAHRE'S GİFT

Tasahre led Myla into the temple where they sat together for Dawn Prayer. The priests and monks stared at her. They knew who she was, she supposed, but that cut both ways. They knew the Shirish who'd crippled a merchant prince and then fled from justice. But they also knew the Shirish who was the youngest Deephaven sword-monk ever to earn her swords. Which probably explained why they looked at her, then looked quickly away, then came back again, despite themselves.

Myla didn't see the contradiction. Both times, she'd gone after men who thought they couldn't be touched. The fact that the first had been an Anvorian elementalist hardly seemed to matter. She wanted to scream at them all: do you know what he *did*? They probably didn't. Sarwatta had written his own story and had made sure it was heard.

"He still deserved it," she murmured, as Tasahre led her away.

"For toying with the affections of a naïve young woman?"

"For believing he had the right."

"Judge one man for that, you might as well judge them all."

Myla shrugged. She didn't see the contradiction *there*, either.

They sparred a while, dancing in the rain, still an edge to the way they fought from the night before, each quietly convinced that the other was wrong and determined not to back down.

As usual, Myla exhausted herself while Tasahre looked like she could have continued for hours. When they were done, Tasahre handed her a cup of water. "They will have their trial soon. My offer still stands."

"Will they hang me?'

The sword-mistress looked away. "Too quick. He wants you to suffer."

Myla bit her lip.

"The law is the law. If we're not beholden to that, what are we? Nothing but killers in fancy clothes."

"That being so, how can you offer me sanctuary?"

Tasahre smiled. "In the eyes of the Constant Sun, the Shirish who committed this crime will no longer exist. In her place, a new Shirish will stand. One who has given her soul to her God."

"A sceptic might consider that little more than playing games with words."

"Is that all our scriptures are to you? Words?"

Myla gave that some thought. "No. Not to me. But to the Hawats, yes. You think House Hawat would be so gracious as to accept such a... rebirth?"

"The law is the law. Grace, I cannot promise."

"He is a master at building castles of lies."

"In that, he is far from unique."

"*Do not suffer a liar. Cast him out.*" She wasn't good at scripture, but some verses *every*one knew. "Isn't that what we're for, more than anything? We are agents of truth, are we not? We even learn to *smell* lies."

"What we are *for* is something of which you have no conception." Tasahre looked at her then, long and deep. "Do you believe that what you did was well-judged, Shirish? Not right or wrong, but *wise*?" She sniffed the air, and now it was Myla's turn to look away.

"No."

"Did you do it to avenge your sister's honour? For that reason and no other?" Tasahre sniffed again.

"Yes! Of course! Because of what he took from her." But there was more. Darker, grubbier reasons. She *had* done it for her sister, yes, but she'd done it for herself, too. For the lies he'd spread about her. And more beneath, for the anger she felt at the world for allowing a man like Sarwatta Hawat to abuse and humiliate whomever he wished and suffer no consequence, simply because he had a name and wealth.

For being a third-born, and thus something lesser than her brother and sister.

"No," she said.

Tasahre nodded. "And there it is."

And there it was. The burden Tasahre kept saying she was trying to escape. Not guilt, but responsibility. The need to protect her sister and her brother. To finish what she'd started. To turn the world on its head if that was what it took. And with that, the weight of inevitable failure.

"Would you have been any different?" Myla asked. "When you were young?" She looked her old teacher in the eye and sniffed, not that she had anything like Tasahre's talent for smelling out a lie. A flicker of a smile played at the corner of Tasahre's lips, then faded. After a few seconds of silence, she got to her feet.

"Your mage will be here by now."

And he was, soaking wet and slouching in the rain near the gates to Deephaven Square, a couple of hostile Sunguard watching from the shelter of the colonnades leading to the Hall of Light. He straightened as he saw Myla and Tasahre, and then Tasahre had her swords drawn, striding at him like she meant to cut him down. Orien took a step back, then held his ground. Tasahre stopped with her blades held level, one point steady in the air a few inches from Orien's face.

"This woman is like a daughter to me, mage," she said. "Had you had any part in leading her astray, I would cut you to ribbons where you stand."

Orien's mouth opened and then closed again, all his words

apparently taking one look at an angry sword-monk and scurrying back down his throat.

"Sword-mistress! Please!" Please *what*, Myla wasn't sure. Tasahre ignored her.

"Well?"

To Myla's surprise, Orien clasped his hands together and bowed deeply, a gesture of supplication she would have thought almost impossible for a man like him.

"Please," he said. "I beg your leave to spend a little time with her."

Tasahre's sword didn't waver. "This man has come here every day for a month, without exception, asking for you. Shirish, would you have me turn him away?"

"I would not," said Myla. "You know that."

"We don't tolerate mages here. Not on holy ground." Tasahre let the words hang on the tip of her sword for a moment, then snapped both into the scabbards across her back. "Be something else while you're here. You have an hour."

She stalked away, not looking back, but Myla saw how she gestured to the lurking Sunguard and had them follow, leaving Myla and Orien alone in the rain.

Alone and only a few dozen yards from the open gates, from Deephaven Square.

I could run…

And then what?

Had Tasahre done this on purpose. Was she *supposed* to run?

But by then Orien was in her arms. They stood in the rain and held each other for a long, long time, and nothing else mattered.

23

TWO TEMPLES

Fings walked behind Seth, chomping his way through an apple. Apples were lucky. They were a bit hard to get hold of at this time of year, what with spring coming on and the Festival of Rebirth not long away, but the Deephaven docks were a cornucopia of wonders and unexpected delights. It *was* an odd-tasting apple, admittedly, shipped up the coast from somewhere in the wild south where, apparently, they fruited late. Truth be told, it didn't *look* much like an apple either… but an apple was what the trader had said it was. It *could* be an apple, Fings supposed, if you closed your eyes and didn't think too closely about the taste.

They trudged into the temple grounds through the open gates from Four Winds Square, past a handful of downcast Sunguard, sodden and wilted-looking in the rain. The way everything was always damp was starting to tick Fings off. Lucius had said Deephaven was like this for months, from late winter all the way through to early summer when the rains would finally stop. It was a shame, Fings thought, because the ever-present drizzle made everything grey and hazy and soggy, and also slippery, all of which took something away from the sight in front of him.

He'd been inside the cathedral in Varr, but in most ways,

the Solar Temple of Deephaven should have been more impressive. It occupied a lot more space, for a start. A long avenue of pillars led from the gates onto Deephaven Square to the domed Hall of Light, ringed with spires. To each side, through columns and arches, spread great open spaces. In one, a company of two dozen sword-monks were sparring. In the other, dotted with statues and other odd pieces of stonework, masked men and women walked in clusters of twos and threes and fours, some with priests but most not, and all apparently oblivious to the drizzle.

Lucius had also drawn a map, back when he and Orien had been trying to tell Fings how to do his job. Fings had studied it; now he was looking at that map in his head and at the temple grounds in front of him, putting the two together. Beyond the Hall of Light, two covered walkways led through a huge yard to the Golden Gate and the Darolith, a needle of crystal set on a pedestal at the very highest point of the city, according to Lucius, who also reckoned that that was where Orien should be, and Myla too, if the priests had kept their promise to the mage. To the left, as Fings looked, were a series of smaller domes. Rising from the middle was the Dawnspire, the tallest tower in Deephaven except for the winged tower of the Overlord, over to his right, which was supposedly exactly the same height because the Emperor had said so. Fings wasn't sure about that. How could an Emperor tell a tower what height it should be? A tower was... well, a tower. Although they *did* say the late Emperor, Sun bless him, had been a mage, so maybe he'd used sorcery to make one of them shrink?

Seth kept walking, a slow steady pace towards the Hall of Light. The thought of shrinking towers put Fings on edge: what if you were *in* the tower when it shrank? What happened then? Did *everything* shrink? Or did whole levels just get sliced out and vanish, and if they did, what happened to the people who were there?

He touched the feather in his pocket, wanting to put it between his teeth so no one would notice him. Sneaking around the temple in Spice Market Square had been fine, but the cathedral in Varr had put him on edge that one time, like there were things there he didn't want to know. This, here? There were *definitely* things he didn't want to know, not to mention mages, and now maybe an enchanted tower and how the whole place was crawling with sword-monks, all of which was making him nervous as a deer in a wolf den. Did sucking a feather even *work* on Gods? Had to reckon it probably didn't, same as most other charms, what with Gods being... well, Gods. What if the Sun saw him and told his priests that some mischievous burglar was here, sneaking about?

He tried telling himself that Gods had better things to do than rat on thieves skulking through their temples but had an uneasy suspicion that maybe they didn't. Especially when it came to thieves with a bit of a history of taking things from those same temples and not putting them back.

On the other hand, Seth was the actual heretic and *he* didn't seem bothered, although he'd managed quite a lot of being bothered earlier. Fings had told him what they were doing and shown him the old Lightbringer robe Lucius had dug up from somewhere, at which point Seth had got it into his head that Orien knew he was in Deephaven and had gone off on one, for some reason. Eventually, when Fings had managed to get a word in edgeways, he'd told Seth no, he hadn't told anyone about Seth being in Deephaven because he wasn't a complete idiot, not like *certain* people who'd apparently been running their mouths to all and sundry about certain books stolen from certain Sunheralds. There had been some glaring, and then Fings had promised not to say anything to Orien about Seth being in Deephaven, and Seth had mostly calmed down.

Mostly. He *did* have a shifty look to him though, even now, and Fings knew that look because he knew Seth like a brother. Seth was already up to something, probably nothing good. A part of Fings was almost impressed. They'd been in Deephaven for what? Two days?

Behind the Hall of Light were the cloisters where the priests and the monks lived. Lucius reckoned this was where they'd be holding Myla. Seth reckoned he was probably right, so that was where they went. With luck, Orien would come back and tell Fings exactly where to look. Fings, after he and Seth had had a good look around of their own, would know exactly how to get there. All he had to do was come back in the middle of the night when the Sun wasn't looking, slip in past the Sunguard, avoid any restless priests, not wake up any sword-monks, flit between shadows to wherever they were keeping Myla, pick a lock or two, and lead her away. It sounded straightforward enough, except the leading away part. *That* would inevitably go wrong because Myla would do something stupid, like not wear the charms he'd bring to make sure she stayed lucky, or not suck on the spare feather he'd bring to make sure no one noticed her, or not wait until they were safely away before stopping to ask a bunch of stupid questions that quite frankly could have waited until later, as if the rest of the world would just sort of stop for a bit until she was done. That was the trouble with stealing *people*. *Things* sat in your pocket and did what they were told. *People* had a way of making life difficult.

Seth walked up the steps to the Hall of Light. He gave a little bow to the Sunguard standing to either side of the yawning maw of a doorway. The space beyond was cavernous – bigger, Fings reckoned, than the Hall of Light in the Solar Cathedral of Varr. Almost empty, too, a handful of novices moving about, cleaning and tidying, and no one else. Seth had chosen his time carefully – Dawn Prayers had ended more than an hour ago; now, he angled for the youngest-looking novice, clasped his hands, bowed his head, and asked to see a Lightbringer who'd died in Varr a couple of months ago.

"I'm sorry, I... I don't know a Lightbringer... Suaresh?" The novice gave him a nervous look.

Seth put on his best kindly smile. "My menial and I arrived from Helhex this morning. Perhaps you could point me to your refectory? I'm sure someone there would be able to put me on my way."

The novice led Seth and Fings through a series of puddle-spattered yards, all separated by covered walkways. She brought them to a low stone building with an angled roof. Fings could smell cooking. There were no Sunguard here, he noted.

"Light be with you," said the novice, and scurried away. Fings elbowed Seth.

"Menial?"

They had a good look around, getting a feel for the place. Lucius's map had been vague about these parts, but Seth simply walked everywhere as though he owned the place. They were challenged once by a bad-tempered old Lightbringer who smelled of kitchen-work, and later by a pair of Sunguard. Each time, Seth trotted out his story of being from Helhex, looking for some Lightbringer no one had ever heard of, and each time they let him pass without complaint. No one here wore a scented mask, Fings noticed, and there wasn't that stink of incense that seemed to hover over the rest of the city. Maybe priests and monks were all too holy to get sick? He wasn't sure.

They were on their way out again when he saw Myla, walking with a sword-monk. He nudged Seth, because only a fool turned up his nose at such a stroke of luck, and they followed, keeping at what Fings reckoned was a discreet distance until the pair disappeared into a low stone hall.

"Sunguard barracks," said Seth. "We can't follow them there."

Fings reckoned he didn't need to. He nudged Seth a different way, had a bit more of a look around, checking ways in and out, and then waited. After a bit, the other sword-monk came out, this time on her own. So that was that: this was where they were keeping Myla.

"Could be better, but I've dealt with worse." Fings took a

long breath and huffed. What bothered him was the way Myla had been walking with that other monk like they were old friends. Hadn't looked very prisoner-like.

The puddles bothered him too. The splash of a poorly planted footstep was all it took for something like this to go wrong. Although better than Varr, he had to admit, with all its snow and leaving trails of footprints everywhere.

No one bothered them as they left the temple and returned to the river-docks teahouse where Lucius was waiting. Seth reckoned on lurking outside, stating flatly that when everything went wrong, he didn't want anyone knowing he was anything to do with it, didn't want anyone knowing he was in Deephaven at all, thanks. Fings reckoned he could see the sense of that, although there *was* something a bit shifty about the way Seth said it, like he had something else on his mind, something he wasn't saying.

Turned out just as well, though, because Orien was in the teahouse with Lucius. The mage looked like someone had cut out his soul and shat in the hole.

"The temple offered her sanctuary," he said, before Fings could say he knew exactly where Myla was being held and didn't need Orien to tell him. "She refused."

"What?" Fings reckoned he must have heard wrong. "I thought you said they'll hang her!"

"It'll be a lot worse than that."

Fings took a deep breath, trying to get his head around what the mage was saying. True, Myla was a bit... odd, sometimes. She had... *views* on things. And she *had* been talking about going back to take what was coming to her, even in Varr. But getting yourself hanged? *That* was just stupid. *Worse* than hanged? He didn't even know what that was!

Orien shook his head. He took another long deep breath. "Can you do it?"

"Yeah. Reckon I can. At least, I can get in."

They shared a few drinks and Fings told them how it could

be done. Lucius made unhelpful suggestions while Orien stayed quiet. As he talked, Fings glanced at the window now and then. Seth was still out there, standing where Fings had left him, sheltering from the rain, looking around and shifting from foot to foot like he was waiting for something. Wasn't the best at lurking, was Seth. Always looked like that was exactly what he was doing.

When he'd finished explaining, Orien and Lucius started arguing about whether Fings should go into the temple tonight or whether to wait. Fings' let his thoughts wander. He didn't get it. The temple had offered Myla a way out, and she'd turned it down? No one *wanted* to be hanged, did they? No one who wasn't a few chickens short of a barnyard, anyway.

His eyes drifted to the window again. Seth had disappeared. Fings, who knew Seth's tells and twitches and quirks well enough to know when he was about to do something stupid, bit his lip. Admittedly, being about to do something stupid was normal for Seth… but there was something about the way he'd been waiting out there, something about the way he'd been all morning that didn't feel right. Also, Fings really wanted to get away from all this talk of Myla being hanged.

He got up. "Got a thing I need to do," he said, and left Orien and Lucius to argue. Outside, he spotted Seth quickly enough, weaving through the crowds on the river-docks, making a beeline for the nearest dark alley. Fings sidled after him, lurked at the corner and listened as Seth talked to someone in hushed whispers, too quiet for Fings to make out what they were saying. One day, Fings reckoned, he'd tell Seth how Seth was a bit shit at sneaking about and should maybe stop trying. What they *could* have done, him and whoever it was, was meet in the teahouse across the street, all out in the open, nothing suspicious at all. But no, it had to be a shadowy alley, all furtive glances and forced whispers. Might as well go all the way and hang a sign on it, Fings reckoned: *shifty goings-on afoot right here!*

He sucked on his feather. Seth walked right past him as he

came out, didn't look back and never saw him. Fings followed as Seth made his way along the docks, heading up-river: this was ridiculously easy, since the man Seth was now walking with stuck out like a priest at a pit-fight – an extravagantly dressed Taiytakei, clearly with plenty of silver in his pockets and wanting everyone to know it. What a well-dressed Taiytakei was doing with Seth, who mostly looked like an accident dragged out of the river, Fings had no idea. He wondered if maybe it was to do with Levvi. Maybe Seth had discovered something? Myla's brother had said something about the Black Ships, after all.

But this was Seth, so probably not.

Ten minutes later, Fings reckoned he had his answer, and no, it wasn't about Levvi. Seth and his new friend walked right along the waterfront close to where he and Fings had first put ashore, to where the crowds thinned and the waterfront jetties sat empty. No boats and almost no people. Further on, around the River Gate, the docks came back to life; but in the middle of this patch of dead-ness stood the derelict warehouse that the old man selling the vomity fish-things had said was cursed. Fings knew it was *that* warehouse and not one of the others because it was the one absolutely swarming with seagulls, and also because the Taiytakei kept looking at Seth and then pointing at it. Two days in and Seth had gotten all interested in a cursed warehouse haunted by angry birds, had he? Knowing Seth, that sounded about right.

Fings watched Seth with the Taiytakei popinjay. Once it seemed like they were only *talking* about doing something stupid and not about to get on and *do* it, he walked away and left them to their business. He got back to the teahouse to find Orien had gone and Lucius well on his way to being drunk. Fings settled beside him and patted him awkwardly on the shoulder. The man cared about his sister, which Fings could understand. He asked about the warehouse and was rewarded with an oh yes, *that* place, cursed as fuck *that* place, it's where the old warlock lived before the monks drove him away.

Riiiight. Fings bought Lucius another drink and poked and prodded in case there was more, but Lucius mostly wanted to talk about Myla, what an idiot she was. Poor bastard was at the end of his wits. Fings let him talk until the drink made him useless, then left.

Not sure what else to do with himself, he made his way back across the city to the sea-docks. Seeing Seth apparently determined to get into the same shit in Deephaven as had almost got him killed in Varr, it got Fings thinking that he'd probably been right about Levvi back when he'd first met Lucius, that Levvi was about the same kind of stupid: wind up in the poorest, meanest place a new city could offer and then walk straight as an arrow into the worst trouble he could find. Thinking that, he set himself to asking after Levvi at every grotty teahouse and scum-riddled tavern he could find. It wasn't much fun because it meant going to a lot of places that seemed to be making a point of looking unfriendly, a few with grey death-banners hanging left right and centre. But he had his hat with its tassels, his scented mask and plenty of oil, his charms to keep the spirits of sickness away, his stone with a streak of silver to oil his tongue and make his words sound sweet. Everywhere he went, the smell of that incense followed, so he reckoned he was probably alright.

For a while, it seemed he might as well not have bothered. No one had heard of Levvi, or of anyone who looked like him. Mostly he just got wet from wandering about in the rain; although he *did* find out a whole lot more about the cursed warehouse on the docks, none of it good. Place had a name: The House of Cats and Gulls. Yeah. Well. He'd seen the gulls. Big fuckers. He couldn't imagine how that worked out with a pile of cats thrown on top.

And then, in a puke-and-sawdust dive called *The Broken Lantern*, he struck gold.

"Levvi? Five years back? Yeah, I knew a Levvi."

24

THE WITCHBREAKER AND THE WARLOCK

Seth was pacing his room when Fings burst in and poked him. "Got stuff to do. Let's go. Where'd you get to anyway? All of a sudden you were just gone." The words had an edge to them that Seth knew. He tried not to groan. Something had set Fings' nerves jangling, and now he wanted a *talk*.

"I got bored of waiting," he said, not that Fings would let it go at that. The trouble with Fings was that once he got the bit between his teeth, he wouldn't stop. Seth could brush him off for days and it wouldn't make a difference. Which was exasperating, because right now he had problems of his own. Myla, for a start, and that stupid vision he'd had in the Moonspire. The House of Cats and Gulls, which he really didn't want to be visiting and at the same time knew he had to. Then there was the popinjay and the favour he was asking, and how in the name of Bloody Khrozus he could keep Orien from finding out he was here in Deephaven and yet still get to talk to Myla once she was free. A hundred and one other things, too.

"Go where?" he asked.

"Got word on Levvi. Get your priest clobber on."

"*Clobber*?" Seth rolled his eyes but changed and followed Fings out onto the streets anyway. "Go on then. Let me guess – you walked into a random tavern and there he was?"

"Not exactly. Well... Sort of."

As they walked, Fings explained. "Suppose it helps, Levvi missing his two front teeth and with a nose like a blacksmith's anvil. Bloke in the *Broken Lantern* remembers him. Got himself in some trouble. Got grabbed by some bloke calling himself the Witchbreaker."

"The *what*?"

"Some old thief-taker, apparently."

"Some old thief-taker?" Seth sighed. He was fairly sure that anyone who called himself *Witchbreaker* wasn't the sort of person he wanted to meet.

"Yeah. Used to be. Got his name by bringing in a witch one time."

"A... thief-taker? Are you sure about this? What with you being... well, not to dress it up, a thief." Seth quite liked witches, on the whole. He knew Fings did, too. Thief-takers... not so much.

"Way I hear it, he gave up thief-taking years ago. Runs a shelter for unfallen women on Denial Street now."

"*Un*fallen women?"

Fings didn't know either. "Can't hurt you being done up like a priest, I reckon," he said. Seth supposed he could see the sense in that. Better having a priest visiting a thief-taker than... well, a thief. An old thief-taker, though? One from back in the days of the warlock, perhaps? Sounded a bit familiar, that did. And yes, he didn't know Deephaven, but he was fairly sure Fings was leading him towards the Maze. Maybe he might have some questions of his own, once Fings was done asking about Levvi... So yes. He'd go along with this.

Fings took his time meandering through the backstreets of the docks, eyeing up the stalls and stands and barrows that littered the alleys between bawdy houses and Moongrass dens and drinking shops and gambling holes, and a hundred and one other places whose sole purpose was parting sailors from the coins burning holes in their pockets. For no reason Seth could see, Fings bought himself a gaudy cap, then some interesting-smelling bread, which he happily exclaimed was delicious, and then something hot and fried that made him retch. After a bit, when it was surely obvious even to Fings that he was dawdling, Seth sighed and stopped. Best get this over with. He had other things to be doing.

"Go on then. Spit it out."

Fings fiddled with his charms. "I saw you," he blurted. "This morning. After the temple. I saw where you went."

"Ah. *That's* what this is."

"The House of Cats and Gulls. That's what the river men call it. Call it a lot of other things, too. Who was that Taiytakei fellow you were with?"

You know, you could *always tell him the truth. See how he takes it. Think of it as testing the water before you tell it all to Myla.*

Seth wrinkled his nose.

Yeah... Thing with Myla, though, was she had that sword-monk gift going on for sniffing out lies. With Fings... Well, frankly, you could have a decent stab at persuading Fings to believe almost anything.

Still...

Fine. Have it your way. "A warlock once lived in Deephaven," he said. "Myla told me about him. A proper the raise-the-dead-and-talk-to-them warlock. She knew because one of the sword-monks who... who killed him was her teacher. I was hoping to find out more about those papers you brought back when you stole the Emperor's crown. That place was where he lived."

Nice work. Hardly had to lie at all...

It's what he needs to hear.

"Yeah. I know all that. What about the bloke you were with?"

"What, the Taiytakei?"

"Yeah. Him."

"Knew the warlock a little. Back when he was alive. That's all. I don't really know anything more about him." Seth gave Fings a steely look, the sort of look that said that there wasn't any more to say on the matter, even when there was. Fings nodded, although he didn't seem particularly happy about it.

"Don't seem clever, is all," Fings sniffed. "Pissing about with stuff that might get sword-monks all over you. Well... more than we already are."

Seth nodded. They could agree on *that*, at least. "Actually... I was thinking I should leave it alone until I can talk to Myla about it. It was *her* story, after all." *That* was probably what Fings needed to hear most of all.

And a lie, but never mind, eh?

It was raining again by the time they reached Denial Street, the evening sky dark with thick grey cloud. Seth could have walked right past where the Witchbreaker lived if it hadn't been for the cart parked outside, but that was enough to catch Fings' eye, and then Seth saw the door in the wall and the subtle warning carved into it. *Thief-taker.*

"That it?" When Fings nodded, Seth opened the door into a weed-strewn yard surrounded on three sides by single-storey stone buildings crowned in moss-covered tiles. Seth headed for what looked like the front door, and Fings followed. It opened before they got there, an old man staring at them, all wild grey hair and tattoos and mad eyes and charms, exactly the way Seth might have imagined someone calling themselves *Witchbreaker* would be, twenty years on from their heyday of breaking witches.

The Witchbreaker looked them over, took in Seth's robes and invited them in. He offered tea and quizzed Seth at length about where he was from. Seth said they were from Varr and kept his story largely truthful, only missing the small matter of him being kicked out of his temple for heresy back in the summer. He wasn't sure why, but he had a sense that this

Witchbreaker might have a nose for untruths, almost like a sword-monk. When it came to why they were there in the first place, he let Fings talk about Levvi, who he was, how he looked, how Levvi was his brother and how he'd heard the Witchbreaker had taken someone about five years ago who sounded a lot like him.

The Witchbreaker listened and then nodded.

"Let me check my ledger." He got up from his chair and slowly creaked away into another room. When he came back, he was holding a short stabbing sword and there was nothing slow and creaky about him at all. Fings jumped up and almost tripped over his own feet in his eagerness to back away, but the pointy end of the Witchbreaker's sword wasn't aimed at him.

Course it isn't, Seth thought, as he went in a blink from surprised to horrified to falling backwards off his stool, completely taken off guard. As he sprawled, the Witchbreaker put a boot on his face, pressing Seth's head into the floor while the tip of his sword poked at Seth's throat. "Who are you really?"

"Urk?" Seth tried to reach for the pocket of his robe where he kept a few handy sigils, but one hand was trapped under his body and the other was on the wrong side. As soon as he wriggled, trying to free his pinned hand, the foot pressing on his head pressed a lot harder. "Ow!"

"Stay still, you. Now answer me: who are you?"

"I'm just trying to find my brother!" Fings was fiddling with something in his shirt pocket.

"Why?"

"Because..." It probably hadn't occurred to Fings that he might have to explain something like that, but Seth reckoned he understood well enough. Probably a lot of thieves had brothers. Probably a good few of those brothers weren't happy with the idea of family members being caught and hanged, or sold into slavery. Probably a few, at least, had decided to express their dissatisfaction over the years with a quiet spot of thief-taker stabbing.

"Well?" The Witchbreaker didn't seem interested in taking his foot off Seth's face.

"Because he's family, and family has to stick together. No matter what. I just want to find him," pleaded Fings. "That's all. I don't know what he did. Something stupid, probably. I ain't looking for trouble."

The Witchbreaker seemed to think about this. Seth felt the pressure on his head ease a fraction. "I took a man who wasn't from Deephaven back about then. Might be who you're looking for. Helped a couple of idiots. Something that should have ended with three new corpses bobbing in the sea, but your boy and one of the others got away. The one that didn't was from the Peak. Thought that would save him. He was wrong about that, but it got a couple of us hired to find who did for him." The Witchbreaker finally lifted his boot off Seth's face and stepped away. Seth scrabbled to his feet.

And now sigil the fucker and let him finish his story as a corpse. He can tell you what he knows about the old warlock, too.

It *was* tempting. But the Witchbreaker still held his sword, and his guard was still up, and even if Seth managed to sigil him without getting stabbed, Fings would inevitably and spectacularly lose his shit. He'd have a *lot* of explaining to do.

He settled for backing away. The Witchbreaker watched him. The words were for Fings, but his eyes never left Seth.

"We did what we were paid for. Hunted them all down, both sides, turned them over, took our coin and walked. Far as I know, they were shipped to the mines, the whole lot of them. That's what usually happens." He pursed his lips and shook his head. "Don't know after that. Don't know, don't care, although still being alive up there after all this time would be a small miracle." He waved at them both with his sword. "If you're honest men, you got what you came for. If I see you again, that means you're *not* honest and I'll kill you without breaking a sweat. Got that?"

Seth reckoned yes, he had that, thanks.

"Well," he said, once they were outside. "*That* was fun. Now what?"

Apparently, *now what* was Fings sloping off to the fort outside the city they'd seen from the barge on their way downriver, breaking in, stealing all the records of slaves passing up the river from five years ago, and then bringing them back so Seth could read them and tell him where Levvi had gone.

"Right then," Seth said, since he obviously wasn't going to be any help with most of that. "When you're done, you know where to find me." With that, he hurried off before Fings had time to start banging on about maybe *not* visiting forbidden warehouses covered in bad-tempered sea birds, or dodgy fancy-clothed sorcerers, or whatever else was bothering him. He went back to his nice quiet room, sat down, and settled in for a good long think. Telling Fings he was going to leave the House of Cats and Gulls and the whole business of the sigils alone until they'd sorted this Myla nonsense had been what Fings needed to hear; but now he thought about it, maybe it wasn't such a bad idea?

"Should I start with the visions?" he asked the air. It had been all very well back in Varr, back at the start when he'd thought he was getting sendings from the Constant Sun, and generally having a religious experience that might get him his old life back, the Path welcoming his return with open arms, a pile of apologies from sheepish priests...

You burned that bridge months ago. When you...

He wasn't sure. He'd done something bad, back in Varr. *Really* bad, worse than the whole business with the hooded woman on the boat and the men sent to kill him. Something, he was fairly sure, to do with Lightbringer Suaresh, only he didn't remember *what*, exactly, because he'd made himself forget so the sword-monks wouldn't get it out of him.

Spread across his table were six sheets of tattered paper, quietly ripped from a temple ledger, each inscribed with a sigil. He imagined Myla standing across from him, looking at them.

This would be the convergence of minds, this confession. There was a chance, Seth supposed, once he finished telling her what he'd done, that only one of them would leave the room alive.

Probably won't be you, either.

If it came to that, Seth had no idea what he'd do. Run like fuck, probably.

"So, what do you think?" asked Seth after a while.

I think I should burn all this, said Imaginary Myla. *And then we should never speak of it again.*

No, no, no. That was *far* too easy. Also not helpful. "Those sigils are literally what you gave me." Which was true enough. "You asked me to find out what they were." Still largely true, although what she'd *actually* said was *see what's here and burn them when you're done;* both of which he'd eventually done, but Myla probably hadn't intended on him committing them all to memory first so he could write them out again here in Deephaven. Then there was the whole business of what he'd done once he *had* found out what they were, and the two rather unfortunate encounters with a pair of sword-monks that had followed. She probably hadn't intended *that*, either.

Maybe don't get into what you did with them after she left Varr?

No! That's exactly what you do *need to get into. You have to tell her everything. Otherwise, what's the point?*

Did other people have voices in their heads? If they did, were they *all* like this?

What do they do? asked Imaginary Myla.

Seth considered this.

He *could*, he supposed, tell her that he'd found himself hiding in a crypt in the under-city with three skeletons of what might once have been half-gods. That he'd been a bit bored, so had slapped the sigil that supposedly made the dead talk onto one of the skulls for something to do, and it sort of did.

Maybe not.

How about that time her lover caught you mucking about with a bunch of Dead Men and you slapped a sigil on him to make him forget?

Maybe not that, either.

How's it going, telling her everything? As well as you hoped?

"The one I gave to the sword-monks in Varr was to end the silence of the dead. I told you that. Draw it on to a fresh corpse and they'll talk. I didn't tell you that the reason I knew was because I'd tried it."

He watched Imaginary Myla shiver.

Alright, but she won't kill me for that.

His thoughts drifted to Varr. To Locusteater Yard in the dead of night, stooping over the body of a dead Spicer...

Still not killing me. Although she might if he told her why he'd done it.

He pointed to another. "That brings back fresh corpses as Dead Men." And not-so-fresh, apparently, which he'd found out by slapping it onto one of the other half-god skulls and having a walking skeleton following him about the place.

Going to mention that bit?

Yes! "Bit inconvenient, all things considered, so after I pissed myself, I put it to rest. Usual priest stuff." She wouldn't like it, but why not? She was hardly going to murder him for *that*. "Do you remember the night in Varr? When the Spicers had you and Fings?"

Imaginary Myla frowned.

"Orien caught me as I was trying to break in. Cleaver punched him in the face. If it's any consolation, I stopped Cleaver from eating him."

Ok. Not happy, but still not stabbing you.

"Yes. Cleaver. About that. See, he was a Spicer when I first brought him back. I only wanted to know where they'd taken Fings, but something got inside him. A former priest of the Living God, whatever that means. Said he could slay a slave with a thought and live through them without them ever knowing, sense the ebb and flow of the powers of creation for miles, create darkness and forge it into weapons, fool and beguile other spirits, travel the outer planes, forge Soul Jewels..."

He caught the horrified look that Imaginary Myla was giving him. Yeah, the dead thing that had got into Cleaver had *definitely* been some sort of sorcerer back when it was alive, definitely *not* the Spicer Seth had *thought* he was resurrecting. But Cleaver was gone now, put down by those two sword-monks in Varr.

Still not stabbing me.

Yeah. But…

Seth quietly added all that to the ever-growing list of things Myla didn't need to know when it came to his big confession. He was beginning to think he had hadn't properly thought this through.

But that's exactly what you're doing, right? Thinking it through and discovering what a fucking bad idea it is.

He forced a chuckle. "Way Fings tells it, you didn't need our help that night. But you need it now, right? Look, I know what these are. I know what they're supposed to do. I wouldn't ordinarily touch them if my life depended on it…"

She's a sword-monk, you turd-farmer. You can't spout bollocks like that and think she won't notice.

Fine. Seth nodded at the sigils. "Yes, okay, I've tried them all. This one is a symbol of death, this is a symbol of enslavement…" He trailed off. Imaginary Myla had taken a candle and was busy setting fire to his sigils.

I suppose that answers that, then.

Imaginary Myla swept the ash and the last fragments of charred paper into an old sack. *Warlocks burn, Seth,* she said.

"I'm not a warlock," Seth snapped, although he had a nasty feeling that he probably was. Even a whiff of this and he'd be up to his neck in priests and sword-monks. Which *was* exactly what had happened in Varr, after all.

My sword-mistress would burn us both to the bone.

Seth wagged a finger at Imaginary Myla. "Point *is*, *any*one can use a sigil if they know it. Point *is* that someone was writing them down. Point *is* that you and Fings took these from the same place as you took the Emperor's crown. Which means..."

Except he didn't know, that was the thing. It sure as shit meant *some*thing, but he had no idea what. Nice to have someone share that particular burden, just for once. Even if Imaginary Myla was... well, imaginary. "Point *is*... What if *every*one knew how to make the dead come back? What if *every*one was doing this shit?"

Imaginary Myla tossed the bag to him. *And there, Seth, you have your answer. You wanted to know the secret the Path was keeping? There you have it, right there in front of you. I'm going to leave now. Take this to the river. Put some stones in, tie it shut and throw it in the water. Let that be the end of it.*

Right, then. Nice talk. Bye. Seth sighed, and that was when he realised that the whole sigil-burning part hadn't been imaginary at all. There was no one else in the room, so he must have done it himself. Didn't remember doing it, though.

I see. Like that, *is it? Sneaky, devious little shit of a conscience. Clever, though.*

You do *realise you're talking about yourself, here?*

He sighed again. He wasn't keen on the idea of crossing the city at night, but that was what you got for waiting until after dark before showing off your shadowy secrets to some made-up idea of someone you vaguely knew. He probably should have shared them over breakfast. Or maybe a nice cup of afternoon tea.

But still, he had his answer. Right there in his hand. A sack of scorched paper and ash.

Was that really the secret the Path was trying to hide? That the power of the sigils wasn't special at all? That anyone could use them, and that the Path thought that allowing this would be a bad idea? He had a bad feeling that maybe it was. Which was a bit upsetting, because he was inclined to think they were right, that this *was* a secret best kept hidden.

So, they were right all along, and you were wrong, and that includes the part where they tossed you out, and you have no one to

blame for the ruin of your life but yourself. Good job. Well done. Off
you go, now, before you change your mind. Probably just as well you
can't remember what you did to poor old Lightbringer Suaresh, eh?

The walk to the river took a while, which at least gave him
some time to think. He'd fled Varr in a rush. Anywhere would
have done as long as it got him away from the sword-monks
trying to climb up his arse and gut him from the inside. He'd
come to Deephaven because Fings was his only real friend.
He'd come because Myla was in trouble and he had a nagging
sense that he owed her.

And all of it for nothing? Everything he'd done? Everything
he'd suffered?

It was all so stupid. So, so *stupid*. Why hadn't someone just
told him?

But then…

He tried to imagine it, some Sunbright coming up to him and
explaining about the sigils and how they were secret because
the whole world would fall over if everyone started drawing
arcane symbols left right and centre and bringing back the
dead and all manner of shit like that. Would he have believed
it? Probably not. If he had, would he have agreed?

Back then… He wasn't sure.

Probably made sense, if he was honest, not going around
telling thousands of goggle-eyed novices, most of whom were,
in Seth's opinion, idiots.

Was that *really* it? The secret he'd been so sure they were
hiding?

He stood at the edge of the docks and dangled the sack of ash
and charred leather over the water. He'd never forgotten Myla's
story of the warlock. A part of him had come to Deephaven
thinking he might find answers; or at the very least, a way to
make the one-eyed god with the ruined face piss off and leave
him alone.

And there he was. The half-blind shit-weasel. Whispering
in his head.

It starts in Deephaven. In the House of Cats and Gulls. All you have to do is open the door and let it in.

Seth looked down the length of the waterfront. The derelict warehouse was almost out of sight, but not quite. It stood quiet and still amid the rain and the thrum of the night-time docks.

A waiting invitation.

No. Not why I'm here.

He let go of the bag and watched it sink into the water.

Whatever you are, I'm not your puppet.

Some things it was better for Myla not to know. Some things, perhaps, it was better for *everyone* not to know, but it was too late for that.

Was *that* who the one-eyed god really was? The warlock who'd once lived here?

I should never have come. Should have stayed in Varr.

Right. And been murdered by sword-monks.

He made his way back from the river, through the spring twilight, passing costumed dancers and groups of revellers getting in some practice for the Festival of Rebirth. They were dressed as Dead Men and carrying lanterns made up into effigies of skulls.

Should have stayed in the Pig *and drunk the voices away.*

Stayed where he was safe.

Later, back in the tavern, he sat in his room and lit a lamp. He cupped his hands and stared into them, focussing his thoughts, driving the light away with his mind until a writhing, boiling ball of darkness began to form, tendrils licking out to touch his fingers. He blew softly into his hands, and the darkness was gone.

Just checking.

After all, even if some long-dead priest of some long-dead god taught you a little dark sorcery, it didn't mean you were going to *do* anything, right? He was still a creature of free will, wasn't he? Still the same Seth as he'd always been?

Wasn't he?

25

THE WRONG SWORD-MONK

Fings had a spring in his step on his way back to the Guildhouse after their little jaunt to the Witchbreaker, whistling a bright tune to himself. True, the Witchbreaker had turned out to be a bit terrifying, but on the whole, the day had gone well: he knew where Myla was and how to break her out, Seth had agreed to stop pissing about with things he ought to leave well alone; best of all, he knew where to go next to look for Levvi.

And then things took a bit of a turn: while he'd been gone, Orien's mistress had shown up.

On the way from Varr to Deephaven, Fings had wrestled with a particularly vexing dilemma: on the one hand, Orien was a mage; on the other, Fings didn't know anyone else and so had nowhere else to go and so the alternative was paying money. Paying money for a room was, he knew, the usual way of things; but when you put that up against *not* paying, Fings had eventually and reluctantly reckoned he could live with Orien. When Orien had offered him a room in the Guildhouse, he'd accepted. It was a nice room, and it was free. He'd made this difficult decision on the basis that Orien didn't do much actual mage-stuff and was a bit crap at it. All in all, he thought he'd coped quite well.

It took exactly one look for Fings to understand that Orien's Mistress wasn't like Orien at all: here was a mage that gave nightmares to everyone with any sense, a sorceress who threw her power about willy-nilly, who couldn't be bothered with doing things the normal way when a bit of Meddling With Things About Which Man Was Not Meant To Know would do the job instead. While Fings spent most of his life trying not to be noticed, Lady Novashi apparently did the opposite, managing to be everywhere, chucking sorcery about the place as easy as breathing and always finding something new to be cross about. It really didn't help that she was permanently angry, mostly with Orien.

After the third round of shouting, Fings decided he'd had enough, possibly forever and certainly for today. He left Orien to his apocalyptic mistress and went back out, with no great plan other than being somewhere else, and wondered what he should do next.

Levvi had been gone for five years, so another day or so wasn't going to make a difference. On the other hand, if Orien and Lucius had ever decided whether it was better to get Myla out right now or wait a few days, they hadn't bothered to tell him.

Sometimes, if you wanted something done right, you had to get up and go do it yourself. If Myla wanted to be hanged, she could say it to his face.

It was fully dark by the time he reached Deephaven Square and, for once, not raining. The temple gates were closed but he was ready for that. One side of the temple faced the square, another faced the Palace of the Overlord – no getting in *that* way, for sure – but the other two looked down on narrow streets flanked by tall houses: the walled compounds of the rich and the apparatus of the city government. Fings had worked out which he wanted back when he and Seth had come by in the morning; now he simply waited until the Longcoats that walked these parts weren't looking and scaled a wall. He

waited some more until the street below was clear, patience
being the difference between a good burglar and a dead one.
Once it was, he tossed a piece of rope across the street and over
the temple walls, the other end tied to a small rusty anchor
looted from the docks. After a couple of goes, it held fast. He
tied off the other end and made it taut, coiled a second rope
around his shoulder, and slithered across. Was just as well it
was Myla inside; if it had been Seth... well, he'd have to have
done it some other way. But Myla could manage a rope or two.

If she'd come.

She *had* to, didn't she? She obviously didn't know what was
waiting for her. That had to be it, didn't it?

Maybe there was more to *sanctuary* than he thought. Maybe
he didn't understand. Although... well, Seth *was* his brother,
and had been a novice for the best part of a decade, so...

Best not to think about that.

Balancing on the temple wall, Fings tied off his second
rope and shimmied to the ground. He danced from shadow
to shadow between the puddles in the yards, sucking on his
feather, until he reached the Sunguard barracks. He paused
there for a moment, muttering prayers to Fickle Lord Moon
and the Goblin King. He checked one last time to make sure
all his charms were in the right places, in pockets or around
his neck.

The door to the barracks wasn't locked. He slipped inside,
tip-toeing between cots of sleeping men. No one stirred. Down
a narrow passage, he found six cells with locked doors. He
started at the far end, not much liking how his only escape
was through the sleeping Sunguard where all he could do was
run like buggery and hope to get out before anyone was awake
enough to stop him. He sniffed at each door until he found one
where the air from inside smelled lived-in. Soft and slow, he
eased his picks into the lock, and pushed and probed until he
felt it click. He touched the charms around his neck again as he
checked behind him.

No movement. He opened the door and slipped inside. Moonlight shone through a tiny, barred window. He could make out the shape of someone sleeping in a cot.

He grinned at the darkness.

The tricky part, he'd been thinking, was how to wake a sleeping sword-monk without getting murdered and without them making a noise. The best way to go about this, he reckoned, was to prod Myla gently and then shove a hand over her mouth as soon as she opened her eyes. He did the prodding part and then it all went horribly wrong. He hadn't even got his other hand halfway to her mouth before she grabbed his wrist and twisted and turned him, and it was all he could do not to cry out. Then she let him go and he saw it wasn't Myla at all. It was the sword-monk he'd seen with her, earlier that day.

Oh. Bugger!

She seemed a bit cross. Oddly, though, not at all surprised.

"Are you Fings?" she asked.

Fings had a bit of a panic then, because how could she possibly know his name? But the monk was between him and the door, there was no other way out, no way he was getting past her if she didn't want to let him, and even if he did, there was a room full of Sunguard outside.

He sighed. "Maybe?"

She beckoned him to sit. Fings sat, seeing as how his choices were apparently that or get stabbed. They had a bit of a talk, then. Quite a long talk, as it turned out. When they were done, the monk told him what she wanted him to do and let him go. He slipped away, sliding unseen through the night, back out the way he'd come. He wasn't entirely sure what had just happened, but, strangely, it wasn't all that bad. Quite the opposite, really.

26

THE THİEF-TAKER'S BOY

Tasahre broke the pattern of their movements and sheathed her swords. The sword-mistress was slow this morning and clearly had something on her mind. They crossed the yard, heading for the armoury. As they did, a knot of novice sword-monks stopped their chatter to turn and stare.

"They can't decide what to think of you," Tasahre said. "Are you a martyr or a monster?"

"Neither."

"No, Shirish. You must be one or the other, now. You will have to choose."

Myla hung her practice swords and watched as Tasahre did the same. In a locked cabinet at the far end of the armoury were the sets of sword-monk blades, twinned pairs of golden Sunsteel, short and sharp and light. They were all different, some straight, some curved, some with hooks at the end, every pair unique. Myla wondered if the pair Tasahre had given her was here. Three years, that was how long she'd held them. They'd been held by other monks before and would move on after she was gone. To the swords, she was a blink in time, no more.

Three years that felt like a lifetime. She'd been a different person.

"Your mage's patroness has arrived in Deephaven. Lady Novashi of Neja. She has demanded immediate audiences with both the Sunherald and the Overlord. Such things are to be expected. Less expected is that she has asked that *I* attend her. Privately. A sorceress requesting the presence of a sword-monk is... unusual. I understand she's a close cousin to the Master of Neja and has the ear of the throne. You'll find little love in this temple for either; nevertheless, your mage may have more power than I thought. More than House Hawat even, if his mistress chooses to use it on your behalf. *Will* she choose to use it?"

Myla thought back to Midwinter night on the bridge in Varr. Orien's mistress had been the one to accept the return of the Moonsteel Crown.

"And will the Autarch of Torpreah recognise his Highness Emperor Ashahn the Second as the rightful ruler of the Empire?"

"You want to know, go and ask him. Do you want this or not?"

Not the most auspicious exchange. And then there had been the look on Lady Novashi's face, right from the start. Hostile and suspicious. The sort of look that was mostly wondering how Myla had been in a position to return the late Emperor's crown in the first place.

She wondered what Orien had told her. The truth, probably, because why wouldn't he?

"No," said Myla. "Not for me."

She half-expected Tasahre to reply but the sword-mistress only nodded, eyes roaming across the infinitely patient swords sitting in their stands.

If Orien came back that morning, Myla didn't see him. One meeting was all Tasahre would permit. They talked instead of the other students Myla had known, and of how Myla had faced the Anvorian Elementalist, the day she'd won her swords.

"There *is* one thing I'd like to know," said Myla, as they sat in a moment of afternoon sun, sandwiched between the rain showers. "How did you really get your scar?"

Tasahre gave her a long stare, then slowly pulled at the collar of her tunic. It was a large scar, jagged and ugly, if faded by many years. It started under her left ear and ended under her chin. As far as Myla knew, Tasahre had never the told the story of that scar to anyone, but there were always rumours. Most were of betrayal by some lover, which struck Myla as unlikely.

"My first pupil was a thief-taker's boy," she said. "I was young and rash. His master…" She sighed, raising her collar, half hiding the scar once more. "It's a very long story, Shirish."

And one she would never hear, Myla thought; but then to her surprise, Tasahre led her back through the cloisters, pausing on the way to her private room for a bottle of wine and two clean cups. Myla had never seen Tasahre drink, to the point of thinking that the sword-mistress never did, but tonight Tasahre poured a cup for each of them and made no comment as Myla drained her own, merely filling it again until the wine was gone. As they drank, she told Myla of the warlock, of the House of Cats and Gulls, of the thief-taker, and of his apprentice who'd been her pupil.

"One moment of hesitation, Shirish." She touched the scar. "I should have died, but there was another sword-monk. He had the healing art to him. He saved me, stayed with me and staunched the blood. I survived – barely – but the cost of my life has doubtless been many others. We had the warlock from the House of Cats and Gulls cornered. Euva should have left me to die and finished our work; but he didn't, and so the warlock escaped. He was punished for that, and rightly so." She sighed. "The warlock of the House of Cats and Gulls lived many years, pouring his darkness into the world. As for the one who cut me, he wasn't wicked, as men go."

"He must have been a good fighter."

"In a dirty sort of way." To Myla's mild astonishment, Tasahre pulled up her tunic, revealing the skin underneath and another scar running across her ribs, as long as the first although not as ugly and deep. "That was him, too. Admittedly, he had two swords at the time while I had none. Another mistake. You see, Shirish. We're none of us perfect."

Around the scar, Tasahre's skin was covered in tattoos. Sigils, born of the same language as the symbol the priests used to still Dead Men.

"What are they for?" Myla asked. She'd seen them on other monks too, but no one ever talked about them.

"Sigils." Tasahre let her tunic drop. "Like those the warlocks use but inverted. Protection against their sorceries." She half-smiled, apparently enjoying Myla's look of astonishment. "And against things far worse. That's why they fear us, Shirish. Accept my offer. Take sanctuary here and I will ink your skin myself."

"You know why I can't."

Tasahre came and sat next to Myla. For a long time, she said nothing, merely put an arm around Myla's shoulder and held her close, stroking her hair. She went away and came back with another bottle of wine and watched as Myla drank it; and then, when it was done, she put Myla to bed and lay beside her. In the morning, when Myla woke, the sword-mistress was gone and it was a pair of Sunguard nervously prodding her; and it was only after they tied her hands behind her back, only as they walked her through the cloister and around the Hall of Light to the foot of the Dawntower, that she understood what Tasahre must have known last night: that now was her trial, and so they would never see each other again except at a distance.

The Sunguard walked her to the Petitioning Hall where the Sunherald held court and made her wait outside; and then six sword-monks, all men and women Myla knew, with whom she'd trained, marched from the Hall of Light and demanded to take their place. When the door opened and a priest beckoned, the sword-monks escorted her, more as an honour guard than as though she was a prisoner. The Sunherald sat on his throne. Myla recognized most of the priests around him. She saw Tasahre, arms folded, her expression giving nothing away. Across the hall were a cluster of hired swords, among them the man she'd knocked down on that night at the *Captain's Rest*. She saw Orien in his orange robes.

In the middle, three men in red and white were being harangued by a woman in orange, the sorceress from the bridge in Varr, Orien's mistress. Another man was shouting at her. It took Myla a moment to recognise him: Sarwatta Hawat. He was changed. Gone was the cocky, preening stance. He stood a little stooped. He'd put on weight. He looked sallow and bitter and angry.

Myla smiled. *He still got what he deserved.*

He looked at her then; and that one glance told her that Tasahre was right, that nothing would satisfy him, even her total annihilation. His face twisted into a snarl as he spat shouted words at her, hurling them as though they were javelins.

"Your sister! Your brother! Everything! I'll take it all. I'll make you watch them all die in agony!"

And it still wouldn't be enough.

"Right here, Sarwatta," she shouted back. Goading him probably wasn't clever, but it wasn't like she had anything left to lose, and there was always the tiniest chance that he might completely lose his shit and end up skewered by another sword-monk.

"I will make you suffer, Shirish! They'll have to make new words for the pain you'll feel."

"Touch my sister again and I will end you, half-man."

It almost worked. He tried to run at her, would have done it too if he hadn't fumbled drawing his sword, which gave his own men time to rush in and hold him back.

The Sunherald banged a hammer. He had to bang it a lot before the commotion finally stopped. Orien's mistress withdrew. Sarwatta too, seething and shooting venomous looks at anyone who caught his eye. The oldest of the men in red and white – the Overlord's judges – cleared his throat.

"Shirish of House Sarcassian, you are hereby sentenced to service to the throne in the Hammerfell mines for the remainder of your natural life, denied the light of the Sun. Upon death, your body will be taken to a field at night so your spirit may be claimed by the Mistress of Many Faces never to return to the Sun's forge."

Myla saw Tasahre's face tighten.

And that was that. No statement of her crimes. No testimony of witnesses, of which there had been plenty. No statement in defence of what she'd done or of its heinous consequences. A handful of words and her fate was sealed.

Orien's mistress strode out, Orien trotting in her wake. Sarwatta shouted something she didn't catch and came at her again, only for the sword-monks around her to fan out, blocking his path.

"You'll never reach the mines," he hissed. "I'll make sure of it. Oh, I have such plans for you."

"Half-man," she said again.

The sword-monks led her to the gates of Deephaven Square where a dozen city Longcoats waited around a wagon that was a cage on wheels. As they walked, one of the monks pressed something into Myla's hand. "A gift from our mistress," he whispered. "She promises it will be quick and merciful."

Poison? She felt at it with her fingers. A bead of wax. Inside, she supposed, would be a sliver of something deadly.

The Longcoats looked her over, uneasy, as she reached the wagon. They opened the cage. The sword-monks stood back and let her climb in alone. Two stayed, walking with the Longcoats and the wagon all the way along the Avenue of the Sun and down the Godsway to the docks and the slave barge that waited by the River Gate. Myla didn't see how long they stayed, but imagined them keeping watch as the Longcoats shackled her with a score of waiting others. The monks were there because Tasahre had sent them to keep her safe for as long as she possibly could; but there were limits to even

Tasahre's reach. And so, as the barge lurched and rocked and pushed away from the shore, Myla understood that she was alone.

Much later, in the dark at the end of a long and terrible day, she squeezed Tasahre's bead of wax and split it open. It would only get worse, she knew, and so the temptation needed to be faced.

But it wasn't poison. Simply a note.

Your burden is to live.

27

THE HOUSE OF CATS
AND GULLS

For pity's sake! Can you at least not do this when I'm with other people? Seth stood in a place he shouldn't be, somewhere deep within the earth. White stone archways lined the walls. An old man in dazzling gold turned to face one, bowed, then both he and the arch dissolved into mist.

Do you know who that was? asked the one-eyed god with the ruined face.

Don't know, don't care, go away.

The Autarch of the Sun. The most powerful person in the Empire after the Regent and the Emperor.

You're *lecturing* me *about the Autarch? Are you feeling alright?*

Now he was on an icy ridge, high between two mountains. He looked for the one-eyed god but couldn't see him. *Care to say what this is actually about, or do you just have a fetish for mountain-tops and lightning?*

He stopped. He was holding a book. It was full of sigils. Sigils to destroy gods.

What about the missing hand? I'm sure you used to have two. Missing anything else I should know about?

The ridge collapsed, and now Seth was flying. An avalanche

of snow chased after him, smothering and destroying everything in its path. Jagged lines of ice raced beside him, cracking the landscape and speeding ahead. Night gave way to a pink tinge of dawn. As he looked back, the world turned silver.

"Oh, just *piss* off, you tedious fucker!"

"I *beg* your pardon?"

Seth blinked. He felt a breath of wind across his face. The world was still black but now it had a slight smell of mildew that reminded him of the *Unruly Pig*. And actually, the world wasn't *black*, simply dark. He was sitting in a boat, tied up to the far end of an abandoned pier on the river-docks, abandoned because it was right outside the House of Cats and Gulls. The popinjay was already ashore. He'd been tying up the boat, but now he'd stopped. He was giving Seth a hard look.

Shit! Did I just say that out loud? Seth blinked again and shook a mental fist at the one-eyed god. *You just come along and throw stuff into my head whenever the mood takes you, don't you?* "Sorry," he said. "Talking to myself there."

"Change of heart? Do you want to turn back?"

What was he thinking, doing this? He didn't trust this man. Hadn't he decided that he was going to wait for Myla? Wasn't coming here with the popinjay, alone, exactly something he'd decided *not* to do?

He climbed out of the boat and stood on the pier and looked around. A faint mist was rising off the river. "Tell me again why we have to do this in the middle of the night."

The popinjay looked annoyed. Which was odd, because until now his expression had mostly been one of amiable interest, flavoured with a slight hint of wanting to dissect people to see how they worked.

Well, you did just call him names. How would you *feel?*

"Why are we here?" he asked.

This seemed to make the popinjay even more annoyed. "*You're* the one who wanted to come here. *I* said we could go in the middle of the day. *You* said no."

I did?

Seth stood and had a think about this. Yes, he'd done exactly that. Why? Had he been drugged? Drunk? But he didn't *feel* either of those things. He felt... enervated. As though on the brink of something.

The one-eyed god?

Did you borrow *me to make this happen? Sun's arse! If there really* are *sigils for ending gods, you're making a fine effort to be first in the queue, you know that?*

He checked his pockets. His slips of paper were all where he'd left them, sigils drawn and ready. If the worst came to the worst, he could simply slap one on the popinjay and make him do exactly as he was told, or make him tell the truth, or simply kill him and bring him back as a Dead Man. Still hadn't tried that on a mage. It would be interesting to find out if it worked.

Useful to know before *you try it out, don't you think?*

Well, he was here now. Might as well take a look. He pushed past the popinjay and stomped down the pier. "So how do we get in?"

"You go up to the door and open it." The popinjay trotted up to walk beside him. "It's not locked or sealed and no one's going to stop you."

"You've been inside?"

"Yes."

"And?"

The popinjay shrugged. "You're not going to find anything interesting. After the sword-monks drove him off, the priests took everything. I've no idea what they did with it. Burned it, for the most part, by the looks of things."

The black shape of a cat darted through the darkness near the warehouse. Then two more. Seth had the sense of a hundred pairs of eyes watching him from shadows and alleys. The entrance, when they got close, had bits of fish and entrails scattered around it. The door was the colour of bleached bone.

It hung ajar, half staved-in. The surviving timber had been daubed with the crude outline of a skull.

"That's a plague mark," said Seth. Going inside a plague house seemed pretty fucking stupid, if you stopped to think about it.

"Yes. A lot of people seem to think this is the source of the River Plague. They're probably right."

"And that doesn't bother you?"

The popinjay shrugged. "Just don't let anything bite you."

"How very fucking reassuring." *I shouldn't be here. I should have done what I said I'd do. I should have waited. I should have come with Myla...*

But he'd watched them take Myla to the slave barge. And that, he figured, had been the end of that.

Around the threshold were a few baskets and pots. They looked new. Seth scrunched up his nose. "Lucky for us it's cold," he said. "Must smell a bit when the sun's gotten the place warmed up a bit."

"People leave offerings." The popinjay stepped inside. "For the cats and the gulls. So they don't... so they don't bite people and give them the plague." He sounded a bit embarrassed. "I imagine that's the idea, anyway. Kuy's been gone a decade and more, yet they still come."

"They?"

The popinjay only gave another shrug. Seth hesitated, reluctant to go inside. "If the priests came, is there still anything worth bothering about in there?"

"Not really."

"Right then." *So why the fuck am I doing this?*

The popinjay pulled the door open and went inside. Seth let out a long sigh and followed. One hand settled in a pocket, around a strip of paper. He could feel the cold and the darkness squatting in the heart of this place. There was something still here. He just wasn't sure what.

So. What are we looking for?

No answer.

Well?

Still no answer. Seth hissed under his breath. "Pseudo-divine shit-weasel!"

The popinjay lit a candle, not that it helped much. The space inside the warehouse was a ruin. It smelled of old and musty clothes, of charcoal and smoke and decay and damp. Walls stood black and, in some places gaping. At the far end, a staircase and some of the inner structure had collapsed. As Seth looked closer, he began to make out the remains of furnishings: a table here, a chair, a partition.

He followed past the gutted entrance as the popinjay led him into a warren of tiny spaces, moving from room to room. A reek of rotting flesh wafted past and then was gone. More than once, he thought he smelled burnt hair. Where there were windows, they'd obviously once been boarded up, although the boards had long since been ripped away to let the light return.

"I came here once before," said the popinjay. "Shortly after Kuy left. There wasn't much to see, even back then. The priests gutted the place. By the looks of it, no one's been here since."

In the deeper rooms, where there was no place for the moonlight to enter, the air carried the tang of candles and incense, of burning tallow and sulphur and a hundred other scents, adding themselves to the stink of rot and decay. The richness of its air seemed all the old house had left to offer except bare walls and floors, streaked with soot and greasy to the touch.

Something wasn't right, though. There had been fires hot enough to melt metal in places. Seth could see the damage. Surely the whole building should be ash?

They stopped deep in the warehouse. The popinjay crouched where a fire had once burned in the middle of the floor.

"Salt." He traced the outline of a dirty black ring circling the pile of ash and embers. "Salt and iron. There are other circles if you look for them. Sun knows what he was up to at the end."

Seth crossed the circle and picked through the ashes. His fingers came away with tiny fragments of parchment, too small to make out anything useful, and slivers of charred bone.

"They said he had a pact with the cats and the gulls who live here. That they were his spies and that he could ride them, seeing the world through their eyes, listening with their ears. Some think he's still here, riding them. Watching and waiting for his day to return."

Despite himself, Seth shivered. "Do *you* think that?"

The popinjay snorted.

"You met him, yes? What did he look like? He didn't have one eye and a half-ruined face, did he?"

"A watery-eyed old man, pale white skin like the men from Anvor." The popinjay led Seth deeper still, into a maze of tiny passages. "Like a ghost, with tattoos on his cheeks and neck, disappearing beneath his robe. Eyes like the night. They both worked, though, and no scars that I remember."

Of course, it *had* been a long time ago. Maybe the ruined face and the milky-blind eye came later?

Is that who you are, fucker? What did that to you? Fire, was it? Did they burn you?

"Here." The popinjay stopped outside a little room with a ladder going down. "If you're looking for something, it's probably down here." He chuckled. "People think he turned into one of his cats or gulls because they never saw him come and go, but I know how he did it."

The popinjay started down the ladder and disappeared into the darkness. Seth shuddered. Everything about this place felt wrong, so why was he here? Why was he doing this? No, really, why *was* he doing this?

Another deep breath and then he followed. He found himself in dank musty space that smelled of earth and water and rot, low and spreading out under the warehouse, filled with wooden piles to support the structure above. The floor was stone but covered in a layer of damp sticky mud. It was a huge space, featureless apart from the piles and seemed to go on forever. A dozen paces in the popinjay's wake and Seth knew that if he turned back, it might take him hours to find the way out. The gaping darkness felt oppressive. Like delving into the bowels of the Earth.

The home of the Hungry Goddess.

He followed the bobbing light of the popinjay's candle until the mage stopped. He was standing at the edge of a wide circle of stone. Almost like a well, except Seth could see the water, only a few feet below. Oddly, in the flickering light of the candle, the water seemed to have a sigil written on its surface.

"That's the river," said the popinjay. "I think this room floods sometimes. Some years when the river peaks. That's how he did it. That's how he got in and out without anyone ever seeing." The popinjay grinned. "As did the wraith of whom he imagined himself master."

Seth froze. "*What* did you say?"

İNTERLUDE:
THE SORCERESS

Lady Novashi wasn't someone you wanted to anger. Annoy her enough and she'd literally burst into flames. Since annoy her was exactly what Orien was about to do, he took a deep breath as he headed for her study, ready to be as humble as he could manage. He didn't get far before he heard a commotion at the front door. When he looked, the front hall had three hooded men in it, looming over an extremely flustered pair of the servants Lady Novashi had brought with her from Varr. Rather, *two* of the three men were looming. The third was a full head and shoulders shorter than the others.

"Hey!" He conjured flames into his hands and stomped down the stairs, all ready to give whoever these idiots were a good talking too. Then one of the idiots threw back his hood and tossed his cloak over his shoulder to reveal black Moonsteel armour and a crimson sash, all of which made him unquestionably an imperial guardsman. Orien didn't know his name, but he'd seen the man in Varr, too. One of the Princess-Regent's.

"Lady Novashi," he said. "Now, boy."

Boy? *Boy?* Orien bristled but the three men were already moving, brushing past the servants and heading up the stair towards him. The other soldier pulled back his hood as he came, and Orien recognised him, too. The third one, the short one, kept her hood down, her face hidden, but by then Orien was fairly sure he knew who she was, although he was surely wrong, because the Princess-Regent was supposed to be in the City of Spires.

"Yeh... yeh... yeh..."

He just about found his wits in time to get out of their way. As they passed, the short one flicked a finger at him. The flames vanished from his hands as the three walked on, heading for Lady Novashi's suite as if they knew exactly where they were going and ignoring him completely. After a few seconds, Orien hurried after in time to see the short one walk into Lady Novashi's study and close the door behind her. The two men in Moonsteel took up positions outside. From beyond the door, he heard his mistress talking. He couldn't make out the words but she sounded deferential. As far as Orien knew, he could count the people in the Empire who qualified for deference from Lady Novashi on the fingers of one maimed hand, and none of them were in Deephaven. Rather... none of them were *supposed* to be in Deephaven.

The soldiers glared at him. Orien glared right back. This was *his* Guildhouse, after all.

The study door flew open. His mistress glared at him as well.

"I'm expecting another visitor. Bring her here directly when she arrives. Wait for her in the hall."

Orien did as he was told, quietly wishing he knew a spell to send one of his ears off back upstairs to have a good listen to whatever was being said. He didn't see Fings wander in until the thief came and sat beside him.

"Morning mage," he said, and carefully turned away. "Is it safe?"

"Is it...? What *are* you talking about? Why *do* you keep behaving in this absurd fashion?"

Fings seemed to think about this for a bit, then swivelled to face Orien. "Who's the toffs, then?"

"The... *toffs*?"

Fings nodded to the door. "Seen them, ain't I. Three of them. Big fancy horses outside, too. Didn't go well this morning, I take it?"

It took Orien a moment to realised Fings was talking about Myla. "They're sending her to the mines," he said.

Fings nodded like he wasn't particularly surprised or even particularly bothered. Orien was starting to think how maybe that was a bit odd, but then there was another hammering on the door. Since that was why he was there, Orien supposed he'd best get up and open it.

Myla's sword-mistress. Orien gawped. The sword-mistress cocked her head. She seemed about to say something, then glanced past him, saw Fings, and looked rather surprised. Orien stepped aside, wishing he could think of something clever to say about how sword-monks weren't allowed in mage places, how she'd have to be something else while she was here, but not finding the words.

A look passed between the sword-mistress and Fings. Couldn't say what it was, only that it wasn't nothing. Orien peered, trying to work it out, but Fings had gone back to picking his nails and studiously ignoring everyone. By the time Orien came back from showing the sword-mistress to Lady Novashi's study, Fings had gone.

Later, his mistress summoned him and handed him a list of names.

"Gather every mage in Deephaven," she said. "Then go to the Temple of the Moon. I require someone who can speak for them. The Moonherald, if he'll come. Then go to the sword-mistress. She will have a message for you."

Orien looked at the list of names. Most he didn't recognise. "And Myla?" He looked around. "Do we stand by and do nothing?"

Lady Novashi didn't look up, but Orien felt the scowl. "The Overlord has passed his judgement. And she *was* part of the theft in the first place."

"But..."

She shook her head. "No, Orien. Now is not the time. Leave her to her own."

Orien closed the door behind him. He stood for a moment, gathering his thoughts. So that was his choice, was it? Everything he'd worked for throughout his entire life? Or Myla. He understood, or at least, imagined he did. The empire was on the edge of war. The Princess-Regent was here. Not merely in Deephaven but *here*, under the same roof. Something was about to happen. Something momentous that didn't need an upstart fire-mage and a disgraced sword-monk making a mess everywhere.

Because for all his mistress's fury, he'd seen how her face changed as he came in, slipping back the mask of her authority over...

Fear? Was *that* what he'd seen?

PART THREE
Wraith

Freedom is the child of unswerving resolve.
– Tasahre

28

THE RİGHT SWORD-
MONK, THİS TİME

Fings had been glad when everyone else buggered off to
Myla's trial, leaving him to his own devices, which was
mostly packing and talking to the servants about the cheapest
flop-houses around the sea-docks. Partly, he hadn't gone
because the priests wouldn't have let him in; but mostly
it was because he already knew how it was going to go,
because the sword-monk who'd turned out not to be Myla
had told him. Interesting chat, once he'd calmed down a bit
and understood she wasn't about to stab him. Had shed a bit
of light on what Seth was up to, as well. For example, he now
knew a couple of things that Seth had somehow forgotten
to mention. One being that the sword-monks *hadn't* killed
the warlock of Deephaven, only chased him off, which he
was sure Seth already knew, the other being that he now
had a shrewd idea who the Taiytakei popinjay really was.
Unfortunately, he couldn't talk to Seth about any of this,
because that would mean explaining how he'd snuck into
the temple without telling anyone and how it had all gone
perfectly well, thanks, until the sword-monk he'd tried to
rescue had turned out *not* to be Myla but the same sword-

monk who'd chased the warlock out of the House of Cats
and Gulls all those years ago and was now quietly keeping
an eye on the place. And if he did *that*, well, then there
were going to be all sorts of questions about how come
the sword-monk had told him all this and then let him go;
and so *then* he'd have to explain the rather uncomfortable
interrogation that had gone *before* they got to all the stuff
about old warlocks and so forth, how Fings had told the
sword-monk pretty much his entire life story, how that had
included all the stuff in Varr with Orien and the Moonsteel
crown and all about Orien's rescue plan. And, too, how
the sword-monk had been very clear that anyone getting
interested in the House of Cats and Gulls was likely to find
themselves on the wrong end of a lot awkward questions
and possibly a stabbing, at which point Fings had had to be
very clear that he was only asking for a friend.

On the whole, Fings reckoned he could be doing without
all that. He supposed Seth might not take the last part terribly
well, either. There might be some shouting.

He wasn't entirely surprised to see the sword-mistress show
up at the Guildhouse. There was obviously something sinister
going on, what with three high lord mucky-mucks showing
up in secret in their swanky armour. He tried to have a bit of
a listen to what they were saying, having worked out which
rooms had walls or floors or ceilings that butted against where
all the talking was happening. Odd things was, whenever he
found a place where he could press his ear to any of those
without being seen, all he heard was a buzzing that crept into
his head and got louder and louder until he had to stop. After
a bit, he gave up. Wasn't anything to do with Myla or Levvi, far
as he could tell, so he was only doing it because he was bored.

He watched, later, as Orien dithered outside his mistress's
door. He pressed his ear against it when the mage finally found
the courage to enter and ask his question. The apocalyptic
sorceress of Neja mostly looked at Fings like he was an unruly

piece of furniture, and apparently thought much the same of Orien; right now, neither the mage nor Lucius were being much use, which left Fings wondering if maybe he *should* tell them about his visit to the temple, just be a bit skimpy on some of the more warlock-related details.

He heard Lady Novashi's answer, that they were going to leave Myla to her fate; and right there was everything broken with the world. There was a right thing to do and a wrong thing; and somehow people kept on coming up with reasons for the wrong thing when they should have simply done the right one.

He left and went to find Lucius.

"No one with money or connections ever reaches the mines," Lucius told him. "Sarwatta will spirit her away before she ever gets there."

Fings nodded. He'd expected as much because that's what the sword-monk had said, too. "Yeah. So, we do the same, right? Only we get there first."

"The sword-monks will stand watch until the barge leaves. Sarwatta will take Myla at the first stop that follows. The soldiers will be bribed and waiting to take her."

"Yeah. At that fort place a bit up the river." The same place he'd been planning on paying a visit anyway, on account of it maybe telling him what had happened to Levvi.

Lucius sounded beaten; and it was a pity, Fings thought. So he told Lucius how it could be done, pointing out that if he could sneak past a company of Imperial Guard to steal the Emperor's crown from literally under their arses – since apparently the whole world and his dog knew about that now – then he could probably sneak past a few second-rate guardsmen to steal a Myla. He *did* have some history, after all, when it came to sneaking onto barges.

And Myla *would* want to come with him this time. The sword-monk had told him that, too, although this bit he kept to himself. In fact, the sword-monk had told him exactly where and when it could be done, along with a good bit of how, right after they'd finished talking about warlocks. Almost like she'd been him encouraging him, really, which didn't seem at all the proper attitude for a holy sister.

Myla dropped her oar. Her arms sighed with relief as she looked down the row of gleaming backs, all glistening with sweat in the half-light. The evening sun poured across the deck, rendering the Oarsmaster in silhouette. A brutish soldier walked between the rowing benches, slow and close, daring any of the new slaves to try something. No one moved. No one said anything. Satisfied, the soldier left.

It could be worse. She could be the young merchant boy caught setting fire to the wrong warehouse, sat at the front. He had enemies here. Even if he survived as far as the mines, he wouldn't last long. No one would help him. Certainly not the soldiers.

She looked again at Tasahre's message. *Your burden is to live.* She didn't understand what the sword-mistress meant by that; what she *did* understand was that her sentence was meaningless because Sarwatta was still coming after her. He'd made *that* very clear. He'd also made it clear that he'd take his revenge on her family no matter what, that she'd surrendered her power for nothing.

Except... Her sentence *wasn't* meaningless. Not to her. She'd come to Deephaven to be punished for what she'd done. She'd never flinched from that. She'd gone willingly, rejecting offers of escape. She would have accepted it, if Sarwatta could have accepted it as well. She'd wiped her slate clean, as best she was able.

Send your men, then, Sarwatta. I'll be waiting.

There wasn't much to see on the riverbank: thick with trees, branches drooping into the water and bright with new leaves; the outline of a small wooden fort; a few fires along the waterfront. She caught a scent of smoke. Once it was obvious that they were being left in the barge for the night, she tallied the men around her. Chained as they were, seven could reach her. Five, she thought, would try to stay out of any trouble. Of the two that wouldn't, she judged that one would leave her alone if she hurt him enough. With care, it wouldn't come to that.

The last… if he decided to test a sword-monk, that one was going to be to the death. Question was, though, would he help if she tried to escape?

When, she told herself. *When* she tried to escape.

Down the front, they were starting on the merchant boy again, telling him what they were going to do to him when they reached the mines. She drifted into an emptiness that wasn't quite sleep, but wasn't quite wakefulness either, waiting for the full dark of night to fall.

Fings watched the barge draw up at the pier by the fort. The fort *was*, he had to admit, a bit of a distraction; if Lucius was right, somewhere inside were records that would tell him where Levvi had gone. He wouldn't have the first clue where to look, mind, or where sentries might be posted. A difficult job without some proper reconnaissance. Impossible, if everyone was all riled up on account of a missing slave.

Just have to make sure they don't notice, then. He was tempted to burgle the fort first and then snatch Myla on the way out. *Things* were always easier to steal than people.

"Can you get us in there?" he asked Lucius. "You know. Like, we're respectable slave-buying folk, or whatever?"

Lucius shook his head. Fings thought about explaining what he was planning, then decided not. Lucius was only interested in Myla. He'd say that what Fings wanted to try was pointless and dangerous. The dangerous bit was probably true. What rankled was how all this was so unnecessary. Orien's mistress was a silver-thumbed high-born from the same house as the soldiers at the fort. All she had to do was tell this lot to let Myla go. Then she could take Fings and someone who could read to where they kept their books and they'd be done. No risk, no mess, no need to even steal anything. But she wouldn't.

He was, he had to admit, glad in a way. Partly because Orien's apocalyptic mistress scared the crap out of him. But partly, too, because he liked stealing things. Got a thrill off it.

If he found their books, he'd have no way to know which were the ones that mattered. He'd have to steal *all* of them. They'd probably notice that.

Could always ask Myla to help. Once she's free. She can read, after all.

He gave some serious thought to that. Sneak her off the barge, then sneak her *into* the fort? Knowing Myla, she might even go along with it, if he told her why.

No. Wasn't fair.

According to Lucius, the road from Deephaven followed the river after the fort to some place called Bedlam's Crossing, then petered out into a mud track and then vanished into the floodplains. The best thing, they both reckoned, was to keep going once Myla was free. Get to Bedlam's Crossing, take a boat up the river and disappear. Well, *Fings* couldn't do that until he knew what had happened to Levvi. Didn't matter, though. If Lucius couldn't spirit Myla away on his own, Fings sure as shit wasn't going to be any help.

The soft sides of the fort were the ones facing away from water. Those would be his way in and out. Surrounded by forest, there were plenty of places to hide.

"Go back to the cart," he said. "Once it's dark, get as close as you can without being seen. When I get back, I'll have Myla with me. Can't say I won't have stirred up a bit of noise, mind. You go on. Don't wait. I'll go a different way. Lay some false tracks. Make a diversion. That sort of thing."

Lucius opened his mouth to protest. Fings walked away,

quick as he could, before the whole *don't-you-want-me-to-come-with-you, no-you'll-only-get-in-the-way* conversation had a chance to kick off. Once he was properly alone, he settled to wait. There were only a couple of sentries out by the river, and they didn't seem particularly watchful. Maybe they weren't bothered about a few slaves escaping. Maybe they were getting ready to turn a blind eye when someone came for Myla in the night. No way to tell, really. Both?

Well, if anyone *did* come for Myla in the night, Fings was here to make sure they had a bit of disappointment.

And then, since he didn't have much of anything else to do with his time, he had a good long look at the fort while he was waiting. Just in case.

Myla's eyes snapped open. She ached everywhere and the world was black. She'd fallen asleep. The men around her were quiet; but *something* must have happened to wake her. She strained her ears. Plenty of snoring. The occasional whimper. The quiet hiss of gentle rain falling on the river and the shore around her. Two distant voices from somewhere on the shore, quiet and unconcerned…

She didn't see Fings until he was almost on top of her. At first, she didn't recognise him, only a shadow moving slowly between the benches. Then she saw the feather between his teeth.

"Fings?"

It made no sense, so she had to be wrong; and yet, when she looked again, it *was* Fings. He grinned and put a finger to his lips and began feeling for the chains that held her to the rowing bench. She watched him work until he found the lock, then put a hand on his wrist to stop him. A part of her wanted to crush him with hugs.

She let go of his hand. *Why are you here?* she signed.

Fings gave her that look he had for people when he thought

they were acting daft, then shook his head and signed back: *Be silent. Be invisible.* He set to work on the lock. In a moment, he had it open.

She hesitated. *What now?*

We run.

No. If she ran, what was the point of it all? Why come back to Deephaven in the first place? Sarwatta had made it clear that Lucius and Soraya would pay in blood for what she'd done. If she ran, he'd make them pay double. She had to stay until he came for her. And *then* there would be blood.

Fings gave her an irritated look, then gave a little sigh, took the feather out of his mouth, bent close and whispered in her ear. "Your burden is to live."

Myla started as though she'd seen a ghost. Fings put his hand over her mouth before she could speak and stuffed his feather back between his teeth.

Be silent. Be invisible. Follow.

It seemed for a moment that her body had forgotten how to stand. Her back creaked and spasmed. Jolts of pain shot through her, a hard day at the oars taking its revenge. She put a hand on Fings' shoulder and slid off her bench. He thrust a second feather at her; after a moment, she took it. Stupid superstition – holding a feather between your teeth didn't make people not see you, it made them think you were an idiot – but here? Now? What harm could it do?

She held it between her teeth. It tasted musty. She almost spat it out again, then caught Fings looking at her and changed her mind. *Let him have this.* It was only a feather, after all. A seagull feather, picked up off the street, most likely.

She winced as they crossed the deck, partly because everything hurt, mostly because all it took was for one slave to stir and wake and that would be the end; either they'd sound the alarm out of spite or demand their own release in exchange for silence; and when one roused, so would another and another. She started a mantra in her head...

And then they were on the pier, the shock of cold rain on her skin, and there were no shouts of alarm and no soldiers standing on watch. Fings nudged her to the shore. The more she moved, the easier it came, and then they were running under the moonlight, past the fort, past smells of horses and old cooking and stale beer, the sound of the falling rain muffling their footsteps, into the trees until darkness swallowed them. There, Myla stopped. In part to catch her breath, but only in part.

Fings took a deep breath, let it out, spat his feather into his hand and grinned. "So. Hello, I suppose."

Myla returned her own feather, mangy manky thing that it was. She had a vague urge to wash out her mouth. "What did you mean, my burden is to live?"

"Yeah, yeah. Me and Seth only came all the way from Varr to get you out of whatever mess you're in. You know, across half the empire and everything, but never mind that, you're welcome." He shook his head in exasperation. "Best we get clear, quick as we can. Been lucky so far. There were a couple of sentries on the pier earlier, but they left. There's men coming for you. Going to take you back to Deephaven. Not for anything nice, neither."

"I know. What are you doing here?" she asked. "How did you find me? Why aren't you in Varr?" She had about a hundred other questions, but maybe now wasn't the time. Although, out here in the pitch-dark, the canopy overhead blotting out the sky, the hiss of the rain…

Fings shrugged. "Orien said you needed helping."

Myla sniffed the air, looking for a bad smell, but he wasn't lying. She listened to the pitter-patter of water falling from the leaves overhead as she let that swirl through her. Orien had sent for help? From Fings, of all people? *Orien* had done this?

The same Orien who'd come to the temple every morning, even though the sword-monks never let him in. Until they did.

Persistent bastard.

Still, it lit a smile in her.

Fings shifted a bit, like there was something he wasn't saying, then let out a long breath. "Thought maybe I might find out what happened to Levvi while I was here."

"Fings... I have to go back."

"To the barge? Don't be daft." She couldn't see his expression in the dark, but she knew what it would be. He'd be looking at her like she was mad.

"If Sarwatta doesn't get what he wants, he *will* take it out on my family. I have to go back. *He* has to be the one to break the Overlord's judgement."

"Yeah. About that." Fings shot a nervous glance behind her. "Look, your Sarwhatever-his-name-is, he's got men coming for you. You know how it goes with these Longcoats. A few coins in a pocket, off you vanish, and he does whatever he likes."

"Yes. I *do* know. I was counting on kicking the shit out of them. What are you *doing* here? What did you mean 'my burden is to live'? Did *Tasahre* send you?" The idea was absurd. How, in Kelm's name, had the sword-mistress and Fings ever crossed paths?

"Yeah." Fings stared at his feet. "About that. I got the wrong sword-monk the first time, alright. She said to say it ain't going to help, you doing what you're doing."

"Tasahre? *Tasahre* said that?"

He nodded. "Yeah."

"And then she sent *you* here?"

Another nod. "Not... exactly. But yeah. Sort of. More... happened to mention some stuff that might happen to make it a bit easier for someone who might have been thinking of doing it already. Would have come anyway, mind."

"She's wrong. I have to go back."

Fings shook his head then put a nervous hand on her shoulder. "Family, right? Look, you came when the Spicers took me. I got you into all sorts of trouble and you still came.

I would have died to protect my ma and my sisters if you hadn't. I owe you for that." He squeezed, gently. "So, listen to me now. I've never met your Sarwhatever but I've met plenty like him. The Mage of Tombland, he was the same. The Murdering Bastard. Blackhand, if I'm honest about it. Others, too. He wants to hurt you, and the best way to do it..." He let her go. "Look, you know him better than I do. But I'm telling you, men like that... you ain't saving anyone trying to bargain, or giving yourself up, or any of that shit. You don't give them that power. What he wants is for you to be there to watch. He wants you helpless. He wants–"

"Fings."

"No, hear me out! He wants you pleading for mercy, begging him to take it out on you, not on them. Promising you'll do whatever he says. He'll string you along, take you as far down that road as he can, watch you humiliate yourself until there's nothing left. But in the end? In the end, he'll do it anyway, because that's the thing that breaks you. Trust me. I know his sort."

"Fings!"

"No! Myla! What you do is you walk away and let him stew, knowing he can't reach you, can't find you, can't touch you. Knowing that if he does anything, you'll hear about it, and the first he'll ever know is an edge of steel opening his throat. *That's* what keeps them safe. There's no making peace with people like that."

"No." Myla shook her head. "I can't take that risk. Not with Soraya."

"Then you murder the fucker good and proper. And then you vanish, so everyone knows you're still out there to do it again if you have to."

"Fings! I *know*, alright! It's just that *he* has to be the first to step across that line."

Fings took a step back, apparently a bit confused by Myla's reply. "Oh. Right. Well, your brother's out here, a few minutes away. Might need a bit more convincing. He wants you to run. Oh, and whatever you do, if you *do* go back to Deephaven, do it quick. I think something bad is about to happen."

"Tasahre told you to say all this?"

Fings shook his head. He held out his hand. "She said how it would go, but... No. Look, me and Seth... You stood for us. Both of us. We ain't tied by blood, but by any other count I reckon we're family. Let us do the same. Your brother's here. You go with him. I'll get your sister and get her safe. And then we run, because there's nothing else to be done."

He wiggled his outstretched hand. Myla stared at it. This, she understood, was what Tasahre had been trying to tell her all along. That the burden she carried wasn't the burden of knowing she could never undo what she'd done, but of carrying on, even so. Stupid really, how Tasahre had been trying to tell her this for weeks and hadn't managed, yet it all made sense, coming from Fings.

Still, *fuck* that. If Sarwatta wanted war, so be it.

Kelm's Teeth but she could do with a drink.

"I have to see Soraya safe."

"No, you don't, but I ain't going to try to stop you. Don't suppose I could even if I wanted. But quick, right? Like, tomorrow. Then we run."

She took his hand – he was probably right – and let him lead her through the forest to where a cart sat beside a road, and next to it a man shrouded in shadow.

"Lucius?"

She ran out from the trees into the falling rain. He turned, and there he was, clear in the moonlight, the brother who'd always stood by her; and yet there was horror on his rain-streaked face, as she came closer, and a desperate sadness.

"Look that bad, do I?" Myla wanted to laugh and cry at the same time. And then she stopped, because Lucius was looking through her, not at her, back along the road towards the fort.

"I'm sorry," he said.

Two men emerged from the shadows, crossbows ready and loaded. When she looked back to Lucius, another had emerged from his hiding place in the cart, a crossbow held at her brother's back.

The sell-sword from the *Captain's Rest*. The one whose nose she'd broken.

He met her eye. "You want your brother to live. You do exactly what you're told, sword-monk."

She looked at him and had to try hard not to smile. *Thank you for setting me free.*

"Only three of you?" she asked.

29

ONE LAST VISION

Seth stared at the popinjay. "*What* did you just say?"

The popinjay's grin didn't waver. "You heard. A wraith. A half-god. A Silver King. Take your pick, although if you really *were* a priest, you'd know there was only one true Silver King."

Seth gave the popinjay an even harder look. He sounded deadly serious, even a little menacing; but the half-gods were stories, long gone if they were ever even real. They belonged to an age of myth, and Seth would have laughed in his face, except...

Except for Cleaver. Except for the skeletons he'd found in Varr.

"Are you saying there's another wraith? Here in Deephaven?"

"I'm saying there *was* one, once. Whether it's still here... That's what you're going to help me find out," said the popinjay. Then he cocked his head. "*Another* wraith?"

Seth slipped a hand into a pocket, trying to be subtle about it. *Here we go.* He fingered the slips of paper with their sigils. With his other hand, he gestured at the gloom-laden space around them. "There's nothing here, is there?" He'd expected something more... well, at least *some*thing. "There's nothing to see at all."

The popinjay shrugged. "I told you that before we left, but you *did* insist we come."

No, I didn't.

The popinjay looked at his feet. "Not *quite* nothing, though."
He snapped his fingers. The circle of stone began to glow, a warm
white-gold light like sunlight that resolved into an intricate
set of sigils, marked into the stone. "The priests found this, of
course. They put up wardings. They're keeping something at
bay. Something Kuy trapped in there." Without ever taking his
eyes off Seth, the popinjay crouched and scratched a symbol
of his own into the stone, apparently with a fingernail. The
wardings flared. The popinjay bared his teeth.

"What the *fuck*?" Seth took a step back.

"That's why you came here, isn't it? With your questions?
To finish what Kuy started?" The popinjay held up a hand.
The lantern flickered as the popinjay's fingers turned into long
curved knives of bone. Seth took another step back. He gave a
lot of thought to running away.

"What *are* you?"

"No one to be trifled with. We both know what *you* are."

Seth shivered. He could almost feel himself shrinking. *Shit.*
"We do, do we? And what's that?"

"I know someone touched by That Which Came Before
when I see one."

"Touched by *what*?"

"The sigils you warlocks so admire. Which brings us to the
favour you agreed you would do for me in return for showing
you this place. If it's still here, my guess is the wraith won't be
able to resist one of Saffran Kuy's apprentices, at which point
I will trap it inside you." The popinjay glared. "Now, take your
hand out of your pocket."

Fuck! FUCK! Seth took his hand out of his pocket. "Look...
I don't know what you think, but I'm just a priest who found
something he wasn't meant to. I got given some papers by a
sword-monk who told me to find out what they were." Might
as well tell the truth, as far as it went. "I didn't know they were
fucking *sigils*, and I'm only here because the same sword-monk

told me about a warlock who used to live in Deephaven. I was looking for some answers, that's all." It hit him then, what he should have seen right from the start. "Fuck! You're *him*, aren't you! *You're* the fucking warlock!"

The popinjay blinked. "Don't be absurd."

He seemed genuinely taken aback. Seth swallowed hard. "Look, there's something going on. The papers came from…" But he couldn't launch into all that, could he? How Fings had found them while stealing the late Emperor's crown? "They came from the Emperor, alright? The dead one. That's all I know."

The popinjay lowered his hand. His fingers turned back into fingers. "A sword-monk gave them to you. You really expect me to believe *that*?"

"Yes!"

That earned him a snort. "Let's find out, shall we?" He grabbed Seth, quick as a snake and strong as an ox, *terrifyingly* strong, too strong to be human. Before Seth could even think about what was happening to him, the popinjay had pressed Seth's hand against the circle of stone. The wards flared again, bright and blinding. Seth whimpered.

After a second or so, when nothing else happened, the popinjay let him go. He looked a bit surprised. "What sword-monk?"

"What the fuck was *that* about?" Seth backed away.

"A little test, is all."

"A *little test*?"

The popinjay's expression was… sheepish? He shrugged. "Had you been one of Kuy's, the wards would have burned your hand to cinders. But apparently, you're not. We can stay friends." He sounded almost apologetic. "What sword-monk?"

"You were trying to *kill* me?" If he'd had any chance of finding the stairway back into the warehouse on his own, Seth would have turned and run. As it was, the popinjay had the only light, and Seth was reasonably sure that turning and running would only mean he tripped over and smashed into a wall, or something equally stupid.

"Good grief, no! Maim you and then use your body to trap the wraith, if it's here, and ask it some questions... yes, but only if you were the one Kuy chose to finish his work of releasing That Which Came Before from its prison. Couldn't be having *that*. If you were his... Well, anyone setting out to rewrite the whole of creation itself can expect a fairly severe critical response, don't you think? But it seems you're not." If anything, the popinjay seemed disappointed.

"*Rewrite creation*?" Seth stared at the popinjay, aghast.

"What else would you call it, trying to rearrange the celestial hierarchy? I'm not saying he ever *got* anywhere. Now. *What* sword monk?"

"She wasn't using her given name when I met her. But I think it's Shirish."

The popinjay blinked in surprise. "The monk who stabbed–"

"Yes!"

"You're really *not* Kuy's apprentice, are you."

"I'm not *anyone's* fucking apprentice." *And he's not the warlock, either. Fuck!* "Frankly, I wish I was, because then maybe I'd have someone who could tell me what *fuck* is going on!"

The popinjay pursed his lips. He took another long look at the circle of stone with its wardings. Then he clapped his hands, as if the whole business of maybe burning people's hands to cinders and turning them into vessels for dead spirits of half-gods was all behind them and could happily be forgotten. "We should probably leave."

Oh no you fucking don't. Not after that! Being cooped up in a dead warlock's cellar beside a pool of foetid water with a psychopathic Taiytakei sorcerer who could apparently turn his fingers into knives and already had a vague go at murdering him definitely *wasn't* how he'd seen himself spending his night. On the other hand... "You say priests from the temple cleared the place?"

"Years ago. What they didn't burn on the spot, they carried away."

"What did they do with it?"

"No idea." The popinjay snorted. "Why don't you ask a priest?"

Yes, well, he *could* do that, but he wasn't at all sure it would end well. Still, tomorrow's problems could wait until tomorrow; right now, he had to live through the night. There was also a conversation to be had about wraiths and warlocks and what the popinjay knew about them, along with the whole 'rewrite creation' business, which frankly sounded a bit alarming, and also how he could turn his hands into murder-weapons. But if they were going to have *that* talk, Seth preferred to do it outside, where he could at least try to run away if it came to it.

The popinjay followed him back through the House of Cats and Gulls, telling him which way to go but always hanging a few paces behind, as though he expected Seth to try and stab him if he got the chance. A bit of stabbing *did* seem a sound idea, but Seth reckoned he wouldn't like the way it went if he tried. Mostly, he was worried the popinjay was thinking the same, so getting back to the open air of the docks was like a weight lifting off him, even if it stank of dead fish. Once outside, he made sure to keep a good distance between him and the popinjay, watching the popinjay snuff his half-burned candle and toss it aside. "Tell me about the warlock and the wraith."

The popinjay seemed to consider this, although possibly what he was considering was whether to murder Seth and dump his body in the river.

After a few seconds, he shrugged. "Why?"

"Because the Path of the Sun are hiding something. It has to do with sigils. They expelled me when I found out, and I want to know why." It all sounded a bit pathetic, out in the open like that, but it was the raw truth.

The popinjay nodded. "Your Gods were not the first. Your

priests do not like to acknowledge this, but it is true. The Gods you worship imprisoned That Which Came Before. In the last breaths of the Shining Age, the Silver King found a way to tap its power and tried to turn it to his own ends. He failed, shattered the world, created the Stormdark and it almost escaped. Both were snared by the Hungry Goddess. The half-gods who defeated the Silver King ascended to Father Moon, while those who'd followed as his acolytes were stripped of most of their power and left to wander like ghosts. What you call wraiths. That Which Came Before remains trapped, but the Splintering left that prison weak. Every sigil is a means to reach through and draw out a little of whatever lies within. Enough of that and perhaps the prison will fail?" He shrugged. "If you were one of Kuy's, you'd already know all this, since he and his ilk seem to have made that their goal. That's what your priests try to hide. Or a part, at least. A dangerous deception, but there you have it." He smiled. "*My* people have known forever, of course, but we keep it to ourselves. How to cross the Stormdark is our great secret, after all. You *are* marked, priest. If I can sense it, a wraith certainly can. If there *is* one in Deephaven, it *will* seek you out." He turned towards the pier and his boat. "My advice? Leave before it's too late."

"Too late? Too late for what?"

The popinjay didn't answer, just kept walking away. As he reached the pier, he stopped and turned. "Kuy's wraith was strong. It had dealings with more than mere warlocks. When Khrozus the Butcher took Varr, when the rivers froze, ask yourself who did that. Then ask why."

"Too late for *what*?"

The popinjay was done talking, it seemed. Seth watched him climb into his boat, wondering vaguely what business the man could possibly have on the river at the dead of night and deciding he probably didn't want to know. After the boat disappeared into the gloom, he walked for a bit, then sat at the end of another pier, trying to make sense of what the popinjay had told him.

*There was a warlock in Deephaven once, a man who could speak
with the dead. My mistress drove him away.* That's what Myla
had told him back in Varr. The same mistress who was still
here, from what Fings and Orien had said. Perhaps all he had
to do was find this sword-monk and ask, and then tell her
everything else, and maybe what the popinjay had said too. If
he could find some way to say it all that didn't end up with a
pair of swords stuck through him.

He fingered the sigils in his pockets. There *were* ways, if he
could take her by surprise...

No. No more of that. Once was enough. Anyway, his sigils
hadn't worked on the monks in Varr, so why would it be
different here? He'd have to find another way.

Myla?

But Myla was on a slave barge.

The mist coming off the river was rising. Thickening. He got
to his feet. It was a long walk across the Peak to the sea-docks
and Orien's Guildhouse.

Stay.

What?

You heard. The one-eyed god with the ruined face. Not a
vision this time, only a presence.

Enjoy all that, did you?

The sigil in the water. You missed something.

Seth thought about this.

"Fuck off," he said.

Although... Now he thought about it, the sigil in the water
had been somehow familiar. He hadn't really taken it in at the
time, what with the whole business of the Taiytakei popinjay
growing claws and vaguely trying to use him to trap a dead
half-god.

It wasn't as if the House of Cats and Gulls was going to be
more terrifying a second time round. Obviously, he'd be alone
this time but... well, that was starting to seem like the best
way to be.

I'm an idiot. He was already searching the cobbles for the popinjay's discarded candle. He lit it and went back inside. Turned out the warehouse wasn't as big as it had seemed, second time around, the space underneath not quite as cavernous. He found the circle of stone and peered over with his candle.

There it was. A sigil, reflecting back at him off the surface of the water, and yes, he *had* seen it before, on the blank sigil-ringed archways of the catacombs under Varr. He had no idea what it meant, seeing it again here, but the more he thought, the more certain he became. Every single archway. The popinjay was wrong, though. The sigil was already complete.

Which was… good, right? He'd learned something. Not that he had the first idea what to do with it.

The wardings flared briefly as he touched them. He felt a pain, but only a slight one. He pulled back and the wards faded. He was left with the vague sense of a presence, somewhere down the well.

Bollocks to this. He picked up a stone and dropped it in the water, watched it splash, watched the sigil vanish in the ripples, and waited to see whether it would come back.

When it didn't, he pursed his lips.

It's quite possible you just did something really stupid. I mean, really *fucking stupid.*

The sense of a presence in the well seemed to be growing stronger. It was probably just his imagination, right?

Riiiight.

Maybe best not to wait and find out, eh?

He left. It was just a well, right? Stuff had to fall in it all the time. And surely, if anything bad had been in there, the priests would have done more than a few wardings.

Outside, he walked to the end of the pier. Stopped and had a look along the river.

Nothing but mist.

Back at the derelict warehouse. Nothing but a lot of feral cats, all watching him.

A *lot* of feral cats.

He almost ran as far as the Godsway, then started up the wide road to the Peak, mostly because he didn't know his way around Deephaven and didn't want to get lost trying to cross the city in the middle of the night. With Myla gone, he'd have to find some friendly priest who could help him make sense of it all, or who could at least make the one-eyed god piss off and leave him alone. Could priests do that? He really ought to know.

He stopped.

Across the water, seven great ships loomed out of the mist like the ghosts of fallen clouds. Like monstrous white birds, with huge prows for heads and great curving sides that might be wings. They were graceful, elegant and unreal, and he'd never seen anything like them. They slid past the city in ethereal silence, distant shapes in the water, heading up the river until they vanished into the night.

I told you something was coming.

And then the one-eyed god was gone.

30

SHiPS iN THE niGHT

The trees were close and it was dark. The rain was cold and getting through her clothes. Fings and Lucius stood paralysed. The sell-sword from the *Captain's Rest* fixed his eyes on Myla and jerked his head at the cart.

"*You're* going back to Deephaven. You even look at me wrong, I put a bolt through your brother."

"But if I come with you, you'll let him go? How stupid do you think I am? You have one chance, here and now. Walk away."

Lucius held his head in his hands. He was shaking.

"Well?"

The soldiers didn't show any sign of walking away. They could probably see she wasn't armed.

"Fine." Myla raised her hands in surrender; as she did, the sell-sword from the *Captain's Rest* squinted and stared along the road back towards the fort.

"What the...?"

Heading towards them, came the outline of a man wreathed in flames.

Orien?

Myla sprang, knocking Fings to the ground, pushing Lucius aside, and leaping for the cart. She shouldered into the sell-sword before he could turn his crossbow on her; it fired into the air. He dropped it, fumbling for a blade. Behind her, she heard the twang as another crossbow fired, but there was no burning lance of pain, no shriek or scream from Fings or Lucius. She dropped to her haunches, wrapped her arms around the man's legs, hefted him over her shoulder out of the cart, fell with him, twisted in the air so she landed on him, felt him grunt, snatched the knife off his belt, and whirled to face the others.

One was frantically trying to reload his crossbow. The other was about to shoot Lucius. Myla threw the knife, hitting the second soldier in the face, gouging a chunk out of him. He screamed and clutched himself. The crossbow fired as it hit the ground, the bolt zinging off into the trees.

Only three? Do you Hawats never learn? She could deal with three.

The soldier she'd tossed out of the cart was groaning, trying to tug a hatchet from his belt. Myla kicked him in the elbow, grabbed his wrist, pulled hard and twisted, dislocating his shoulder, kicked him again, in the head this time, and helped herself to the hatchet. Lucius was on the last sell-sword, the two of them sprawling to the ground together. Orien was running, his wreath of flames wavering and dying. Myla ran to Lucius, hitting the man grappling him twice in the head with the blunt of the hatchet. The sell-sword dropped. Stunned or dead, she didn't know.

"Hold him! Orien! Help Lucius!" The sell-sword with the maimed face was trying to run. She chased him down, jumped on his back and threw them both to the dirt, sliding the haft of her hatchet around his neck as they fell and throttling him. By the time his struggles died, Lucius had the sell-sword from the *Captain's Rest* pinned against the side of the cart with the blade of his own knife pressed to his throat.

"How much is he paying you?" Lucius hissed.

The soldier spat.

"It doesn't matter," said Myla. "Let him go."

Lucius shook his head. "So he can go running to the fort shouting about an escaped slave? I don't think so."

"Then tie him up!"

"With what?"

"I..." She stopped, because the sell-sword's face had changed. Hostility and defiance were draining out of him, leaving a fear that spread to terror. When Myla looked back, she saw why. Orien had reached the sell-sword she'd choked and was crouching over him, wreathed in fire again. He gripped the man's head in his flaming hands and held him tight. The sell-sword screamed as he caught alight.

"Orien! Stop!"

The screaming stopped. The flames flickered and died.

"Why did you do that?" Myla hissed. "Why?"

Orien ignored her. He went to the sell-sword Myla had clubbed, toe-poked him a couple of times, then scooped up the man's knife.

"Orien!"

The knife came down. Once, twice.

The sell-sword from the *Captain's Rest* stopped struggling, eyes wide. "The Hawats! It's the Hawats! They offered an emperor for each of you!"

Myla planted herself in Orien's way as he approached, a dark smear on his hand and carrying naked steel.

"We know that!" she heard Lucius hiss. "Tell me something else!"

Orien stopped in front of her. His face was murder. "These men saw me. This *can't* come back on my mistress."

Myla stamped her foot, pointing to the bodies in the road. "You think Sarwatta won't work it out when one of his men shows up charred to the fucking bone? Not exactly a sword-monk trick, that!" Behind her, the sell-sword was gasping something to Lucius. She couldn't make out the words.

"We put the bodies in the cart and dump them in the river," said Orien. "No one will ever know."

Myla shoved him. "The fight is done. I won't be a part of murder."

"You don't have to be."

From behind her, she heard a strangled gurgle. When she turned, the sell-sword from the *Captain's Rest* slid down the side of the cart and fell to the ground, his throat gouged open.

"You! *You!*"

Lucius bowed his head. "They would have taken us both to our deaths and thought nothing of it."

"And that makes it right? You're *better* than them!"

Lucius's eyes flashed in fury. "They took Soraya. Sarwatta has her." He turned away and set to helping Orien load the bodies onto the back of the cart.

Myla stood still, stunned. "Soraya? He's taken her *already?*"

She looked around for Fings, but Fings had obviously had the sense to run into the trees when the fighting started. She wouldn't begrudge him that.

"You're my sister," Lucius said, when they were finished. "It had to be done."

He offered his hand. Myla flinched away. "Soraya? You're sure?"

Lucius nodded and turned to Orien. "We're going to Bedlam's Crossing. The thief and I will take a boat back to Deephaven and find you there. Myla, you head for Varr."

"I will not."

"Myla–"

"No!" Myla shook him. "Not if Sarwatta has Soraya!" He'd get Lucius too, and discover what had happened here. And then?

She didn't want to know. Didn't want to think about it.

"You shouldn't have killed them," she said again, but left it at that when Lucius didn't reply. It was done, and he was her brother. "Where's Fings?" she asked instead.

"Laying a false trail for when they find you gone. He'll meet us at Bedlam's Crossing."

"But we're not going to Bedlam's Crossing."

"Yes," said Lucius, "we are."

"Well then goodbye and good luck." Myla turned to walk away.

"Myla!"

She spun back to face him. "You're not going to save Soraya with clever words and cunning deals, with legal arguments and carefully curated influence." She gestured around her. "We are swords-drawn, brother. This is my world now. Not yours."

She watched as Lucius and Orien exchanged a look. They both clearly wanted to disagree; but equally clearly, she was right.

They turned back for Deephaven, then, past the fort where everything was quiet, until it was out of sight behind them. A few miles later, Orien guided the cart off the road. The rain had stopped but they were all damp, shivering and cold. Orien and Lucius took a body each, hauling them into the woods. Myla reluctantly took the third. Not that they expected it of her, but the alternative was to leave an abandoned cart with a dead body in the back; and yes, there wasn't much chance of anyone coming past, but it was good few hundred yards through the trees to the river and why take the risk? She hung back, avoiding Orien. He'd come to the temple every day while she'd been held there. He'd brought Fings from Varr to rescue her. He was here, no matter the trouble it might cause him. He'd killed a man in cold blood. Two, in fact, and he'd done it all because of her.

Lucius stopped. Ahead, the whole river seemed to glow with fog. Out in the middle, seven white ships drifted among the swirls. A shiver of dread danced up her spine. Born and raised in Deephaven, Myla had seen every ship ever built come and go, from the clumsy flat-bottomed barges of the empire to the knife-like Black Ships of the Taiytakei that sailed between worlds, but she'd never seen ships like these. They were as white as ghosts, curls of icy mist swirling around them, gliding across the water like giant swans. She felt her eyes held, locked in hypnotic fascination. They were beautiful.

Through the mists, she thought she saw men jumping over the sides and running across the river. Which couldn't be right... She rubbed her eyes and they were gone. Except, as she stared, she kept thinking that maybe she saw them again. Maybe...

She walked on, slow and entranced, until she stood next to Orien.

"Whose are they?" he asked.

"I don't know."

"They reek of sorcery."

Orien let the dead soldier he was carrying drop into the underbrush. The fog from the river was rising, lapping at the trees, reaching out until it touched their feet and then then their knees, and then it was up to their waist, and Myla realised she could barely see Lucius at all; while on the river, all she saw were the prows and masts of the ships, rising from the curling whiteness. She felt eyes, watching her.

"Lucius! *Lucius!*"

He was labouring his way through the mist towards her.

"This isn't right."

"No sails," he said. "They have no sails. And no oars."

"I have to get back to Deephaven," said Orien. "Right now."

It was only when they reached the road that Myla remembered what else wasn't right. Fings; except he was probably well on his way up-river by now, on his way to Bedlam's Crossing.

31

THE KEEPERS OF SLAVES

Fings wasn't exactly surprised when it turned out Lucius had been caught, and he wasn't exactly surprised when a burning man suddenly appeared on the road either, since that was obviously Orien. He certainly wasn't surprised when Myla started a fight because that was who Myla was. Fings saw something dangerous, he did what any sensible person would do: ran the other way. Myla? *She* went straight at it.

Being a burglar and not a sword-monk, Fings rolled and lurched and scampered into the woods before anyone found the wits to shoot at him. He darted behind the cover of a nice big tree and watched. He wasn't much use in a fight, after all, and he'd seen Myla take on worse odds and come out the last one standing. After the first two went down, he had a moment of thinking maybe he should go and help while Lucius was grappling with the last; but by the time he decided that yes, maybe he should, Myla had already dealt with the problem, so he stayed where he was.

Which was fine until Orien started murdering people and Myla started shouting at him. Fings reckoned they both had a point. Of course, it *was* wrong to go around murdering people after you'd beaten them. But it was *also* wrong to be taking slaves and bribes and abducting people. As long as Myla was safe, and they all got away with all their bits still properly attached, he found it difficult to care about the rest.

What *wasn't* fine was the two of them yelling at each other in the middle of the night with three corpses strewn about, right next to a fort full of soldiers. *This* was why he didn't steal people.

He watched as Lucius and Orien loaded the bodies into the cart. He saw Myla look around and reckoned it was him she was looking for, which was nice. It was a bit *less* nice, mind, when they all drove off without bothering to find him and make sure he wasn't hurt or something; but then again, he *had* told Lucius all that bollocks about making a diversion, and he *could* have come out from where he was hiding and let them know he was alright; which he hadn't, because that would mean an argument with Myla about what he was about to do next, and he wasn't sure he fancied that, not with the mood she was in.

What he was about to do next, he reckoned, was go back to the fort and look for those ledgers that might tell him what had happened to Levvi.

He thought about that, watching Myla and Lucius and Orien on the cart as they vanished into the darkness. They'd tell him not to, which was why he hadn't asked. They'd say he might get caught or raise the alarm, or something equally stupid. Lucius would probably come up with a perfectly reasonable-sounding idea about how he could use his connections to get inside without any sneaking around at all. Thing with *that*, though, was that Lucius and Orien and even Myla didn't actually *care* about Levvi, and it would all take time, if it even happened at all; and sneaking around in the dark was about the only thing Fings did really well, apart from running away, and he had a feeling that something bad was coming, and so maybe it was best not to wait.

So he watched them go, and then turned back to the forest and made his way to the fort and the piers and the slave barge. He sat there for a good long while, because if he *did* get caught, it was only fair to make sure that the others had a good head start. It crossed his mind that he could raise the alarm about a slave gone missing and use the chaos to slip inside; but on the whole, Fings preferred to let the soldiers sleep. He didn't like chaos. Chaos was, well... chaotic.

He fished in his pocket for his feather and stuck it between his teeth, sucking on it. He fingered the charms around his neck to make sure they were all still there, and then the ones in his pockets. As an afterthought, he put on the chicken-foot he'd brought with him from Varr, black and shrivelled now, the one that was supposed to keep sorcery at bay, not that he'd need it, not in a place like this, but you never knew, right?

The gate from the fort facing the river was open but no one was going in or out at this time of night. Fings supposed they'd have a sentry, so brazenly walking in probably wasn't clever, not that it hadn't worked other times. Which left scaling the walls, and so that was what he did. Wasn't even difficult, since whoever had decided they wanted a fort had done a bit of a rush job, felling trees and banging them into the ground and lashing them together with ropes, not bothering to even strip the bark, leaving them so any fool could climb if they wanted. Presumably, there were supposed to be soldiers keeping watch at the top to make sure that didn't happen, but if that was the idea, someone had forgotten to tell them. Probably weren't expecting trouble. That was always the thing. People put up walls and fitted locks and thought that was enough.

At the top of the wall, he hopped onto a creaky wooden platform that ran along the inside, then hunkered down to have a good long look at what he was dealing with. Sure enough, he spotted a pair of soldiers leaning on their spears inside the river gate, propped up by a glowing brazier and looking like they were mostly asleep. Another soldier stood watch in a little tower in the far corner. Fings couldn't tell whether this one was awake, but he didn't have a fire to keep him warm like the ones by the gate, so he was probably cold and miserable and shivering, none of which made for a good watchman.

Looking out for boats on the river?

Yeah. Probably that.

At the bottom of the wall, arrayed against the base, was a row of wooden shacks: stables and barracks and stores and the like. Against the far wall, under the watchtower, was a two-storey stone building, which Fings reckoned was where he needed to be. This was Deephaven, after all, where the weather didn't seem to have the imagination for anything other than rain, rain and then maybe some more rain. The stone-built house had a nice, tiled roof to keep it dry, while the wooden huts didn't; and, as Seth liked to point out, books and damp didn't go well together. The house had a chimney, too, a steady wisp of smoke rising from it, which was probably no fun at all for the poor sod in the watchtower above.

Whoever was in charge, they'd be there too, keeping nice and dry and warm.

Right then.

There were no sentries on the walkway, so he made his way along until he was level with the roof of the stone house, then lowered himself down. He lay flat and inched his way to the edge and peered over, then eased sideways until he was level with a window. The window was shuttered but the shutters had warped from the constant damp. He climbed down, slipped the edge of a knife between them, lifted the latch, and gently pulled them open, the same trick he'd done for years in Varr, getting in and out of the temple on Spice Market Square when Seth had been a novice there.

Almost too easy.

The thought made him frown. Easy was bad. Easy meant a stupid mistake lurking nearby.

The air coming from the window was warm and smelled of sweat and wine. He heard a grunt, and that was when he realised the window was right over someone's bed, someone who was busy waking up.

Oh, crap!

He dropped, hanging from the window ledge by his fingertips, sucking hard on his feather as whoever it was swore and came to the shutters. They didn't bother to look out. Just closed them and slipped back the latch.

So. Not *this* window. *Now what?*

He peeked over his shoulder, trying to see the ground, but it was too dark to see what he'd land on if he let go. From where he was hanging, he couldn't climb back to the roof without making a noise. There was another window, further along the wall; but he didn't fancy his chances of swinging across and managing to reach it, never mind holding on.

Bollocks.

Nothing else for it. He muttered a prayer and let go. The ground hit him hard enough to leave him sprawled flat and winded. He lay still, taking his time, listening in case someone had heard while he worked out whether anything was broken. He tried his arms. They worked. So did his legs. He tried getting up. When that worked, too, he stooped and felt around until he found his feather, stuck it back in his mouth and sucked hard...

"Hello?"

Crap! One of the guards from the gate, coming with a burning torch to investigate the noise. Fings had a look about for a place to hide and he saw he'd missed a pile of stacked crates by less than the span of a hand.

Lucky.

He ducked behind the crates and fingered his charms. People thought luck was something that either happened or it didn't, but they were wrong. Luck was a thing you made.

The guard stopped almost exactly at the spot where Fings had landed. He held his torch high, peering into the darkness.

"Hello?"

Fings waited. The guard didn't seem interested in having a proper look. After a few long seconds, he shrugged and turned away, heading back to his post. Which was all very well, but

Fings knew he'd just used his luck for the night. Mostly, people shrugged off the first out-of-place noise. They rarely shrugged off a second, though. He waited for the guard to get back to his post, then waited a while longer.

Now what?

He liked windows. People tended not to watch them. But since he was down on the ground now, there was always the door. Which – some more luck – was out of sight from the sentries at the river gate and the soldier in the watchtower. When he tried it, it wasn't even locked.

He slipped through. Inside, everything was the sort of dark where you could barely see your own hand in front of your face. He could feel the space around him, open, not some narrow passage.

Best bet, Fings reckoned, was that whoever ran this place was a lazy sod who liked to sit around not doing much, and certainly didn't like going up and down stairs for no good reason. If this was where he worked, everything would be close to hand, ledgers and the like included. Fings felt his way around the edge of the room, slow and careful, because slow and careful was how a good burglar didn't get caught. He found steps going up, definitely *not* where he wanted to go. He found a stand with a set of what felt like heavy leather clothes hanging off it, and a pair of swords in scabbards. He found a cabinet, locked shut, easily picked but yielding only a few bottles and the smell of cheap wine. He found a desk. Inside the drawers were papers and a glass bottle of something, and a feather with a metal nib. A quill and ink? He stuffed the papers into his shirt. There were candles, too, and a fire steel and a tinderbox.

No books.

Behind the desk he found a door. He gave this a bit of a think, counting the steps he'd made around the room, and decided it wasn't another way out but must lead to a second room. When he tried the handle, it was locked.

Here we go...

He pulled a trio of crude clay figurines from his bag and set them carefully on the floor, three charmed figures to make sure no one disturbed him while he worked. That done, he set about the lock with his picks. It was a good lock, better than he'd expected, and it took several minutes to feel his way into it in the dark. But, like they always said in the *Pig*, no point locking away your valuables when Fings was around. It opened; he gathered his figurines, stashed them away, and slipped inside.

He wasn't sure what he'd found at first. There were no windows, and so no shutters he could open to let in a little starlight. He could smell spices, familiar scents from Varr's Spice Market where he'd grown up.

Why were there spices?

He felt his away around, shelf after shelf of sacks and boxes, sniffing each as he went. Some he recognised, some he didn't. Some didn't smell of anything much at all. A lot of the sacks smelled like old earth. One pile of boxes, stashed carefully high up in a corner, smelled like the Glass Market in Varr, specifically the part of the Glass Market that tended to explode now and then because that was where the alchemists went. He paused, wondering whether whatever was in these boxes might explode, too. There was nothing like a good bit of something exploding for getting everyone's attention and putting it where you weren't when you needed to make an escape.

No need. He'd slip out like he'd slipped in, unseen, no one any the wiser. First thing anyone would notice was when they looked for the ledgers he was about to steal. Assuming he could find them.

A bit more searching and he found a strongbox. Not big but heavy and, when he tried it, locked. Had to fight a bit to resist temptation there, but no, for once in his life he didn't need money. What he needed was to find out what had happened to Levvi.

A horn sounded, somewhere not far away, most likely from the soldier in the watchtower. Fings froze, almost panicked and ran, then realised that running was about the worst thing he could do. They hadn't sounded the alarm because of *him* because no one had the first idea he was here. Which meant it had to be something else.

Myla. They'd found she was missing. Had to be.

He took a deep breath. *Stay where you are. No one's going to come looking for her here.*

He crept to the door, got out his picks and locked it again. *Wait it out.*

He clenched and unclenched his fists. What he *ought* to do, he supposed, was go back to feeling his way through the shelves, looking for ledgers. But he couldn't. Couldn't bring himself to move or to do anything except listen. After a bit, he resigned himself to that.

Feet running down the stairs. A sliver of light from the crack under the door. Someone with a lantern.

"What is it?"

"Ships! On the river."

"Where the fuck else would they be?"

"Sir… I've never seen anything like it."

"Like *what*?"

"You need to see this."

The light faded. Fings heard a door open and then slam shut. Followed by shouts in the distance, *wake-up-get-up-get-out-here* shouts.

He stayed where he was. The shouts died away. For a minute or so, everything went quiet again. Then more shouts. Sharper. Fings, something of an expert on other people shouting, reckoned these were *what-the-fuck-is-that* shouts.

Not good.

"*Dead Men!*" He heard *that* shout clear as a bell.

"Close the gates!" And that.

They were under attack? By Dead Men?

Yes, that *was* how those shouts had sounded. Under his breath, Fings swore. This was luck taking the piss, this was.

Right, then. Two ways this could go. Either the soldiers saw off whoever this was, in which case they could be at it for hours and it would be daylight and he'd be stuck here, hoping no one happened to come by. Or else they didn't, in which case presumably whoever was out there was going to make a beeline for anything valuable, in which case Fings needed to be somewhere else before that happened.

Whoever he'd disturbed opening those shutters had since come down and gone outside. Maybe he could slip up the stairs, out that same window, and climb onto the roof. Then he could jump onto the walkway, hop over, climb down the walls and get out the same way he'd come in. Job done.

Yeah. Except the walkway was going to be crawling with soldiers, on account of that being the whole point of it at times like this.

He thought about this and discovered he didn't have any better ideas. He picked the lock a third time, prayed the room outside was empty, got ready to run in case it wasn't, and threw open the door.

The room was empty. The shouts from outside shifted into *stand-your-ground* shouts. The calm before the storm. A parlay?

Ledgers!

Fings grabbed the candle from the desk, lit it with the fire steel and tinderbox, and dived back into the storeroom. Now, with a bit of light, he saw what he'd missed: in the corner by the door was a small stack of books. He grabbed them and stuffed them in his bag; then, because they were there, he pulled down one of the crates that smelled of sulphur and opened it. Inside were six glass globes, stuffed with black powder. He'd been around the Glass Market enough to know an explody thing when he saw one, so he stuffed those into his bag too.

The tone of the shouts outside had shifted again. More *what-*

the-fuck-is-that shouting, with a *Kelm-preserve-us-we're-going-to-die* edge of hysteria.

Not good.

He took the stairs three steps at a time, found a window and threw open the shutters. Outside, a few soldiers were clustered around the riverside gate, fixing a bar across it. The rest were on the walls or scrambling up ladders to get there, pulling on pieces of armour as they went. From where he was, Fings couldn't see what was outside the walls, but it was dark and the soldiers were all looking out at the river, so it would do.

Yeah. Not my problem.

He went to other side of the building and climbed out, feet scrabbling for purchase as he pulled himself to the roof. There were soldiers only yards away but they all had their backs to him, all looking out at the water, transfixed by whatever was there – some sort of big white ship, by the looks of it, and a lot of mist and fog.

Still not my problem.

With his heart in his mouth, he pulled himself onto the walkway behind them and crept away...

Almost crept away.

"Hey!"

Fings turned, ready to come up with some ridiculous excuse for being there, but the soldier who'd seen him didn't get any further because that was when the gate to the river exploded, throwing men and splintered wood right across the fort, and that was quite enough. Fings reeled and gawped, then turned and ran.

Before he went over the wall, he glanced over his shoulder. He knew, even as he did, that he was going to regret it. What he saw was Dead Men pouring through the ruined gate. He saw the river, buried in mist. He saw more ships like giant swans out on the water. And all of that was bad, but for an instant he saw something far worse: he saw a man in silver, striding among the Dead Men as though they were his minions, hands outstretched, one casting beams of moonlight that turned men to dust, the other casting a darkness blacker than night.

He knew exactly what *that* was: a faerie-king.

He climbed, he jumped, he ran. He didn't stop.

INTERLUDE: TASAHRE

Tasahre should have been asleep when Sunbright Shwen knocked on her door. Should have been, but sleep had been elusive these last few days. Shwen found her sitting on her cot, a candle lit, reading the same letter she'd read over and over these last few nights. It had arrived almost eight years ago, the letter telling her that the warlock Saffran Kuy was dead, killed in another world in some trivial battle for a tiny kingdom no one really cared about. Killed by the mercenary commander known as the Bloody Judge.

She touched her scar. The Bloody Judge had had another name, once.

"Sword-mistress. I'm sorry to disturb you." Shwen bowed.

Tasahre put the letter down and poured cups of water for them both. "Shwen..." She hesitated. "There's a new warlock in Deephaven. He's been to the House of Cats and Gulls. The wards remain but... The sigil Kuy put there has gone. I don't know what that means."

"If the Dead Men come, we'll put them down."

"Take some monks."

Shwen nodded. "Will you join us?"

"No. If the wraith is loose, it will strike here."

Shwen stopped at the door on his way out. "You asked to be told at once of any sightings of White Ships," he said. "Seven have been seen on the river. Heading inland."

It had begun in Deephaven decades ago. Perhaps even before the civil war. She wasn't sure. It *should* have ended sixteen years ago but it hadn't.

One hesitation. One mistake.

"Thank you, Sunbright," she said.

PART FOUR
Fiпgs

Freedom is seeing the chance to run away and bloody well taking it.
— Fings

32

A COΠFLİCT OF
İΠTEREStS

The morning rain was lashing down when they reached
Deephaven. Myla didn't speak to Orien as he left to go back to his
Guildhouse. Didn't speak to Lucius, either. If Lucius hadn't been
in such a hurry to open the man's throat, the sell-sword from the
Captain's Rest might have been able to tell her more about Soraya.

It *was* the truth, though. She felt it in her bones, even before
they reached Soraya's house, its door ajar.

"He did it," she said, as much to the air and sky as to Lucius,
who could plainly see for himself. And then she couldn't wait
any longer. She jumped off the cart and ran, pushing her way
inside. "Soraya? *Soraya!*"

But Soraya was gone.

She searched the house anyway, and then went back out into
the rain. She'd been ready to die. She'd been ready to let Sarwatta
do whatever he wanted, and he'd taken Soraya anyway, just like
he'd said he would. And yes, her head had understood that he'd
do this, but she hadn't felt it in her heart, not until now.

"He took her," she said again.

He must have done it right after the trial. Probably before
Myla had even left the city.

Bastard!

Lucius stood mute. There was no one in the house to ask how it had been done. She hadn't found any blood, at least.

"I was in chains. I couldn't stop him."

"I know."

They tracked down one of Soraya's servants. Sarwatta had come on the night before Myla's trial, not after. He'd offered promises: Soraya would be his wife. The child she carried – *his* child – would become the Hawat heir. After the birth, Soraya would cross the sea to Anvor, to Caladin or Brons or some such place, to another world and a comfortable life as an exile. When Soraya turned him down, he'd taken her at the point of a sword instead.

Myla listened in numb silence. She knew what Sarwatta had *really* been thinking: treat Soraya like a princess until the baby was born, and then torture and murder her while Myla looked on, begging for him to stop.

Soraya had said no. She'd seen through him, then? Finally?

"I'm going to get her back," she said. "And then I'm going to kill him." How long before he realised she was free? The end of the day? He'd be waiting for word from his sell-swords by now, getting impatient. He wouldn't hurt Soraya until the child was born, though. How long did she have? Days? A week or two?

Less time, perhaps, before he took her out of the city and hid her where Myla would never find her.

"Once I have her, we have to run," she said, when she and Lucius were alone again. "Send your boats up-river. Sell whatever you have warehoused for whatever you can get. Find a ship sailing south. You won't have much time before he comes after you, so you need to do it all today. I'll see to Soraya. We'll go to Torpreah. I don't care *how* much religion mother and father have found, they'll take her in, and the child too."

She was asking him to abandon everything they'd built and everything he knew. The troublesome little sister, the one who stood to inherit nothing and so had nothing to lose, telling him that he had to throw it all away. And why? Because of what she'd done. *Her* fault, all of it.

No. She'd accepted her guilt and her punishment for what she'd done. Extending that punishment to her family was Sarwatta's choice, not hers. She had to keep telling herself that until it stuck.

"What are you going to do?" he asked.

"He'll know I'm free soon. He needs to understand that if he hurts her, I'll hunt him to the ends of the empire. Further, if I have to."

Lucius had always looked out for her. And for Soraya too, not that she'd needed it. She took his hands in hers.

"We'll build it back, I promise. In Torpreah, or in Helhex, or somewhere across the sea. I know I brought this on us. I did what I thought was right but..." she looked away.

"I know," he said at last. "And yes, we will."

He hugged her, and she took it because she needed it, needed someone to tell her it was all going to be fine in the end, even when it wasn't. Someone to tell her it wasn't all her fault, even when it was...

No! He deserved it!

"We need to find a place," Lucius said. "Somewhere safe for a few days." He took her to a tavern at the seedy end of the river-docks, a place close to the River Gate, not far from the House of Cats and Gulls and where no one would ask questions. They hid their faces behind scented masks, same as half the workers on the docks, and used names from their favourite stories. He told her to rest, but there was no chance of sleep, not now.

Sword-monks don't hide.

Where would Sarwatta keep her?

Sword-monks don't hide.

She thought about where they might go, the three of them together to start a new life in the South.

Sword-monks. Don't. Hide.

What, then? Storm House Hawat right here and now? Single-handed and in broad daylight when she didn't even have her swords? If Tasahre had been with her, she'd probably observe that a good sword-monk understood the virtue of patience, at which point Myla would have observed right back that she *wasn't* a good sword-monk, and that smug-arsed comments were likely to get you a punch in the mouth, even if you were a sword-mistress.

But still... Maybe this time she had a point?

Eventually, Lucius returned, Orien with him, about as inconspicuous as a big red flag even if Orien wasn't wearing his orange robe. Myla bit her tongue. She still wanted to shout at him for killing those men, and at the same time to kiss him for being there in the first place; but as it turned out, Orien had plenty to say of his own, how she needed to leave Deephaven right away, that it didn't matter whether they didn't have money or whatever else they might throw in his way as an excuse because this wasn't about Sarwatta, this was something else, something much worse, a feeling in the air and the white ships on the river and some impending catastrophe. Then he told her he'd find a boat to take her up the river if he had to, or a ship to take her down the coast, as if he somehow knew this city and its ships and barges better than she did.

Eventually, he stopped. Maybe because of the way Myla was looking at him like he wasn't there.

"No," she said, when he gave her space to speak.

"Myla, this isn't–"

"He has my sister."

She watched as he wrestled with something. His expression confused her at first, until she understood: he was scared.

"Myla–"

"Orien, no. I can't leave without her. Not even the end of the world will change that." Should she ask him for help? It couldn't hurt, could it? A mage could make a difference... But no. It wasn't fair, and, bluntly, mage or not, Orien had never been much use in a fight. "I promise this won't come back on you, if that's what you're worried about."

"Bit late for that." Fire flashed in Orien's eyes. He tried to smile but couldn't seem to find much enthusiasm for it. "Wherever you go..." He shook his head. "I wish this wasn't happening. I'm going to miss you, Shirish."

"You can't escape a sword-monk," she said. "And I'm not gone yet." She still wanted to shout at him, but maybe now wasn't the time.

"You can't escape a mage, either." He took a deep breath and huffed it out and shuffled his feet.

"I'll... see about those... things we talked about." Lucius slipped away.

"Get away, Myla," said Orien once Lucius was gone. "Do whatever you must, but get out of Deephaven as fast as you can. Those ships we saw... they carried nothing good."

"As soon as I have my sister."

He touched her cheek. Myla took his hand in her own and held it there.

"Come with us," she said.

"I can't."

"Yes, you can."

"No, Myla."

She let go and took a step back. "Why? Because you'll lose your place in your precious Guild? Because your precious Mistress won't love you anymore?" As soon as the words were out, she regretted them. "I'm sorry. That wasn't fair."

"Well." He smiled, a little more real this time. "There *is* that."

They stood and looked at each other, neither seeming to know quite what to do. Then Orien took a step back.

"Your duty is to your family. I understand. Mine is to the Empire. I wish I had your courage. I wish..." He shook his head. "You know what? Most of me *does* want to come with you. But I have to stay, because I think some terrible storm is about to break upon us, and because some stubborn pig-headed sword-monk once taught me that when you see danger, you face it, you draw your swords, and you dare it to do its worst. Beyond stupid when you look at it, yet here we are."

He turned away.

"Orien!"

He stopped and turned back, and she opened her arms to him and pulled him in, holding him tight.

"I can't help you with your sister," he whispered. "I wish I could, but I can't."

"You don't need to," she soothed. "But you hear this, mage. You stay safe. You do whatever it takes. Because I *am* stubborn and pig-headed, and if something happens to you, I might have to go on a murderous sword-monk rampage of revenge, and I don't think any of us wants that." She laughed, because not to laugh would mean to cry.

"Well," he said. "That's me told. And… Yes. Yes, you'd best do the same. I'm not sure a furious fire-mage would be much better."

"That depends on whether you've learned to set fire to anything more than yourself."

They were both laughing now, damp-eyed, unwilling to let go, yet both knowing they must. She kissed him, long and slow and lingering and full of promise for the next time. And then she pushed him away.

"I still want to shout at you for what you did out there," she said.

"It wasn't because they'd seen me." He shook his head. He didn't say the rest, but she knew. He'd done it because they'd tried to hurt her.

"I'll find you again before I leave," she said. "I promise."

"Thank you," he said.

"For what?"

"For being you."

She turned away. Hadn't Arjay said much the same, back in Varr that time?

No matter. She was Soraya's sister now, nothing more and nothing less, all and everything.

33

THE LEDGER

It was a long way back to Deephaven on foot. Miles and miles
and hours and hours of walking, all of which wouldn't have
been so bad if Fings hadn't spent most of it almost shitting his
pants in terror at what he'd seen. Dead Men swarming out of
the river was bad enough. But the rest? Those things on the
water, were they even ships? The ghosts of ships? Something
else? Since when did ships look like giant birds? Weren't they
supposed to have masts and sails and stuff…? And as for the
other thing…

A faerie king!

The memory was burned into him. A brilliant silver light
flickering through the night, turning to ash whatever it
touched. He saw it over and over, whenever he closed his eyes:
Silver over dead white skin.

Shouldn't have looked back.

But he *had* looked back, and he *had* seen the faerie king
dressed in silver, and the faerie king had seen *him*, too, and so
he'd run until he couldn't, and then he'd hidden, shaking like
a leaf, wondering how long before a horde of Dead Men came
after him. After a bit of that, he'd discovered he *could* run some
more after all, and so he had, and it wasn't until dawn that he
let himself stop.

He was exhausted.

Dawn and daylight. Daylight was the scourge of Dead Men. The light of the Sun took their souls to where they belonged, to the great forge in the sky, melting them down and hammering them out anew. Or at least, that was how Seth put it. Something like that. Except water was supposed to put a Dead Man to rest every bit as well as sunlight, thanks. Burn a body or set it out under the daylight sky to send its soul to the Constant Sun, the Lord of Light and Fire. Sink a corpse in water to give its spirit to Fickle Lord Moon, the Ever-Changing One. Leave your dead at night in the open under a wind and a starlit sky and the Infinite Mistress of Many Faces would come, the Lady of Stars. Bury the wicked in the ground, the irredeemable, the heretics and the iconoclasts, destroy their souls and feed their essence to the Angry One, the Hungry Goddess of the Earth. But *these* Dead Men had walked *out* of the river. Fickle Lord Moon hadn't taken them. Did that mean the Sun wouldn't have them either? Did that mean Dead Men who could walk about in daylight and not worry about it?

Don't think about it.

The early morning sun was warm, the air crisp but with a tinge of spring to it. For once, it didn't rain, which was nice...

Don't *think about it!*

And then the clouds came, and it *did* rain, hard, and soon he was cold and wet on top of scared and miserable.

He couldn't help himself sometimes, glancing back at the road behind him. Partly in case someone came with a wagon or a cart, someone willing to let him sit on the back in exchange for a few bits; but mostly in case he saw a cloud of Dead Men cresting the horizon, telling him it was time to run again.

Neither came. No one at all coming down the road behind him: no wagons, no carts and no riders either. People going the other way, sure, heading out the city, but heading in? He wasn't sure what to make of that. It was early spring. It rained all the time. Every track and trail that wasn't the Imperial

Highway was a mud-slick. On top of all that, a city riddled with plague? Stood to reason people would avoid the place.

But no one at *all*?

Deephaven, when he got there, didn't seem to think anything was amiss. The River Gates were open, the sentries bored and not paying attention, sheltering from the pissing rain, the same hustle and bustle along the river-docks, everyone with their masks and their charms and waving their incense burners, the same emptiness outside the House of Cats and Gulls past the Godsway, all as if nothing had changed. Everyone was talking about the white ships, of course, but the white ships had passed far out across the river, a curiosity and nothing more.

He had to tell someone. That was the thing. Tell someone what he'd seen. Get it out of him and put it on the shoulders of someone who could *do* something. Myla, maybe, except he had no idea where to look for her.

Seth, then? But what was *Seth*, of all people going to do about a bunch of Dead Men and ghost ships and the king of the faeries? Knowing Seth, he'd get all curious and want to go and look for himself, dragging Fings with him to show him the way, and Fings was *not* going back out there, thanks, not after what he'd seen.

So. Not Seth?

There *were* a couple of other choices. Better ones, if he was honest, even if he didn't much like them. Best of all was probably that sword-monk, Myla's teacher... but someone like him, showing up at the great temple of Deephaven, demanding to see a sword-monk? He could already see the Sunguard laughing at him. Probably wouldn't even let him through the gates.

Orien's mistress?

Bollocks to that. Mages were the worst kind of luck. He could manage Orien, just about, but that apocalyptic nightmare of unnatural happenings that he called a mistress? No. Besides, this was for priests and monks. So it *would* be Seth, because Seth could dress up in his stolen robes and get him into the temple, just like last time, and tell them all what Fings had seen using all those fancy priest words he knew. Yeah. That might work. Just had to make sure Seth didn't get any of those stupid ideas of his.

He crossed the city, eyes and ears wide for the first sign of anything out of place. All around him, the world was carrying on like nothing had happened. It made him want to jump onto the back of a cart in the middle of the street and shout at everyone, but what was he going to say? They'd laugh and jeer and throw things at him because who was he? Just some crazy foreigner in rags.

He reached Four Winds Square, trotted down the Avenue of Emperors, got lost in the sea-docks for a bit, and eventually made his way to Seth's room. There, he let it all pour out: getting Myla off the barge, the fight with the soldiers waiting to take her to Deephaven, sneaking into the fort looking for anything that might tell him what had happened to Levvi, and then the mist and the ships on the river, the horde of Dead Men storming the gate, the faerie king in his silver armour who'd been...

"Say that again." Seth was suddenly paying attention. "*Silver armour?*"

"Yeah. All shiny, almost like a mirror. Made weird, too. All plates and strips and funny angles that moved over each other. Bit like a beetle or something."

Seth, he noticed, had gone pale.

"What? What is it?"

"Did anyone else get away?"

"What? *I* don't know! Didn't stop to hang about, did I, what with people being turned into ash and Dead Men everywhere! Look, I don't know where Myla is but... We got to do something! We've got to tell people!"

"Like who?"

"Priests! People who can *do* something about a horde of Dead Men! Them monks at the temple! Like, maybe the one Myla knows. The one who was her teacher and stuff."

He mostly expected Seth to not like the idea of sword-monks after what had happened in Varr; but to his surprise, Seth was nodding, even if he wasn't looking happy about it. "Yes."

"Thing is… Well…They're hardly going to let the likes of me talk to some silver-thumbed priest, are they?"

"Since when has people not letting you into places ever actually stopped you?"

They looked at each other. Fings had to accept that Seth had a point.

Seth shook his head, chuckling for some reason. He glanced to the window, at the grey afternoon sky, tutted and hissed between his teeth. "Twilight Prayer," he said. "We go to the temple and find a priest and ask for–"

"I… Don't need to ask," said Fings, and then wished he hadn't. "I'll… I'll know the sword-monk when I see her. You know… From when we were following them around."

"Riiight." Seth was still nodding. "So… You don't know where Myla is?"

"What? Yeah. No, not yet."

"When you find out, tell me. I need to talk to her."

Flustered by the Dead Men and everything else, Fings had almost forgotten: he took the ledgers out of his bag and thrust them at Seth. "Got these. Don't know if they're the right things. It's what was there. I can… I can't read them."

Seth looked at the ledgers. "What are you even talking about?"

"Levvi." Fings pushed the books at him. "He was sent to the mines, right? Like Myla!" He nodded at the books. "Lucius said they keep records. You know? Of who gets sent where. Same place they took Myla. So… that's what they are. Them books of records. Ledgers. Whatever."

Seth was giving him an odd look. "So… You stole them. While all the rest of… while the place you were in was being swarmed by Dead Men and a…" he squinted at Fings, "a… faerie king?"

"Yeah. Right. So… would you look?"

"Fings! Fuck's sake! He was *my* brother too! Of course I will."

Fings nodded and huffed as Seth took the ledgers. He tended to forget that Seth and Levvi had been tight before Levvi had left, the three of them all getting into trouble together whenever they levered Seth out of his temple.

"Make yourself useful and find Myla. Come back in a couple of hours. If I find anything, I'll tell you on the way up to the temple."

Fings nodded some more and left the ledgers behind. He slipped back to the Guildhouse, carefully avoiding any mages, reckoning that if Myla was hiding somewhere, as likely as not it was there.

Couldn't get the memories out of his head, that was the thing. Close his eyes and there he was, the faerie king in silver, grinning at him and surrounded by Dead Men.

Myla wasn't at the Guildhouse. Frankly, Fings was glad. Place was crawling with bloody mages now. As the sun sank towards the sea, he made his way back to the *Mended Net* and found Seth where he'd left him, sitting at his table, a lantern beside him, poring over the ledgers.

"Found Myla?" Seth asked.

Fings shook his head. "Not yet."

Seth pushed a ledger across the table and tapped on the open page. "Can't spell his name for shit, but I reckon that's him."

"You sure?" Fings blinked. Despite everything, he'd mostly expected the ledgers to be a dead end.

"Levvi left Varr towards the end of Floods, five years ago. Even with the spring current, it would have taken a few weeks to get here. Say the middle of Lightning. A couple of months to find his way into trouble and get caught: Flames, Answering Prayers, Learned Discourse… This is the entry for a batch of slaves intended for the mines who were delivered at the end of Learned Discourse five years ago." Seth tapped the book again with a finger. "There's a Levvi… something-or-other. I think it could be him. It's not a common name. There aren't any others that fit."

Fings leaned in closer. "It say where he was sent?"

"Yes. Not one of the mines. Something else. Sold to… B.S., I think it says."

"Sold to bullshit?" Fings frowned.

"It's probably someone's unfortunate initials, Fings." Seth sighed, then shrugged. "No idea who they are but they buy a lot of slaves. They're still doing it, too." He pulled the ledger back, snapped it shut and pushed another at Fings. It looked recent. Cleaner. Seth opened it and tapped the page. "These are the slaves that came before Myla. Three weeks ago. Same initials. Whoever it is, they bought the whole consignment. Which means, Fings, that they're in Deephaven."

"Which means…!" But Seth was wagging a finger.

"Could mean anything. Could still be that Levvi died years ago. Could be they sold him on. Could be that this isn't him in the first place. Could be anything."

"But–"

Seth gripped his arm. "Yeah. *Could* be he's still alive. *Could* be, he's right here in Deephaven. Knowing *your* luck, we might just find him."

34

ONCE UPON A WARLOCK

Seth walked with Fings up the Avenue of Emperors in the twilight amid a procession of the faithful. It was a big crowd, most in scented masks and adorned with charms against the plague. A good few carried sticks of burning incense and the air was full of the smell of it; whoever was selling it was surely making a fortune. Which annoyed him, because the idea of sickness being caused by bad spirits who could be shooed away by a smell they didn't like was obviously daft. Although he wasn't sure the Path's remedy of prayer was any better. He sighed quietly. It all just went to show how stupid people were.

There were chapels scattered through the docks; even then, most people stayed in their own homes and bowed towards dawn and dusk with only their own family to see them. It took a special dedication to make this trek up to the Peak, yet here they were, all of them trudging up the hill to reach Deephaven Square in time to watch the setting sun. It took an equally special dedication, Seth supposed, to be one of the staggering drunks already trashed from a day of drink before sunset. The scatter of them, lurching across the Avenue, made for an odd journey; it was hard to know who was more uncomfortable, the devout or the debauched.

Parts of the crowd moved slowly, labouring to make the

climb even though it wasn't all that steep. He wondered if some here were already sick, hiding blisters behind their masks, the stink of corruption behind their incense. He tried to keep his distance, but it was difficult as more and more joined the throng.

About halfway up the hill, a commotion started ahead. He heard a shout: *Unclean! Unclean!* He pulled Fings to the centre of the Avenue, in among the relentless train of wagons heading up and down between river and sea. He had Fings drop a quarter-moon into a carter's palm and they sat on bales of cloth. Other people, it seemed, had had the same idea. The crowd left the wagon-trains alone; from his perch, Seth saw where a sick man had been unmasked. The fool was being mobbed. Most likely he'd be beaten and stoned if he couldn't get away.

Yeah. Remember what that was like?

He hadn't been into a temple to pray for… what was it now? Almost a year since they'd thrown him out? No. Less. It had been coming up to the Solstice of Flames. He tried to think of the person he'd been back then and found he couldn't. The Seth they'd kicked down the temple steps – *literally* kicked, thank you very much – had been stupid and naïve and horrified. The man he was now knew so much more, even if sometimes he wished he didn't.

The sky was getting dark, the sinking sun hidden behind a horizon of black cloud. He wondered whether Myla would be at the temple tonight. Probably not, not if she had any sense. He was glad Fings had rescued her, though. He felt like he needed her. A growing sense that his time was running out.

The wagon carrying its cloth reached Four Winds Square. Seth hopped off and followed the crowd along the Avenue of the Sun, dragging Fings with him. A makeshift podium had been built near the gates in Deephaven Square, a dozen priests already on it, surveying their flock. A full phalanx of Sunguard stood nearby, blocking the temple gates to the crowd but for but a select few. There were, Seth realised, simply too many people, even for Deephaven's vast Hall of Light.

His stolen Lightbringer robes got him through, pulling Fings behind him. The yards of the temple were almost as crowded as the square outside, more makeshift altars and more makeshift priests. He'd never seen anything like it. There were Sunguard here, too, and monks; but they saw his robes and merely nodded him along, all the way into the Hall of Light. He knelt and listened to the Sunherald of Deephaven speak the Rite of Dusk, words which had once moved him to tears, and found they meant nothing. He listened to the homily and found it empty, found himself picking at the hypocrisies buried under trite exhortations to honour one's neighbours, one's lords, the throne, the Empire, and above all, the Sun. All in the expectation, of course, that such honours would be reflected back on any soul that was righteous, an expectation Seth reckoned was a stinking pile of crap. By the end, he had to bite his lip not to laugh. He knew better, now, how the world really worked.

And then the Sunherald spoke of the seven white ships seen in the night, and Seth's blood turned cold. He spoke of a darkness falling upon them. A corruption from within, begun when the Usurper made a pact with a warlock to bring down the righteous emperor Talsin, brought now to fruition with a sorceress on the Sapphire Throne. All who were soldiers, all who were strong, all who were righteous, he exhorted, must stay and fight against the coming evil.

A declaration of war. No other way to take it. To Seth's way of thinking, it was also probably about the best way the Sunherald could have come up with to get people to flee Deephaven in droves.

"Fings..." he whispered. "I think we might be in a bit of shit here."

Sunset ended, and with it the last Twilight Prayer. The congregation in the Hall of Light began to disperse, a lot of them in a hurry – maybe some were uplifted, but most seemed terrified. Seth stayed, not wanting to imagine what it would be like outside in the crowded square. Fucking mayhem, probably. He watched Fings watch the sword-monks file from the back of the temple to some private unseen yard. As the crowd thinned, he found a young Lightbringer, suitably fresh and wet around the ears, told the Lightbringer he was a priest from Bedlam's Crossing – the only place nearby whose name he knew – and that he must speak at once with a sword-monk. His robes and the authority of his words, his warning of Dead Men on the road out of Deephaven, was enough to make her listen.

"Tasahre," said Fings, hopping from one foot to the other. "We need Sword-mistress Tasahre. Tell her we know Myla." He frowned hard. "Shirish, I mean. Tell her it's about Shirish."

Tasahre. Seth made sure to remember the name, surprised Fings knew it. Sword-mistress Tasahre. That was the one. The one who'd driven the warlock from the House of Cats and Gulls.

He fingered the sigils in his pockets, although trying to slap a sigil onto a sword-monk in the middle of the most holy temple in Deephaven didn't seem likely to end well. What he needed was someone else. Someone old enough to have been there when it all happened but who wasn't a murderous sigil-proof, hair-triggered warlock-killer with a penchant for sniffing out lies. He waited with Fings; as soon as he saw the Lightbringer heading back, a sword-monk striding alongside, he made his excuses. The last time he'd tried to tell a sword-monk something useful, they'd had a good go at killing him.

"I'll wait outside," he said.

Fings didn't seem happy, but he didn't kick off and make a fuss, which was maybe better than Seth had expected. It was almost a little odd, in fact, how he didn't protest, only looked... *bothered*. On his way out, Seth peeked over his shoulder. Sure enough, the sword-monk and Fings were standing together;

and there was something a little too comfortable about the way Fings wasn't keeping his distance, the way the sword-monk wasn't all folded arms and frowns and superior hostility...

They *knew* each other? They did!

Shit. How?

Right then, the sword-monk looked straight back at him. Seth hurried out of the temple, not daring to look in case the monk was following. He didn't need that, not coming in here wearing a stolen robe and with a pile of warlock sigils in his pockets.

The yards outside *were* fucking mayhem, much as expected, filled with people, worshippers and priests and Sunguard, all in a hurry to be somewhere. They were dark, too, which helped, the gloom broken by the dazzle of dozens of lamps and lanterns and candles as people scurried this way and that. He zig-zagged among them and hid behind a pillar. After a second or two, when it occurred to him how stupid he probably looked, he stepped out and risked a peek back at the temple doors.

The sword-monk hadn't followed. Seth swore under his breath and moved on, dodging between people, skirting through the colonnades towards the cloisters. Easy to lose himself in this confusion of lights and shadow and movement. The two Sunguard watching the entrance to the priests' quarters barely even looked at his robe, never mind his face. They didn't challenge him.

He stopped and picked on the oldest.

"I've come from Varr," he said. "I'm looking for anyone who remembers the warlock who used to live here. The one that was chased off by the sword-monk Tasahre."

It seemed reasonable that everyone would know a story like that. Sure enough, the Sunguard nodded. After a few suggestions that obviously weren't going to work – the Sunherald of Deephaven might have been the temple Dawncaller back then, but most likely wouldn't have time for some scruffy-looking Lightbringer from Varr moments after having declared war on the Sapphire throne – the younger Sunguard suggested the temple archives. He even offered to show the way, which Seth didn't have much choice but to accept. He winced a bit as they walked back through the Hall of Light, but neither Fings nor Tasahre were there. He wasn't sure what to make of that.

The archives lived in the domes surrounding the Spire of the Sun. The Sunguard introduced Seth to a grizzled old Lightbringer who seemed to take an immediate dislike to him; although, from the way the Lightbringer dismissed the Sunguard with a wave of his hand like he was dismissing a bad smell, maybe it was just people in general.

"All the way from Varr in the middle of winter? You're still going to tell me it can't wait until morning, I suppose?"

Seth put on a sickly grin. 'If it were *profoundly* important, I dare say they would have sent me here to carry the robes for some preening Sunbright."

The old Lightbringer seemed to like this. His demeanour changed a little, moved more towards a mild dislike rather than open hostility.

"We have a concern. May I?" Seth nodded to a chair. The grizzled old Lightbringer reluctantly nodded and lit another candle. Seth sat down. "One of our novices was dismissed for heresy last summer. Going to places he wasn't supposed to go, reading things he wasn't supposed to read. A bit more than that, maybe. In the end, he was expelled." Seth settled into his chair and into his story. There was nothing like the actual truth for a bit of authenticity.

"Oh yes?" The old Lightbringer had an air of tired resignation, like whatever story Seth was about to tell, he'd heard it all before.

Well. Not this *one you haven't.* "Yes. Cut off from the light. Kicked down the cathedral steps by the Sunherald-Martial. It seems he scratched a living as a forger for a while, working for some thug who thought he was a criminal mastermind. At some point, heretical texts found their way into this novice's possession. *His* story is that he acquired them from a rogue sword-monk. He showed up at his old temple with these papers and tried to hand them over. Unfortunately, there was a, ah... misunderstanding. The temple monks tried to kill him, so he ran away, leaving one of the papers behind. I've got my Dawncaller saying it was nothing, merely some heretic trying to cause trouble out of spite; and at the same time, our renegade novice is hiding and I've got two sword-monks acting properly bothered that they can't find him. So here I am: apparently, there was a warlock on the loose a dozen years or so back who got chased off but not killed? Do you know anyone who could help me with that? Any danger he's in Varr now?"

He stopped and waited. The old Lightbringer seemed to think about this. He picked his teeth with a fingernail, slow and careful not to miss any out.

"Sixteen years ago," he said at last. "The year this new Regent was born." His lip curled, making it clear what he thought about Princesses who studied sorcery and came from a family whose devotions largely went to Fickle Lord Moon.

Happy with having a new war then? Easy to say when you're not going to be fighting it. Seth didn't say that, though. Instead, he shrugged. "Well. I already know more than I did. Is there anything else?"

"I was there. After the sword-mistress fought him. Stuck both swords right through him, she said. Sunsteel blades, too. Still didn't kill him."

"Nice trick."

The old Lightbringer narrowed his eyes. "Not really. Weakened him enough to drive him away, though. But he's not in Varr. He died in another world, years ago. Never came back."

"I've seen where he used to live," Seth said. "We passed it on the way down from Varr. On the waterfront. The house of..."

"Cats and Gulls." The old Lightbringer spat a gobbet of

phlegm to the floor and stared at it. "Should have burned the place to the ground years ago."

"Yes. Why *didn't* you?"

The only answer he got to that was an angry grunt.

"I've heard..." Seth took a deep breath. *Choose your words carefully and don't be an idiot.* "Did you find anything? Something this warlock left behind?"

"I can tell you what I saw. Lots of candles. Symbols on the walls drawn in soot and blood. Dark sorcery. Room by room, the sword-mistress had us take everything that would burn, pile it up and set it on fire."

The piles of soot and the rings of charred salt. "What sort of things?"

The old Lightbringer shook his head.

"Was there anything taken out? Brought back to the temple, perhaps?"

That earned him a sharp look. *Yes, there was. And you know where it is.*

"You'd want to talk to the sword-mistress about that."

No, I really don't think I do. In fact, I think I'd very much rather talk to you. "The sword-mistress?" Seth tried to feign surprise. "The one who fought the warlock? She's still here?"

A nod.

"It does seem to me that... Well, after what the Sunherald said... Might she not be a little... busy?"

A shrug. Seth sighed. *Fine. Be like that.*

"Did she... did she ever say anything about a wraith?"

The old Lightbringer looked startled. *There we are. She did, didn't she.*

"No."

Liar.

The Lightbringer's eyes narrowed some more.

"You're right. Of course. If she's here... well, I should ask her myself." He got up and smiled and bowed and thanked the old Lightbringer for his time, then went as far as the door to the yard so he could have a good look around in case anyone else was near. The yard outside was... well, not deserted, but the last few remnants of the crowds were dispersing and there was no one nearby.

"Lightbringer?" called the old priest.

Seth stopped. "Yes?"

"Don't you want to know her name?"

Shit. He could see the suspicion in the old priest's eyes. He turned back. Took a couple of steps closer.

"One thing before I go..." He drew a strip of paper from his pocket. "I was given this. I'm supposed to show it to anyone who might remember from back then."

He walked to the old Lightbringer, holding out the strip of paper with the sigil written on it, which was almost a catastrophic mistake, because at the last moment, the old man's eyes widened as though not only had he seen it before, but knew exactly what it was.

"Warlo–"

Seth jumped him, clapping one hand across his mouth while the other slapped the paper sigil to the side of his head. "Quiet!" He held the old Lightbringer for the second or two it took for his struggles to stop. Until he sniffed the slight smell of burned skin as the sigil etched itself into the old man's face.

"Be quiet. Be still. Behave. Do as I say and take no action to raise any alarm or indicate any distress. Nod if you understand."

The old man nodded.

"I never quite know with this one whether you're still in there. If you are, I'm sorry to do this to you. I'll let you go when I have what I need and when it's safe. But... you will never speak of me to anyone. You will never speak of this conversation or of what I'm about to ask you to do. Nod if you understand." Even as he said it, he knew it was bollocks. The moment sunlight next touched the old man's face, the sigil would fade, and with it, Seth's power over him.

The old Lightbringer nodded.

"I'm not a monster. I could have killed you and brought you back as a Dead Man. But I'm not like the other one, the one from the House of Cats and Gulls. The worst I'll do to you is see that you never remember any of this. Now, did the sword-monk say anything about the warlock and a wraith?"

"No."

No? Fuck!

"Really? Nothing at all? Nothing about a man in silver? Silver armour?" Because a wraith *was* what Fings had described.

"No."

Now what? Shit. SHIT! "You brought things back from the warlock's lair. What were they?"

"A chest. A bronze statue of a lizard. A goblet made of bone. A flask of powdered dragon-scale. A–"

"I don't need a complete list."

"–glass orb of memories. A–"

"Stop!" That was the problem with people when you made them mindlessly compliant. They took everything so literally.

No, the problem with making people mindlessly compliant, you fuckwit, is that now he knows you're a fucking warlock! When the light of the Sun does undo this, you're going to have every sword-monk this side of the Godshome Peaks hunting you!

I'll just make him forget it all, won't I! It had worked on himself, after all. Even now, he didn't remember whatever it was he'd made himself forget back in Varr. Just remembered that he'd done it.

Oh, and you really think that'll be enough?

Why not? Take him to a tavern, make him drink himself into a stupor and then make him forget!

"Is any of it still here?" What's done was done. Might as well make the most of it.

"Yes."

"Can you bring any of it to me without raising suspicion?"

"Yes."

"Go do that, then." It would be a start. Probably most of

what they'd brought back had been dismantled or destroyed. Or melted down, at least, because you could always count on the Path not to throw away any gold or silver or anything of any real value just because it was tainted with something as trivial as dark magic.

The old Lightbringer shuffled off. He was gone for a while, long enough for Seth to wonder whether he should have asked how long it was going to take, in case the old man happened to know of something he could retrieve without raising any eyebrows but which also happened to be in Torpreah or Varr or Tzeroth, or maybe across the sea. It was so bloody easy to make mistakes, that was the thing. You sent someone off on what you thought was a trivial errand, the next thing you knew they'd set off halfway around the world because you weren't careful enough with your words.

So maybe... don't use it?

The old Lightbringer came back dragging a chest. It was clearly too big and too heavy for either of them to carry alone. It was also locked.

"Don't tell me it's all in there."

The old man said nothing.

"Oh, for fuck's sake! *Is* it all in there?"

It was. Of course it was. Seth sighed. Why did it always have to be *difficult*?

He sent the old Lightbringer off to fetch a handcart, told him where to take it and when, and then left. They could have wheeled it out together, or he could have sent the old Lightbringer ahead, but there were far too many people in the temple yards right now, and in the squares outside, and if anyone was going to be stopped and asked awkward questions by some angry sword-monk who happened by, Seth was damned sure he was going to be somewhere far, far away when it happened.

He had a quick look for Fings on his way out, but there was no sign of him in the darkness, or in the milling crowds and their thousand lanterns.

35

BLACK SHİPS

Waiting around for other people to get things done had never sat well with Myla. She paced in small circles, telling herself over and over to be patient. It didn't help. She wanted to kick in the doors of House Hawat and find her sister, before Sarwatta knew she was free. She wanted to find Tasahre and ask what in Kelm's name she was thinking, and how she'd reached Fings, and why she'd sent Fings to set her free.

She was surprised when Fings showed up, since no one was supposed to know where she was. He came running in, banging on the door all out of breath as though the world was ending, looked about her room, threw some books onto the bed, then stared at her.

"Fings! What are you doing here?" It *was* a weight off her to see him alive.

"Did you see? Did you see what happened? Did you see the–"

"Fings! Aren't you supposed to be in Bedlam's Crossing?"

"What? No. Where? Oh, right, yeah, aren't *you*? Anyway, never mind–"

"Did Orien tell you where to find me?"

"Orien?" Fings snorted. "You're not *that* hard to find. I wouldn't stay here if I were you. You're not very good at this. Anyway, shut up a minute. You saw them white ships on the river, right?"

Myla raised an eyebrow. It wasn't often that a sword-monk got told to shut up. "You look like shit." Like he hadn't slept for days.

Fings glanced to the ledgers on the bed. "Yeah. Well. Busy busy. *Any*way. Them white ships. You saw them too, right?"

"Yes."

"Yeah? And what about piles of Dead Men coming out of the water and some faerie king all dressed in silver? You see *that*, too? Throwing rays of moonlight that blow gates to smithereens and turn men into ash?" He told her his wild story, how the faerie king had seen him, how he'd run all the way back to Deephaven, sodden and scared. Myla sniffed the air as he talked, but he wasn't making it up.

"Bit like goblins, eh?" she said, when he was done. She gave him a sharp look. Couldn't resist.

"No, *not* like bloody goblins. Goblins is just a nuisance. Goblins ain't ancient sorcerers that go about with hordes of Dead Men at their beck and call, chucking about magic that turns people into dust! *Goblins* just nick stuff. Not like goblins at all! If it was like goblins, how come your priest lot were telling everyone this evening about some great doom coming down on us all and how it was all the fault of the Emperor?"

"*What?*"

He told her about going to the temple then, Twilight Prayer with Seth and what the Sunherald had said, about finding Tasahre afterwards and telling her what he'd seen; then how he'd snuck into the temple a couple of nights earlier, planning to rescue her, and had found Tasahre in Myla's place, how they'd had a good long chat about Myla and Deephaven and what she'd done, before Tasahre had let him go.

"Oh, and Seth's looking for you. Says he's got something he needs to talk about."

Myla stared, aghast. "The Sunherald... declared war?"

"Look... Thing is, there's this big sorceress from Varr now,

Orien's mistress." He shivered, hesitated, then walked in a tight circle on the spot for some reason. "I've been listening to her and Orien talking when they think no one else can hear. Some bad shit is coming. I don't know what, but we need to get out of here, all of us. Like, *now*! Except I can't. Not until I find Levvi."

"Nor I until Soraya's safe. And I've already talked to Orien." Myla closed her eyes. "Fings... The barge... *Did* Tasahre send you?"

"Not flat-out told me to go." Fings fidgeted. "Like I said. Was more... some helpful observations in case I might find myself thinking about it." He fidgeted some more. "Quite a lot, really, when you look at it..."

"What does she want from me?"

Fings shrugged. "Didn't say."

That was the sword-mistress for you. Tasahre had guessed the truth and nudged things the way she wanted them to go. She *did* want something, even if she wouldn't say what it was.

She eyed Fings up then, pursing her lips, wondering whether to ask if he'd help her do something difficult and dangerous that might get them both killed. The way his eyes darted around the room stopped her. He looked ready to turn and run.

"Fings... I want to get out of here too," she said. "But I need your help. You help me, I help you. Alright?"

Fings nodded enthusiastically, then cocked his head at the ledgers on the bed. "Seth says Levvi got sold to someone called... Well. Someone with the initials B. S." He tried and failed to supress a smirk. Myla sighed.

"Black Ships. It means the Taiytakei ships that cross the Stormdark between worlds. I'm sorry, but if your brother was sold to a Black Ship... He could be anywhere."

Fings nodded, apparently taking in his stride the idea that he didn't have to search only Deephaven but was going to have to search entire worlds. "Suppose I need to know which one, then. Where do I find one of these Taiytakei blokes?"

"Around the sea-docks and in the trading houses. Places like the *Captain's Rest.*" Myla closed her eyes. The sort of places she'd gone looking for Sarwatta.

"You help me find one? Talk to them when I do?"

"Yes." Not that it would do any good. "Fings... I might know where to look to find out which ship took your brother, and Lucius may be able to get in, but... Sarwatta Hawat has my sister. I need your help to get her back."

"You know where?"

Myla shook her head. "That's the problem. I can't think of anything to do except take Sarwatta himself and make him tell me. And I don't know how to do that."

There was some more waiting while Fings went to find something for her to wear that wasn't the same tunic she'd been wearing since that night on the Avenue of Emperors. She half expected him to come back with a smelly old rag that was too large and had spent too long near the fish markets, but he was gone quite a while. When he returned, he was carrying the robes of a sword-monk. Myla looked them over.

"Do I want to know?"

Fings shrugged. "People want to keep their stuff, they shouldn't leave it lying about the place, right?"

The robe was still a little damp. "You raided the temple laundry?"

Fings examined the room, carefully not looking at her. "Thing is," he said, "you wear that and all anyone ever sees is a sword-monk. They don't look at your face. Especially when it's dark." He offered her a feather. "Keep this between your teeth and no one will even notice you."

Myla swatted it away. "A sword-monk trying not to be seen?"

"Point."

He hadn't thoughtfully stolen a pair of Sunsteel swords to go with the robe; but sword-monks didn't always go armed, and it felt good to be dressed this way again. Like... coming home. Then they went out, and she felt the wrongness in the air at once. The river-docks heaving with people, despite being the middle of the night. Barges at every pier, heavily loaded, refugees fleeing the city. Even away from the waterfront, she felt a charge in the air. Knots of people hurrying for the river, pushing handcarts, moving with tense purpose. Other than that, the streets were almost empty.

Everyone in Deephaven remembered the siege. Even if they hadn't been alive, they knew the stories. First the River Plague, now this?

In Deephaven Square, Myla pointed to House Hawat. "That's where he'll be. Soraya might be there too. I need to get her out. Tonight, if I can. Can you do that?" Because if he couldn't, she'd have to do it herself; and for that, she *would* need her swords, and there would be blood, and probably quite a lot of it.

They crossed the square, almost empty now, Fings taking in House Hawat and the houses around it. "It'll be the rooftops, I reckon," he said, when they reached the other side. "Because that's what it always is."

"I've been inside," Myla said. She told him everything she could remember, from the yard behind the gates, the three wings of the house itself, luxurious halls behind gilded doors, Sarwatta's study and his suite of rooms at the top of the house. She pointed out the windows that led into his quarters, and the stumpy signalling tower on top of them. Fings took it all in and then wrinkled his nose.

"You ever see where his servants live?" he asked. When she said she hadn't, he looked disappointed.

"He'll keep her close," she said. "He's like that. He'll want her near, in a gilded cage, some place he can go and look at her whenever the fancy takes him. He'll treat her well until the baby comes. Then he'll hurt her."

"I can try. Least I can do is see if she's even there. Can't make any promises about getting her out if she is." Fings sucked air between his teeth. "Ain't going to be easy, either. Best wait a while." He nodded up at the sky, at the near-full moon high overhead. "A couple of hours before sunrise. When the moon's heading for the horizon and maybe there's more cloud. People always at their worst that sort of time. So, where's this place I can find some of them Taiytakei?"

Myla led him through the streets of the Peak towards the sea-docks and then down the Avenue of Emperors. She stopped a little way from the *Captain's Rest* and pointed.

"Black Ship captains come and go here a lot." She stilled him as he started to move. "That's one place they'll be sure to know me. And *you* can't go in, either. They won't let you. Maybe Orien. Maybe." What Fings really needed was Orien's mistress, with her noble blood and her title and carrying the favour of the throne. "But... Fings, they won't know. They don't know the names of their slaves. You're never going to find him that way."

"I got to try."

"I know. But I have something better."

She led him through the Maze then; even here, the city felt quiet and tense. She felt eyes watching her, hungry. No one who lived in this quarter would have money for passage on a ship. It made her glad of the robe Fings had stolen for her: no one was desperate enough to try mugging a sword-monk.

When they reached the sea, the docks were again crowded, soldiers and sell-swords and Longcoats trying to keep order. The tension was different, like the edge of a riot, everyone with money trying to bribe and buy their way out of the city all at once. She pushed through the throng, out the other side of it, past the warehouses to the end of the harbour, to Reeper Gate and the road out to Wrecking Point, to a building almost like a castle, with tall stone walls and windows that were high above the ground and barred tight enough that not even Fings could have slipped between them. The gate was open and the guards here were the Emperor's men, the sword and burning falcon emblazoned on their chest. An arch behind led into gloom between black walls of shadow. There were no ships at this end of the bay, and so no crowds.

Fings twitched.

"The House of Records," said Myla. "Where the harbour-masters keep their secrets. Stay behind me and stay quiet. Leave this to me."

She walked to the gate. The soldiers stiffened as she came close, eyeing her robe. "State your business," said one.

"The Sunherald has questions for our harbour-masters and their ledgers," said Myla coldly.

The guards stood aside, despite the hour. Myla marched haughtily between them, down a vaulted passage into an open square. She paused in the darkness, looking around, taking it all in. The buildings here were stone, not like the rest of the docks. Some had lanterns burning over the doors and hired swords, slouching half-asleep by the threshold. She'd been here before, but it had been a long time ago, and things changed.

"You think Levvi's *here*?" asked Fings.

"No. But… This is Deephaven, Fings, and these are the trading houses of the merchant princes. If the city is selling slaves to the Taiytakei, there will be records. That's how it works. Records and ledgers of everything, even things that shouldn't be allowed to happen."

She crossed the square and walked past the hired swords, ignoring their stares. Then down a narrow street, through an arch and into a dead-end alley. She stopped outside a door emblazoned with a dark triangle on a pale field and a burning falcon; not the arms of the city Overlord but the arms of the throne. She banged on the door. Like the ship and the barges and the never-ending trail of wagons across Four Winds Square, the House of Records never slept.

The door opened. Myla thrust Fings' stolen ledgers at a short balding man and stepped inside.

"Get out!" said the balding man.

"I'm looking for a man who was sent to the mines as a slave five years ago."

The balding man gave her a blank look. "And?"

"The temple requests the help of the Guild of Merchants in locating him."

"Maybe you missed the message, monk, but these are the emperor's halls, and your Sunherald just declared war on the Sapphire Throne." The balding man's look didn't change. "You're not welcome here."

"Welcome or not, here I am." Myla pressed a finger to the middle of his forehead and gently pushed him back. "You're going to tell me that I'm in the wrong place. You're going to tell me that the mines are a thousand miles away, in the far north. Before you do, know that I have already *been* to those mines, a thousand miles away in the far north, and in the middle of winter, and I have not found him. And before you say anything to *that*, my God-fearing friend, I will share with you what I *did* find: the man I was looking for was not there, because the man I was looking for never *reached* those mines."

She had him back through the door now, and an audience too – clerks and the like from two large rooms on either side of the hall beyond. She pushed further, towards a single passage that led into the back of the house, pitch black stone walls lined with strong heavy doors. Each carried a coat of arms, the heraldry of the city merchant princes. All the secrets of the harbourmasters.

And all the secrets of House Hawat. There had to be something, didn't there? Something she could use to free Soraya?

"Did you not hear me?" shouted the balding man. "Your Sunherald–"

"Does not speak for the Autarch in Torpreah or for the Constant Sun whose purpose I serve." She threw the ledgers at him. "The man I was looking for never reached the mines because he was sold before he got there by men of Neja who trade in slaves – *imperial* property, I remind you – for their own profit. To the Black Ships." She smiled then, all teeth. "My purpose is to find this man. The Nejans who sold him chose not to assist in that purpose. As a consequence, they will no longer be trafficking in stolen imperial property. Or indeed anything else."

She could almost feel Fings wishing himself invisible behind her; but this was who she was, who she was meant to be, and a sword-monk was nothing if not relentless.

"I prefer not to waste my time assessing the complicity of this house with crimes against the throne. *That* is a matter for the Overlord, should it become necessary for him to hear of it. I am interested only in this one man. May I be assured of your aid, or must I return armed?"

The balding man took another step back and bobbed his head. "I'll... find someone who can help you." He darted down the black passage. Myla supposed he meant for her to wait; but sword-monks weren't good at waiting, everyone knew that, and so she followed past the iron-bound doors hiding their secrets and tried not to look too closely. *Those* doors would remain closed, even to a sword-monk, and she knew better than to try.

The balding man scurried up a flight of stairs. Myla stayed on his tail, Fings trotting behind. They emerged into the office of another man, fat and with more hair and who looked like he was used to getting his way, an angry expression on his face that melted as Myla stared him into oblivion. He tried some bluster at first – what did she think she was doing coming to a place like this with such an accusation, how he'd be raising a complaint to the Overlord, how the Sunherald would hear about it, that sort of thing, the last of which must have struck even *him* as faintly ridiculous. She looked him in the eye through every word until he faltered and fell silent. Then she smiled and put Fings' stolen ledgers on his desk, opened one to the page that mattered, pointed to the name she was looking for, and looked him in the eye. You didn't bargain with a sword-monk. Everyone knew *that*, too.

"One man," she said. "One name. Or must I look for myself?" They didn't have records of names. She'd expected as much. What they *did* have – what she'd known they'd have – were records of every cargo delivered to every Black Ship since the siege of Deephaven when the old House of Records had burned down and the new one had been built in its place. The harbourmasters were meticulous with their books, always. The trades of slaves were disguised, but not well if you knew what to look for, and the hours Myla hadn't spent in the Temple, she'd been a merchant's daughter. She knew how ledgers worked as well as she knew the feel of a Sunsteel sword in her hand.

"You understand," the harbourmaster said, after she'd found the name of the ship, "that all of this is perfectly within the law."

"Then why disguise it?" She could have said something more reassuring, maybe reiterate that her purpose was simply to find this one man, nothing more. But she preferred to let him stew. *Let* him be afraid. Let him send his secret warnings to the Overlord and complain to the Sunherald. Let him do that and bury himself in his own coffin.

She was about to leave, to tell Fings it wouldn't do any good knowing the name of the ship to which Levvi had been sold, that the Black Ships appeared and disappeared as they pleased, sometimes for years. But something about the harbour-master's agitation told her there was more to this.

"When was that ship last in harbour?" she asked.

There. Right there. She loomed towards him, sniffing the air. "You know we can smell lies, yes?"

He'd gone very pale, and she knew exactly why. "I could... find out. It will only take a moment."

"No need," Myla said. "You've already told me. It's here right now."

"Well," said Fings, as they left the House of Records behind and crossed back through the Sea Docks, heading for Deephaven Square and House Hawat. "That's handy."

He sounded quite chipper.

36

HOUSE HAWAT

Things just sat in your pocket and did what they were told. The thought kept buzzing round Fings' head like an angry wasp. He was good at slipping in and out of places he wasn't supposed to be, but that was *him*. Admittedly, Myla hadn't made life too difficult when he'd snuck her off that barge, and Levvi would probably do his best – presumably, if he were a slave, Fings would end up having to steal *him*, too – but a heavily pregnant merchant's daughter who'd never sneaked across a rooftop in her life? How was he supposed to do *that*?

Shouldn't even be here, not really. Where he *should* be was fixing a way to get out to the ship that had taken Levvi, and then maybe stay on it and scarper out of Deephaven before that death-throwing monstrosity of a faerie-king and all his Dead Men minions came calling. Yeah, he'd seen the face Myla's teacher had made when he'd told her. Grim, that was the word for it.

But a promise was a promise. Myla had found the ship that had taken Levvi, so he'd do this one last thing before he was gone. All he'd *promised*, after all, was to find out whether Myla's sister was even here. Not that he'd stop at that, if the chance came to get her out.

The alleys around the back and sides of House Hawat

weren't looking hopeful. A few doors into the compound, but all closed. They didn't have locks either, which meant they were barred from the inside. Coming in over the rooftops was going to be fraught too, it turned out, since the buildings to either side were mini-palaces much the same as House Hawat, and equally well guarded, and when he *did* manage to get a look at the rooftops from up on the walls of the Temple of Light, he saw guards standing watch, almost like they were expecting something.

He thought about that. This Hawat fellow had sent sell-swords to steal Myla off the slave-barge. They'd never shown up with their prize. On the other hand, everyone *else* there was dead too, as far as Fings knew. Did the Hawats know that? Did they think Myla among the corpses? Had to reckon they probably didn't, not yet. That being the case, he had to reckon on them thinking Myla was loose and so would be expecting trouble. It *was* possible, he supposed, that they were imagining Myla having gone on a rampage and slaughtering an entire fort full of soldiers down to the last man. Would explain them being all a bit jittery.

On the way to the harbourmaster, he'd seen wagons packed full of chests and sent with squads of armed men heading down towards the docks. Had got him thinking about a bit of quiet breaking and entering, that had. No doubt the rich princes fleeing the city had left more guardsmen behind to make sure there wouldn't be any of that nonsense while they were away; still, it was never quite the same when the mistress or master of a house was gone.

No sign of that from House Hawat. Probably thought a nice wall and a few blokes with swords was going keep them safe. Not from what Fings had seen last night it wouldn't, but they didn't know that. Yet.

So: their guard was up and it didn't look they were planning to flee like half the rest of the city, none of which was helpful. If he couldn't get through a door or across the rooftops, that left climbing the walls. They were twice his height and too well built to climb without hammering knives into the mortar between the stones, and presumably someone would notice lots of loud hammering coming from a dark alley in the middle of the night. On the other hand, it was perfectly easy to lob the anchor-on-a-rope he'd used to get into the Cathedral of Light and scale them that way, so that was what he did. Myla wouldn't have much trouble with that either, he reckoned. Her sister would, though. When it came to getting out, he'd have to find another way.

He crested the wall, sucking on a feather as he always did, peeking over the top in case one of the rooftop guards had heard the noise of the grapple and was looking right back at him. Once he was sure no one had noticed, he dropped into what looked like some sort of ornamental garden, hid his rope and anchor under a bush, and started searching for an entrance into the part of the house where the servants lived. That was a thing he'd learned in Varr: rich folk didn't bother with guards for their servants because servants had nothing worth stealing. So that was how you got in, then crept about while everyone was asleep until you found the doors into the expensive bits. If you were lucky, you found yourself some servant livery; if *that* happened, you got to walk about the place like you owned it. If anyone saw you, they mostly assumed you had a right to be there and didn't bother with a closer look.

Mostly.

The first problem, it turned out, was that House Hawat *had* put a guard on the door from the garden where Fings found himself. Fortunately, the garden was full of bushes; Fings picked up a stone and tossed it into one and waited. The guard took a few steps and poked at the bush with the butt of his spear, and that was long enough for Fings to slip through the door behind him. He reckoned Myla could pull the same trick, although maybe not on the same guard on the same night twice in a row.

If it came to it, Myla would probably just hit him.

Inside was quiet. Fings crept around, mapping the place in his head so he could tell Myla where to go and where not to bother, until he reckoned he'd found all the ways into the main house, as well as some into the central yard. He found two exits to the alley alongside House Hawat, too. The first was by the kitchens, separated from the servants' wing by a small yard surrounded by storehouses with two swordsmen standing watch. The light of their brazier showed the door to the street held shut by three heavy bars. As a way out, it wasn't promising. On the other hand, the second exit was a tiny passage with an iron-bound door at one end and Kelm-knew what at the other. The iron-bound door was locked, which wasn't a problem for *him*, but was no good if Myla was the one doing the rescuing.

Best do it myself, then.

He had a go at the lock, not much fancying having to deal with it while a nervous pregnant woman fluttered around him. He wondered, as he started, whether he might be able to knock up a key for Myla, but the lock turned out to be a tricky bugger, so that wasn't going to work. Still, he got it open. He cracked the door ajar, enough to glimpse a narrow passage and another barred door at the far end, this time with another soldier sat on a chair right in front of it, head bowed in sleep.

Shit.

If the fellow stayed asleep, maybe Fings could deal with him. But if he woke up, if there was any sort of commotion… yeah, all in all this House Hawat place was starting to get annoying, what with all its guards everywhere.

Like they're expecting trouble.

Yeah. Like they were expecting sword-monk trouble.

This is why you steal things *and not* people.

He tried one of the doors from the servants' quarters into the main house and found it wouldn't move. Barred from the other side. This whole business of using bars and bolts instead of locks was *also* starting to be annoying, almost as though whoever had designed this place had known what they were doing. He tried the door into the main yard. *That* wasn't barred, but the yard had four guards standing watch. *Four,* for Kelm's sake! And yes, it was dark, and yes, part of the yard was covered on each side, the roof held up by narrow columns, but they weren't exactly good for hiding. Even with a feather between his teeth, Fings didn't fancy his chances sneaking through without being seen; and even if he *did* somehow get through, the doors into the main house were closed and, judging from what he'd found so far, likely barred from the inside like everywhere else and with sixteen guards standing on the other side.

Bollocks to this.

He sucked a breath through his feather. There were times when a good burglar had to accept that a job couldn't be done, not without a good chance of getting caught. This was starting to look like one of them, never mind getting out again with someone who probably didn't have the first idea about hiding and sneaking and couldn't climb a rope.

If it was Levvi in here, what would you do?

He'd take his chances, that's what. So that's what Myla would do, too.

Come on Fings. You're supposed to be good at this.

Maybe there was another way, from somewhere else?

He made his way to the second storey, crept into a bedroom overlooking the ornamental garden where he'd come in, slipped outside, and levered himself onto the roof. The roof guards were all on top of the main house, two storeys up. None of the ones he could see were looking his way. Yet.

Now what?

He couldn't reach the shutters on the next storey of the main house. Even if he could, they looked too well-made for his usual trick of slipping in a blade and opening the latch. What he needed was his rope and anchor, which he'd left in the garden where he'd come in. Up from this roof to the top of the main house. Not that *that* would work either, not with that walkway around the edge of the roof and guards standing at each corner. Even if they didn't hear him climb... well, they were still *there*, and you still weren't in the actual house, and they weren't blind, and there was nowhere to hide.

He squatted on the roof for a good long time, trying to see a way in and gradually realising there wasn't one. The place was locked up tight. And if he couldn't get *in*, him on his own, how the Bloody Khrozus was he – or Myla, for that matter – supposed to get *out* again with Myla's sister in tow?

You only promised to find out if she was here.

He checked the sky. The first glimmer of dawn was on its way. He waited around a while longer, hoping he'd get lucky, that something would happen to change the way it was, or maybe he'd overhear some conversation that might be useful, but no. As the sun crested the horizon, he dropped to the ground, left as he'd come, and slipped away into the night.

He'd been beaten by places before. Places where prudence said to walk away and not try. Prudence wasn't keen on telling Myla she'd most likely have to fight her way into the main house and that she'd certainly have to fight her way out again, even if her sister *was* inside, which he still didn't know. But he went back to where she was hiding near the temple anyway and told her exactly that, told her everything as he'd seen it, saw how she didn't much like it. What *he* didn't like was what the look in her face when he was done. He made a point of how many guards there were, quietly doubling all the numbers in the hope it might put her off, but it didn't make any difference. She was going to try it anyway.

He didn't bother trying to change her mind, simply wished her luck. If it had been Levvi, he'd reckoned he'd be the same.

37

THE ORB OF MEMORIES

Right on schedule in the middle of the night, the old priest showed up pushing his handcart. "They'll find you, warlock," he said, as Seth took it. "You've shown yourself. They'll find you and kill you. They always do."

"Be quiet and still until I release you."

The old priest fell silent and still. Seth looked at the handcart – a pile of motley bits and pieces all covered in a moth-eaten blanket – and then at the priest. He'd had a bit of time to think about this since leaving the temple; and the trouble was, the old priest was right. Sooner or later, the monks would notice an empty space where their collection of warlock memorabilia used to be. Maybe it would be a while if they were all distracted by suddenly being at war with the Sapphire Throne, which presumably meant being at war with the city Overlord as well, but sooner or later, they'd notice. When *that* happened, it would be like someone had kicked a nest of hornets. Angry monks looking for anyone who might know anything. His priest would be one of the first they questioned. Seth wasn't sure what would happened then.

He'd make the priest forget tonight. He'd put *that* sigil somewhere subtle, but the scar of the first sigil would always be there on the old priest's face. Faint, after the sun burned it off, but there to anyone who knew what they were looking for. The sword-monks would see it, and then what? They'd ask the Sunguard. The Sunguard would remember the priest from Varr who was asking about anyone who remembered Deephaven's warlock. The sword-monk Tasahre would surely remember how Myla's friend Fings, when he'd come with stories of Dead Men and white ships on the river, had come with a priest. A priest she'd seen walking away. A priest she didn't recognise, walking away.

She'd remember *him*.

And then? She'd go after Fings. When she didn't find him, she'd go after Myla and Orien. She'd track them down and find out who Seth was and then she'd hunt him. She'd find him and stick her two Sunsteel swords through him, and Seth reckoned he had a way to go before he mastered the trick of not dying when someone did a thing like that.

"Follow me," he said. "Bring the cart." He was sweating. Felt hot and his eyes didn't seem to keep up if he turned his head too fast. Felt a bit sick, too. That, he reckoned, was the fear.

He had the old priest push the cart to the *Mended Net* where he was staying and carry the contents to his room. There was a sigil painted on the wall beside the door now. It was the sort of thing you only noticed if you knew what you were looking for.

"Stand still and be quiet," he told the priest. "Actually no. Answer me this, first: did you find anything with funny writing on it?"

The priest gave him a blank look.

"Like the sigil I used to bring you here."

"Everything paper was burned," said the priest through gritted teeth.

He'll find a way to give you up. You know he will. Whatever you say, he'll find a way to twist it.

Seth scanned the glassware and pieces of metal that the priest had brought. He had no idea what any of it was and already knew he couldn't keep it. Even if he made the priest disappear, those two Sunguard would still remember him. It wouldn't make any difference. It all had to go back so the monks never knew.

And he *would* have to make the priest disappear. Fortunate that half the city was trying to flee. Best thing, probably, was to tell this poor idiot to get on a ship and sail south like all the rest. Could say all he liked about there being a warlock back in Deephaven once he was safely on a ship; Seth would be long gone before any word got back. Yes, that would do it. Put everything back. Send the priest away on a ship. No harm done, right?

"What of all this scares you most?" he asked.

The priest gave him a baleful look, then pointed. "The skull."

A regular human skull, adorned with silver fixings. "Why?"

"They say it's the skull of a wraith."

Seth picked up the skull and had a good look at it. There was nothing particularly unusual other than the fact that someone had gone to the trouble of drilling holes through the bone and wasting a fair bit of quality silver turning it into a morbid work of art. Being scared of a skull struck Seth as almost Fings-like.

He considered using a sigil and talking to it, then decided not. On the whole, he'd had his fill of consorting with the skulls of long-dead half-god sorcerers.

He looked at the biggest piece instead, a lump of bronze, scarred by fire. It was shaped like the limb of some terrible lizard, covered in scales, the craftsmanship smeared by heat hot enough to make the metal turn soft. It was half as tall as he was and ended in a claw holding a clear glass globe. When Seth touched the metal, it felt warm.

"What's this?"

"A memory orb."

The words hissed out from the priest as though he'd fought them all the way. Seth peered at the globe. There seemed to be something inside, but only when he saw it from the corner of his eye. He picked it up, held it to the light of a flame, and looked deeper. There *was* something there. Like the glimmer of the moon in a piece of Moonsteel. A tiny picture, buried in the heart of the glass. He peered closer…

…He was standing on a dark plain of bare blasted rock in the midst of an annihilation of sorcerers and of silver knights murdering one another and of dragons scorching the sky. He was at the end of the world, while overhead hung the thin silver disk of the sun, blotted out by a black moon. His power was limitless. He cracked the earth to swallow his enemies. Petty priests and sorcerers called fire from the Sun and he barely felt it. He held high a helm of ice imbued with a fragment of his own soul. As he did, he called it to him. That Which Came Before…

Seth wrenched himself away. That was a *memory*? Fuck's sake! *Whose* memory? He turned to the priest. "You're a fucking idiot, you know? *That* should scare you more than some decorative piece of bone. Have you seen what's *in* there?" He picked up the silver-inlaid skull and hurled it to the floor. The bone cracked but didn't shatter.

He poked around and picked out a few things that looked interesting. There were pouches and glass flasks of powder, although he had no idea what they were. He'd have to work that out for himself. The rest? A treasure trove of dark secrets or a pile of arcane nonsense. He had no way to know the difference.

It crossed his mind that he knew a mage who might be able to help with that. Not Orien, because *his* questionable moral flaws were more vanity and arrogance and ambition than a true quest for power. But the popinjay…

Are you really *thinking that? After what happened last time?*

No. Besides, the popinjay would probably want it all for himself.

Seth, if he was honest, wanted it all for himself too.

He looked at the pile of the banished warlock's possessions. It was a shame to let any of them go. But he had to keep the sword-monks from hunting him, and that meant giving them back.

Maybe there was a way to keep the orb, at least?

He told the priest to sit down, and then squatted in front of him. "Answer my questions. You said you went into the House of Cats and Gulls after the sword-monk chased the warlock away. Is that true?"

"Yes," growled the priest.

"Underneath the warehouse, there's a large dark space with a mud floor. There's what looks like an old well, rimmed by a ring of stones. Did you go *there*? Did you see it?"

"Yes."

"Did you see a sigil in the water?"

"I don't know."

"How can you not..." Seth sighed. "Fine. Did you see an odd-looking symbol that seemed to be somehow marked into the surface of the water?"

"Yes."

"What does it mean?"

"I don't know."

"Did anyone say anything about it?"

"We were told not to touch it. The Dawncallers and Sunbrights placed wards on the stone. The monks knew more but they wouldn't tell us."

Seth felt an odd moment of glee and disappointment. Here it was, the schism between the priests and the monks. "Why not?"

"They were new and from Torpreah and the sword-mistress had just betrayed the Sunherald's aide. We didn't trust them, nor they us."

"What about later? Did you ever hear anything to suggest what it was?"

"Yes."

When that was all there was, Seth clenched his fists. "What did you hear?"

"That the sign was the lock. That there was something trapped in the water. That it was something the warlock held prisoner. That the wards were placed in case the sign in the water failed."

Seth felt his blood freeze. "I see," he said, almost in a whisper. "And what would happen then? If the sign in the water failed?"

"I don't know."

"Speculate!"

"Something bad."

Seth rolled his eyes. "Fuck's sake! Speculate better. Be specific. *What* something bad."

"Whatever was trapped would get out."

"Obviously! *What*?"

"I don't know."

"Then guess!"

"Dead Men."

Seth rocked back on his heels. "Dead Men?" That was *it*?

"The corpse of once-living man or woman reanimated by a remnant."

"Yes, thanks, I know what Dead Men are. *That's* what you think was down there?"

"Yes."

"Dead Men, trapped in water? You *do* realise that makes no sense? Water is supposed to set them free."

"Yes."

Seth got up. *Well. That's not so bad, is it?* Worst came to the worst, all he'd done by breaking the sigil in the water was set a few Dead Men loose, and there were Dead Men loose in Varr all the time, and everyone got on with things because they weren't much trouble, easily dealt with by monks and by priests with their sigils. Frankly, hardly anyone even noticed. And that was only if the Sun priests' wards failed, and why would they fail?

Dead Men. Yes. Nothing to do with what Fings saw. Nothing to do with that at all.

He told the old Lightbringer to stay where he was, went

out onto the docks and never mind that it was the middle of the night, and bought himself a keg of whale oil. When he went back, he had the Lightbringer carry everything except the orb and a few other interesting-looking bits and pieces and put them back in the handcart. Outside, they walked together through the night, crossing the Maze and up the Avenue of Emperors and Four Winds Square and along the Avenue of the Sun, the old Lightbringer pushing the handcart with a burning brand wedged at the front to light their way, Seth following behind with the keg of oil under his arm.

"Stop." At the entrance to Deephaven Square, Seth stood behind the old priest, making sure he couldn't be seen, and touched a second sigil to the Lightbringer's skin, one to make him forget everything that had happened in the night until now, on the chance something went wrong later, because knowing *his* luck, something inevitably would.

"Close your eyes," he whispered. He took the burning brand, set it carefully aside, opened the keg of oil and poured it over the cart. "Give me your hand."

The Lightbringer offered his hand. Seth gave him the brand. "I was going to let you go. Make it all like this never happened, I really was. But sometimes things must be done. It's for the greater good."

He told the priest what he had to do. It wasn't for the greater good at all and they both knew it. But the priest would do what he was told because Seth hadn't given him a choice, and no one was going to get hurt, so it wasn't *so* bad, was it?

He walked away, keen to put some good distance between himself and the temple before the old Lightbringer got back to his archives and set the whole place on fire. He reckoned the Sunguard would be quick noticing a thing like that, and then it wouldn't be long before some sword-monk was up and asking questions about why some confused old Lightbringer had decided to experiment with being an arsonist and then run off into the night shouting something about the sea. Hopefully that last bit would be enough to send any sword-monks off towards the sea docks; meanwhile, the old Lightbringer would be heading for the river, fast as he could, and a barge to Varr.

At least, that was what Seth had *told* him to do.

He hadn't gone far enough not to hear the shout as some Sunguard at the temple bellowed a challenge. And then he heard a scream, and then more screams. He tried not to turn and look but couldn't help himself; he already knew what he was going to see.

And there it was, framed by the arch of the Deephaven Gate: the sight of an old man standing by a handcart, both wrapped in flames, ablaze in the middle of the temple yard.

No! NO!

The old Lightbringer's arms flailed as he burned. Someone was trying to help him. Pushing him to the ground. Rolling him over, trying to put out the flames. One of the Sunguard, probably.

No! Shit! Fuck! Why?

Now the Sunguard was on fire, too, rolling around the yard. Someone else came to help him. Another Sunguard, probably.

This wasn't how it was supposed to be!

The burning Sunguard managed to put himself out and was getting back to his feet. The old Lightbringer was still on fire. He wasn't moving.

Why? Why does it always *turn like this?*

He walked quickly away, before anyone in the temple had a chance to look out across the square and maybe notice a horrified stranger looking back. Ran, mostly, telling himself the same thing over and over all the way to the docks.

I'm not a monster.

This *wasn't* how it was supposed to be! He'd told the old Lightbringer *exactly* what to do! A little fire in the archives. A confused old man waking up in the morning on a barge to Varr, not sure why he was there. That was all. Nothing worse. Not this!

I am not *a monster.*

He wasn't fooling anyone, least of all himself. But maybe, if he said it enough times, he'd start to believe it; and if he could believe it, maybe one day he'd be able to sleep with the knowledge of what he'd just done.

38

MIRROR, MIRROR

In Deephaven Square, the faithful were gathering for Dawn Prayers, far more than usual, a sea of fearful faces and masks and charms. Myla pushed through; they saw her sword-monk robes and moved aside. Forty or fifty men, Fings reckoned, well-armed, vigilant and with crossbows. She'd need a distraction, then. Something to make them open the gate or get those men off the roof. Also, she needed a sword.

The main temple gates were closed, only the side gate open. The Sunguard keeping the crowd at bay let her through, and by then she could smell the reek of burned flesh. In the yard between the gates and the Hall of Light, four novices were lifting a charred body, one at each limb, while Tasahre and a priest and another sword-monk looked on. Beside the body were the remains of a wooden handcart and whatever it had contained. Most obvious was something made of bronze that had started to melt from the heat. It looked like it had once been a large, clawed hand.

Tasahre's face was murderous. She strode to stand in front of Myla. She didn't draw a blade, but the edges on her words were sharp enough that she might as well have done.

"Why are you here?" Tasahre hissed.

"Because you clearly want me to be," Myla snapped. "And

because Sarwatta took my sister, so tell me what you want and be done with it."

"What I *want*, Shirish, is for you to live a life of purpose." Tasahre sniffed pointedly at Myla's face, then withdrew a pace. "You should not be wearing those robes."

"Shall I strip and walk naked?"

"Don't be foolish."

Myla looked at the blackened body as the novices laid it out onto a stretcher and started to carry it away. "What happened?"

"An old friend inexplicably doused himself in whale oil and set himself on fire," snarled Tasahre. She looked past Myla and waved to the Sunguard at the gate. An angry gesture. They opened the gates and the crowd beyond surged forward, hurrying to the Hall of Light. "He was with me at the House of Cats and Gulls after I fought the warlock." She touched her scar. "Before this. We burned what would burn and brought back what would not. It seems he chose last night to gather the last artefacts and destroy them. Along with himself. First, though, he took them out of the temple, and I have no idea where he went or why. He returned an hour before dawn. When the Sunguard challenged him, he set himself ablaze. He was dead before anyone could stifle the flames."

"Why? Why would he do such a thing?"

"I don't know, Shirish," Tasahre growled. "Although I wonder if he perhaps did not *choose* to do what he did." She turned to Myla, eyes boring in. "I was wondering whether *you* might know. Because it does seem strange to me that the ghost of that monster should lie at peace for sixteen years, only to become suddenly restless at the same time as my most errant student returns."

"I'm sorry for the loss of your friend, mistress," said Myla, "but I know nothing of this except what you've told me."

Tasahre sniffed the air and then gave a sharp nod. "I cannot help you with your sister. You must know that. But since

you're here, I'd have you at my side tonight. It's the full moon.
The storm is about to break."

"Storm?"

"There's a warlock in Deephaven again. He's been to the
House of Cats and Gulls and opened Kuy's prison. The wraith
has returned."

"Wraith? *What* wraith?" Myla had heard Fings' story too.

"The one you'll help me slay. After Dawn Prayer, I'll ink
your skin. There's a lot you don't know, and you will need to."

Myla clenched her fists and shook her head. "No. If you got
me off that barge to help fight something you can't be bothered
to explain, fine. I'll be here. But *after* I save my sister."

"No."

"Yes. My sister first. Then I'm yours."

"Then you will be useless. I will seek help elsewhere."
Tasahre spat. "Do as you must, although know that I am
unlikely to be a match for it alone. Will there be violence in
House Hawat tonight?"

Myla looked away. "I will not answer that, mistress."

"And thus you do. Get out before someone recognises you."

Myla turned away. Despite Tasahre's warning, she walked
past the smouldering cart and on with the crowd into the Hall
of Light. She stood quietly near the back, taking Dawn Prayer
for what she knew might be the last time.

She'd have to wait until tonight, but she still needed
something to distract the Hawat sentries on the house roof.
Orien? Maybe, if she pushed him...

Fires make a good distraction...

Orien didn't have to *help*, exactly. Just... make a scene. If
she put it that way, he'd agree... Wouldn't he?

Yes, he would. But no. If she asked for help, he'd give it,
and then it would slip between them, that chance he might
be discovered and become an outcast like she was. If he *was*
discovered, it would poison them. In the end, he'd blame her
for asking, and he'd be right.

So best *not* to ask. Besides, what she *really* needed was someone who could help her get Soraya away, and all Orien could usefully do was set fire to the place, and how exactly was *that* supposed to help when her sister was still inside?

After Prayer she went back to the river-docks. They were quiet now. Far fewer boats and barges at the piers and only a handful of dockworkers. Mostly it was families, little clusters of humanity huddled around a few boxes or bags or the occasional handcart, waiting, despondent, for the first boats to come back from yesterday's exodus. That was the problem with Deephaven: apart from the one paved Imperial Road, everything around it was a sea of mud at this time of year. The only other way to leave was by water, and the far bank of the river was nothing but mudflats for miles and miles. The nearest places to put in were Fewport and Bedlam's Crossing, both a full day up-river. Yesterday's barges wouldn't be back until nightfall. If they came back at all.

She went to her room, gathered what possessions she had, and left. The morning rain had started by then, but if Fings had found where she was staying then Sarwatta could find it too, so instead she went to Deephaven Square and settled in the shelter of an alley to watch House Hawat. The rain faded to drizzle, then picked up again. Shortly before midday, the house gates opened, and a dozen soldiers filed out. They formed a guard, and then Sarwatta followed into the square, dragging Soraya beside him.

Myla forced herself to be still and watch. They hadn't seen her. At least, that was how it seemed. They stood there, out in the open in the rain, Sarwatta and Soraya, surrounded by soldiers, for a full minute, and then they went back inside. Myla understood perfectly. This had been a display, a lure, Sarwatta letting her know that he had her sister, daring her to try and take Soraya back. Out of sight behind his gates, he probably had another dozen men, waiting for her to break cover, armed with crossbows.

She forced herself not to move. When he did the same thing

again, a couple of hours later, she knew she was right. She knew something else, too: he didn't know she was already here, watching.

He'd expect her to come at once, or else in the dead of night. In the small hours after midnight...

Dusk, then. Let it be at dusk.

The Guildhouse, when she reached it, was quiet, still asleep despite the fact that it was almost mid-afternoon. An unfamiliar servant let her in, seeing only the robes of a sodden sword-monk dripping all over the doorstep. He offered to fetch the lady of the house. Myla declined and asked for Orien instead. She didn't have to wait long before the fire-mage appeared, still in his night clothes and yawning. He smiled when he saw her. Myla looked him up and down.

"Look at you! Half the day already gone. Are mages suddenly nocturnal?" They embraced. She let it linger. Orien didn't seem to mind how sodden she was.

"I thought you'd be gone by now," he said.

"I told you I'd see you again before we left. Lucius has arranged a ship for us. We leave tomorrow morning. I..."

Are you really going to ask him to betray himself? For you*?*

"Did you find your sister?"

She nodded. "I know where she is. Is Fings here?"

"From the snores coming from his room, yes. Do you need him?"

If only to say goodbye, but that could wait. "I wanted..."

Don't! Don't you dare!

"You wanted?" He raised an eyebrow. Obvious enough what *he* wanted...

"I think you should go back to bed."

"I won't go back to sleep."

"No," Myla smiled, "you won't. These robes are sodden, clammy and uncomfortable, and are sticking to my skin as though they're made of leeches. You can help me out of them." She took him by the hand and led him, still yawning, back up the stairs, thoroughly enjoying the look on the face of the servant who'd let her in. A mage and a sword-monk? Scandalous!

And now you can't *ask because that wouldn't be fair.* It was a compromise she could live with. A relief, too. She'd survived temptation and given herself a fine way to kill the afternoon while she was at it.

"Our ship is the *Speedwell*," she said, much later, as they lay in bed together. "She leaves from Ygalla's dock. You could still come with us. Although you probably shouldn't."

His answer was to roll her onto her back and lay a trail of kisses that started at her neck and made their way down across her belly and kept right on going. He was good at that. Good at giving pleasure. Arrogant and conceited and full of himself, and too ambitious, and not particularly good at being a mage, but he wasn't selfish, and he was good at *that*, oh yes, and she was going to miss him.

And then, for a bit, she stopped thinking at all.

"I'm going to take my sister from Sarwatta tonight," she said, later. "I came here to ask... I'll need a sword. Do you have one?"

Orien took her hand and showed her that he did, which wasn't what she'd had in mind at all, but oh well, why not?

"I meant one made of steel," she said. "And Orien..." She trailed off. She'd been about to say something important, but suddenly all her words were gone, her eyes locked to the mirror on the wall behind him. There was something else in the room with them, in the reflection, some creature; and then the mirror cracked, a crack that widened as the creature reached at it from the other side, two hands with long-taloned fingers pulling it open. As her voice caught up with what she was seeing, the mirror splintered and then shattered, and half a leg had come through the crack, and a head, bulbous and white, with protruding golden mirror eyes and a snout the length of her forearm, ending in a mouth large enough to swallow a mailed fist and ringed with jagged teeth.

"Shit!" She pushed Orien away. "*Shit*!"

She dived off the bed, looking for anything that could be a weapon. What did he have? A book. A candlestick. A fire-steel... *He's a fire-mage! Why does he have a fire-steel?*

"What the...?" Orien turned and froze. The creature was almost through the mirror, its eyes fixed on him as though Myla wasn't there. She grabbed the candlestick and jumped past him, smacking the thing on the snout, then aimed for the creature's eye, ramming the candlestick into its face as hard as she could. It hissed and swatted at her with a slash of a claw. She danced back but not quite enough as it ripped a slash across her belly.

"Myla!"

Fire exploded from Orien's hands. Myla felt it sear her cheek and smelled scorching hair, but none of that mattered. The creature pulled free from the wrecked mirror, rearing up, all segmented legs and insect-like body, and yet the way it stood upright was almost human. Myla smashed the candlestick onto the back of its head as it was about to bury two of its claws into Orien's neck. It swatted at her again, but she was quicker to dodge this time. Orien rolled sideways and pointed his burning hands; flames leapt from his fingers with a ferocity she'd never seen. They bathed the creature up and down. As it burned, she hit it again and again. It screamed and shrivelled into itself and staggered back. Orien's fire didn't stop, a torrent of flame driving it back, until it turned and scuttled into the ruined mirror from which it had come and disappeared.

Like a wheel-rut in thick clay mud, the glass of the shattered mirror oozed back together behind it. Orien kept pouring fire until it was gone...

And then the mirror was as it had always been, not broken at all, its frame and the wall around it blackened and scorched. The reflection was nothing more than the two of them, staring back at themselves, shaking and panting. She had blood smeared across her. Her own. Orien had a streak of white in his hair that hadn't been there before. He looked as pale as death.

"What was that? What was *that*? What the *fuck* was that?"

"I don't know." Myla tried to catch her breath, to slow her heart. "Orien... The... The room is on fire!" She heard a scream from outside, and then panicked shouting.

"But what the *fuck*...? Was that Sarwatta?"

"Are you *daft*? No! No, it wasn't!" She ran out, still naked. To her right, the corridor opened into the wide space of the grand staircase which spiralled lazily up the four storeys of the Guildhouse. Two... *things* were bounding up from below, a little like whatever it was that had come from the mirror, insofar as they were a mish-mash of all sorts of bits and pieces that didn't belong together, but that was as far as it went. One had four vaguely human limbs but the head of an oversize wolf and was running on all fours. The other looked a bit like someone had lopped the head off a giant spider and replaced it with the head of a small dragon.

So: not that way.

Down the corridor to her left, a door exploded as something that looked a bit like a gorilla made of boulders slammed through it, careened into wood-panelled wall on the other side, roared, saw her, roared again, and charged.

"Oh fuck!" Not that way either, then. Didn't look like either fire or a candlestick was going to be much use, so all she could do was make sure it chased her and didn't go after Orien. She turned back to the stair, already running, but now there was a figure further up the staircase. Despite everything else, Myla stared: the Regent, of all people, in white and gold and her long dark hair loose and wild, arms outstretched, one palm pressed into the back of her other hand...

She raised her hands towards Myla. Myla dived and rolled as a flare of dazzling moonlight lit the stairwell. The creatures on the stair shrieked in unison and both exploded into clouds of ash. Behind her, the gorilla thing made of rocks spasmed mid-charge and then collapsed to pieces. Pebbles and chunks of stone rolled along the hall, a few reaching Myla's feet as she stared in disbelief.

When she looked back up the stair, the Regent had gone.

Riiiight, then...

Orien! She dashed back to the bedroom. Orien was where she'd left him, sitting on the floor by the bed, rocking gently back and forth. She started hauling to him to his feet, shaking him. "Orien! Get up! Orien! Fuck's sake, snap out of it! The *room* is on *fire*!"

She started to drag him out. The door flew open. Orien's mistress, Lady Novashi, crashed in. *She* was on fire too, although in her case it seemed to be deliberate. She scanned the room, saw the slashes across Myla's belly, hissed, clenched her fist, and then opened it. The flames spreading across the room leapt to her hand and died.

"Here too? Where is it? Did you kill it?"

Myla shrugged. "I shoved a candlestick in its eye and hit it a lot and Orien set it on fire. We drove it back into the..." she faltered then because she didn't know what to say. It was sinking into her now, the enormity of it: something she could only describe as a demon had come through the mirror and tried to kill them; there were more of them outside; what she'd seen the Regent do – the Imperial Regent, here in Deephaven; and she was naked, a candlestick in her hand still dripping some sort of ichor; and she was bleeding from the three shallow scratches across her belly. "Dead? I don't know. What *was*...?"

Lady Novashi had gone.

"I'm going to be sick." Orien threw up in a corner.

39

PARTIПG WAYS

After a whole night in the docks and then sneaking around House Hawat, Fings reckoned he was due some rest. He went back to the Guildhouse and tried going to bed but couldn't sleep, too busy thinking about Levvi and the Black Ships and how he needed to get out of Deephaven before the faerie king came and murdered everyone. After a bit, he gave up and went to the sea-docks, wandering up and down, talking to people about how someone might, hypothetically speaking, get to a Black Ship that happened to be anchored out in the harbour and how someone might – and this was absolutely definitely *only* hypothetically speaking, mind – sneak aboard. A lot of people, it seemed, were interested in sneaking aboard ships right now, so it took a while; but eventually he sniffed out a couple of men who reckoned they could do it, rowing out under cover of dark with muffled oars. Money changed hands and he went back to the Guildhouse. Since it looked like he didn't have much choice but to wait another day, he reckoned on trying the whole sleeping business again.

He'd always thought of himself as the sort of person who could leap from his dreams and out the nearest window in a gnat's heartbeat, spurred on by nothing more than the heavy tread of a Longcoat's boot outside his door. Apparently, this talent didn't extend to the building he was sleeping in catching on fire in several places and a pitched battle between a handful of mages and several dozen… well, whatever they were. He woke up with the vague idea that something was going on, aware that the air smelled of smoke and, bizarrely, rotting meat. When he went outside to see what was happening, he rather wished he hadn't.

"What the…?"

Some priests came by and bustled away again, and then a handful of other strange-looking fellows, the sort of mage-type people Fings preferred not to think about, one of whom was Seth's Taiytakei popinjay. He was just getting over that when four servants, wide-eyed and gagging, came hurrying by, carrying the charred remnants of something that had too many limbs and teeth and was put together all wrong, and which Fings knew was going to give him nightmares. Some sort of demon-thing was about the best he could describe it; by the looks of it, some sort of demon-thing that had made the mistake of bothering Orien's mistress and been largely turned into charcoal for its troubles.

Turned out there had been quite a lot of demon-things. Apparently, they'd come crawling out of all the mirrors about the place, which made Fings jolly happy he'd turned his own to face the wall. He slunk out, trying to keep out of everyone's way while he went looking for Myla, mostly because he reckoned she might tell him what the bloody Khrozus was going on. He found her downstairs in the biggest room in the house. She was standing beside Orien, stroking his hair. Orien was sitting in a chair looking like he'd seen a ghost. Fings reckoned he could sympathise with that. Unfortunately, also in the room were a dozen mages, all clustered around Orien's apocalyptic nightmare mistress. They all seemed a bit stressed.

The apocalyptic nightmare sorceress cocked her head. She was talking to Myla. "*You*, of all people, should know," she said. "The wraiths, sword-monk. The remnants of the Silver Kings who didn't ascend. Isn't that what you've all been waiting for?"

Wraith? That was what Seth had called the thing he'd seen at the fort. There was more than one of them? Kelm's bloody Teeth! Yeah, he needed to get Levvi and get out of here, and fast, before this shit got even worse than it already was.

He hung around long enough to discover that Myla had had a go at fighting one of the demon-things while stark naked and armed with only a candlestick, both of which Fings preferred not to contemplate and added to his general opinion that sword-monks were as mad as a barrel of badgers. No one seemed sure that more weren't about to show up, or maybe something worse, so he left her to it and went to check on Seth instead, where hopefully the world was a bit more normal. When he got there, he found himself starting to question his life choices.

First was the dead thing, same as the one he'd seen in the Guildhouse only not all burned, which was worse, because there was no hiding how it was mostly teeth and claws and too many eyes and limbs, how it looked vaguely assembled from a collection of parts each of which seemed slightly familiar but which certainly didn't belong attached to one another. Then there was Seth being all evasive, apparently with no idea how it had ended up in his room or how it had ended up dead, all of which, Fings was fairly certain, was bollocks.

"Myla's at Orien's Guildhouse, if you're still looking for her," he said.

Seth gestured vaguely at the dead demon-thing. "I need to get rid of this."

They rolled it up in Fings' carpet, Seth banging on about wraiths and half-gods and something to do with the old warlock who once lived here. As far as Fings could tell, it all added up to how they should both get out of Deephaven as fast as they could, something Fings had already worked out for himself just fine, thanks.

"I ain't going without Levvi." Fings wrinkled his nose.

"There was more of these things at the Guildhouse. Myla had a go at one." He looked around. There was a lot of stuff he didn't recognise. "What *is* all this crap?" Mostly it looked like junk.

"It used to belong to the warlock who lived in the House of Cats and Gulls." Seth gestured around the cellar and shivered – there was clearly something wrong with him: he was pasty-faced and sweaty and out of breath like he had a fever. Having a demon-thing come wandering through a mirror would do that, Fings supposed.

"Right. So… what's it doing *here*, then?"

"There's something going on. Something to do with what happened years ago. And the papers Myla gave me that you found from that barge, and the Moonsteel crown and the late Emperor and the Usurper and the Autarch and the Path of the Sun, and maybe a wraith was here once too, and something to do with Dead Men; and oh, did you know that our Gods weren't the first Gods and there's something else and maybe it's all to do with *that* as well and…" Seth ran out of breath and sat heavily in a chair, gasping for air.

Fings thought about all this for a bit. "So… there's monsters coming out of mirrors, and faerie-kings attacking forts, and hordes of Dead Men climbing out of rivers, all that crap happening all around us, and what *you've* done is swipe the shit some evil wizard left behind when a bunch of priests and sword-monks chased him off half a lifetime ago, because just maybe the same evil wizard has something to do with it all. Have I got that right?"

Seth pursed his lips. "I wouldn't call him an *evil wizard*, exactly."

"And I suppose you want me to keep quiet and not bang on about how bloody stupid that is? How bloody stupid it is for us having anything to do with any of this, frankly."

Seth nodded, then shook his head, then threw his hands up in the air and let out a sigh of exasperation. "I… I don't know, Fings. I don't know anything. You're right. We shouldn't be here. I shouldn't have come. Shouldn't have done any of this."

Fings wrinkled his nose in suspicion. "Done any of *what*?"

"Will Myla still be at the Guildhouse later?"

"Until dark at least, I reckon. Probably not much after." Fings frowned, looking around Seth's room. "It ain't the best time, what with everything that just happened, and... Well, good chance she'll flip her lid if she sees all this. Look, I know you're my brother and everything, so this comes from a good place, but... are you *trying* to be stabbed and burned to death by a horde of angry monks and mages?"

Seth gritted his teeth. He was breathing hard, like he'd just run up the stairs. "Look... Go and find her and ask her to come, would you? Please? Just give me a chance to get rid of this... *thing* before she gets here."

"Fat-eared Abdeen," Fings muttered under his breath. The thing rolled up in the carpet was far too big to be a goblin and he'd already seen a faerie king two nights ago. *Demon-thing* it was, then. "He does charms against this sort of nonsense."

"*What?*"

"Doesn't matter. Listen, there's a ship in the harbour. The *Speedwell*. It's leaving on the morning tide. Got space for all of us. Myla's brother sorted it."

Seth nodded.

"I'm going to find what happened to Levvi tonight."

Seth nodded again, clearly not listening.

"It's probably something I should be doing on my own anyway. You know. Creeping around and stuff. Not your thing."

"Hmmm." Seth was back to staring at that glass orb.

"But he's *your* brother, too. So... you know. If you want to come..." He shivered and paced the room, careful to step around the thing in the carpet, even while his eyes kept being drawn to it. The creature had bled before it died. Its blood was an almost luminous pastel blue. Didn't seem likely that Seth, of all people, could have done a thing like that.

The evening air outside felt like Varr. Cold, with a touch of ice in the wind.

"You know, you really don't look well. Reckon you should stay here," he said, when Seth didn't reply "Probably safest."

He looked at the carpet and wondered if he might be a bit wrong about that.

"Right then," he said, when Seth still didn't look up. "I'll leave you to it, then, shall I? I'll come find you once I get Levvi, right? Otherwise... I'll see you at dawn, yes? On the docks. The *Speedwell*. I'll ask Myla to drop in for a bit. If she's got time. Yeah? Oh, and bring the carpet, would you? Once you've got rid of that thing." The carpet was a present for Ma Fings and his sisters. It seemed like the sort of thing to make them giggle and titter and be all impressed. Carpets were for rich folk, not for *their* sort. They were going to have a stain on it to remember Deephaven by, he thought, and then chuckled. They'd probably think it was there on purpose. Best not mention how it was demon-blood.

He was about to leave when Seth caught his arm. "Yes. Tell Myla I... I need her help."

Fings looked at Seth, squinting. Poor bastard looked terrible. Only natural, really, given what was on the floor.

"Yeah." He nodded and patted Seth on the shoulder. "I will."

He trotted back to the Guildhouse, frowning all the way. Myla was talking with Lucius; as Fings came in, Lucius said his goodbyes and left them alone. Fings found himself looking Myla up and down.

"Well," he said. "Don't know what *that* was all about."

"It was an attack. They were–"

Fings held up a hand. "No, I don't want to know nothing about it. Not my business. Glad you're alright, but that's as far as it goes; I got my own problems tonight. Oh, and Seth wants to talk to you. Don't know what but... Yeah. Probably good if you could. He's in the tavern at the end of Sour Street. The *Mended Net*. Something..." He frowned again, because there was something in the way Seth had asked that had almost been scary. "I don't know. Yeah. Like I said. Probably good if you could. He's..." He sighed. "He's mucking around with shit. Needs someone to set his head straight, I reckon." Someone who wasn't Fings.

"Why did you come here?" Myla asked. Fings looked around, in case there was someone standing behind him, but no: apparently Myla was talking to him.

"Er... what?"

"To Deephaven. Why did you come to Deephaven? Was it really because of Orien's letter? Only... well..." It wasn't often Myla struggled for words, but then it *had* been a very strange day. "You know. You and mages."

Fings fidgeted a bit. "Bit of all sorts, really. Been sort of thinking of seeing if I could find what happened to Levvi for a while now. And Seth needed to get out of Varr for a bit." Which was true, as far as it went.

Myla was still looking at him. Fings fidgeted some more. That was the trouble with sword-monks having a nose for words that weren't quite honest.

He took a deep breath and huffed. "So, yeah, there was all that, but... yeah. I reckoned I owed you, alright? Look, there's–"

"What, for sending me off looking for buried treasure in the middle of the winter Sulk with a bunch of soldiers on my trail?" Myla cocked her head. "A treasure you knew perfectly well wasn't there? Yes, I reckon you did."

Fings frowned. "That? No, not *that*. That was business, that was." He didn't understand why she'd still bring *that* up after all this time.

Storm-clouds were gathering in Myla's face.

"Um... Maybe?"

The clouds weren't going away.

He stared at his feet. "Because of what you did for Yona."

"Who's Yona?"

"My little sister. The one Red had a knife to. The day before we left Varr with the Murdering Bastard. You didn't know her. And the thing was, I *did* steal Red's silver, even though I kept telling her I didn't."

The storm-clouds turned into a wry smile. "I know. I could tell you were lying to her."

"Red probably would never have done it. But… you didn't know that."

"Are you coming south with us?"

Fings nodded. "If I can find Levvi. If I can't…" He didn't really want to think about that.

"I'd be glad of your company, but…" Myla made a sour face. "If I succeed tonight. If I get Soraya out… House Hawat will hunt me. Being near me could get you killed. Once we get to Helhex, you should go back to Varr. Get away from all this. You must still have a pile of silver stashed from the Emperor's barge."

Fings looked sheepish. "Well, that mostly got spent." Mostly it had stayed with Ma Fings and his sisters, truth be told, because Fings had understood perfectly well that it would simply fall through his fingers if he kept it. Which of course it had, a good chunk on a carpet rolled up in Seth's room with some sort of dead monster inside, most of the rest about to go to a bunch of dodgy boatmen, but that didn't seem the sort of thing to mention. He shrugged. "Thing is… Well, if I'm honest, sneaking onto a barge full of soldiers to help *you* made a whole lot more sense than sneaking onto a barge full of soldiers simply because Sulfane said so. And since I'd already done *that*…"

"But you don't have to do *this*. Whatever debt you think you owe me, you've paid it. We're square. Clean."

"Oh, yeah, I know *that*. Ain't about debt, not really." Fings shrugged. "Probably won't find Levvi tonight anyway. If that happens, suppose I'll stay and keep looking."

Which was enough to make Myla smile, and so Fings relaxed a little, and then she got up and hugged him, which he had no idea what to do with, and so was a bit relieved when she let go. Thing was, watching Myla leave Deephaven chained up on a slave-barge, he'd found himself wondering if it was the last time he'd see her. The idea had troubled him. Quite a lot, actually. Like the looming spectre of a death in the family.

She didn't look too bad, now, all things considered, given what she'd gone through. A bit scorched at the edges, wincing now and then from the scratches that demon-thing had left on her. Nothing that wouldn't heal.

He shook his head. *Mad as a barrel of badgers.*

"I know what you're going to do," he said, because it was bloody obvious, and it was what *he'd* do, too. He fished in his pocket and pulled out a charm, a bit of bone on a string. "Wear this," he said. "You know. For luck. And don't forget Seth. Reckon it might matter, you and him having a word. Keep an eye on him. He's looking a bit peaky."

"After Soraya's safe," said Myla.

Fings flailed his arms a bit and mumbled something about seeing them both on the docks next morning and backed away. He was never good at shit like this.

And anyway, he needed to find Levvi.

40

A WARLOCK'S END

She won't forgive you the priest. Myla *was* a sword-monk, after all. Maybe not a good one in a lot of ways, but it was still what she was. And *he* was a warlock, like it or not, and he'd killed a priest, even if he hadn't meant to.

Fuck.

He kept telling himself it had been an accident. The old fool was only supposed to set his archives alight along with all the old warlock's stuff. That was all. Then run away. Leave it so no one knew anything was missing. He'd seen it all in his head, how it was going to go. A neat and tidy mystery and an old Lightbringer waking up on a boat with no idea how he'd ended up there. Kelm's Teeth, Seth had known people in Varr for whom waking up with no memory of the night before had been almost a way of life!

He'd done things back in Varr, too. Whatever he'd done to Lightbringer Suaresh. If he was going to tell Myla everything, he'd have to forget this one, too.

Is that how you clean your conscience? Pretend it never happened?

Maybe that was the answer. Not just the priest. Forget everything about the House of Cats and Gulls. Forget about Deephaven. Or back further. Forget the Moonspire. Forget everything that had happened in Varr after Midwinter. Or further still. Forget Myla had ever given him those papers. Forget Sulfane and sigils. Forget Blackhand. Forget he'd ever been a novice. Forget everything.

When Myla left Deephaven, Fings would go with her. Seth reckoned he might stay behind. Probably better for everyone that way. Probably better if Myla didn't come to find him either, even though he'd asked; yet some part of him still wanted it, like she was the last open door to something he'd almost lost. He wanted to tell her what was happening to him. He wanted a way to explain it, a way to ask for help. And she *would* help. He knew it. All he had to do was ask, and then tell her everything.

You know you can't stay here.

No. Not after what he'd done. People might remember the priest with his handcart. There was the dead thing rolled in Fings' carpet, too. He needed to do something about that. How could he explain it?

He looked at the warlock's orb. He was tired. He was aching and he was hot and he was shivering and his head throbbed and he couldn't concentrate. What he needed was to lie down for a while. Get a good sleep. Get some rest.

No time for that.

The orb was filled with secrets. The warlock's knowledge and memories. When he had the time, he'd unlock them all, one by one; but right now, he *didn't* have time. So after Fings had gone, he skipped to the end, to the last memory the warlock of Deephaven had left behind...

He found himself in the House of Cats and Gulls. The sky outside was clear, the sun bright but the windows were boarded and shuttered, only a few feeble rays poking through the cracks. Candles lit a short hallway and then an expanse of space, of shadows and shapes and more candles, candles everywhere, so many of them and yet all so dim. A boy was talking to a pale-skinned man. A severed head lay on the floor; the boy only noticed when it rolled past his feet. The old man's mouth gulped air. He started to rant about how the boy hadn't brought any fish.

Seth squinted. *Fish?*

The boy said something. The old man replied, jabbering about tools and craftsmen, then ranting names: The Bloody Judge, the Black Moon... Seth didn't really catch it, too busy realising that *this* was the warlock. The warlock of Deephaven. The man he'd come here to find. Saffran Kuy.

He broke away, let the orb go. His heart was racing.

The warlock of Deephaven was long gone. Wasn't he?

A few deep breaths, and then he returned to the memory and watched the warlock write the sigil to make the dead speak. The boy asked questions and the head answered. Names Seth didn't know. Something about black powder and betrayal. A lot of the warlock venting his spleen against the Path of Light, which Seth supposed was understandable... and then, without warning, the warlock hurled the head at the door at the exact moment it burst open to reveal a sword-monk, swords naked, sunlight like a halo around her.

The same monk Fings had gone to see, back when she'd been Myla's age or maybe even younger. She sprang and struck at the warlock, then stopped, frozen by some invisible hand.

Nice trick.

The warlock drew a knife. The boy turned on him. Seth watched the warlock press the knife into the boy's skin. He saw the desperation on all three of them. The warlock determined to prevail, the boy and the monk desperate to save one another. Were they... were they in *love*? A sword-monk and a warlock's boy?

Shadows swirled around the warlock. The boy screamed but his hands were no longer his own. He cut himself three times.

"Three little cuts. Three little slices. You. Obey. Me."

And then the warlock screamed because the sword-monk had broken free – Seth hadn't seen how – and driven both her swords through him. Shadows swirled, shifting and morphing so Seth caught only glimpses of the forms they sought, of eyes that glared and teeth that snapped, of claws and spines and withered hands. They strained, as though tethered to the warlock and seeking to be free. They looked, he thought, a lot like the dead thing lying behind him, wrapped in carpet.

He shivered.

The memory filled with dazzling light. The warlock staggered and disappeared into darkness. The sword-monk gave chase and the boy followed. Seth saw the look in his eye, poor lad, a desperate infatuation never to be returned.

Minutes passed. The boy and the monk came running back and vanished outside into the afternoon light. The boy's left hand was bloody, half his little finger missing. Seth felt almost sorry for him, moon-faced over a sword-monk. He didn't know how that story ended, but Tasahre was still here in Deephaven. The boy? He wondered whether he might ask Myla if she knew, then decided not. He wasn't interested, not really. The boy wasn't important. All in all, the memory was more annoying than useful. He hadn't learned anything.

"I see you," whispered the warlock. "Watching me."

Seth jerked as if stung; and now, there was the warlock again, pale and ghost-like, almost translucent, with two Sunsteel swords still skewering him, the orb cupped in his hands, face close, looking Seth in the eye.

How was that possible if these were the memories of a warlock who'd died sixteen years ago?

No. Not dead. Driven away. He'd survived this, remember?

The crippled warlock picked up his orb and carried it through the House of Cats and Gulls. Seth winced at the treasure trove of books and papers, all about to be destroyed when Tasahre returned with her priests. So much knowledge...

Don't think about it.

They reached the cellar steps, descended, and crossed to a far corner, to a small hole dug out of the mud. Inside the hole was a plain iron box.

"The secrets of That Which Came Before. Here they hide. The Book of Endings. The book of the Black Moon's herald!"

The mud began to flow, uncomfortably akin to how the mirror in his room had oozed open when the demon-thing had walked out of it and straight into one of Seth's sigils.

A few seconds and the box had gone.

Hidden.

Seth waited to see if there was more. When there wasn't, he put the orb back on the table and covered it with a cloth. Then changed his mind and stuffed it into a satchel and slung it across his back. He wasn't sure why, but he had a nagging sense that whatever was waiting for him in the House of Cats and Gulls, he was never coming back here. That he had to go there...? He didn't even question it.

That Which Came Before? The same name the popinjay had used. But what did it mean? Every novice knew the story of creation, of the four divinities, of the half-gods and the Shining Age, of the Black Moon. But something that came before?

He stood and swayed, momentarily light-headed. He caught himself on the table, waiting for the room to stop spinning.

Definitely over-doing it.

He wished Myla would come. He felt like shit and wasn't entirely sure this wasn't a trap; and if it *was* a trap, it never hurt to have a sword-monk stand beside you.

Stupid fool. No one ever stands with a warlock. Least of all a sword-monk.

She stood with me once before.

Fings would probably forget to ask. Too preoccupied with Levvi. And if he *did* remember, Myla wouldn't come. No point waiting.

Yet still, there it was, the sense of one last door to something. And of Myla, holding it open, beckoning him.

He turned his back on it and left.

41

FİTGS MAKES A DETOUR

Fings decided that he really, *really* didn't like Deephaven. When there weren't mages, there were faerie-kings and Dead Men. When there weren't faerie-kings and Dead Men, there were monsters from the nightmares of mad people, and cursed warehouses, and a plague that had everyone hiding in masks and burning incense, none of which he'd had to put up with in Varr. Even when there wasn't any of *that* nonsense happening, it was almost always raining. Everything about the place was a bit shit, really – he'd been looking forward to going on a journey and having an adventure and seeing somewhere new, even while he'd dreaded it on account of expecting Levvi to be dead. Now, frankly, he was quite ready to be going back home to where demons didn't walk through mirrors and attack people in the middle of perfectly ordinary afternoons.

There *were* some problems with that, unfortunately, starting with how the road to Varr had a faerie-king and a horde of Dead Men lurking somewhere, and he hadn't much liked the look of those ships on the river, either. If he was lucky and found out what really *had* happened to Levvi tonight, he reckoned he'd take Myla's offer and go with her and her brother. But in case he *wasn't* lucky – and Fings knew well enough never to take luck for granted – he went to the sea-docks looking for other ships willing to take an extra pair of hands, all of which turned out a bit more difficult than he'd hoped. Half the ships in the harbour had already gone, the rest weren't taking more passengers, and about half the city was looking for a way out.

He thought about this for a bit and decided the best thing would be to find a ship going somewhere he fancied, get onto it without bothering about asking, and take it from there. The place he most liked the sound of was Syradrune, which was apparently a part of the empire but far away across the sea. He'd heard that treasure ships sailed into port every few months from Syradrune, and what wasn't to like about a place full of treasure? He thought about this for some time, lining it up beside other places where strange and unlikely customs were apparently normal, places beyond the Empire where they had four moons instead of one, places where there were no sorcerers but where songs had the power to change the world. That sort of thing.

Lined them up, then settled on sticking with Myla and sailing to Helhex, the Empire's second port. As far as Fings could tell, Helhex was mostly notable for how much they hated the imperial family, followed shortly by being a place where anyone who didn't meticulously adhere to the Path of the Sun was likely to be thrown onto the rocks by the sea. It didn't sound like the sort of place he'd enjoy, but it *did* sound like a place that wouldn't be full of sorcerers, faerie-kings, Dead Men and sundry other abominations; also, it rarely rained. So Myla's ship to Helhex it was, because he'd had enough of all that, these last few days. From Helhex, he could do like she'd said and make his way north, have a few adventures and be back in Varr by summer with an empty purse, a hatful of stories, and a carpet with a messy stain, assuming Seth remembered to bring it.

Decision made, then; which left him with tonight and a ship moored out in the harbour which probably didn't have Levvi on it; but before that, there was one more thing needed doing.

The Taiytakei popinjay. The so-called healer, except if the popinjay was a healer, then Fings was a donkey. If he was going to leave and Seth had another one of his daft moments and decided to stay, Fings reckoned he should get to the bottom of whoever this popinjay was. He owed Seth that much, at least.

A few discrete enquiries later and Fings reached the old Moon Temple where the popinjay supposedly lurked. It crossed his mind that he *could* simply knock on the front door and ask a few questions and see what happened; but Seth was the one who was good with words, so Fings did what *he* was good at: waited until dark and then crept in across the rooftops. Finding the popinjay wasn't even difficult – a light in the window of a ramshackle lean-to propped up against the old Hall of Light. Fings crept up and looked in, and, as was turning out to be a bit of a pattern today, rather wished he hadn't.

The least disturbing part was the dead demon-thing. This one lay on a table, neatly slit open, its insides arranged in a careful order around it. Unless Fings was mistaken, beside the mound of gore was a slate with words scribbled in chalk. Somewhat *more* disturbing was the second body. A man who'd been skinned, which was bad enough, but the fact that the popinjay was actively finishing the job made Fings almost retch.

The popinjay was wearing the same extravagant clothes he'd worn to the Guildhouse, albeit a bit bloodier now. He was humming to himself.

A sensible person, Fings reckoned, would sneak off at this point, tell Seth what he'd seen and then never come back. But this was looking a lot like warlock stuff, and Fings was getting a bit concerned about that sort of thing when it came to Seth. So he stayed a bit longer.

The popinjay finished skinning his corpse. He stood back to admire his work, then stepped forward again and put something on the flayed man's head, at which point the flayed man sat up and started talking. Fings almost fell over, then rubbed his eyes in case he was seeing things; but the corpse's lips were moving and he could hear words, even if he couldn't make them out. The flayed man was still alive, then, although there was strangely little screaming for someone with no skin.

Whatever the flayed man was saying, the popinjay didn't seem particularly interested, mostly poring over the man's skin which, Fings now saw, was covered in tattoos. After a while, Fings reckoned the popinjay's questions were about the tattoos too, because he kept making sketches in a book and taking notes as the flayed man spoke.

He saw robes on the floor by the flayed man's table. Sword-monk robes. *Could* have been coincidence, he supposed. Maybe.

The moon was rising, which told him it was time to be heading to the docks. He slipped away as he'd come, silent and unnoticed. In the morning, Myla was going to hear about this. Orien too.

Seth?

He wasn't sure. Hard to say. Best thing for Seth, Fings reckoned, was probably to whack him on the head, drag him onto a ship and him get out of Deephaven before he did something spectacularly stupid.

If it wasn't already too late for that.

42

THE BOOK OF ENDINGS

As the streets fell quiet for the Twilight Prayer, Seth slipped out and stole a handcart. He took his satchel, heaved the carpet into the cart, and headed for the river-docks. By the time he got there, he was gasping for air, shivering and sweating, exhausted and light-headed. Everything ached, down to the tips of his fingers. It was alarming, how badly he wanted to simply lie down and close his eyes.

In the darkness, the river docks were busy again, a steady stream of empty boats returning from up-river, the piers jammed with fractious crowds all trying to get out of Deephaven. Plenty of shouting, a bit of looting and robbing, people getting pushed into the water, all that. No soldiers or Longcoats to keep order, either. Seth kept away from the waterfront, trying to have nothing to do with it. If someone *did* mug him and stole his handcart and Fings' carpet, he wasn't about to stop them. They were going to get quite the surprise when they unrolled it, though.

The House of Cats and Gulls stank. The half-devoured remains of fresh fish lay scattered around as though heaped in ritual offering, noticeably more than when he'd come with the popinjay. Flocks of seagulls still roosted in the eaves while feral cats patrolled the perimeter, the cats and the gulls seemingly having formed an unlikely territorial alliance. As Seth came close, he felt the pressure of their thousand tiny eyes, watching him. He felt his hairs prickling and his skin crawling as if both were trying to escape. There was a charge in the air tonight, something new, a sense of wrongness.

The door hung ajar as he'd left it. He looked again at the offerings. How long had the warlock been gone? Sixteen years? Declared an abomination by the Path of Light, and yet still people left them. Begging for favours, or were they trying to appease an angry ghost?

He forced the door open wide enough for his handcart and pushed it inside. Deep in the House of Cats and Gulls, he hefted the dead thing out of the cart and rolled it out of its carpet. He set a lantern beside it and stopped to have a good long look. He didn't know what to make of it. It had come at him upright, like a man, but hunched. It had scaly skin like a lizard, talons for fingers and toes. It had a long dog-like snout, lined with flesh-tearing fangs. It even had vestigial wings, although they weren't more than flaps of skin with flimsy bones no longer than Seth's arm and which seemed to serve no purpose. All in all, the dead thing looked as though someone had started with a crippled hunchback and then done an appallingly bad job of trying to turn him into a miniature dragon.

The strangest thing wasn't the wings, though. The strangest thing was the way the glass in the mirror had turned almost… pulpy, as the thing had pushed its way through. He'd been looking right at it as it started to emerge. One claw, then another, then the two of them pulling the opening wide, pushing its snout through. Seth had stood frozen to the spot until the first leg had squeezed though; and then for some reason, he hadn't run away screaming, but had calmly reached into a pocket and slapped a killing sigil onto its snout. The sigil had worked. Not just killed it but split it open. He had no idea why. Now, thinking back, he wondered if he'd made a mistake. The thing was monstrous but there hadn't been anything hostile about it. The look it had given him, just before he killed it, had been... servile?

Maybe *that* was the strangest thing.

The mark of the sigil was still there. Seth took two more and placed them on the creature's flanks. One to bring it back as his servant, the other to make it talk, if it could. He watched until the creature stirred.

"What are you?" he asked.

The creature looked at him, all baleful golden eyes. Did it even understand?

"Where did you come from? What are you doing here? What *are* you?"

The creature only stared. And then Seth heard a noise from somewhere deeper in the House of Cats and Gulls. The creak of an old wooden board, and then footsteps. Heavy boots, and then a voice, not far away.

"Lightbringer? That you?"

Seth froze. Lightbringer? There were *priests* here?

Shit. What were priests doing here?

He hissed at the creature. "Lie down and stay still."

The creature lay down and stayed still. It understood him, then. Maybe the problem was that it couldn't talk?

The footsteps came closer. Seth picked up his lantern. "Hello?"

A figure loomed from the shadows down a burned-out passage, and then stopped. "Who are you?" The voice sounded deeply suspicious.

"Lightbringer Seth. Did sword-mistress Tasahre not mention I might come by?" It was the only name he could think of they might know. "Come into the light where we can see each other."

The figure came cautiously closer and turned out to be a burly Sunguard. Rough and tough and pushing twice Seth's bulk, which Seth supposed was why the man's caution loosened as he came closer and saw what he was dealing with.

The Sunguard squinted. "I don't know you. Lightbringer *who*?"

"Lightbringer Seth. I have a message for you from the sword-mistress." Seth held out his hand, offering up a strip of paper with a sigil drawn on it. As the Sunguard bent to take a closer look, Seth pushed it against his face.

"What the...?" And then he froze as the sigil burned into his skin.

"Stay still. Be quiet. Protect me from harm," said Seth quickly.

The Sunguard didn't move.

"Good. How many of you are here? Tell me."

"Just the two of us." The soldier's voice had gone blank now, toneless, like the old priest from the temple. The thought gave Seth a pang of something he didn't want to think about.

He was old. He was going to die soon anyway.

Yes, but quietly and in his sleep. Would you like to remember his screams again?

Shut up! He was doing what needed to be done. Finding the truth so it could be exposed. Had to, so he could show the Path of Light for what it was: lies and hypocrisy, like the popinjay had said. For there to be a reason, in the end, for everything he'd done, so that things like some old Lightbringer accidentally going up in flames at least had some purpose instead of being pointless acts of random...

Evil?

He shook the thought away. Great deeds demanded great sacrifices. Someone had said that once. Khrozus, was it, after he took the throne?

*Oh, that's *your* role model?*

The Sunguard was staring at him, standing slack. Waiting to be told what to do.

"Are there sword-monks here?" Seth asked. "Or priests?"

"No."

Just as well. "Alright, I you need you to..."

To kill your friend and then slit your own throat? Is that what you want to say? Quick and easy and out of the way?

He *did* need these men gone.

"Sword-mistress Tasahre has asked me to stand watch tonight. You and whoever's with you, you can leave. Go home. Or go and get drunk. Yes, do that. Go and get drunk. Have fun. You'll still get paid. In fact..." He took a couple of Fings' silver moons from his pocket and pressed them into the soldier's hand. "A little extra for your time and trouble. Go. Do it now. Get out of here and get your friend out of here too."

He watched the Sunguard trot back the way he'd come. *Better, now?*

Shall we listen again to the screaming priest as he burned alive?

What if the second Sunguard didn't *want* to leave? What if he saw the sigil burned into his friend's face? What if the first Sunguard told him exactly what Seth had said and done – Seth hadn't told him not to, after all? What if they went back to the temple, and then the next thing he knew, every sword-monk in the Empire was hunting him...

He'd almost worked himself into a proper panic, torn between chasing after the soldier to tell him to kill his friend after all, or else running away from the House of Cats and Gulls and getting on the first ship he saw to somewhere else; and then he heard footsteps again, and the burly Sunguard was back, with an equally burly friend. The second Sunguard tipped him a salute.

"Much obliged to you."

Seth forced a weak grin. "You're welcome." He watched them go, walking quickly, glad to be away. Hopefully that would do it.

Hope? He'd had a lot of hopes, once. He'd watched them burn, one by one.

Could still go after them. Put them both in the river. Just another pair of corpses for Fickle Lord Moon.

Instead, he went back to the dead creature and told it to follow him and protect him from harm and went down to the cellar. Once there, he set the Orb of Memories on the ground, sat down and pressed his hands around it.

"Show me again where you hid it," he said. "Show me where you hid your Book of Endings."

He dived into the memories of the dead warlock and listened again to the last words. *The secrets of That Which Came Before. The Book of Endings. The Book of the Black Moon's herald.*

Deep breaths. *Yes, yes, yes!* That was why he was here! Why he'd come all this way! He felt sick. But that was the anticipation, right? And hot, so hot he was constantly sweating. The air down here, probably. And his head, pounding and so full of fog he could barely think…

Still feels like walking into a trap.

Yet here he was.

The book of the Black Moon's Herald. The warlock's words hadn't been meant for him. Someone else was meant to find this. But the Path of the Sun had come to the House of Cats and Gulls and the orb had been taken, and with it the message. Whoever had been meant to hear it, they were long gone.

The boy with half a finger missing?

Don't know. Don't care. Doesn't matter.

He went to the corner of the cellar where the warlock had hidden his iron box and started to dig. It didn't take long, only a few scrapes at the soft wet mud before his fingers found metal. It took a while longer before he had it free and he had to stop several times to catch his breath. Why was it so hard to breathe down here? His hands were shaking, slippery with mud. It took him three goes to open the catch. He couldn't think. His head was thumping like an oar-master's drum.

The Book of Endings. The secrets of creation.

Only that *wasn't* what was in the box when he finally got it open. Not a book of anything, only a single sheet of fine vellum inscribed with a solitary symbol; not even a new sigil but a piece of heraldry: a winged serpent rampant wearing a solar halo wrapped around a sword.

Seth clenched his fist.

"You *fucker*!"

He knew that symbol. Back in Varr, Fings had stolen a ring with that same mark and had tried to fence it. The symbol of the twelfth House of the Empire, the House that no longer existed. The House that history claimed had never existed at all.

Valladrune. The warlock was telling him to go to the ruin of a city more than a thousand miles away, sacked and flattened more than thirty years ago.

"Fuck. *Fuck*!"

He sat in silence for a bit, wondering how in the name of Khrozus the Murderer he was supposed to search an entire ruined city when he didn't even know for sure, if he was honest, what he was looking for...

A splash from the pit in the floor, from the flooded tunnel into the river.

Seth turned to look. There was a Dead Man pulling himself out of the water.

Of course there was.

"*Fuck* you."

He pulled a sigil from his pocket as the Dead Man hauled himself half out, strode towards it, all ready to put it down, and then stopped as the wards on the circle of stone flared and the Dead Man fell still.

"Yeah. That's right." Seth let out a long sigh of relief.

The wards flared again. And again and then again, brighter and brighter. Seth frowned and went to have a closer look.

The water in the pit was seething. There wasn't just *one* Dead Man trying to come out of the river. There were hundreds.

And then the wards faltered and died, and everything went dark.

İNTERLUDE:
ORİEN

Orien wasn't good at goodbyes. He didn't want Myla to leave, and he *really* didn't want her going to House Hawat. Having a living nightmare ooze through a mirror to try and kill you changed your perspectives on things.

"I have to do this," she said.

He clutched her arm, then let go, paced a tight circle, clawed at his chin, then stopped and looked her in the eye. "Get out while you still can. Come back when this is over. By then, there might not *be* a House Hawat."

She smiled but obviously didn't get it. "I *will* find a way back, I promise." She held him and made him stand still. "Say what I say. Light of the mind and strength of the limb and warmth of the heart and courage of the soul." She repeated the mantra until Orien's reluctant lips moved in time with the words.

"Better?"

"Yes," he said, although it wasn't. He wanted to tell her what was out there. What he *thought* was out there. About the Silver Kings, or wraiths, or half-gods, or whatever you wanted to call them.

White of skin and red of eye, see them once and then you die.

He wanted to tell her that his mistress was scared. She

who had the power to melt castle walls, and she was *scared*, and so was he, and yet he couldn't turn and run and didn't know why. He wanted to tell her how he needed her strength. Her courage... But none of that would stop her from going after her sister. Why would it?

"You know where to find me, come dawn," she said, as though she could taste his fear. "There's a place for you if you want it. Sometimes it's best to run away and fight another day."

"Does a sword-monk ever run away."

Her smile faded. "No. Though perhaps, sometimes, we should."

He watched her leave and head away towards the Avenue of Emperors and Deephaven Square and whatever fate awaited her. He heard his mistress call then; and for a moment, he hesitated. He'd given up so very much to get where he was. The worst mage in the Empire? Maybe. But still a mage.

If turned his back on everything now, what would he think of himself. More to the point, what would Myla think? She'd think he was a coward.

He closed the door, turned to go back inside and he saw he wasn't alone. A short figure, hooded and cloaked and shrouded in shadow, stood watching. He knew who she was, although he guessed he wasn't supposed to mention it, otherwise she wouldn't be hiding her face.

"The wraiths will come tonight, mage Orien." She touched a finger to her temple, then stood aside to let him pass. "Your mistress calls."

PART FIVE
SWORD-MONK

*Freedom is a sugar-coated fairy-tale. No one really wants it once
they understand what it means.*
– Seth

43

HOUSE HAWAT

Myla left the Guildhouse at dusk, Fings' anchor-on-a-rope coiled over her shoulder. There wasn't much she could do about getting a sword, but she could help herself to one from the Hawat guards if it came to that. Before she left, she put on the charm that Fings had given her. Not that she believed in that sort of thing, but it could hardly do any harm. And, well, Fings *did* have way of coming through things.

She detoured via the sea-docks to the *Mended Net* and asked after Seth, since Fings had managed to make it sound like it was important. After some confusion, once Myla discovered she should have been asking for *Brother* Seth, the slightly weird priest from out of town who worked some very odd hours, they let Myla into his room to see for herself.

There were stains on the floor. Ichor, still tacky to the touch, the same shit she'd had dripping from the end of her candlestick earlier that afternoon. As far as she now understood what had happened, the demon-things had gone after the temple as well as the Guildhouse. Not much luck among the mages, but with the priests it had been a different story. Odd that one had appeared *here*, of all places, although perhaps not as odd as Seth getting the better of it. She could only assume he'd had some help.

Either way, he was gone, and it didn't look like he was coming back. She asked around and discovered Seth had left not long before she'd arrived, pushing something heavy in a handcart. He hadn't said anything about leaving, never mind where he was going.

She left the *Mended Net* behind. The arteries of Deephaven were clogged with people trying to leave, with Longcoats and soldiers trying to keep the wagons flowing back and forth between the river and the sea; the back-streets, though, were quiet and empty, and so she crossed the Avenue of Emperors and climbed to the Peak through a ladder of side-streets and tiny squares, taking her time, enjoying the twilight air, the hint of warmth now that spring was on the way, the smells, the sounds, the sights. No one bothered her: a lone sword-monk walking home to the temple, that was all she was, but she felt eyes on her, nonetheless. The way the people watched her as she passed. What she saw, when they looked at her, was both hope and fear.

She found a quiet place to change clothes as the sun set. The temple gates were closed, something she didn't remember ever seeing before. She quietly left the sword-monk robes Fings had stolen outside. Tasahre was right: they weren't hers. Then she slipped into the alleys and the side-streets, picking her way around House Hawat and the surrounding houses, looking for a distraction. The air was turning cold now, no one about except a skeleton-watch of Longcoats in the square. The quiet reminded her of Varr and the Sulk, with snow and ice three feet deep in its alleys, muffling every sound. There was no snow here, but the air had a familiar crispness to it.

She might start a fire, she mused. Steal a wagon and set it ablaze, but so what? It wouldn't make the Hawat guards open the gates. Fings thought she needed a distraction but she didn't see how it could be done.

She looked up at the sky, at the rising full moon. An hour after dawn, the last boat would leave for the *Speedwell*. Soraya would be on it.

Soraya. The sister who hated her.

No matter.

She used Fings' rope-and-anchor and climbed the wall of the Hawat compound where he'd said. She dropped into the unguarded garden and followed his path to the guard at the servants' door and walked towards him, hands out in front of her, letting him see she was unarmed. He didn't notice until she was almost on top of him: when he did, he took an abrupt step back.

"I'm here to see Sarwatta Hawat," she said. "My name is Shirish."

She'd expected some sort of reaction. A recoiling, a look of horror, maybe even fear, at least *some*thing.

Nothing.

"The Shirish who stabbed him, in case you know a lot of Shirishes," she said, and then punched him, because if she was going to be dragged to her doom by some anonymous house guard, it could at least be an anonymous house guard who knew her name. She punched him again, kicked him in the knee, grabbed him as he went down, locked her arm around his throat and settled to choking him. After he'd thrashed and kicked and then fallen limp, she dragged him into the bushes. The safest thing would be to slit his throat, but that wasn't who she wanted to be. Instead, she held a knife to his neck and waited for him to come round.

"Be quiet and give me your clothes," she said, as he opened his eyes. When he didn't move, she pushed the knife into his skin. "I *will* cripple you, if you make this difficult."

She left him trussed up, tied with bits ripped from his own shirt, the frilly cuffs stuffed into his mouth. With luck, someone would find him in the morning, cold and miserable but alive. If he put his mind to it, he'd probably work himself free long before then. She took his coat and his knife but left his stupid cavalry sword, all very well for posing and duelling but not nearly as handy in a small space as the short stabbing swords she preferred. Then she collected the anchor and rope, remembering what Fings had told her about the roof, and slipped inside.

The roof. The roof and its signalling tower, that was the way. And yes, there were more soldiers up there, keeping watch, but what were they going to see when they looked at her? In the darkness, they'd see one of their own.

This was going to work. It had to.

44

THE BOATMEN

Whatever the popinjay was up to, Fings reckoned it could wait until morning. He wasn't happy about it, but he'd come a long way and waited a long time to find out what had really happened to Levvi. He trotted across a few rooftops, dropped to the street and darted through alleys and scruffy cluttered yards until he reached the waterfront. For the most part, the sea-docks were still swarming with people trying to leave and – unlike the river-docks – with soldiers and Longcoats stopping them. He kept away from all that, pushing through until he reached the far end, the cheap and smelly end where it was all fishing boats and nets hung up to dry and about as far away from the Avenue of Emperors as it was possible to get, close to the Hall of Records where he'd come with Myla.

Well... Where there *would* have been fishing boats. There had certainly been enough of them a few nights ago, before they'd all buggered off.

He found the pier where his three helpful boatmen were waiting. Fings reckoned they had to be smugglers, because who else would be up for some nefarious sculling about the harbour in the dead of night; in fact, who else with a boat would even still *be* here. A part of him reckoned smugglers was good because it meant they knew all about how to get around at night without being seen. Another part wasn't so sure: smugglers, like thieves, presumably had a bit of a tendency to take their money and then not bother with the actual earning it. He wasn't *sure* about that, not having met any smugglers before, but he knew plenty of thieves and reckoned the same principles applied.

He'd promised them a *lot* of silver.

He fingered the lucky charms in his pockets, especially the bone one, popped an old silver coin in his mouth for a touch of Silvertongue, then put on his best gap-toothed grin. They came at him with some expected haggling, demanding the rest of their payment here and now. Fings pointed out how they'd have no reason not to smack him with an oar, heave him into the sea and head home for an early night if he did that, gave them a third of what he'd promised and swore on his life that they'd get the rest when they brought him back to shore, turning out his pockets to make it clear he didn't have the other two thirds on him, because what idiot would head out on a boat carrying a great pile of metal? There was a grudging acceptance of this arrangement. Fings explained how the rest was hidden not far away; the boatmen explained how it would be a quick stabbing and a watery grave if Fings didn't make good the debt the moment they were back on land, and off they went, two of the boatmen on the oars, the third standing at the prow, keeping a look-out. The oars, Fings saw, had cloth wrapped around them where they sat in their rowlocks, and moved without a sound.

Definitely smugglers.

The boat pitched and heaved through the waves. For a while it didn't seem like they were getting anywhere – at least, they didn't seem to be getting any closer to the ships, even if the land got steadily further away. After a bit, he tried some conversation. When ignoring him didn't work, the smugglers told him to shut up and stay quiet.

Eventually, as the ships finally drew closer, Fings saw how

some of the lamps they hung were moving. Men on watch. He hadn't expected that. A ship, he'd thought, was a bit like a castle, only one with such a huge moat that there was hardly any point in setting any guards, was there?

"They're not looking for *us*, are they?" he asked.

"They're looking for whoever might be coming," hissed the man at the prow. "Time was, a wily crew could boat right up close, scale the anchor chains and help themselves. The Black Ships got wise to that long ago, but there's always some knob desperate enough to give it a try." He gave Fings a pointed look. "Way things are tonight… surprised there aren't more out."

Fings thought about this. Trouble was, he'd rather assumed they were going to do exactly that: come up alongside, he'd shimmy up one of the ropes they all seemed to have dangling into the water, have a good look around, see whether Levvi was there, and then…

And then *what*, exactly?

All this time he'd been thinking about how he'd find out what happened to Levvi, but what *did* happen next. They'd bought Levvi as a slave. What did you do with slaves? You sold them. So Levvi *wasn't* going to be on that ship, not really, and all those hopes he was carrying, they were going to be ash in his heart. And then what? Did the Black Ships keep ledgers like the slaving fort and the harbourmasters? Maybe they did, but suppose he found them, then what? Suppose – not that he'd even know what he was looking for – he managed to steal them and then found someone who could make sense of them. Suppose he found out where Levvi had been sold, and to whom, and for how much, and when. Suppose all that. What was he meant to do about it? Get a ship of his own? Sail to another world and keep on looking?

If that was what it took then yes, he reckoned that was exactly what he was going to do. Small problem with that being how he was spending the last of his money from Varr on these smugglers.

He wondered if Myla would help; but Myla had her own problems. A sister and a brother to look out for. She'd go south with them like she'd said. In her place, Fings knew he'd do the same.

Seth, then?

Didn't seem likely. Seth was the closest thing he had to family here in Deephaven, at least until he found Levvi; but Seth was on his own path now, and not a good one.

He'd be on his own and broke, then. And sure, he was used to having no money and he always worked alone because no one else could do the things he did. But he'd *also* always had someone to go back to. Always had a family. His Ma and his sisters. The Unrulys, back in the *Pig*. Myla and Seth, here in Deephaven. Even Myla's brother. Even Orien, at a pinch.

Well, maybe not Orien, what with him being a mage.

They were among the Black Ships now. The man at the prow hissed and pointed.

"There she is. The *Servant On Ice*."

The Black Ships were big. Bigger than the ships anchored closer to the shore.

"I'm looking for someone," said Fings. "Someone they took as a slave."

The boatman at the prow nodded. It was hard to tell in the dark, but did his face soften a little? "You wouldn't be the first." He studied the ship and then shook his head. "Shit."

"What?"

He pointed to the lamps on deck. "Strong watch tonight. Someone on the anchor. Some on the rudder ropes. A man looking out either side. Be a couple more of them on the decks somewhere too." He shook his head again. "You ain't getting aboard without them seeing."

Fings begged to differ. The boatmen quietly explained how he was wrong, how the men at the ropes and chains would have their hands on them, so even if their eyes somehow didn't spot him, their fingers would feel the movements of anyone trying to climb them. That the sides of a Black Ship were almost impossible, the wood hard and pieced together without a crack for as much as a fingernail.

"Where do they keep their slaves?" asked Fings.

The smugglers all looked at him like surely that was something everyone knew. "New slaves? In the hold, chained up. You got something with you for breaking chains?"

If there were locks keeping those chains in place, Fings reckoned he did. *New* slaves caught his ear, though. He didn't want *new* slaves. "What about old slaves?"

None of the smugglers had an answer to that. Fings told them to get as close as they dared, then settled in for a bit of praying. A little to the Sun and a little more to the Moon, because it was night and the moon was full and so the Fickle Lord was in charge right now, and anyway was more the sort to dish out a bit of luck if it took his fancy or else spit some ill-fortune in your face if he was in a bad mood. But mostly, Fings prayed to the little gods that no one else remembered. The spirits of this and that who rarely got a mention, and so maybe sat up and took some notice whenever a prayer passed their way. He prayed to all the sprites and all the faeries for whom luck was currency – not the faeries like the one he'd seen in the middle of a horde of Dead Men, mind – *that* was an entirely different type of faerie; no one in their right mind would ever pray to *them*. He prayed to the mischievous King of the Goblins, who, he had to admit, probably wasn't real, because in his heart of hearts he knew that goblins probably weren't real either; but if they *were* real then the King of Goblins was the King of Thieves, and why take the chance of being wrong?

When he was done, he stripped off his coat and shoes, made one last prayer to the Moon not to idly drown him because it felt like it, and dived over the side.

45

THE HORDE

Seth stumbled back to where he'd left his lantern and shone it at the well. The first Dead Man was already out of the water and coming at him. It came fast, which Dead Men didn't usually do, and with obvious purpose, which Dead Men didn't usually have, neither of which filled Seth with joy. Fortunately, it had the usual Dead Man stupidity and lack of reflex. Seth ducked a flailing arm and slapped a sigil on its wet chest. It dropped like a sack of cabbages.

"And fuck *you*, too."

Not that it was going to help. More were climbing out of the water, dozens of them, their sheer numbers the only thing slowing them down. Seth, on the other hand, had precisely three sigils prepared for felling Dead Men, after which he was royally screwed unless they decided to form an orderly queue and come at him very, very slowly.

Run like buggery it is, then.

He was halfway through turning when a shape barged past him coming the other way and ripped into the first wave of Dead Men climbing out of the water. The demon-thing he'd told to protect him; he'd almost forgotten, wrapped up as he was in hunting for the warlock's iron box.

He gave himself a moment to take in the flailing claws,

the flying dismembered limbs, the speed at which the dead demon-thing moved, then wished it luck and legged it.

The box was still in the cellar, the cruel joke of its contents beside it. Didn't matter. Seth had the warlock's orb in his satchel and knew what the symbol was telling him, even if he didn't like it. He ran through the House of Cats and Gulls, a part of him wondering where to go once he got out and what he was going to do when he got there, but mostly occupied with not smashing into walls and tripping over charred beams in the dark. Getting *out* was what mattered, and so it never occurred to him that there might be more Dead Men swarming from the river in other places as well, until he burst onto the waterfront and saw that that was exactly what was happening. Clambering up the piers, swarming over boats, the fuckers were everywhere. Not that he could see terribly well, what with all the mist suddenly rolling in off the river.

Mist?

Shit! He took a moment to peer for any white ships looming out there. He didn't see any.

Doesn't mean they're not coming, though.

The howls and wails and screams coming from up and down the waterfront made him feel a bit better – at least the Dead Men weren't coming specifically for *him*. From the way his day had gone this far, they just might have been.

He took a moment, tried to catch his breath and found he couldn't. He was gasping and wheezing, sweating like he was staked out under a desert sun. He felt like death. The pounding in his head and the cloud that came with it was getting worse. And what was he supposed to do? The waterfront was covered with screaming running people, with Dead Men, with men fighting them, and how long before the horde rushing from the cellars of the House of Cats and Gulls caught up; and all the while, the loudest thought in his head was screaming that this wasn't possible, that sinking a body in water was a sure way to stop it from coming back, sure as fire, that Dead Men coming out of the river shouldn't be happening.

Get a grip! He looked up and down the docks. Telling a horde of Dead Men that they were theologically incorrect wasn't going to help him get away from them without being ripped to pieces. He settled for running, as best he could, helped along with some swearing, wishing that he could sprint like Fings, and why did it have to be today, today when he had no air in him, when all he wanted to do was collapse in a heap and close his eyes?

Fings would have made for the rooftops where the Dead Men wouldn't be able to follow; and Seth had run from bad shit with Fings leading the way more than once, and they'd *always* found some way to get up high. Like Fings had a knack for it. He bolted down alleys and side-streets, looking for anything he could climb: a ladder, boxes, barrels, crates, anything...

Nothing.

Fuck's sake!

What he could really do with right now was a sigil for ending being visible to Dead Men. However Dead Men saw, with their dead eyes. How *did* they see? He'd never given it any thought.

He'd lost track of where he was. Away, that was all that mattered. Up, towards the Peak, away from the river-docks and towards the sea.

Unless they were swarming out from the water there, too?

Anywhere where he could stop and lie down and close his eyes...

The temple! The priests and the sword-monks would have something to say about a horde of Dead Men. He'd be safe there.

You don't think they'll have something to say about a warlock?

Let them. He was done. Spent. He just needed everything to stop.

He paused, trying again to catch his breath, and again it didn't make any difference. He was sweating and his head was swimming and he felt ready to be sick and he couldn't think straight. He had no idea where he was; all he could tell was which way *not* to go from the shouting and the screams. He kept on, heading uphill, and then something absurdly large and low and with wings like sails blotted out the moon as it passed overhead and disappeared behind the rooftops; and, for a moment, the sky turned as bright as day and filled with fire. An almighty *CRACK* split the air. The stone walls of the building beside him bulged and buckled and started to fall. He skidded to a stop and turned back, but now the whole side of the street was splitting and fracturing and coming down, and all he could do was dive into the shelter of a doorway as shattered stone and splintered wood rained down, and hope that it would hold...

Something hit him on the back and sent him sprawling, a crushing shock of weight and pain. He tried to roll back into shelter and found he couldn't move. He saw glimpses of cold, brittle sky, of heavy stone walls and wooden timbers falling, of dust and choking smoke, of remembered faces, smiling down at him...

He moaned softly, closed his eyes, and sighed as the world turned a blissful black.

46

A FAMILY MATTER

Myla followed Fings' path to the roof of the servants' wing. She saw the shutters that wouldn't open and the silhouettes of the guards on the rooftop walkway.

She bared her teeth. *All for me.*

Fings said it couldn't be done. The house was locked up tight and the roof walkway had a guard on every corner. From where she squatted, Myla could see the stubby spire of the signalling tower, little more than an extra room tacked on to the top of the house with a balcony looking down towards the sea-docks and a mage-made crystal that shone with the light of the sun hidden in a box for when the Hawats wanted to send messages to their ships in the harbour. She knew this because Sarwatta had shown it to her on the night she'd come here, about an hour before she'd punched him in the face. His "box of light."

That balcony was an entrance straight into the top of the house Hawat's private rooms. *If* she could get there without being seen, which meant passing at least two of the sentries in plain sight, which Fings reckoned couldn't be done.

Fuck you, Sarwatta.

She'd tried running. She'd tried repentance. She'd tried accepting punishment for what she'd done. Nothing had been enough; and maybe Tasahre was right, but it was too late for that, and so this was all she had left.

Your choice. Not mine.

"Hey! Did you see that?" The shout came from above. Myla flinched, thinking someone had spotted her; but what she saw when she looked up was a streak of light like a shooting star, fired from the heavens, coming straight down at the city. She didn't see where it went. Somewhere towards the river-docks.

Another flash seared the sky. Then another, striking at the city towards the river.

The river, which was on the opposite side of the house from where she crouched in darkness.

You'll need a distraction...

She squinted. The guards on the rooftop walkway had turned to watch. They all had their backs to her, eyes fixed on the horizon and the sky. She touched Fings' lucky charm, threw his anchor and rope, scaled the wall, and vaulted over the parapet. She landed low, ready for a fight, but no one had noticed her. The sentries on the two corners nearest to her only had to turn their heads, but they were all looking...

Up.

The fire from the heavens had stopped but they were still looking. Then she saw it, as it arced past the moon. Bat-like wings, a long tail like a whip and far enough away that it must be huge. Like a dragon, except dragons didn't belong in this world, they belonged in another, and only the Black Ships could cross between. She didn't know what it was or what it meant except that Orien had told her that something was coming, and that it was hard not to stare...

Soraya! Whatever it was, it could wait. She slipped along the walkway, hunched low towards the one guard who would surely see her when she climbed the roof to the stubby tower. She never took her eyes off him; but he never stopped looking at the sky, not until she had an arm locked around his neck, dragging him silently down.

She looked back to the sky as he fell still in her arms. Was *that* why Tasahre had wanted her at the temple tonight? To fight *that*?

Focus!

She looked at the unconscious guard on the ground. Whatever their faults, these were ordinary men with brothers and fathers and wives and daughters to mourn them. A swordmonk never brought suffering if they could help it, so she ripped the sleeve off her shirt and tied it tight across his mouth, hooked the anchor in his belt, tied the other end of the rope to the parapet, and heaved him over the side to dangle until someone found him. She wouldn't be coming back this way, not with Soraya.

She muttered a silent prayer and scaled the roof. The thing in the sky was still there. The flashes of fire had started again. No one turned, no one saw her, no one shouted an alarm. She vaulted onto the balcony. When she tried the door into the house, it wasn't even locked.

Best burglar in Varr, eh Fings?

The wooden lightbox with its enchanted crystal sat exactly where Sarwatta had shown it to her on the night he'd thought he was taking her to his bed. She lifted it from its plinth and looked away and closed her eyes as she opened it a crack, and yes, it still worked, still shone dazzling bright.

Mine.

The stair down from the tower was a creaking wooden thing. She remembered that, how the steps had groaned under Sarwatta's feet. It led straight into the uppermost storey of the house, where Sarwatta and his brother Jeffa had lived, where only the most trusted staff ever went, and then only rarely. She walked carefully, feet planted at the edges of each step, willing the wood not to give her away as she descended into darkness. It didn't matter that there was no light, she remembered this place like she'd been here only yesterday. The hall at the bottom of the stair, dark polished wood inlaid with gold. The walls with their silk tapestries from across all the worlds where the Black Ships sailed...

They're the ones with the real power, Sarwatta had said. *The Black Ships that sail between the worlds. The Emperor thinks he rules all creation from his Sapphire Throne, but their empire is greater, awash with marvels we can only imagine. One day, Shirish, I will show it to you.*

He'd made the same promise to Soraya. The same words, only days before. That was the moment she'd known she was going to hurt him.

A dozen steps to his door. She found it without even having to feel at the walls. Beyond was what he'd called his Seashell Room, a narrow room, walls covered in shells from the beaches of a thousand different shores. Apart from the shells, it had a long bench for waiting guests and nothing much else. Beyond was the room he called his study but which he treated as though it was a throne room. And beyond *that...*

You're not here for him.

She tried the door anyway, but it was locked, and she wasn't Fings.

Just as well...

The day she'd been here, nearly a year ago, this floor of the house had been split half and half between Sarwatta and his brother Jeffa. Jeffa was gone now. Myla had cut off his head, because, like his brother, he simply couldn't accept when he'd lost. Would Soraya be there? No. Too fresh a wound. Sarwatta would keep her close, though. One of the guest suites, then?

She remembered how there was another door into the Seashell Room, small and with a solid lock on it. He'd never told her what it was and she'd never thought to ask. Access to another suite? The place where he kept his lovers?

She followed the wall, feeling her way across the silk of a tapestry that probably cost more than her entire family had ever been worth, drawing a map in her head, working out where that door must go, how any rooms beyond might open into this hall. She found another opening. An arch into a nook, with a door at the back, small and low.

Locked, again.

She brushed her hand against the wall, wondering what to do. Smash it down? The noise would give her away…

Her hand touched something metal. A key, hanging on a hook.

Locked from the outside. Not to stop anyone from getting in, but to stop someone from getting out.

Soraya!

She took the key and turned the lock and eased the door open and stepped inside.

Yes! The air carried a scent. The fragrance of her sister.

A breath of movement made her duck and dart forward. She felt something heavy skim the skin of her back.

"Soraya?"

"*Shirish*?" A hiss of disbelief and anger and hope and resentment all rolled together.

"Yes! It's me."

A long silence. Myla strained her ears, listening for any sounds from the rooms around them. When she didn't hear any, she turned very slowly, and whispered:

"Are you going to try and hit me again?"

Another long pause. Then: "How did you get in?"

It would do for now. "Over the wall and through the light-tower on the roof. There's a ship. The *Speedwell*. It sails an hour after dawn. It'll take us to Helhex. We'll go to Torpreah. Lucius is coming too. He'll take you to mother and father."

He'll take you. Like Myla wasn't going. But she *was* going. Wasn't she?

"You know he won't stop coming for us," whispered Soraya.

"I know."

"Because of you."

She couldn't see her sister in the darkness. Knew where she was but couldn't see her.

"Are you going to kill him?" Soraya asked.

"Would you like me to?"

A long pause. "I don't know. I loved him once."

"You know he's going to murder you after the child is born."

"He said exile."

"He lied. He does that."

Soraya didn't reply.

"Can you climb the roof? Scale a rope?"

"A rope? No, I don't think so."

No. That was always going to be too much to ask. "Soraya... I came to get you out. You *do* want to get away from him, don't you?"

"Shirish... *Fuck* you! Yes, of course, but how?"

"I'll show you." Myla locked the door to the hallway nook and carefully pocketed the key. Then she went to the door into the Seashell Room. She felt around its edges and gently pressed and pulled on it, looking for the bolts. It was locked, of course, but the lock was a flimsy one. When she thought she had the measure of it, she took a deep breath and tensed.

And now the fun starts.

She kicked the door, square at the lock. Wood splintered, shattering the quiet. A second kick and it gave way, and the door flew open.

"Close your eyes," she said.

47

THE BLACK SHİP

The sea was kind enough to let Fings reach the Black Ship without drowning him. He clung to the hull as best he could and made a mental note to give thanks to Fickle Lord Moon when he got back to shore. The side of the ship angled up out of the sea over his head, unexpectedly smooth under his fingers. The smugglers had it right: he had no idea how to climb it. Which was annoying, because he was used to being able to climb almost anything; and because the sea was cold as shit and the waves were knocking him about, and there was a good chance he'd drown if he didn't get out soon.

Anchor chains and rudder ropes. That's what the smugglers had said.

Yeah, and that they're all watched.

He'd seen the anchor chain angling out from the front of the ship and reckoned there was no climbing it without being seen if someone up on deck had their eyes open. Which left the rudder ropes. He had no idea what rudder ropes were for or where to find them, but they weren't the anchor chain, so they'd have to do.

He thought for a bit. Ships had rudders at the back, which was usually the less pointy end. Well, he could find *that*, and then see about things. Except when he got to the back of the ship, what he found was a wall of wooden planks that went up nice and straight and with various windows and assorted bits sticking out that made it perfectly climbable without needing any ropes, and so that was what he did, all the way up until he peeked his head over the wooden rail at the top.

Two sailors were keeping watch, both with lanterns. One leaned against the back of the ship in the middle of the rail, his hands resting on a pair of ropes, one to either side of him, his lantern at his feet. The other was sitting on a wooden box, a few paces away. They were talking, chattering away in some gibberish language Fings reckoned he hadn't ever heard in Varr. They were smoking pipes.

He grinned to himself. Their lanterns were on the deck between them, which meant they couldn't see anything in the gloom outside their circle of light. He hung from the rail, eased his way to a corner over the deck, hopped over and crouched in the darkness, wondering what to do next. Search the ship from top to bottom looking for anything that might tell him what happened to Levvi?

He took a good long look at the two men standing watch. They had slave brands on their arms and yet here they were, standing guard. Did that mean they'd *been* slaves but now they weren't? Was that possible? If it was, how did it work? A brand was a brand. Once you had one, there was no getting rid of it.

He thought about that. In a pinch, he supposed he could simply ask?

Best leave them alone.

He tiptoed off and found some steps that ran to the main deck. He skulked his way across the ship, keeping a watchful eye on the lanterns of the watchmen, slipping between their circles of light as they moved, looking for ways down into the body of the ship, because how else was he going to find anything?

He found several hatches, all shut tight. Presumably, they had ladders or stairs, probably steep ones, difficult to take at speed. He didn't like the look of them, not one bit. Too easy for the watchmen to seal them if someone raised the alarm while he was below. Keeping a clear run to a clean escape was always the first rule of good burgling.

If Myla was here, she'd have stood guard for him, held the exits while he made his escape, if it came to it. Or even Seth, who would somehow have pretended to be important and in charge, who would have talked the men standing watch into doing all the work of finding Levvi and then letting them walk away. Probably would have had them help him into the boat so he didn't get wet.

But Seth *wasn't* here, and nor was Myla, and he really wasn't liking those hatches. Felt like traps, they did.

Two man job, this.

The bone charm was still there, stitched into his pocket. He rubbed it as he crept to the watchmen on the stern deck and walked into their circle of light.

"Hello," he said, and held up his hands.

They almost jumped out of their skins. One went for a knife, holding it out in front of him, pointing it at Fings. Fings cringed and dropped to a crouch, making himself small, and put a finger to his lips, begging them with his eyes not to sound the alarm. They looked at him with narrow-faced suspicion but they didn't shout.

"What the fuck are you?" hissed the sailor who'd been leaning against the railing.

"Fucking *thief*!" The other moved to shine his lantern over the side, searching the water.

"Nah," said the first. "Stowaway, I reckon."

"No! Well... yeah, but... Look, I'm looking for my brother. He was sold to this ship. Name's Levvi. Was years ago but... I don't know where else to look."

He saw how their expressions changed. *Levvi.* The name meant something to them. He felt his heart skip and jump. Slowly, he got back to his feet.

"Please... I'm not here to steal anything and I don't want

passage or nothing. Don't want to make any trouble. I just want to know what happened to him."

"You're... Levvi's *brother*?" The sailor who'd been shining his lantern down at the sea now shone it in Fings' face, looking at him, incredulous.

"What's your name?" asked the other sailor.

"Fings."

"And your *other* brother."

Fings frowned. His *other* brother? What kind of a question was that? "Seth. Although he's not a real brother." He looked at the two sailors, trying to figure them out, and then suddenly he understood. "You... Levvi? You knew him! Right?" Didn't only *know* him, they were talking about Levvi almost as though he was a friend. "What happened to him?"

"*Happened* to him?" The sailors looked at each other, then at Fings. "You *really* his brother? Fings?"

Fings nodded. "Yeah."

They looked at each other again, and now they were almost smiling. "The brother who could sneak into the Emperor's bedroom and swipe his clothes while he was still wearing them and somehow get away with it?"

Fings swallowed, finding an odd lump in his throat. Thing was, he remembered Levvi saying exactly those words before he left, standing by the River Gate in Varr. *You'll do all right, Fings. You could sneak into the Emperor's bedroom and swipe his clothes while he was still wearing them...* "Do you...? Do you know what happened to him?"

The sailors exchanged another glance. One shook his head. He was smiling to himself. "See for yourself," he said, and headed off into the gloom, leaving his lantern.

The other looked Fings up and down. "Five years," he said. "Kelm's fucking teeth. Five years and you came looking?"

"I just... want to know. What...? What's going on? *Do* you know him?"

The sailor didn't answer. For a few minutes, they stood in

silence; and then Fings heard footsteps coming towards them. He turned. Two men this time; the watchman from before and...

Levvi?

In the months after Levvi left, arguments had raged through the extended family as to what he'd make of himself. Sometimes Levvi was across the oceans, working his way impossibly fast to be captain of some great merchant ship. For a while, Ma Fings got it in her head that Levvi had followed Seth's footsteps and become a priest, already the ruler of an exotic kingdom full of the converts he'd created; or else he was in Torpreah, serving the Autarch. Sometimes he *was* the Autarch by now. But Fings had always known better. Levvi had gone to Deephaven to do the exact same shit he'd been doing in Varr before he'd tried working an honest job as a tanner.

And he'd been caught, and sold as a slave, and here he was.

Fings stared through a blur of tears. It *was* him, it really was. Leaner, stronger, all muscles now, standing upright in a way Fings didn't remember. Like he was proud. Like he was free.

"Fings?" Levvi stared.

"Levvi! I thought... we all thought..."

Fings caught a glimpse of the slave-brand on Levvi's arm, and then Levvi launched himself, grabbing Fings in a crushing embrace. He looked to the other sailors, one to the other and back again. "See! What did I tell you? Steal the—"

"Emperor's clothes while he was still wearing them," the others finished, and they all laughed.

"Fings! What are you *doing* here? How'd you *get* here?"

Fings sniffed. "Swam, didn't I?"

"But..." Levvi shook his head in disbelief. "Told you I was going to sea to make my fortune, didn't I?" He stood back and looked Fings up and down, and then grabbed him by the shoulders again and shook him and swore under his breath.

"Five years, Levvi," said Fings. "You said two."

"Yeah." Levvi looked away. "Didn't... quite go the way I

thought." He took a deep breath and huffed it out. "So... How's Ma? How are my sisters?"

"Doing alright. All as difficult as ever." Fings forced a smile. Most of him was still struggling with the idea that Levvi was here, right in front of him. The rest was struggling with the absurdity of the two of them lurking on the back of a Black Ship in the dead of night. "Levvi... what happened to you? What you... What you *doing* here?"

Levvi screwed up his face. He turned away and spat.

"I know some of it. Found the thief-taker who caught you. I know you got made a slave and then sold. But..."

"Took us across the sea," Levvi said. "Across the storm-dark to other worlds. Things you wouldn't believe." He chuckled. "Not that we got to see any of it, not the first few times. Chained us down in the bowels of a galley. Two years as an oar-slave. But we stuck together. Seven of us, all taken on the same day from Deephaven. We kept each other going and came out the other side. After that..." he looked back at Fings, and this time Levvi was the one with tears in his eyes. "They here? In Deephaven?"

"Who?"

"Ma. My sisters."

"No. Still in Varr."

"Fings! I told you to look after them!"

Fings frowned at that. "They're fine. We got money for a bit. Enough to get by."

"Do I want to know?"

The other sailors drifted away. Fings told Levvi about Varr, about how things were, how they'd been, the years of running jobs for Blackhand in the *Unruly Pig*, barely making ends meet, about Seth being thrown out of the Path of Light. Levvi lapped it up and begged for stories, although he simply refused to believe the one about stealing the Emperor's crown and Blackhand being dead and all the other stuff that had happened in the month up to Midwinter. And Levvi had his own stories too, of all the places he'd seen, the worlds that were out there, the places the Black Ships went, worlds where there were dragons, where there were castles made of gold and glass. Palaces and crystal ships that could fly and men who could turn into air and water and fire. How he'd been a slave, but it wasn't like that now, not really. How he was a sailor.

How, though he never came out and said it, he'd finally found his place in the world.

One of the sailors pointed to the sky. "You see that?"

Fings looked up. At first, he had no idea what he was supposed to be looking at, but then it came again. A streak of light, arcing from the sky, flying over the Peak towards the far side of the city.

They all stopped what they were doing and stared. Another came, and then another, lines of fire falling from the sky. The sailors exchanged a look. From near the bows, a bell started to ring.

"You better go," said Levvi.

"Alright," said Fings. "There's a boat waiting. Not far. You can still swim, right?" He grabbed Levvi by the arm and tugged, and then didn't quite understand when Levvi didn't move.

"I ain't coming with you, Fings."

"Oh Xibaiya!" One of the sailors again. "You see *that*?"

"What do you mean, you ain't coming?" Fings held Levvi's arm tighter and tugged again, and still Levvi didn't move.

"What the fuck is it?" The sailors were gawping open-mouthed up at the sky. Whatever it was, it would have to wait.

"Levvi! There's a boat! You can come home!"

"I can't leave," Levvi said.

"You *have* to!"

"No, Fings. I can't."

Fings shuffled his feet. He was the wrong person for this. Myla, with the strength of her conviction. Seth and his way with words. But not him. Not Fings, who believed in goblins half the time and couldn't even read.

Levvi took Fings' hand and gently pried him loose. "Fings... This is my place now."

"That's a fucking dragon," said the first sailor. "Seen them before."

"Liar."

"Truth! Port called Furymouth. Dozens of the fuckers. Levvi... Your brother's got to go."

"Levvi!" Fings made another grab for him. Levvi took a step back.

"Maybe we should take him with us?" suggested the other sailor.

Levvi backed away. "Fings... I was never any good in Varr. I tried, but... When I got to Deephaven, I went right back into the same mistakes. The first years on a Black Ship are... well, never mind that. But now... It's like I'm free. Back home...? I wouldn't know what to do."

The deck hatches were opening. Men were coming out. Shouting at one another and pointing up at the sky. Fings turned away.

"I love you, brother, and Ma and my sisters. But this is my home now. This is where I belong."

A black-skinned Taiytakei in white robes hurried up the steps, carrying a golden glass rod. He shouted in a language Fings didn't understand, and then his eyes landed on Fings and snagged there. He shouted something else.

"Refugee, sir," snapped one of the sailors. "Swam all the way from the city."

Fings didn't understand the next words either, but he got the gist. *Not on my ship!*

The sailors looked at Fings. He saw pity in their eyes. He didn't mind so much, what they were about to do. But Levvi... he saw the same pity there, too.

"Thank you, brother," whispered Levvi. "I won't forget this." He grabbed Fings and pushed him towards the rail. "Tell my sisters I think of them. Tell them I've found my place. Tell them I'll find you again one day, when I'm ready. Tell them not to waste their prayers on me until I do."

And then he tossed Fings back into the sea.

48

JUST RUN

Seth opened his eyes to find a Dead Man trying to eat his face. It wasn't the sort of Dead Man Seth was used to seeing in Varr. It stank and was half rotted. A bit like it had been lying at the bottom of a river for a good long time.

He screamed and kicked the Dead Man away. It raked jagged fingernails along his leg, tearing skin, gurgled something and tried again to bite him. Seth screamed for a second time, mostly to convince himself that he was still alive, and wriggled a hand free to snatch a sigil from his pocket. He slapped it in the Dead Man's face as it lunged for his ear.

It dropped.

Seth took a moment. He didn't know where he was. His wits were scattered. He felt hot and sick and breathless. Everything hurt and his head seemed to have an army of bad-tempered soldiers marching through it, occasionally stabbing at him with their knives. Eventually, he pulled himself to his feet and stood, quivering. Everything ached and his leg was burning from the Dead Man's scratch. When he looked down the street, through the settling dust, he half-expected to see a swarm of them pouring towards him; instead, all he saw was rubble and darkness.

From off in the distance, he heard shouting and screams. Muffled, though, and not close.

Fuck this.

Whatever had hit the warehouse beside him had hit it hard. There was nothing left except a mound of rubble strewn across the street. He doubled back, took the first alley he found that wasn't full of broken stone, and kept on going, heading uphill. He didn't like scurrying through narrow alleys at night even at the best of times. Now? In a city he didn't know? With a horde of Dead Men roaming the streets?

Why did a horde of Dead Men have to swarm out of the river on the exact same night he went to the House of Cats and Gulls? Sixteen fucking years they'd had to choose from, and it had to be tonight? What the fuck, exactly, had he done to deserve this level of shit?

I'm cursed, that's what.

Valladrune. Sulfane had been from Valladrune. All the business in Varr, all the shit Myla and Fings had gone through with the crown, somehow it all tied back to something in Valladrune before the civil war. Sulfane had had a book, written in cipher, that might even hold answers. Fat lot of use now. Seth hadn't ever cracked it. He'd left it behind in Varr. Presumably, the sword-monks had it now, along with everything else he'd ever owned...

Concentrate!

He had one sigil left to put a Dead Man down. As good as useless, given what he'd seen by the river, so he kept heading towards the Peak. Not that he had much idea what to do once he got there, only that it was somewhere where he could get his bearings, and where the Dead Men weren't.

It has sword-monks. And priests. Maybe you could help them?

He had a bit of a laugh at that. Even now, after everything he'd done and everything he knew, a part of him still wanted to go back.

That ship Myla said. What was it called again?

He couldn't remember. Hadn't been listening. Hadn't had any intention of leaving.

Pity, that. Might be handy to know, eh?

He heard a hubbub ahead. Running feet. A few people came hurrying past him, heading the other way. He wondered if he should warn them what was coming from the river but the thought seemed to get stuck in his head. They trotted past and were gone and he still didn't have an answer.

Still, they'll slow the Dead Men down a bit, right?

He had absolutely no idea where he was.

A noise cut through the night. An unearthly shriek from somewhere high. It came again. He ducked into an alley as more people came running, faster than the first few. Once they were past, he kept going, rounded a corner and found himself in an abandoned market. He pushed on. Another scatter of people came, and then the trickle turned to a flood, all noise and screams. He wedged himself into a gap between two empty stalls as people tumbled by, helter-skelter, pushing each other down, trying to run through each other, raw fear and nothing else. Shouts and screams swept through them like waves. Stalls were battered and shaken and overturned. Seth had no idea what they were running *from*, but he knew damn well what they were running *towards*.

He pushed himself deeper between the stalls. Joining the stampede was only going to get him trampled. He ducked and crawled and went the other way, and then he saw why everyone was running, and wished he'd taken his chances.

Walking down the street towards him was what looked like a man made of metal. Silver, darkened to black by the night, glinting from the light of the moon and from firelight cast through windows. It had a curved sword in each hand, and shone with an inner light; quiet, calm, white moonlight. It came in peaceful silence, a trail of blood and murdered corpses in its wake. It didn't seem in any hurry. Seth couldn't be sure, but it looked a lot like whatever Fings reckoned he'd seen. A faerie-king, Fings had said, but Seth knew better.

The warlock's wraith.

He ran. Not into the bottleneck of the market because that was a death-trap, but through an open door, through a house, out into a yard, through a gate and down the nearest alley, running and not thinking about much else as long as where he went was away from that... *thing*... Anywhere was good enough, right up until *anywhere* spat him out on the waterfront of the river-docks, half a mile downriver from the House of Cats and Gulls.

Fuck's sake! *How am I back here?*

He stopped. Ahead, a crowd of men and women, frightened and confused, milled uncertainly, unsure what to do or where to go. No Dead Men, though.

But they came out of the river. You saw them. If they're not here, where are they?

He had to stop. He was exhausted. His head was spinning and pounding. He couldn't think. He tried to blink it all away, but nothing worked. He looked back the way he'd come. No sign of the wraith but he had no doubt the thing was still there, heading closer, calmly and leisurely murdering whoever got in its way.

Right. But where's it going? What does it want?

He looked again down the river towards the House of Cats and Gulls. Still no Dead Men.

So they went somewhere else? Right. Great. But where?

Somewhere up-river, that much was sure, so he wasn't going *that* way. And he wasn't going back the way he'd come, either, which left heading further downriver and trying again for the Peak, or else diving into the river itself and taking his chances with the...

Skiffs started drifting out of the mist. A handful, then dozens, then hundreds. Seth's first thought was they'd come to take people away. The crowd on the waterfront obviously thought so too as they surged to the piers. Seth watched the first skiff pull up, a dozen mud-spattered sailors on board. Hairy and ragged, so dirty it was hard to say where skin ended and clothing began. As soon as the boat was secure, they jumped out, swarmed up the steps, pulled out knives and started stabbing. Seth stared, open-mouthed. There was no design to it, no purpose, only murder and raw carnage.

Oh for fuck's... really?

His ears were ringing. He couldn't stop shivering. The air felt icy cold. Something stank, not the estuary reek of rotting fish, but worse. A reek of corruption and decay. The river-docks were turning into a pitched battle, a no-quarter fight to the death between the men coming off those skiffs and the river-workers and dock-hands and whoever could pick up a weapon; in between, men and women ran and screamed, while the smell of decay grew stronger, tinged with iron. The air felt so cold he felt his skin burn...

And there they were. Now he saw them. Further up-river. The prows of seven white ships rising from the mist.

He picked the most likely-looking alley and ran.

49

SARWATTA

"Close your eyes." Myla squeezed hers shut and looked away and opened the lightbox. Only for an instant, but enough for the guardsmen in the Seashell Room to yell and curse. Then she closed it and went for her knife. There were five. They'd been sitting half-asleep, a pair of lamps hanging on the walls. Kicking in the door had stirred them like she'd kicked a nest of wasps; they were on their feet, half-drawn swords tangling between their legs, hands raised, reeling from the blaze of the lightbox, and the Seashell Room wasn't big, and so it was going to get crowded. They had gaudy uniforms, but they weren't soldiers. They were ornaments, these men, dressed in fine shirts and with gilded steels to show off the wealth of their masters. She knew their sort. Men from families like hers, serving a merchant prince in hope of advancement. She might even know their names, some of them, if she stopped to look at their faces.

They were between her and Sarwatta. Better, then, that they stay faceless. She grabbed the nearest, slammed his head against the wall, cracking shells, and down he went.

You could have simply left. Taken Soraya and gone back out the way you came.

She jab-punched the next on the nose, kicked him between

his legs, grabbed his hair as he doubled over and slammed her knee into his face.

And then what? Hope the guards on the roof keep staring at the sky while Soraya labours over the balcony and tries not to slip and fall as I lower her down the roof. And even if they did, what then?

The third must have been turned away when she'd dazzled them. He had his sword drawn, quicker than the others. He took a clumsy swing. She ducked and dodged past him and slashed her knife across the back of his knees.

"I'm sorry." He'd never walk again but at least he wasn't dead.

The last two were blinking away the light from the lightbox. She kicked one in the knee, bending his leg at an angle legs weren't supposed to bend. He screamed.

"Stay down," she growled. That one *might* walk again, one day. "Soraya! Make sure they stay down!"

One more to go…

The door to Sarwatta's study flew open. There he was, still dressed, wearing a heavy leather jerkin studded with metal. He saw her. His eyes went wide, and his mouth gaped. He ducked back. Myla crashed into the last guardsman, barging him half through the door before Sarwatta could close it. The guardsman tried to throw her off, but Myla was having none of it. She pressed her stolen knife to his throat.

"Drop your blade." She pushed him on, driving them further into Sarwatta's throne-room.

The guardsman dropped his blade.

"Now turn and run away before–"

A sharp pain lanced into her belly. The guardsman's eyes went wide, and then he gagged and sagged into her. Sarwatta had run him through. Run them *both* through. Stuck his slender prick of a sword right through his own man and stabbed her.

Oh.

She looked down at herself. Pressed a hand to her stomach and felt her shirt wet and sticky. For a second, Sarwatta

simply looked at her, waiting to see what would happen. He
should have struck again, without hesitation, but he didn't.
If anything, he looked surprised.

Myla raised her stolen knife and fixed her eyes on his. Had
he killed her? She wasn't sure. Impossible to tell how deep
his sword had gone. An inch? Two? Even an inch could be
enough; but if he *had* killed her, it would be slow enough for
her to get Soraya out of here. After that… After that, they'd
both go down together.

"Not good enough." She looked him in the eye. "But that
was always you. Simply not good enough."

He lunged then, fast and precise and straight for the heart.
Myla twisted, parried, made a lunge of her own and squealed
as fresh pain tore from where he'd stabbed her. Sarwatta
ducked back; and now her knife, so perfect in the crowded
space before, lost its virtue. He had space, his sword gave him
the advantage of a better reach and he was smart enough to
use it, retreating deeper into his study to circle behind his desk;
when Myla followed, he slashed at her face and then jabbed
at her chest, then cut at her feet and then another slash that
turned into a lunge. She dodged them all, looking for a chance
to close the distance between them. The moment she got inside
his reach was the moment this fight would end; but he knew
that as well as she did, and she'd put four men to the ground
behind her and hadn't killed any of them. Two wouldn't be
getting up any time soon, but the other two wouldn't stay
down forever…

"You're trapped, Shirish. Lay down that blade and I'll spare
your sister."

"Liar." She scuttled around the side of his desk, picked up
some papers and threw them at him, but they merely scattered
in the air. She heard a squeal and a cry from where she'd left
his crippled guards.

Soraya! And now she heard a shout from deeper in the
house, and thumping footsteps, and then a fist pounding on

the door to the Seashell Room outside, and a man calling to his master.

"She's here!" shouted Sarwatta. "Break down the door!"

He edged closer. Myla jumped around the desk, a flailing arm across it, sweeping its contents at him as she jumped in and slashed. He danced away, keeping his distance.

"You took me by surprise last time," he said.

"No, I was just better than you." She kept at him, advancing slowly, drawing his attacks, parrying each as it came, slowly pressing him around the desk until he had his back to the door into the Seashell Room once more. She supposed that made him feel safe, knowing it was where his guards would appear. "Your brother had more men when he came at me in Varr, and I still took his head." Myla stayed where she was. She held up her hands. "Take me if you can, half-man." The walls shuddered as someone tried to shoulder through one of the locked doors.

Sarwatta's lip curled. "Everything you hold dear, razed to ashes before your eyes. Your brother first. I'll have him skinned while you watch. Then your sister, after she gives me my heir. Long and slow, both of them, so you can hear them scream and beg for it to end. But not you. *You* can live, a plaything on a chain, knowing what you brought on those you love."

The walls shuddered again. The shouts outside the Seashell Room grew louder.

"I'll give you the same chance I gave you before," said Myla. "Say you're sorry and I'll let you live."

"Sorry? For *what*?" Sarwatta laughed as he shook his head. Myla saw movement behind him. Soraya, in the doorway to the Seashell Room.

"Was my sister only ever a toy for you?"

His lip curled as the door shook again. "But that's what your sort are *for!*"

"*My* sort?" Soraya hit him round the back of the head with a scabbard. Sarwatta stumbled forward, dazed; as he did,

Myla stabbed her knife into his sword arm, straight between the bones behind his wrist, in and out again. As he screamed and dropped his blade, she grabbed him and pulled, let his momentum take him past her, wrapped an arm around his face, pulled back his head, exposing his throat, raised the knife ready to bring it down...

No!

No. She was here for Soraya, and so she needed Sarwatta alive to get them out of here. She stopped the blade, holding it against his skin, pulling him tight against her.

Sarwatta stared at the blood running down his fingers. "My arm! You bitch! You fucking *bitch*!"

Myla pressed the edge of her knife into his skin, enough to draw blood. She might have replied, but Soraya got in first, jabbing him twice in the face with the end of her stolen scabbard.

"*My* sort?" she spat. "Arsehole!"

Outside the Seashell Room, someone was shouting Sarwatta's name. Myla heard wood splinter, then caught the look on Soraya's face. She turned Sarwatta and backed away, holding him as a shield. The guard she'd kneed in the face was standing in the doorway, leaning against it, staring in like he couldn't quite understand what he was seeing.

"Kill them!" hissed Sarwatta. "Both of—" He gasped as Myla dug the knife into him again.

The soldier took a lurching step into the room, sword drawn. He stared at Sarwatta, and then at Myla, and then at Soraya. He blinked a few times and staggered and nearly fell, catching himself on Sarwatta's desk.

"Don't!" warned Myla.

The door outside shook again, then again. Someone was taking an axe to it.

"I will kill you if you take another step!"

The soldier took another step, waving his sword towards Soraya. Myla hissed into Sarwatta's ear.

"Call him off or lose half the fingers on your right hand."

"Fuck you!"

The solder took another step. Myla hooked a foot around Sarwatta's ankle, let go of his throat and pushed; as he stumbled, she slammed his head into the desk and let the movement carry her on into the soldier. He didn't seem to quite understand what was going on, even as she rammed the knife up under his jaw.

She watched him fall. Another corpse on her conscience.

"No. Fuck *you*!" She grabbed Sarwatta, pinned him, pulled his arm free, knelt on his wrist and hacked off two of his fingers. He screamed and screamed; Myla screamed right back: "I told you! I fucking *told* you! You even breathe wrong and the next time I will *blind* you!"

Sarwatta was still screaming as she grabbed him by the hair and pulled him to his feet. From the sounds outside, Sarwatta's soldiers were about done axing their way into the Seashell Room.

"Now what?" asked Soraya.

Myla shrugged. She'd vaguely thought of tying the sheets from Sarwatta's bed into a rope and going out the window, leaving Sarwatta hanging from a noose; but that was never going to work, not for Soraya with her great belly. Books and words and numbers and ledgers, that was the world she'd been raised for, and Lucius too. And besides, escaping to the yard outside was no escape at all. They still needed to get through the gates into Deephaven Square, and those gates were firmly closed, at a least a dozen men still standing in her way.

"We walk out the front door," she said. "And they'll let us, because if they don't, I'll kill him."

"And if they don't?"

Myla bared her teeth. "Then we'll all die together."

50

BROTHERHOOD

Fings didn't remember swimming back to the boat, but here he was, sitting in it, soaking wet. He had some vague notion of the smugglers hauling him out of the water, then a conversation along the lines of: *did you find him? Yeah, but he wanted to stay,* and then: *well, shit.* And *yeah.*

Now they were heading to shore. Fings would give the smugglers the money he'd promised – partly because he didn't want to be stabbed, but mostly because they'd turned out to be a decent lot in the end, and it was only fair. He didn't know what he was supposed to do after that. Go back to Varr and tell everyone that Levvi was alive? Tell them what Levvi had said, that he'd abandoned them? Settle down in the *Unruly Pig* with Dox and Arjay and whoever else was left of Blackhand's gang? What else was there?

Felt empty, though.

Find Seth? Seth wasn't ever going back to Varr, but Seth was his brother too. Close as made no difference, anyway.

The boat was heading to the same pier it had left. On the way out, Fings had been looking to sea and so hadn't really noticed how far it was from one end of the sea-docks to the other. He was glad they were making land away from the Peak. From out on the water, the docks at the end of the Avenue of

Emperors looked like a riot in full swing, the roar of the crowds carrying in peaks and troughs with a rhythm like the waves. He could see the lights of a thousand torches and lanterns, of what must have been a hundred boats and more, tied up to the piers or rowing out to sea and the waiting ships, or back again. Looked like everyone was in a hurry to get away.

He looked up, not sure how he felt about being on a boat when there was some flying monster about and fire falling from the sky. Glancing at the smugglers, they didn't like it any more than he did.

"Where's the rest of the money, then?" asked the one who did the steering and, for the most part, seemed like he was in charge.

Fings told them. The tillerman changed course and they eased up to a different pier. Fings showed them where a small bag of silver was tied by a bit of string to one of the wooden posts rising from the water. He supposed there was still a chance they'd cut his throat and heave him into the sea, but he couldn't bring himself to get particularly excited about it. He watched them count the coins, nod, and split it between them. If anything, they seemed to pity him.

"Sorry about your brother," said the tillerman. "Still, could have been worse, right? I mean, you found him."

Fings shrugged. "Reckon you might not want to hang around," he said. "One of them sailors reckoned that thing in the sky was a dragon."

Didn't need saying, really: these were the sort of people who knew trouble when they saw it and already seemed keen to be leaving. It took Fings a moment to realise that that meant without him. He climbed onto the pier and had a good long look back.

"Hey," he called when the smugglers' boat had already cast off. "You know where to find a ship called the *Speedwell*?"

One of the oarsmen called back: "Her boats will be going from Ygalla's dock, if she's still here. Bottom of the Avenue of Emperors and this way a bit. You can't miss it."

Fings reckoned he probably could, but he gave the oarsman a nod and his thanks and headed off, trying not to think about Levvi and thinking of nothing else. All this way, that was the thing. For all he'd put on a big face about it, in his heart of hearts, he'd mostly reckoned on going back to Ma Fings and all his sisters with nothing to say except that Deephaven had swallowed Levvi whole and then forgotten him. Ma Fings would carry on thinking Levvi was dead, his sisters would keep chattering about how he'd come back one day laden with riches, and nothing very much would change. Maybe he'd make some story for his sisters while quietly telling Ma Fings the truth.

If he hadn't reckoned on finding Levvi's fate, he certainly hadn't reckoned on finding the daft bugger. But if there was one thing that was king of all the things he hadn't reckoned on, the emperor of unexpected outcomes, it was finding Levvi and talking to him, and discovering that he was fine, just didn't want to come home, that was all.

The more he thought about it, the more he didn't know what to do; fortunately, the growing riot on the docks ahead gave him something else to think about. Somehow, he was going to have to get through that if he wanted to find Myla's ship.

Seth first, though. Yeah, and Seth could write him a letter. Or Myla, maybe, if Seth wouldn't come. Yeah, Myla. A letter from Levvi to his family, telling them about all the wonders he'd seen, the stuff he'd told Fings back on the ship. How he was on his way to being an admiral with his own fleet, how he was sorry he hadn't a had chance to write before but was busy doing important things and knew Fings was looking after them all. How he missed them and wanted to come back, but the world needed him, and all the important stuff he was doing to keep it safe.

Something like that. Stuff they wanted to hear.

There'd be a second letter for Ma Fings. Not from Levvi but

from Fings, telling her the truth, although maybe with a bit of polish on it.

He was getting close to the piers where the mob was surging, pushed back by lines of soldiers and Longcoats. Wasn't quite a riot, not yet, but Fings knew a thing or two about mobs. A big mass of desperate people never needed much of a spark. Then came the looting and the setting fire to things, and Longcoats swarming everywhere, kicking the shit out of anyone they could lay their hands on. He didn't much fancy that, so he turned his back on the sea and meandered his way through the warehouses and The Maze. He passed Denial Street and the Witchbreaker's House for Unfallen Women. It looked empty now.

Good for him.

He tried looking for Seth in the *Mended Net*. The streets were quiet, though he could hear the hubbub filtering from the waterfront. He'd be glad to be away from this place. Dead Men and slavers and faerie-kings and monsters that came through mirrors and brothers who didn't want to come back to their families. Yeah. Get on Myla's ship and make his way back to Varr, although the whole business, which had all seemed such a fine adventure only a few hours ago... it seemed a bit pointless now. Really, he just wanted to go home.

When it was obvious that Seth had abandoned the *Mended Net*, Fings went to the Guildhouse instead. The Guildhouse was about the safest place he could think of, so maybe Seth was there with Myla; except Myla *wasn't* there, of course, off getting herself in trouble trying to save her sister. He hoped she had better luck than he'd had with Levvi.

He found himself wandering aimlessly between rooms, hoping to find Seth and wondering where in the name of Bloody Khrozus the idiot had buggered off to *this* time, until he went up a flight of stairs to what should have been some attic rooms but turned out to be sky. There wasn't even any rubble. Where stone and woodwork and a roof had been, a good chunk of the Guildhouse had been sheered clean away. Like it had been made of cake, and someone with a giant knife had helped themselves to a chunk of it...

Oh.

The thought reminded him he hadn't eaten for hours; but that would have to wait, because as well as an absence of walls and ceilings and an assortment of comfortable furniture, here was Orien's apocalyptic mistress, wrapped in brilliant orange Taiytakei silk embroidered with flames, fire in her eyes and a cock of the head that burned aristocratic scorn at everything around her. Beside her, the two of them holding hands, was the short woman in the heavy cloak that Fings had seen about the place a couple of times. Her face was shrouded by a hood but there was a light coming from under it, a moonlight glow. A circle of motley men and women Fings had never seen stood in a ring around them; although now he came to think about it, maybe he *had* seen a few of them, creeping around the Guildhouse these last few days. They were holding hands. Apparently, he'd walked right into the middle of some proper Grandmaster-level Messing With Dark Forces, all going on right in front of him. He could feel the charge in the air.

Oh, he thought again. Then: *Bollocks!*

See? This! This is why you don't get messed up with mages. This is exactly the sort of goings-on you don't want to be anywhere near!

Fortunately, they hadn't noticed him. What he *should* do, he reckoned, was turn right around and bugger off pronto before someone *did* notice him. Or before monsters started appearing through mirrors again, or something even worse; and yet he paused, and frowned, held by a macabre fascination. There were Moon priestesses in the circle. Two... No, three. It occurred to him that he hadn't seen any Moon priestesses in Deephaven until now. Come to think of it, he hadn't seen any temples, either.

Probably *were* some. Just hadn't seen them, was all.

A rumble shook the air, like distant thunder only without

any lightning. The hooded woman pointed across the city. As she did, Orien's apocalyptic mistress raised a hand. The air around her seemed to shiver. Somewhere over towards the river, a column of flame exploded from the night sky and smashed to the ground.

Definitely *time to go, Fings, my boy!*

The hooded woman looked at him. "Shit," squeaked Fings, and turned his back. "Morning, mage!"

He could feel them all looking like he was some mongrel dog brought home by a rebellious child. He cringed and closed his eyes, half expecting to be disintegrated or set on fire or turned into a cloud of bats or something. When none of those things happened, he turned back and bowed, and kept bowing, backing away and keeping his eyes closed to make sure he didn't look at any of their faces in case they hadn't bothered with their mage-masks.

They didn't try to stop him.

Back in his room, he sat in a corner, figuring there was nothing to be done but wait; and while he waited, he prayed. Not to his usual host of sprites and spirits and the Goblin King, but to the proper Gods for once, the Lord of Light and Fickle Lord Moon, the two great Kings. He prayed for Seth to come back safe, because Seth was a brother too.

51

ASH AND SAND

Valladrune… Valladrune… Seth was sweating like he was being roasted, trotting up the hill in a crowd, half the speed of most of them, constantly being shoved out of the way. He couldn't think, gasping and panting even when he stood still. The angry soldiers tromping through his head had stopped; now his skull felt like it had been stuffed with wool from a particularly prickly sheep.

Fucking Dead Men. Fucking wraiths.

All this way and what had he got?

You know the answer to that.

Yes, fine. He was supposed to go to Valladrune. And then what?

Valladrune was where the truth was hidden. He could feel it. Except… Why was he even considering it? Because some up-himself servant of darkness had decided that the best thing he could do after being stabbed twice by an angry sword-monk was bury a cryptic clue in his cellar for someone to find sixteen years later?

Another refugee bashed into him, hurrying past, almost knocking him down. He dragged himself to a doorway, gulping for air.

You think that message was meant for you?

No, it obviously *wasn't* meant for him, but did that matter? The fever in his head seemed to be doing some good, at least, because he was thinking now, really thinking, mind racing, putting the pieces together. What had the popinjay said? That Khrozus had made deals with more than just the priests of Deephaven? And then the freezing of the River Arr in the middle of summer, his quick and sudden route to seizing the throne. And then a year later, his favourite general, the Butcher of Deephaven, had shown up at Valladrune with an army. He'd burned the city to the ground, slaughtered everyone, salted the earth, or at least that's what the Bithwar woman claimed. Khrozus had written Valladrune out of the history books. It didn't exist. It had *never* existed. Something had happened there, then, something Khrozus wanted erased, something to do with the warlock of Deephaven and his wraith, and the sigils that the sword-monks tattooed onto themselves that the Path of Light pretended didn't exist except for the one that put Dead Men to rest.

He forced himself to move again. He was going to find it. *He was going to find the truth and expose it to the light and bring the whole fucking world crashing down.*

Something fell from the sky and shattered on the street in front of him. And then again, and again, more and faster. Ice. Not hail, but slivers with vicious points like knives. He shrieked as one hit him and sliced his skin, then bolted up an alley, arms wrapped over his head, hands to his ears against the thunder of ice shattering on stone. Others ran past him, half-blind, pushing him out of their way; and then he was carried along, running as fast as he could run for fear of being crushed underfoot. He saw a man sprawl flat right in front of him, on his back. He caught a glimpse of the man's eyes and the terror there and then trod on him and almost fell.

I can't do this.

He ducked through an arch, out of the heaving mob before they accidentally killed him. He looked for another way out and found there wasn't one. He was fucked. Fucked if he went back out there, fucked if he stayed, and so he squashed himself into the shelter of yet another doorway, hoping the darkness would hide him, and waited as the ice fell ever harder. He watched men and women running past, screaming; and then he saw one man crash down, another man on his back, stabbing and stabbing and stabbing, oblivious to the flying ice that was flaying his skin; and then more men with knives swarmed and bounded past, barefoot and spattered with gore, their skin slashed to ribbons by the falling knives and yet they didn't care.

And then they were gone.

A distant flash of light. A loud boom, an explosion only a few streets away. As suddenly as it had started, the ice stopped.

The screams faded. The alley fell silent. Seth forced himself to breathe. He closed his eyes and then quickly opened them again as his head spun, because if he didn't then he'd simply pass out and never get up again. His leg burned where the Dead Man had gouged it. His head was spinning. He had nothing left. He was done.

Probably ought to have that looked at.

Which made him almost laugh out loud, because, by Kelm's codpiece, didn't he have bigger things to worry about right now than a few scratches?

Breathe in. Breathe out. Breathe in.

He looked up. Saw the full moon overhead and shook his fist at the Fickle Lord. "Why me? What did I do? What the *fuck* did I do?"

The moon didn't answer. Seth stayed where he was until he thought he might be able to at least walk without collapsing. Then waited a bit more, half-sure there would be someone lurking outside the yard, right at the corner, waiting for him.

He could see the corpse of the man who'd been stabbed, staring back at him with empty, uncomprehending eyes. The alley stayed silent. Seth pulled a sigil out of his pocket, one to bring the corpse back as a Dead Man, because anything would do if it might keep him safe. He crept to the archway out of the yard, crouched and poked his head out, looking both ways.

Empty.

Thank fuck for that. He slapped the sigil onto the corpse and watched it groan its way back to some semblance of life. Unlife. Non-life. Whatever you were supposed to call it.

"Right, you. Let's go. Anyone or anything tries to hurt me, you kill it. Got that?"

The Dead Man nodded. Seth got up.

And right there, where the end of the alley had been perfectly empty only a second earlier, was the wraith. For what it was worth, Seth got a good look this time. A huge, billowing white cloak; under it, silver armour made from hundreds of overlapping segments. An ornamented closed helm that hid the creature's face. Up close, Seth could see what Fings meant, how it looked like a beetle's carapace. What Seth saw that Fings *hadn't* was how the whole armour was etched with lines and curls that formed shapes as the silver man shifted...

Sigils.

He only knew a handful, but he knew how they looked. Different sigils formed by the different movements of the segments depending on how the silver man stood. A part of Seth had to admit to being fascinated. It was clever. Very clever. *Most* of him, though, was too busy staring at the curved swords in the wraith's hands, and how the way he held them reminded him of Myla.

The Dead Man got up and charged. The wraith shifted posture. A sigil formed and flared across his armour; the Dead Man disintegrated into a vague cloud of dust.

So much for that.

So, this was it, was it? He was going to die. After everything he'd been through, after all the good reasons he'd had to get himself killed, he was going to die in some random act of sorcerous warfare, not knowing the first thing about why or what it was all for. It made him...

It made him angry.

"What the fuck *are* you anyway?" he asked.

He wasn't exactly expecting an answer, but it crashed into him like someone had blown a trumpet inside his head. He staggered and reeled and almost fell...

A blink, and the wraith had vanished. If it wasn't for the waft of ash still settling from the disintegrated Dead Man, Seth might have wondered if it had been real, or merely conjured from his fever-raddled imagination. And then a column of fire crashed out of the sky exactly where the wraith had been standing only moments before. It smashed through everything around it and blew the houses either side to rubble. The blast sent Seth flying backwards, landing on his arse, skittering and rolling until he fetched up against something hard.

He lay there for a bit. It was tempting to stay put. Close his eyes and welcome oblivion and see whether he ever woke up. Except... he was dimly aware that something was hurting and getting worse.

Oh. Right. Now I'm on fire.

Not really, only a smouldering ember of something that had landed on him, but enough to make him get up and jump about and brush it off.

For the time being, at least, nothing was trying to eat him.

Now what?

He thought about this, and reckoned it had to be Myla's ship.

If only he could remember its name.

52

SHİRİSH

The door from the Seashell Room broke apart under the blows of the axes. It was strong and took its time about dying. Long enough to let Myla have a look at herself, at the dark red stain, wet and sticky, spread across her shirt. She was still bleeding, but not as much as she'd feared. Of course, that didn't mean much, not when it came to being stabbed in the guts. What mattered was how deep Sarwatta's blade had gone. She didn't know the answer to that.

Sarwatta had passed out. While she was waiting, she opened the shutters of his study and peeked outside. In Deephaven Square, a crowd had gathered outside the Solar Temple, despite it being the middle of the night. There were sword-monks there, too. Mostly, they were all staring up at the sky, looking for the winged monster, wondering what it could mean. If they had any sense, Myla thought, they'd find shelter; but this was Deephaven, where those with power thought themselves invincible.

The axe blows stopped. She heard the remains of the door crash open, then a voice: "My Lord?" Myla slapped Sarwatta until he groaned. She hauled him to his feet, although it was a bit like trying to keep hold of an over-sized sack of rubbish. Which was, when it came down to it, largely what she thought of him. He was as white as a ghost, blood oozing out of the wound in his arm and from his severed fingers. He was barely even conscious.

Maybe the fingers hadn't been such a good idea, even if he *had* deserved it. He wouldn't be much use if he dropped dead.

She held him, a knife to his throat, waiting for the first soldiers to enter the study, and looked to Soraya: "Whatever happens, you get away if you can. Go to Ygalla's dock. Lucius will be there. You need to get away from Deephaven. Our ship is the *Speedwell*. The boat will wait until an hour after dawn."

Soraya looked down at Sarwatta, then back at Myla. "I'll take your ship, Shirish. I'll bear Lucius singing your praises. But when my son asks about his aunt, I'll tell him the truth: that she was a jealous, angry and spiteful sister. That she brought ruin on our family, and we all paid the price."

Myla closed her eyes. Angry? Yes. Jealous? Yes, that too. The jealous anger of a second daughter, unexpected and unwanted, with no easy place in the fortunes of her family. The truth Tasahre had always tried to make her see; that unlike her brother and her sister, she'd have to forge a path of her own making.

A soldier pushed open the door from the Seashell Room. He stopped as he saw Myla with her knife at Sarwatta's throat. His sword was already drawn. Myla saw his hand tighten on the hilt as he saw the blood, saw the state of his master.

"Come any closer and he dies," said Myla. "And then so do you."

The soldier stayed where he was. Another came to stand behind him. This one had a crossbow.

"This is what you're going to do," Myla told them. "You're going to clear the house. Then you're going to go outside into the yard. You're going to open the gates. When you've done that, my sister and I are going to walk down the stairs and out the front door and across the yard. Once we're in Deephaven Square, my sister is going to leave. None of you are going to follow her, because if you do, your master dies. Once she's gone, I'll let him go. You can decide for yourselves whether you want to come after me then, but if you do, I *will* kill you. If I see anyone with a weapon in their hand as we leave, he dies. If I see another crossbow, he dies. If anyone does anything at all to try and stop me, he dies. Nod if you understand."

The soldiers glared at her.

"Nod if you understand!" said Myla again. "If you don't, I might as well kill him now and we can set to it. Ask your friends out there how it went for them, standing in the way of a sword-monk."

"You're no sword-monk," hissed the soldier with the sword.

"Try me." She met his eye. "Or nod if you understand."

Reluctantly, the soldier nodded. He took a step back.

"If the gates aren't open by the time the moon moves one hand across the sky, he dies." She bared her teeth. "Everyone is fleeing Deephaven. You've seen that. It's worse than you think. There are demons here. They come through the walls. I've seen them. Half the priests in the temple are dead." She switched her gaze to the second soldier, the one holding the crossbow. "My advice? Open the gates and let us go and then forget this one. Take whatever you want from here, find those you love, and get away. I doubt anyone would hold it against you. I doubt anyone will even notice. Now move. One hand of the moon or he dies, and so does anyone who gets in my way."

The soldiers backed away, grudging and slow. As soon as they were gone, Myla hauled Sarwatta back into his bedroom and dropped him on his own bed.

"Watch from the door," she said to Soraya. "If you see them come back, scream." She'd retreated here partly so she could watch the gates from the window, but mostly because Sarwatta was slipping in and out of consciousness, face as white as fresh snow and still bleeding. She was starting to worry that if she didn't do something, he was going to die before he'd finished being useful. She began ripping sheets to bandage his hand and arm, and then felt suddenly dizzy and stumbled. She caught herself easily enough, but still…

"Is that your blood or his?" asked Soraya.

"Both." Myla shrugged. "He stabbed me through his own man."

"Is it bad?"

"I don't know." Myla took a deep breath, then another and another. "I'm not dead yet. It's the surge of the fight wearing off, more than anything." She hoped it was true.

Soraya moved to the door. Her eyes flicked to Sarwatta. "They'll hang, draw and quarter you for this."

Myla smiled. "If they do, it'll be quicker than what *he* had in mind."

"Are you really going to let him go?"

Myla grunted something at that. She'd been wondering the same, even as she'd told the soldiers what they had to do. *Would* she let him go? He hardly deserved it. But she'd given her word, and, well… murdering a helpless man, in cold blood? So yes, she supposed she probably would.

She set about bandaging Sarwatta's arm, starting with a strip tied nice and tight above his elbow, cutting off the blood before it could leak out. She'd ruined his sword-arm. Likely as not, it wouldn't heal, not properly; even if it did, those fingers would never grow back. He'd never hold a blade again, nor a quill. If she let him live, he'd bend his entire life and fortune to hunting her down. Probably Soraya and Lucius, too.

"Do you really think they'll let us go?" asked Soraya.

Myla shrugged. "It's all I've got. When we leave, I'll have Sarwatta held in front of us, leading the way. If they try anything, they'll do it in the yard where they can surround us, and they'll use crossbows. If it comes to that, I want you to scream and run. I'll keep them busy for as long as I can."

"What will you do? If we get out?"

"I'll be joining you on the *Speedwell*."

"So you'll be the one to tell mother and father of the ruin

of everything they built?" There was no accusation this time, only a dull recognition of an unpleasant truth.

"I suppose I will." Myla finished bandaging Sarwatta's arm, then went to look from the window, watching the gate and the moon. What if the gates stayed shut? Would she really murder Sarwatta? How, then, to keep Soraya safe?

It didn't come to that: the gates in the yard below swung open. Beyond, in the square, the crowd by the temple were surging forward. She heard shouts, too distant to make out anything more. She went to the bed, found the chamber pot, and tipped it over Sarwatta's face, rousing him to some sort of consciousness.

"So far, so good." She hauled Sarwatta to his feet, keeping the knife to his throat so his men would see the threat, even if Sarwatta himself was barely aware. "Let me go first."

Soraya stepped out of the way. "Why, Shirish? Why did you do it? Really?"

"Anger. Jealousy." Myla sniffed. "There *was* a bit of both of those, I suppose, but mostly it was because he hurt you, and you're my sister, and I love you. It really was that simple."

She pushed Sarwatta ahead, out of the study and through his Seashell Room and into the upper hall surrounding the house's great stair. Soraya wouldn't believe her, not now. But maybe, over the years, she might think about the last words she'd heard from her troublesome sister and wonder if perhaps it wasn't all as petty and straightforward as she thought.

A handful of soldiers waited, all watching with hard stares. Myla made them go ahead, then paused, wary of men with knives slipping out from closed doors behind her, or that Sarwatta might not manage to negotiate his own stairway. He was quietly muttering to himself now, all the things he was going to do to her and to her family, almost like it was a mantra.

They managed the stairs. Sarwatta didn't fall and his soldiers didn't try anything. The doors to the yard were open, as were the gates into Deephaven Square. A score of soldiers looked on, reluctantly keeping their distance, weapons sheathed, no sign of any crossbows. Myla pushed Sarwatta ahead and felt the hate following her, launched from their stares.

When they reached the middle of the yard, Myla told Soraya to go ahead, then turned and backed her way towards the square, keeping Sarwatta between her and the bulk of his men. The soldiers began to follow, keeping pace with her retreat.

Deephaven Square was almost empty. Now and then, figures emerged from streets or alleys or doorways. None paid attention to Myla and Soraya. Every one of them was running for the temple. Something was happening there, but Myla didn't dare turn to see what it was. A dozen yards into the square, she stopped, before the soldiers could follow through the gates and fan out around her.

"Hold there!" she shouted, then hissed to Soraya. "This is where you–"

A flare of light erupted from a figure hurrying towards her. Myla stared in disbelief, because there was only one person it could be, and yet how? But it *was* Orien, fire dancing from his fingers as he raised his hands to the heavens, as flames raced up his arms and jumped at the sky.

"Surrender, Shirish," boomed Orien, in such a portentous way that it was an effort not to let Sarwatta go simply so she could give Orien a slap. "The mines await! Let your hostage go and no harm will come to your sister, for she has done no wrong!"

Myla cringed. The Hawat guards seemed impressed, though. Soraya, too.

"He's a friend," Myla hissed, since Soraya was still holding her pilfered scabbard and seemed to have taken to trying to hit people with it. "Go to the temple. Now! You'll be safe once you're inside. Then Ygalla's dock. The *Speedwell*. Don't delay."

She felt Soraya's hand on her shoulder. A light touch, trembling and uncertain and then gone. When Myla dared a glance over her shoulder, Soraya was running for the temple. She didn't turn to look back. There were no last words.

Keeping the knife firmly at Sarwatta's throat, Myla pulled him deeper into the square, backing towards Orien. "Keep your distance, mage. I'll surrender to you when my sister is safe in the temple." She rolled her eyes and mouthed at him: *Fucking idiot, what are you doing?*

Orien did as he was told and kept his distance. The Hawat soldiers followed her retreat, spreading out into the square. Orien had startled them, but they were finding their wits again.

"This one's ours, mage," called one.

"This slave is the lawful property of the Sapphire Throne," snapped Orien. His voice had a petulant edge. The soldiers kept coming, following Myla's every step, spreading further around her.

This isn't going to work. Had Orien seen that too?

"I warn you—"

"Fuck off, mage."

Well. Presumably, he saw it *now*. They were going to have to fight. It was always what she'd expected, from the moment she'd come up with the idea. And there were too many, and so she'd lose, but she'd see to it that she took Sarwatta with her, and so Lucius would be safe, and now Soraya would be safe, too. She'd have done what she came to Deephaven to do.

"Back away, Orien. This has nothing to do with you." No point in getting himself killed.

A boom shook the air like a bolt of lightning striking close. The whole square shuddered. Then something crashed to the ground beside her, like a piece of glass dropped from high above. Then another and another. Something hit her on the back, like being clubbed, hard enough that her grip on Sarwatta faltered. All around her, knives of ice were suddenly smashing into the ground, faster and faster; one of the soldiers screamed and clutched his face, blood pouring between his fingers; and then the world filled with a noise like thunder as the square turned into a blur of ice-blades slicing down from the sky, smashing on the stones, shards flung everywhere. The Hawat soldiers scattered, bolting for shelter, screaming and howling. More screams from the temple, almost lost under the roar of shattering ice. Myla dropped to her haunches, curled up, gripping Sarwatta and holding him above her as a shield. He screamed, shrill and desperate as he writhed and tried to tear away. She looked wildly for anywhere to run to but there was nowhere. Sarwatta bit her hand, or perhaps it was a flying shard of ice. She let go, reflex, and Sarwatta pulled free. She lunged for him and missed as something stabbed her in the side...

And then Orien was with her, wreathed in fire, looking like a wild animal. "Get down! Get down!" He hunched over her as she curled up, putting his body and his flames between her and the falling ice. A shard hit her shoulder, slicing her open. Another caught her leg.

"Soraya!" She cringed trying to make herself as small as possible. "Did she get to the temple?"

"Yes!" She heard the strain in Orien's voice; when she tried to look, she had to turn her face away from the flying splinters of ice that filled the air.

"What is this?"

The sound of the hailstorm suddenly changed, a deafening rattle adding to the thundering roar. She tried again to look up, saw that Orien's flames had died and that someone new was standing beside them, holding a huge shield over them all as shelter.

Tasahre.

"Mistress?"

"Get up! Get a hold of your mage before he falls."

Myla got shakily to her feet. Ice had cut her in a dozen shallow wounds. Orien was worse. He was barely standing, swaying like he was about to fall and bleeding from a score of cuts. His fire had been strong enough to melt the worst of the edges from the falling ice, but not all. She pulled his arm over her shoulder and started him towards the temple. Tasahre walked behind, holding the shield over all their heads.

"What is this?" shouted Myla over the noise.

Another boom shook the air. Somewhere towards the river, a column of fire flashed from the sky, bright as lightning. The hail of ice petered into nothing almost as abruptly as it had started, leaving a carpet of broken crystals in its wake. Tasahre stopped, Myla too, shocked to stillness by the sudden silence.

"I've smelled this taint before." Tasahre sniffed the air and spat. "Go to the temple. He's on his way to finish what began sixteen years ago."

"*Who's* on his way?" asked Myla, then looked back. The Hawat men were emerging from their hiding places.

"Move!" Tasahre pushed Myla onward. "There is a warlock in Deephaven again. The Dead have risen from the river."

Bodies lay scattered around the temple gates, littered where they'd fallen, racing for shelter from the hail of ice and not quick enough to reach it. Others crawled and staggered, alive but lacerated. A trickle of men and women rushed from the temple to help, some priests, a few monks, mostly the ordinary people of Deephaven. Beyond the gates, Myla saw hundreds more, men and women huddled in the shelter of the temple's covered walkways, too cowed to move. All around her, broken shards glittered in the moonlight. She looked up, but the sky was clear, only the stars and the moon and, now and then, the far-distant shape of the circling monster.

She was shaking, quivering from the memory of thunder as the ice fell. "What *was* that?" she asked again, then realised that Tasahre wasn't with her. The sword-mistress had stayed where she was, out in the middle of the square, leaning against the shield she carried.

A man struggled to his feet nearby, arms and legs covered with blood. One of his hands was little more than a stump. He stared at it and screamed. Myla went to help him, but a monk pushed her towards the temple. Another thunderclap shook the night. She flinched. Another flash of light, another column of fire from the sky. Closer, this time.

"Shirish!"

A figure, running from the gates: "Soraya!" Myla pushed Orien ahead of her, rushing to join her sister; but now Soraya had stopped and was backing away, not looking at Myla but looking past her, and now Myla felt the air go taut, as though the city itself held its breath and clenched its fists in anticipation.

A single figure in flowing white over silver armour was crossing the square, slow and serene, heading towards the temple.

Fings' faerie king. A wraith. She understood, now, his dread.

Tasahre stood in his path, waiting. The wraith spread his hands; as he did, the bodies strewn across the square began to rise. Myla felt a rushing inside her, as though her ears were clogged with water, as though an invisible crowd was standing all around her, jostling her, pressing her, stifling her.

The wraith came on as the dead rose. She began to chant to herself: *Guide my thoughts and warm my skin, feed my heart and light my soul...* The monk who'd pushed her towards the temple now walked past the other way, slow and calm to stand at Tasahre's side; she saw other monks moving too, putting aside the injured and the fallen and heading out into the heart of the square where Tasahre waited.

For a moment, the wraith looked at Myla. A glance, nothing more, and too distant for her to see its face, or any of its features save the flowing mane of white hair. But she felt its eyes momentarily lock with hers, and as they did, it seemed as though something was ripped out of her, and that all her energy and the force of her spirit was flowing freely away, out through the hole that was left behind.

"Shirish!"

She sagged. Her chin dropped to her chest as the strength ebbed from her limbs. She clung to the mantra, repeating it over and over. Fings' faerie-king. Seth's wraith. Not that it really mattered any more.

"Shirish!" Soraya stood back at the gates, waving and shouting, beckoning. Myla shook the torpor away and grabbed Orien by the hand, dragging him after her; and then they were running for the gates, and even here, all around her, the dead were rising. She saw where the falling ice had peeled flesh from hands and faces so it hung in loose strips and fluttered, as corpses hauled themselves to their feet and turned towards the temple, only to be struck down by the Sunsteel blades of the sword-monks who moved among them.

The wraith drew two swords from his back and pointed; with that gesture, Dead Men swarmed into the square from every street and alley, a horde like Myla had never seen. They came like rabid slavering animals. They slipped and skidded and tumbled on the carpet of shattered ice, a great wave rushing towards the waiting monks. There were hundreds, thousands, a mere dozen sword-monks all that stood in their way.

And I should be with them. She felt it then. Her calling. Who she truly was. But she had no sword with which to face them, never mind a blade of Sunsteel.

Tasahre had known this was coming.

Soraya pulled her through the temple gates. Myla felt another wave of dizziness. The wound Sarwatta had given her was bleeding again, the ache growing worse. She felt the pain of the cuts from the ice. The gates began to close, leaving the monks in the square to face the onrushing dead. A sea of them, the stench of rot and the river carried before them; and then, as Myla watched, the air shivered and thundered, and it seemed as though the whole sky burst into flames as a column of fire crashed from the heavens. The wraith vanished, drowned in a torrent of heat and light that smashed to earth, scattering Dead Men around it like leaves in a storm, tossing bodies through the air, the searing wave of fire setting light to hundreds more. Myla watched them burn and falter and fall.

The wraith walked out from the flames, untouched, unhurried, swords drawn. As the fire flickered and died, he made a single gesture and vanished; as the monks braced themselves for the rush of the dead, Tasahre suddenly turned and dropped her shield and raced for the temple gates, faster than Myla had ever seen her run. She watched as the first wave of Dead Men were cut down by Sunsteel, as first one monk then another was overwhelmed and fell, as a second column of fire struck from the sky into the midst of the horde, as the whole city seeming to shudder, scattering them in flames...

Tasahre reached the gates and ran on without stopping. A single other monk turned and raced in her footsteps; and then Myla discovered that she, too, was running, chasing after the sword-mistress, dragging Orien after her, not even sure why she was doing it except that she'd sworn herself to Tasahre as soon as Soraya was safe. The sword-mistress rushed into the Hall of Light. The great doors hung open, as they always did. A cluster of priests crowded around the altar. They looked they were praying; but then they turned, and Myla saw their black empty eyes.

The wraith stood over them, one palm outstretched, a thin silvery glow around it, reaching into them. Myla saw, for an instant, a boiling sphere of black shadow cupped in his other hand, and then his head snapped up. He hissed and the dead priests threw themselves at Tasahre, scrambling and tripping over one another in their haste.

"No!" Tasahre screamed. "No!" The two monks drew their swords as the dead priests came, cutting them to pieces with their Sunsteel. Myla scurried away, still gripping Orien's hand.

"Take my sister! Not through Four Winds Square. Cut down the side of the Peak. Head towards the sea and right. To the bottom of the Avenue of Emperors. Soraya knows the way. Ygalla's dock. Get her onto the *Speedwell*!"

"But–"

"Orien! If you would ever do one thing for me, do this! And *stay* with her!"

"You come too."

"No. *Go!*"

The wraith slammed his palm into the altar and then jumped and sprang across the hall, covering the distance in two impossible bounds. He had his silver swords in his hands and arcing through the air towards Tasahre's neck before Myla had time to blink, yet somehow the sword-mistress caught the blows and blocked them both. She turned on him, flinging cuts faster than Myla could follow while the second monk sliced through the last of the dead priests. As they fought, Myla saw the altar crumble into dust, decay spreading into the stone around it, running across the floor in lines of black and grey as the altar dissolved into ash.

"Tasahre!" She saw Orien and Soraya disappear out through the temple doors.

"Go, Shirish! Go with your sister!"

The wraith jumped, leaping over Tasahre, slicing at her as he did. Tasahre twisted and parried but the strike was only a feint. Myla saw the silver blade cut at the second monk as he put down the last of the dead priests. The slightest scratch across the side of his head but he dropped like a stone, a darkness spreading across his face. He tore at his skin; and then the darkness was spreading up his fingers, too, and then he fell back and lay still as his head and hands crumbled to dust.

The wraith turned to Tasahre.

"I know you," hissed the sword-mistress. "He's years dead, you hear? Your herald is dead. You missed your chance!"

The wraith raised his sword and threw a shaft of moonlight that struck Tasahre square in the chest. Golden light flared around her, brighter than sunlight. The moonbeam faltered and died.

"You are but a shadow," Tasahre growled, "and shadows cannot survive the light." She crossed her swords and her own light flared brighter, driving the wraith back until he mirrored Tasahre's pose. A shield of cold silver light burst around him.

For a moment they were still, gold and silver driving into one another.

Tasahre's stance shifted. Only a fraction, but enough for Myla to recognise the glimmer of desperation. She was going to lose. And she knew it. She'd said as much that same morning.

No.

Myla ran to the fallen monk and snatched up his swords.

53

FAMİLY

Fings tried to think where Seth might have gone. What Seth would *probably* do, if he had any sense, was work out where all the dangerous shit was happening and then be somewhere else as fast as he possibly could. Although you could never quite be sure with Seth these days. Seth and sense seemed to have had a bit of a falling out since the whole business in Varr with Blackhand and the Spicers and the Murdering Bastard.

He'd seen what it was like out there. How there was a riot about to start on the waterfront.

Best stay right where you are, Fings my lad.

Yeah. But Seth...

Yeah, and also a cabal of mages on the roof, half of which was inexplicably missing.

Fair enough. Maybe not.

What if Myla's ship didn't wait? What if it went without them? Then what? He needed to get out of here.

Best head for the docks, then.

Yeah. But Seth...

Maybe Seth was already on the *Speedwell*? It made sense. Safest place to be, probably. Of course, there was no answering that except by going to see for himself.

Or maybe Seth was on a boat on the river. Maybe he'd left

hours ago, making his way back to Varr. Well... Not Varr, Seth wouldn't be going back to Varr, not after the way he'd left. Somewhere else, then. The City of Spires, maybe?

Fings took out all his charms and touched them one by one, offering a little prayer to each spirit in turn, hoping they might tell him what to do, and that was when the ruckus started outside, with a roar that sounded like the Guildhouse was being pelted with stones. Fings opened the shutters in his room to have a look and discovered that it was raining icicles. Or possibly glass knives – anything was possible when you had a cabal of mages lurking on a nearby rooftop throwing pillars of fire about the place and Sun knows what else. It lasted a minute or two and then abruptly stopped.

There was a hammering at the door. Fings ran to open it in case it was Seth and found himself confronted by a wild-looking man wearing the livery of Orien's mistress and looking like he'd narrowly escaped a thorough beating. He was bleeding from a nasty gash on his calf, eyes half-mad with something that was part fear and part fury and part some feral excitement Fings couldn't begin to understand. Outside, the street was covered in broken ice. Or glass. Or maybe the Moon had shattered and fallen from the sky; the way the last few days had gone, seemed like almost *anything* was possible as long as it was something bad. He darted outside and grabbed a handful just in case; turned out it *was* ice; when he looked up, the moon was still where it belonged, nestled among the stars.

He frowned. He wasn't a stranger to hailstorms, but usually ice fell out of the sky round and white, not like long sharp knives. This looked like some new kind of weather. He supposed he shouldn't be surprised.

He closed the door. The wounded man in the hallway stared at him like he was crazy. "Do you not feel it? The air so thick with power you could cut it with a knife and butter your toast with it?"

Mostly what Fings felt was miserable to be in a city he was beginning to think was cursed. Miserable that his whole journey had been pointless.

"You seen Seth?" was all he could think to ask.

"Who?"

A couple more servants arrived who apparently had some idea what to do about someone bleeding all over the hallway. The bleeding man shook his head.

"The ships are all leaving! Our Lady needs to be told!"

One of the servants ran off. Fings shouldered his bag.

Bollocks to all this. Time to go.

His feet crunched on broken ice all the way through the Maze. There were people lying dead on the street; and others, hurt, sitting in doorways like they were trying to understand what had happened. Every now and then, a flash of light lit up the sky somewhere higher up in the city, followed a clap of thunder.

Dead Men, demon-things walking through mirrors, weird weather, weird ships, faerie-kings, cabals of mages? He wished he'd never come.

Brothers who didn't want to come home...

The sea-docks, when he got there, weren't much better. No ice, which was something, but a seething mess, people everywhere, all trying to get away, Longcoats and soldiers trying to keep order. He asked three different people where he could find Ygalla's Dock and got three different answers. In the end, he settled on pulling himself out of the crowd and climbing onto the back of an abandoned cart. From up there he could see out to sea. The Black Ships had left already. Best he could tell, the others were all busy buggering off as well, fast as they could and hang waiting for the morning tide.

He stood there for a bit, taking it all in, wondering what to do. And then, of all people, he spotted Orien, standing out like a sore thumb in that orange robe of his, hurrying along with some woman Fings didn't recognise. Fings jumped down his perch and ran into the crowd, catching Orien and tugging at his robe.

"Morning, mage," he said, careful not to look. He was a bit startled when Orien grabbed him.

"There was a wraith! A wraith at the temple!"

Fings let out a deep sigh. Temple-bothering wraiths now, was it? Although it struck Fings how a temple was probably the best place for wraiths to bother, if they had to bother anywhere at all. Somewhere with plenty of priests and monks and so forth for dealing with them. Better than lurking in forts. Definitely better than anywhere near Fings, at any rate.

"You seen Seth?"

Orien gave him a confused look. "What? He's here too?"

"Er..." Fings finally got around to noticing the woman Orien was with, pregnant enough that she looked ready to pop. Looked a bit like Myla, only frightened and somehow more cross. "That Myla's sister?"

Orien nodded. "We need to go."

That sounded right. "She did it, then." He was a bit impressed. "So where is she?"

Orien nodded back up the Avenue of Emperors. Fings rolled his eyes.

"Seriously? She *does* know these ships ain't waiting?"

"No, probably not."

The Temple seemed the last place to go if Seth had any sense, and yet... well, Seth and sense. And there *was* still a part of him that thought he was a priest. And Seth *had* been looking for Myla.

He sighed. Myla would be up there, right enough, probably trying to pick a fight with a faerie-king who made people disappear into dust. Or a wraith, or whatever it was – did it even matter what you called it? And yes, Myla had said they were square, but by his own reckoning, he still owed her a favour or two. For Yona, yes, but for a bunch of other stuff as well.

"Bollocks," he said, and then got Orien to tell him where

to find Ygalla's Docks before the mage buggered off into the crowd. On the whole, the temple sounded like about the last place he wanted to be. But sometimes there was a right thing to do, and you just had to get on and do it.

"Bollocks," he said again.

54

THE AVEПUE OF EMPERORS

Seth was close to the Peak, in some rich part of the city. It should have been quiet but it wasn't. He passed bleary servants rushing this way and that, frantic messages going back and forth between the houses of power. Carriages blocking streets, being loaded with goods, fat men in rich silks and their bejewelled women buzzing anxiously. Scattered here and there were the bodies of people caught in the open when the ice fell. They lay where they'd been cut down, clothes shredded, and skin too. Flayed red.

A boom of thunder. A flash of fire crashing down from the sky. Somewhere near Deephaven Square, Seth guessed. He started to laugh. These people, desperately trying to salvage their wealth, they had no idea. They'd barely glimpsed what was coming. All that money, all the precious gems and cloth, all the power they thought they had, it was all going to burn tonight. Every design, grand and petty, would crumble into nothing; in the end, the merchant princes of Deephaven would be like everyone else: scared and shitting themselves and begging to live. And then they'd die, and what was the point of all that wealth when it made no difference in the end?

Nothing.

Let it happen. Let it turn to ash and sand. Let them reap what they sow. Let them have what they deserve.

You including yourself in that? Because you should.

Another thunderclap. Another flash of fire. Seth trudged on across Four Winds Square. Down the Avenue of the Sun, Deephaven Square was empty, the temple gates closed. Beyond them, something was happening. Flares of silver moonlight. Flashes of fire. Whatever it was, he didn't want to know. He felt utterly shit, and the end of the world – if that's what this was – was clearly getting on fine without him.

He staggered on across the square, fragments of shattered ice crunching under his boots. Everything was carnage. Broken ice and blood, and strips of flesh, and sometimes eyes and ears. Carts and wagons lay strewn at twisted angles. He gritted his teeth and started down the Avenue of Emperors. Half a mile long, arrow-straight, wide as a palace, the easiest and quickest way to the docks and Myla's ship, and all of it more of the same. From top to bottom, the Avenue looked as though a crazed storm of knives had roared through. Which, Seth reckoned, was largely what had happened.

He stumbled on. He didn't want to. Didn't want to move at all if he was honest. Everything ached. His legs felt like they were on fire. His head was packed with madness, thoughts all spinning around too fast to make any sense.

He leaned against a wagon lying on its side. He needed to sit down. Just for a bit.

No you bloody don't. You stay up and you keep going.

He wasn't alone. There were animals, exhausted from pain and fear, that had somehow survived the knives of ice, trapped, harnessed to abandoned wagons. He saw men, lying where they'd taken refuge under upturned carts, or under the statues of the Emperors that lined the road. Some were still, their stares the only sign of life. Some wandered in a daze, unable to understand what had happened. There were no Dead Men, at least.

He saw the sea, out beyond the waterfront at the end of the Avenue, and three great white ships on the horizon. Far too distant to make out any detail but he knew them anyway. Each had a giant curved prow as tall as a castle, each ending in an exquisite dragon's head, all of them different.

How do I know that?

Where was he going? For a moment, it slipped his mind; then he remembered: Valladrune. Myla's ship. That was why he was heading for the harbour.

He stopped to catch his breath. What he really wanted was to sit down. Just for a few minutes.

You sit down, you'll never get up again. Now move!

His head felt like it was being pounded on an anvil. His vision wasn't right. He was burning up and shivering with cold, all at once. He took a few more steps. For some reason, it seemed to be getting difficult to walk in a straight line. He barely heard the pleadings of dying men as he passed.

The air turned cold. His heart paused and then pulsed so violently that the whole world seemed to shudder. He looked back, half expecting to see the wraith at the end of the Avenue behind him, arms outstretched with a river of Dead Men ready to rip him to pieces.

Nothing.

Move!

The wraith had taken something from him. He could feel its absence. He was lost and small and helpless, all his courage and bravery traded for a single memory of shimmering silver and of two ruby pits of eyes.

A few more steps. He stopped again. Leaned against a wagon.

Move!

A little rest. That was all. Then he'd push on. Get to the ship.

Move, you useless fucker!

He closed his eyes. His legs buckled and gave way. He thought he briefly woke again, later, to see the popinjay walk past, pushing a handcart with a headless body hanging out of it. The popinjay saw him and paused for a moment, as if thinking something through, then walked on.

And then all his thoughts fell into a deep black hole.

55

SWORD-MOΠK

With the familiar weight of a Sunsteel blade in either hand,
Myla threw herself at the wraith. There was no thought behind
it, only the certainty of what needed to be done. She was a
sword-monk in her heart, whatever Tasahre said.

The wraith swatted her away, parrying both her swords at
once. He drew back to lunge at her, quick as lightning, then
staggered and hissed and slashed like a drunkard swatting at
a hornet as his moonlight shield faltered and Tasahre's golden
light enveloped him. Myla parried a blow struck so hard that
it knocked her down; he could easily have finished her, but
Tasahre was on him now in a rain of cuts and slashes.

"Shirish! Get away!"

Myla picked herself up. The wound Sarwatta had given her
was bleeding again, enough that it had soaked her shirt for a
second time; but a sword-monk fought until they couldn't, and
she wasn't done, not yet. Tasahre was back on the defensive,
weathering attack after attack. She was giving ground but she
was turning the fight as she retreated, drawing the wraith
away from Myla, making him put his back to her.

Leading him away so Myla could escape? Or was it something
else…?

Myla launched herself again, fast and furious, wondering

where to strike at that silver armour, where her Sunsteel might find a weakness. *The neck. Always the neck.* She leapt high and came down at the wraith, swords sweeping together to take his head. The wraith whipped around and smashed her away; but as she crashed down, she saw Tasahre move, a lightning-fast lunge, saw the wraith jerk and arch; and then Tasahre was right behind him, up close, driving a sword through his armour as though it was nothing but paper. The wraith staggered and crashed to its knees as Tasahre impaled him with her second blade. As it tried to rise, she howled in triumph, snapped both blades free, raised them high and sliced the wraith's head from his shoulders.

"And here you end," Tasahre hissed.

Myla lay on her back, dazed, staring at the gorgeous detail of the temple dome overhead, seeing the cracks grow, remembering what the wraith had done to the altar, how the decay had been spreading. She gave a little sigh. So now the roof was going to come down, was it? The whole temple was about to fall, and she really ought to get up before it crushed her, but she didn't know how...

Then Tasahre had her, scooping her up and carrying her, running out as the temple fell in a roar of dust and rubble. They fell together, sprawling through the doors in a cloud of dust and a hail of flying stone. Tasahre, of course, was on her feet again in a blink.

"Get up, sword-monk."

Myla got up.

"Disobedient as always. I told you to run."

"You were losing," said Myla.

Tasahre pursed her lips and frowned, and then, quite to Myla's surprise, burst out laughing. "Yes. I was." She looked down, seeing for the first time how Myla was injured. Her smile faded. "You were always a superlative swordswoman, if a terrible monk. Did you save your sister?"

Myla nodded.

"And is the Hawat dead?"

A shrug this time. "Probably. He was in the square when the ice fell."

A nod. "So be it. Shirish died here, among so many others. Go. Find your sister and get away. I have more of these creatures to kill."

"What *was* that?"

"A wraith," said Tasahre, and for the first time Myla could remember, the sword-mistress looked almost afraid. "The remnant of a half-god. Years ago, the warlock called them, and now they've come."

"There are still the Dead Men," said Myla. "I can still fight."

Tasahre shook her head. "The Dead Men will be gone with the rising sun. How many ships did you see, Shirish?"

"Ships?"

"The White Ships you saw on the river. How many?"

"Seven."

"Then I have six more wraiths to kill."

Myla didn't move. "And I will fight at your side."

Tasahre ripped the arm from her robe and held it out, a finger tracing the sigils tattooed there. "Shall we spend the rest of the night inking your skin to protect you from the sorceries of these creatures while they run amok? Or shall I watch you killed by a mere glance? No, Shirish, I offered you that chance and you chose a different path. You *are* brave, but we are legion enough without you. You were lucky, this time."

Myla bit her lip. Without a word, she handed her Sunsteel swords to the sword-mistress. Tasahre took them, then traced a sigil with her finger into the blade of each. The sigils burned bright for an instant before they vanished into the steel. She handed them back.

"Go to the water-monks in Torpreah. Tell them I sent you and show them these swords. They're yours now, for as long as you choose to carry them. Become what you have in you to be." She pushed the swords into Myla's hands and then turned, twirling her blades as she stalked into the night, the slayer of warlocks and half-gods, to face whatever dared stand in her way.

"Tasahre!"

The sword-mistress stopped. Half-turned and looked back. When Myla raised her new swords in salute, Tasahre gave a little tip of her head.

"I will return, sword-mistress."

"And I will be waiting."

Myla watched her go, then turned and ran the other way, towards the sea-docks.

56

THE MULE

The further he went, the more Fings wondered what he was thinking. Any moment now, the seething mass of people at the sea-docks would flare into riot, everyone with any sense desperate to get on a ship and get away. As soon as that happened, the last ships would bugger off as fast as they could. Yet here he was, heading straight towards whatever shit everyone was running from. The crowds thinned as he left the waterfront, but it was hardly an improvement: he passed corpses lying lacerated, surrounded by shattered ice – for some reason only the docks themselves had been spared – or else he passed men and women sitting in doorways or under arches, rocking back and forth with dull dead eyes, some bleeding from dozens of wounds. Mostly, though, what he passed was people running the other way. Which, Fings reckoned, was what *he* should be doing.

Ain't never going to get back on that ship.

Halfway up the Avenue of Emperors, he almost convinced himself to turn back. It was oddly quiet now, mostly because anyone out in the open was only there because they were dead. It was the animals that got him. Many were still alive, still roped to whatever cart or wagon they'd been pulling, unable to break free when the hail had come. They'd clearly run amok

– Fings reckoned this being a perfectly reasonable response to having knives rain from the sky – but now they were simply exhausted, just standing, breathing hard and bleeding from hundreds of cuts, almost like they were resigned to whatever would happen next.

He passed a few like that, and a few that were dead, and then he couldn't stand it, and so he moved among them, one to the next, setting them free. A few looked past any help but he cut them loose anyway. As he did, he offered quiet prayers that they might find safety. Now and then, when an animal particularly caught his eye, he threw a coin over his shoulder for luck. Would have done it for all of them if he'd had enough coins. But he didn't.

Whatever happened next was up to the gods. Although if Fings had been asked to venture an opinion, it was that they were doing a pretty shitty job just at the moment.

A knot of people ran past. They looked at him as if he was daft. One shouted, telling him to run, that end of the world was coming, that the temple had fallen. Then, of all people, he saw the Taiytakei popinjay, trotting down the other side of the avenue, pushing a handcart, and there was something of an eagerness in the way he ran that didn't sit right, and so Fings paused and turned and stared, because he'd been around long enough to know a thief when he saw one.

There was a headless body in the cart the popinjay was pushing. Arms and legs hanging over the edges. All clad in silver.

The popinjay must have felt the stare. He threw Fings a glance and then looked away, too wrapped up in his own business to care who Fings was. Fings eyed the popinjay a while more, then kept going. He freed a few more animals, then went and sat on his haunches against the statue of some dead emperor he didn't know. It crossed his mind that he probably looked the same as the men he'd passed earlier, dead eyes and staring at nothing much, trapped in the horror of what they'd seen.

Would be easy to give up. To sit here and wait for whatever was coming. Of course, once it *did* come, well, then he'd most likely shit his pants and run like buggery, only to find it was all too late.

Couldn't believe it. Couldn't get his head around it. Everything that was happening. But most of all Levvi, staying on that ship.

"Stupid plonker," he said, not sure whether he meant Levvi or whether he meant himself, coming all this way and thinking any good would come of it. He'd been happy in Varr. Well... maybe not happy, but he'd sure as shit been more comfortable.

A little further up the Avenue, a mule brayed, trapped between the shafts of a wagon. A pitiful sound; and as Fings looked, he saw it fall, collapsing sideways so it was held half upright by its harness. He picked himself up. Least he could do, wasn't it, before he turned back?

The mule lifted its head as he reached it. It didn't move as Fings cut it free; but as soon as he was done, it was suddenly back on its feet, nowhere near as close to dead as Fings had reckoned, running away down the avenue.

Cheeky bugger, he thought, but the idea that a mule had played dead just to get his attention was somehow cheering.

If a mule ain't giving up, nor are you.

So he set back to work, freeing the last few animals, still no sign of any Dead Men or any faerie-kings, until suddenly he almost tripped over Seth.

"Seth!" Fings bent down, stricken with dread, half expecting to turn Seth over and see him all slashed open. But apart from some scratches on his leg, he didn't look like he'd been hurt.

Wasn't moving though.

Fings shook him and then jumped back in surprise at how hot he was, like he had a raging fever. Seth's head lolled. He opened one eye. The other was swollen shut. Half his face had turned crimson, peppered with white spots. Fings clenched a fist at the Fickle Moon because this was really taking the piss, this was. Everything that was happening, and Seth had gone and managed to catch himself the River Plague?

Didn't matter. He knew what he had to do. Knew what that mule had been telling him. Knew his prayers to the small gods of luck had been heard. He rummaged around the abandoned carts until he found a nice heavy blanket, wrapped Seth in it, picked him up, threw him over his shoulder, and then turned and headed back down the Avenue of Emperors as fast as he could, hoping he wasn't too late.

Sorry, Myla. But he didn't feel too bad about it. Myla, of all of them, would find her way to wherever she wanted to be.

Ygalla's dock. Orien's directions got him most of the way. After that, he spat the name at everyone he passed as he elbowed and shoved his way through the crowded piers. Most didn't even hear. Didn't matter. He got the odd startled look. The occasional nod. It was enough to get him to the quayside, and then to the pier, and then to a boat where Lucius stood waiting for Myla. Far out in the water, the *Speedwell* floated high, empty of cargo for her return trip south. The docks still swarmed with people and soldiers and sailors and Longcoats trying to keep order. Half were bewildered refugees who had no idea what was going on; but mostly what Fings saw were the faces of those who'd seen *exactly* what was going on and had somehow survived it. They all had the same expression: blank dread.

The riot he'd been expecting still hadn't broken out. Minor miracle, really, when you thought about it.

Lucius grabbed him and shook him. "Where is she?"

Fings shook his head. Myla was Myla. She'd find her way. She always did. She was good at that, better than any of the rest of them. He got Seth down into the boat, carefully kept wrapped in his blanket so no one would see the state of him, and then followed; and then after a bit more, Lucius came too, although he had to be dragged from the pier to make him leave.

Aboard the *Speedwell*, Flings paid no attention to anything but Seth, carrying him to the most out of the way place he could find, up near the bows, curling him up, wrapping him as warm as he could, making sure no one saw the welts on his skin. Probably wouldn't go down too well, bringing a plague victim aboard. Shouldn't matter if everyone had a properly tasselled hat and a properly scented mask and plenty of those incense sticks and all the right charms and so forth but, well, thing was, most people didn't.

Down to me, then. Which was alright. He was used to that; and so he stood beside his brother, fingers clenching the rail, and waited.

57

THE SEA DOCKS

Myla chose her own way from the Peak, down deserted alleys and through plazas, eerily quiet, avoiding the carnage of the Avenue of Emperors, crossing it and making her way through The Maze instead. She felt dazed and dizzy and numb; and yes, some of that was the blood still leaking out of her, but mostly it was the weight in her heart. The dead priests she'd seen had been people she knew, people who'd been almost family until last summer. The sword-monks who'd been her friends, as close to her as anyone except Lucius and Soraya, were out across the city, fighting an enemy she didn't understand. From what she'd seen, many of them would die tonight.

I should be with them.

Here and there, she crossed paths with bands of men. She heard them coming from the crunch of their footsteps on the shards of ice littering the streets, slipped into the shadows, and waited for them to pass. Parts of the city felt dead, the air so cold that her breath was left hanging frozen in the air as she passed. In those parts, she saw Dead Men, shambling and aimless until they saw her, and slavered, and came at her. When that happened, she put them down with her sun-blessed swords. An alley or two later and she'd crossed some unseen boundary into a part of the city untouched by the wraiths.

Even deserted, she could feel the difference. In such places, the dead had the decency to lie still.

Sometimes she thought she caught a glimmer of silver in the distance, of another wraith, its moonlight gleam reflected in the shattered ice. She hid from those, too.

Close to the sea-docks, she found a horse, wandering alone and frightened, saddled but with no rider. She coaxed it closer and stroked it, and told it that everything would be fine, even though the horse surely knew it was a lie. But a horse meant speed; and on a night like this, speed could mean life.

She half expected to find the sea-docks deserted, the ships either gone or wrecked. But no, it was still thick with people. She stopped short of the crowd, took one deep breath after another, and began slowly to push her horse forward. She could see the *Speedwell*, close to the shore, probably closer than its captain would have liked. She could see other ships, too, and myriad longboats with their lights, pushing their way back and forth through the waves, ferrying people to safety.

And out on the horizon, three white ships, taller and wider than anything except the Black Ships of the Taiytakei.

She stayed where she was, eyes fixed on the *Speedwell*, its blue and yellow pennant fluttering high in the air, dulled to shades of grey in the moonlight. She ignored the shouts and pleas around her, trying to make out figures on the deck, looking for Orien and Soraya, for Fings and Lucius and even Seth. The thought came that if pushed on, right now, she'd reach the pier in time for the last of the *Speedwell*'s boats.

She found herself thinking again of the last words Sulfane had said to her in Varr: *The Crown. If she has it, they will come for her. It will be a war like nothing you can imagine. A war of mages.*

Looked like he was right.

Behind her, the Spire of the Sun peered over the city, still intact, not fallen like the great dome of the Hall of Light. She remembered sitting there with the sword-mistress, years ago, watching the ships, listening to the monks training in the courtyard below. She caught a glint of light at the top of the tower and wondered whether it was someone she knew. Was the Sunherald up there? Did he understand what was happening? Was he afraid?

She saw a flash, brilliant sunlight, and then a flare of silver, and then a column of fire.

Tasahre. Still fighting. And she wasn't alone.

The *Speedwell* was still there. She still had time.

She didn't move.

She heard it before she saw it, fearful shouts back and forth and then a strange quiet. People moved aside for her more easily, hypnotised by the electric air of something about to happen. She saw the silver figures, wrapped in moonlight, winking into being, a guardian for each entrance to the waterfront. And swelling behind them in turn, a swarm of the mad and the dead, glittering with knives. She felt the hairs on her arms rise. The air tasted of metal.

Out at sea, the *Speedwell* had lowered its sails. She was moving, a few hundred yards out into the bay and pulling slowly away.

Close, but irrevocably out of reach.

No matter. She'd made her choice.

Then the shrill howls at the edge of the crowd, the screaming of flying daggers and falling blood as the final massacre began. She drew the Sunsteel blades and turned her horse to face the onrushing tide of Dead Men. She'd come to Deephaven to face her fate, whatever it was, and so that's exactly what she would do.

58

THE DEPARTED

Fings saw the faerie-kings, dozens of them, lit up in silver light. For a while, they simply stood, a ring encircling the docks. Behind each, another crowd massed; and even though people were being crushed to death, or falling to drown in the sea, no one went near them. In some places, men with swords – from this distance, Fings didn't know whether they were street militias or Longcoats or even the Overlord's guard – formed a line, nervously standing their ground. Somewhere behind him, Lucius was in a right shouting match about whether they were leaving or not, which seemed a bit pointless when they very clearly were, and it was only later that Fings realised it had been because Myla had never come.

He hadn't noticed. Too busy with Seth, who was giving every sign of being right up to death's door and giving it a good hard knock to see if anyone was at home.

He saw the Dead Men fall on the crowd. He tried to close his eyes, but his eyes wouldn't have it. He saw the lines of soldiers crumple like paper before a fire. He watched as men with knives threw themselves at anyone who moved, until only the very mass of bodies, living and dead, began to slow them. Among the mayhem, he saw a figure on a horse, slicing this way and that, cutting the Dead Men down. Her swords glowed softly in the night, the Sunsteel blades of a sword-monk. She stayed fighting for a long time, despite the numbers. Made him sort of wish Myla had been there to see it. She would have liked that, he thought.

The last boats put away from the docks before they were overwhelmed. Everywhere, people were throwing themselves into the sea, to drown or else be crushed. On one ship, he saw a pitched battle between crew and boarders swarming up the sides. Another was burning. He gave mute thanks that the *Speedwell's* captain had managed to avoid all that. And then he had to stop and look the other way, because some things you didn't want to see, so you didn't have to remember them.

The Black Ships were long gone, and Levvi with them.

Eventually he did look back to the dying city. He couldn't make out much by then, except a few haloes of silver light as they moved through the mounds of the fallen, as the dead began to rise. Up on the Peak, someone was still fighting, judging from the flashes of light and the columns of fire. He wondered if it was Orien but reckoned probably not. His mistress, more likely.

The figure on the horse was gone. He hadn't seen her fall. He hoped she'd found a way out, but it didn't seem likely.

After that, he turned his back on Deephaven once and for all, largely thinking good riddance to the place, and settled in to looking after Seth, his brother, and whatever it took to keep him alive.

EPILOGUE

THE ONE-EYED GOD AND THE HERALD OF THE BLACK MOON

Seth ached. He burned, like that time in Varr when the Spicers had caught him, on the night Blackhand butchered half their men, only this time it was as though Brick hadn't stopped them, and they'd got on with stabbing him a few times and then set him on fire.

Am I dying?

He had a dim notion that he was on a ship, everyone watching with morbid fascination as a city died. He moved to join them and stood next to Fings, but Fings never noticed. Seth realised that that was because his actual body hadn't moved. It was still lying curled up at Fings' feet.

Ah. That would explain it, then.

And then: *Am I dead?*

And then: *Fuck.*

He watched as the colour drained from one part of the city after another.

You did this. All this ruin and more to come. You.

He pushed the thought away. The idea that the old Silver

417

Kings had come walking out of myth and history to murder an entire city just because he, Seth, had happened to be there, was obviously deranged.

Every ending is a beginning. The city dies and will be reborn. The Necropolis of Deephaven will grow. A wonder of the world is being created here. They have been waiting, all of this has been waiting for sixteen long years for someone to take the final step. You, Herald. You're the one.

Seth rather preferred the idea that no, no he fucking wasn't.

You're not dying. We both know what comes next. You're going to Valladrune. You'll finally find what you're looking for. You'll think yourself so clever, slipping the shackles of fate, sidestepping your own prophecy right until it slaps you in the face. The return of That Which Came Before. The Black Moon rising into the sky once more. The end of everything, and the start. You trip it all into being. It's all you. I know, because I was there.

A part of Seth screamed something wild and incoherent, the part that still remembered what it was to follow the Path of the Sun. But it was a small part now, and so he quietly boxed it up and put it away in a corner, where its rantings wouldn't be a nuisance. If he was dead, presumably it was too late to be worrying about stuff like that. And the Path had been wrong about so many other things.

Although maybe it hadn't been as wrong as he'd thought. Maybe now, of all times, was *exactly* the time to be worrying about stuff like that.

After a bit, he settled on a terse *fuck off*. Oddly, it seemed to work. The voice of the one-eyed god faded, and so did the visions, and then, for a long time, so did everything else.

When he woke again, he was at sea. He knew that from the way the whole room was swaying from side to side. He tried to get up so he could find out for sure, and immediately fell over. There was something wrong with one of his eyes. Probably because he was ill. Or the swaying of the ship. Something like that.

He tried again. Still didn't work. He felt like shit.

Fever. Sickness. Nearly dying. All that?

Right.

He stopped. Squinted. Forced himself to look around. It was a cabin in a ship, to be sure, with a pot to piss in and a window and bowl of water and even a little mirror on the wall. In the mirror he could see himself, lying in a hammock. Except the thing in the mirror, lying in a hammock just like Seth's own, was the one-eyed god with the ruined face.

He touched his own face. In the mirror, the one-eyed god did the same.

He closed one eye. He had no idea what the one-eyed god did because he suddenly couldn't see.

What the fuck?

He closed the other eye. In the mirror, the one-eyed god winked his blind eye. Seth stared, and the one-eyed god with the ruined, plague-wrecked face stared back.

Oh.

Oh, shit.

Oh, FUCK!

Imagine how I felt. State of you. The One-Eyed God held up the stump of his mutilated arm. *I did tell you I was you. You want to hear how we get this? Or do you want it to come as a surprise?*

Fuck off.

If it helps, the way your life goes after, losing a hand is the least of your worries.

What do you want? Whatever it is, I won't do it.

But you already did. I'm just here to tell you to enjoy it while you can. Go murder some more priests. Set fire to some villages. Drown some kittens, I don't know. Whatever lights your fire. There's nothing you can do to stop it now.

The One-Eyed God tapped a finger to his ruined face in mocking salute.

I'll be waiting for you.

No. No you won't.

Yes I will. Except by then, it'll be you, looking back in time at who you used to be, wondering in disbelief at what a colossal fucking knob you were.

No. Seth shook his head. *Never.*

You can't run away from what you've done. You can't run away from what you are or what you'll become. Which means you can't run away from me.

Really? Sure of that, are you?

Seth fumbled through his pockets until he found a stick of charcoal. Then he rolled back his sleeve and started to draw a sigil.

ACKNOWLEDGEMENTS

Thanks to Eleanor Teasdale, Sam McQueen and Paul Simpson and everyone else at Angry Robot. Thanks to all of you who read and poured love onto *The Moonsteel Crown* and so made this possible. Thanks again to Nigel, Matt, Michaela, Sam, Ali and Pete, and forgive me, if you will, for the liberties taken.

The story of how Tasahre got her scar is in *The Warlock's Shadow*, volume two of my Thief-taker series. If you want to know what really happened to the warlock of Deephaven, *The King's Assassin* will tell you. If you want to know more about wraiths and dragons and Black Ships, it's *Dragon Queen, The Splintered Gods* and *The Silver King*.

Myla, Fings, Seth and Orien will (hopefully) return in *Herald of the Black Moon*.

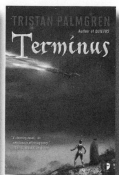
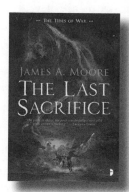
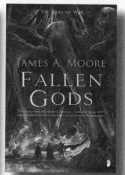
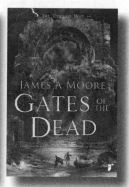

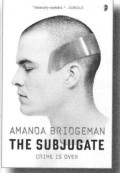

We are Angry Robot

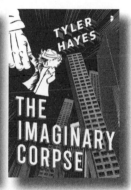

angryrobotbooks.com

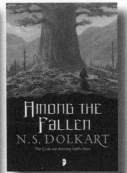